HELEN DALE

KINGDOM OF THE WICKED

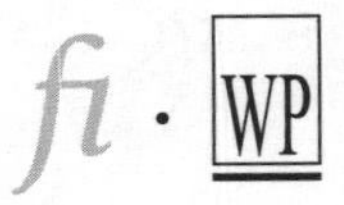

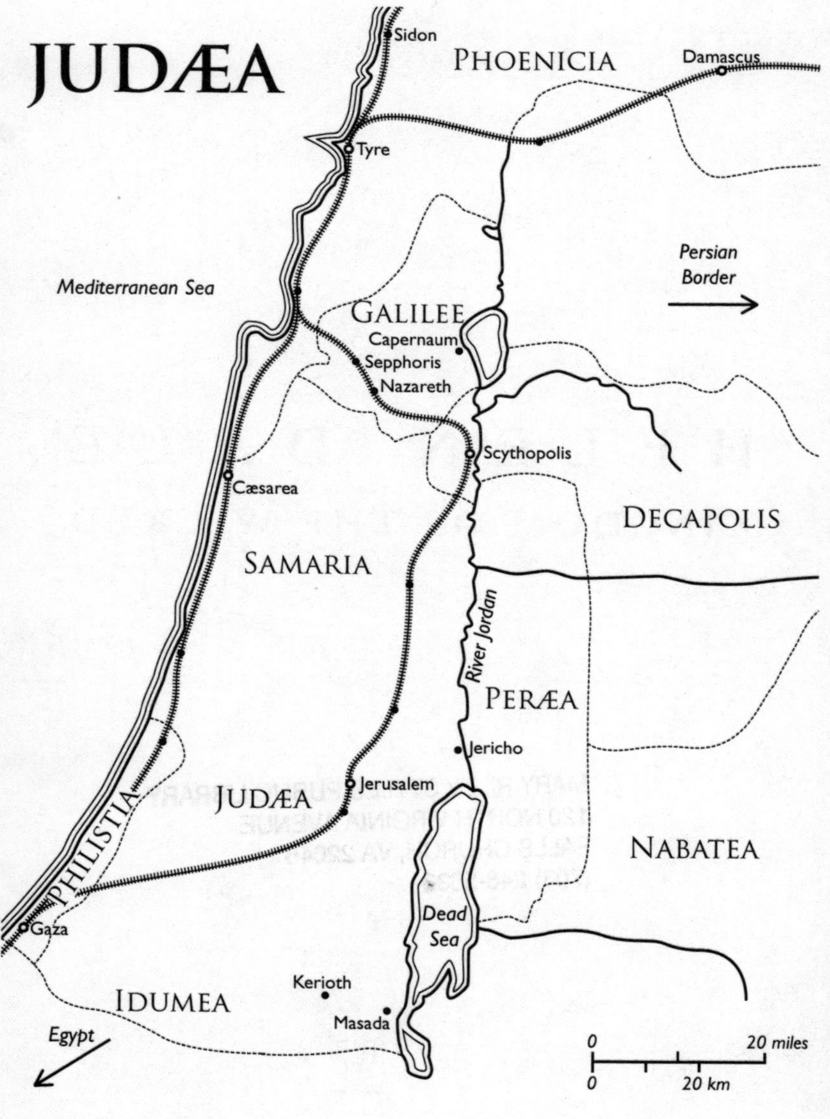
JUDÆA
Sidon
Phoenicia
Damascus
Tyre
Persian
Border
Mediterranean Sea
Galilee
Capernaum
Sepphoris
Nazareth
Scythopolis
Cæsarea
Decapolis
Samaria
River Jordan
Peræa
Jericho
Jerusalem
Judæa
Philistia
Nabatea
Dead
Sea
Gaza
Kerioth
Idumea
Masada
Egypt
0
20 miles
0
20 km

JERUSALEM

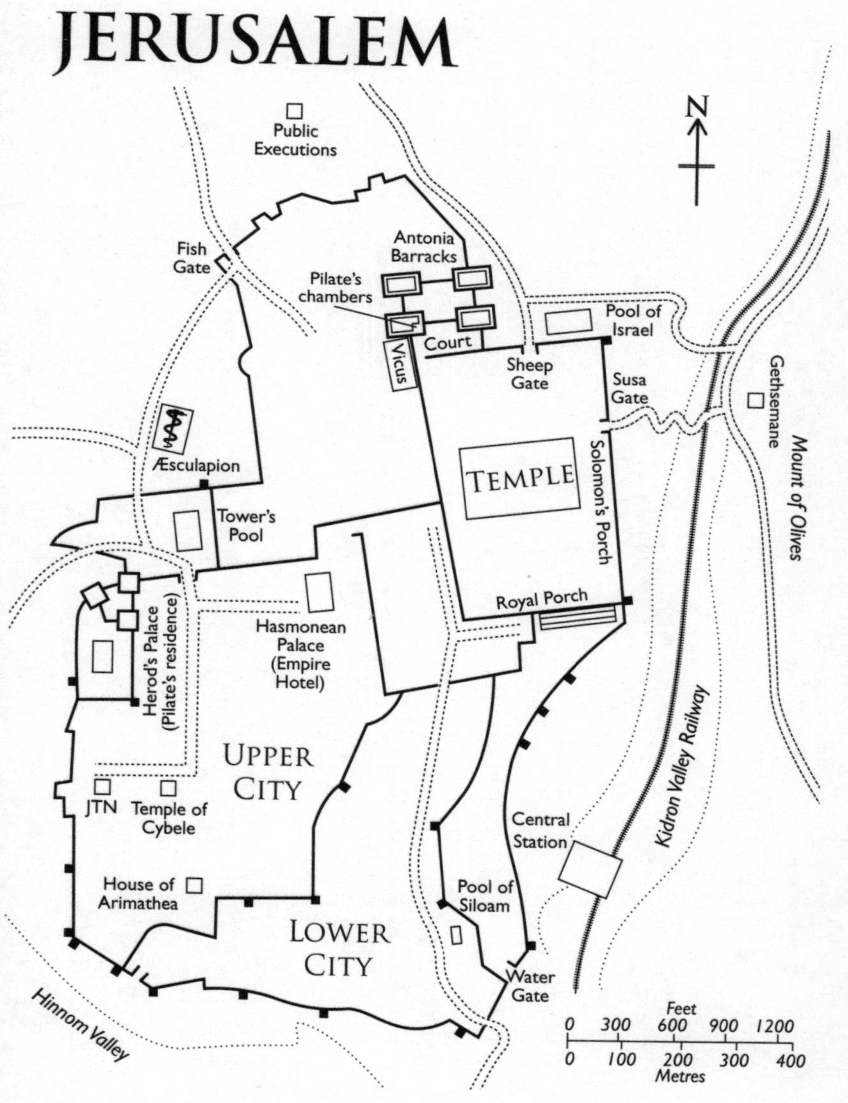

Public
Executions
N
Fish
Gate
Antonia
Barracks
Pilate's
chambers
Court
Vicus
Pool of
Israel
Sheep
Gate
Susa
Gate
Gethsemane
Mount of Olives
Æsculapion
TEMPLE
Solomon's Porch
Tower's
Pool
Royal Porch
Herod's Palace
(Pilate's residence)
Hasmonean
Palace
(Empire
Hotel)
Kidron Valley Railway
UPPER
CITY
JTN
Temple of
Cybele
Central
Station
House of
Arimathea
Pool of
Siloam
LOWER
CITY
Water
Gate
Hinnom Valley
Feet
0 300 600 900 1200
0 100 200 300 400
Metres

BOOK ONE

RULES

Factories in fantasy stories are all in Mordor.

— John C. Wright

KERIOT
METALLVM
κεριοτ
μεταλλο
קריות

PART I

On the god-shelf below the stairway, alongside the tablet from the Great Ise Shrine, were set photographs of their Imperial Majesties, and regularly every morning, before leaving for duty, the lieutenant would stand with his wife at this hallowed place and together they would bow their heads low. The offering water was renewed each morning, and the sacred sprig of sasaki was always green and fresh.

—Yukio Mishima, *Patriotism*

Men and women vie with one another to honour their shameless goddess; husbands and fathers let their wives and daughters publicly prostitute themselves to please Astarte.

—Eusebius of Caesarea

'This,' says Yehuda, 'this is the antenna. When you bury it, you have to leave some of it sticking out of the ground, or it won't explode.'

The young boy, Saul notices, is standing, hands in pockets, watching. Yehuda tells him to go and mind the counter. He agrees, reluctantly, shrugging.

'This is the transmitter.' Yehuda picks up the bomb: it's a smooth dull-grey cylinder, filled with nasty stuff. He points to the side. 'This is the receiver, and this is the detonator. You need line of sight for it

to work, so get up high.'

'Line of sight?' Saul asks.

Yehuda shakes his head. 'You have no idea, do you? You need to be able to point this at the receiver, no obstacles, so they can talk to each other.' He flaps his thumb and fingers together like a puppeteer. 'Like so.'

'So that means it'll go off?'

'It should go off. Pick a remote spot, that way you get the signal through urban radio interference.'

Saul struggles with himself, wondering at the course he's chosen. KERIOTH SCRAPWORKS, SEPPHORIS *the sign outside reads, in Aramaic and Greek. The fenced yard is filled with rusted metal, the detritus of industrialisation. It's piled up next to the office with the sign, and there are even bits of it scattered around the entrance. He supposes the men of* KERIOTH SCRAPWORKS, SEPPHORIS *go around the villages shouting* 'ANY OLD IRON!' *until people come out with bent cutlery, burnt-through cooking pans, rusty chains and the occasional corpse of an ancient sewing machine. He can even see the odd car chassis, which means a rich Roman or Greek has responded to the call and the scrap merchants have loaded it up on their wagon or cart—or it's stolen.*

'We were going to hit the Jerusalem–Jericho road,' Saul says. 'It's pretty remote down there.'

'And another thing, when you send the signal through, make sure you send all of it.'

'What do you mean?'

Yehuda holds the transmitter in his hands and mimes the holding gesture.

'It's a pulsed radio signal, randomised to avoid jamming. If you don't send all of it, nothing happens.'

'Why do you have to do that?'

'What?'

'The randomised signal.'

'Because,' Yehuda says with infinite patience, as though teaching a slow child, 'the Romans don't like us blowing them up, so they have tactical communications jammers. They invented all this stuff, and they like to make it difficult, see?'

'I see,' Saul says.

'You better see, Saul, sooner rather than later, because we need you alive. On account of that piece of parchment you've got hanging on your wall.'

Yehuda turns and fishes in among the greasy rags hanging on the door, handing Saul a twenty denarii note.

'If you succeed, you get another twenty. This is your reward on earth. God will reward you, too, in heaven.'

'Fuck,' says Saul, 'a Roman checkpoint.'

'You knew it was coming,' the woman tells him, 'and I already tell you what you have to do. You just act casual, you my Leno, remember.'

She bangs on the back of the driver's box, attracting his attention.

'You just be casual, too,' she says, 'they have to lift up you seat if they going to find it. So don't give them a reason to make you lift you seat. You get out nice and relaxed when they frisk you, and if he tell you to suck his dick, you suck his dick, but don't you lift you seat.'

The driver jiggles the reins into one hand, looking at her, then out over his two donkeys. His face is so lined it's difficult to see his eyes. Saul thinks he can see dust in the lines.

Saul winces every time the woman speaks; the Samaritan accent grates on him. The driver is Samaritan, too, and Saul worries about his loyalty. He's been paid to do this, and Saul doubts his willingness to give some randy Roman soldier a blowjob. He turns to the woman again. A Samaritan guerrilla, there doesn't seem much that she won't do in order to get the 'package' through. It's an alliance of convenience, this, Zealots and Samaritan insurgents.

Saul suspects that if and when the Romans are expelled, the two groups will turn to killing each other. She's unpeeling her veil now and shaking her head; lustrous long curls flow over her shoulders and down her back. She folds the veil and hands it to him, then drops her black cloak on the floor.

Saul admires the pale-blue dress, gathered at the waist, and her painted nails. She's very beautiful, something he can appreciate without wanting to go any further. She likes him for this, although he can't tell her the reason why. He can see the soldiers up ahead searching each vehicle, clambering through drays and opening trunks, ordering drivers and passengers—even small children—to the side of the road for frisking. They're being careful, but not too careful. He can't see anyone looking to rip apart any upholstery, but you never can tell. Sometimes they'll let five carts through and then roll a mechanic with a hammer under the first car they see, looking for explosives. Other times, they'll wave the cars through without a glance and dump bales of hay on the side of the road, determined to prove that some Judaean farmer has hidden detonators in his produce. He hears the telltale saw of a hunting knife cutting through heavy cloth. Ah, he thinks, the thoroughness is starting. A coach seat is flung into the roadway with considerable force. Two horses drop a big pile of turds next to each other.

The woman leans over the side of the cart; it comes to just below her breasts. She rests them on the top of the wood and fiddles with her hair. He can hear the Romans kissing their teeth and passing comment.

'What they saying?' she asks him.

'That they want to fuck you,' he says in Aramaic, 'what do you think they're saying?'

'What else?'

He stands beside her. 'They want to know how you're so clean. They also like your dress and hair. You should wave and say "hello" now. Be cheerful. A whore is happy in their country; she makes a good living and has a whole festival in her honour, the Floralia.'

'What do I say?'

'Salvete milites,' *he says, 'then* quid agit. *Make your voice go up at the end of that, it's a question.'*

She yells his words at the three soldiers; he watches as their faces light up. One of them lets his carbine hang loosely at his side and saunters across the sand towards the cart. Saul notices he looks first at the woman. He has decurion's flashes on his sleeve and a lean, beaky face.

'What do you want for her?' he asks.

'My driver doesn't want his cart hacked up,' he says, careful to speak the man's language properly. 'Not like you just did before. You can search us, that's all right, but he's just a poor farmer. He can't pay to fix it if you hack it up.'

The soldier waggles his head from side to side, considering the implications of this. He looks at the woman, licking his lips. Saul can sense fear under her bravado. He looks at Saul and points to the two men standing behind him, then points at his own chest.

'She service them as well, all of us together?'

She looks at Saul; the gesture is appropriate and the soldier waits patiently while they talk, but Saul can see the terror in her eyes.

'Please,' she says, 'I do one, the officer, no problem, but not three of them at once.'

'He's not an officer,' Saul says, 'only a decurion.'

'She just wants you, Decurio,' Saul says. 'Says she thinks you'll be promoted soon. She's a good class of whore.'

The decurion grins at this; he likes the play to his status, Saul can tell. He turns to the two men.

'I'll pass you out overnight,' he says. 'This one's for me.'

Saul can see sour expressions on their faces, but also drilled obedience. They nod as he orders them to conduct the search, frisking Saul and the Samaritan driver and looking under tarpaulins and piles of rags. The decurion watches as they do this, then lets the driver break out of the line and move further along and across the road, stopping on the opposite shoulder. In the meantime, he strips off his body armour and hands it and his helmet and rifle to one of the two men. The woman watches as he unbuttons his jacket and runs his hands over his chest.

'He nice looking,' she says, 'maybe this not so bad.'

'Yes,' Saul agrees, his voice strangled, 'he is. You know, see if you can get him to give you a tip.'

She turns on him, winds up and slaps his face. The decurion and his two subordinates roar laughing at this, the whore hitting her Leno like something they've seen at the commedia. The decurion stretches his hand up and helps her down from the cart, the gesture gentlemanly, turning his left arm out and showing her something there as he does so. 'I'm chipped,' he says.

She waits as he pours water from his canteen bottle into his hands, washing them and his face, then rinsing out his mouth. He kisses her and guides her towards the MRAP parked beside the checkpoint. Saul can see him lay his jacket on the floor inside and pull her in after him, slamming the door.

Saul and the driver wait for half an hour or so. They're both conscious of the opprobrium directed their way from those behind them in the tailback; Saul can hear people hawking and spitting, and burbling invective. He rubs his sore cheek, aware that there's a visible handprint there. At length the soldier leads the woman towards them, her blue dress intact but her hair dishevelled, make-up smeared and one of her silver hoop earrings crooked. He repeats the movements with his canteen bottle, this time not only washing his own face, hands and mouth but encouraging her to do so as well. When they've finished he kisses her again and helps her into the back of the cart, then starts buttoning his jacket. Saul sees that the name stencilled across the top of his left pocket—opposite the S.P.Q.R. on the right—is Clodius.

'You can go now,' he says to Saul, smiling.

JERUSALEM

Claudia stretched out on the bed, wriggled her toes and stared at the ceiling. She pulled the pillow into a friendlier, more comfortable lump underneath her neck and shut her eyes. The headache hovered just above her eyebrows, knotting the muscles in her forehead. She flung her arms wide and licked her lips, tasted lipstick and remonstrated with the pain.

Just back off. Just leave me alone.

A little later, she heard the downstairs front door slam, and the dog bark in response—a deep, booming retriever's bark. Voices murmured softly at the base of the stairs.

'Beer's in the kitchen.'

'Any cold?'

'Two in the fridge.'

Camilla. My baby girl. And Marius. The boy.

Claudia watched the lazy motion of the ceiling fan. *So that's where we are, the beery prelude to a night's amusements. Brought to you by Marius the Human Adding Machine.* Marius thumped up the steps, past her door, glass in hand, massive in his battle dress. She picked out the purple S.P.Q.R. stitched across his tan and sand sleeve.

'Here's yours,' he said, looking into Camilla's bedroom. 'Nice artwork in here.'

Camilla sniggered. 'I thought you'd say that.'

Claudia listened to their smutty chitchat, watching the fan blades cut across an immense central marquetry roundel of a bronzed man—his skin darkened by means of stained wood grain—performing cunnilingus on a pale woman, her skin light because she was made from some fair timber, perhaps ash. Camilla's room was, if anything, even worse. Claudia promised herself again that she would redecorate.

Camilla poked her head around her mother's door, her top lip covered with beer froth. Marius stood behind her, one hand on her hip; Claudia could see his dark, bristly scalp. The other hand reached down, scratching the dog's head. Camilla turned her face upwards, smiling at him. He kissed the tip of her nose. She looked into the bedroom.

'You awake, Mama?'

Claudia sat up, her eyes raw and bleary.

'Trying to sleep. Not doing very well—the usual monster Jerusalem headache. I've had it all day.'

Camilla frowned, concerned. 'We'll order pizza for dinner, Mama. Keep sleeping.'

'It's bad enough that we've had to come for a whole month, with the backlog of cases.'

'Do you want some canine company?'

Claudia nodded and tried to smile. She patted the spot beside her. Nero jumped up, resting his glossy black head on her stomach. She scratched his ears. They meant well, these two. Cheery, efficient Marius who bonked her daughter every time they came to Jerusalem; Camilla who was so in lust with him she seemed happy to lose her brain for one month in twelve. *My baby Camilla of the red-varnished fingernails and purple streaks and pierced nose. It'll be a Celtic tattoo next.* When it wasn't outré clothing, it was an obsession with strength training—aided and abetted by Marius, no doubt. She'd walked past the weights room downstairs often enough to know that Camilla could do twenty chin-ups; both pronated and supinated. She'd had to ask Marius what those words meant. Camilla's breasts pushed out against her fitted waistcoat.

Claudia could see Marius staring over her shoulder, eating

her up.

They turned to go. Claudia pulled herself upright.

'Where's Antony?'

'In the den next to the baths.'

Claudia sank back into the bed. *My other baby.* She stared at the ceiling again and started to count mammoths. 'Maybe I should count black retrievers,' she said to Nero. His tail thumped the bed in response. Counting sheep, she found, just didn't work these days. A fine specimen ambled from the bottom of her mind, tusked and hairy.

Pontius Pilate tucked the swollen dossier under his arm and grunted at the two soldiers on duty outside his front door. The taller of the two smiled broadly. Both snapped to attention.

Really not used to that. Really not.

'Hail Caesar, sir!'

'Just open the door.'

The soldier's smile remained unaltered.

'With pleasure, sir!'

Pilate pushed inside, fingers scrabbling at the file, trying to avoid spilling its contents everywhere. He dumped it on the table in the foyer and stretched his hands towards the ceiling. He unhooked his formal collar as he walked through to the smallest of his dining rooms and looped it over the back of a chair, leaving the gold chain that sat beneath it flat against his throat, then kicked off his shoes. Nero bounded downstairs from the bedroom and danced around him, his tail high. He bent down, bringing his own face level with Nero's, smoothing back his ears.

'Terrible smart dog.'

He stood and stretched his fingers over his head and down his back, hauling his long smoke coloured formal robe off with both hands; it caught the thumb-width leaf-shaped links in his chain, and he had to fiddle in the dark for a moment to pick them apart.

Barbarians have much more sensible clothes than us.

He succeeded in removing the gown, draping it over his arm and trotting naked up the stairs to his bedroom. Claudia was asleep on their bed, her eyes flickering. Taking care not to disturb her, he found a pale-blue cotton tunic draped over a bedside chair—he sniffed the armpits to make sure it was still acceptable—and dropped it over his head. It came to his knees. He thought about adding a pair of barbarian knee-length trousers, but decided against it.

In Caesarea, yes. Not here.

Two empty bottles and two frothy glasses littered the stone bench in the smaller kitchen. The remains of a cheese and olive platter sat on the side. He yanked open the fridge door. *Good. More beer.* He twisted the top off one bottle and rocked his head back. *Nice and cold, good imported German beer.*

'Yes! Track record! Ooooo!'

Antony's voice floated up from the den. Pilate clumped down the stairs to investigate, Nero at his heels. He paused outside the door. *At least the den'll be neat,* he thought. *Supervised the cleaning myself yesterday.* He opened the door.

Every object Antony owned had been dumped on the tiles. Pilate looked at the floor, then Antony, then through the far door; it opened onto a terrazzo recreation area. The *frigidarium* beyond rippled and glittered under an open skylight. Antony was running his remote-controlled racer around it with no little skill. Nero barked at the buzzing sound, his tail high. Antony smiled and scratched his ear when he saw his father.

How, in the midst of this, can he have such an innocent look on his face?

Antony settled on his haunches and looked up, endearing,

his green eyes so light they were almost blue.

'Couldn't find my racer.'

'Try to avoid dumping it in the baths. You'll wreck it.'

Antony guided the toy to his feet and picked it up. He polished the brass fittings with his sleeve.

'I like it here, Papa.'

Pilate looked at his son, his face pained.

'I wish the *materfamilias* agreed with you. There are worse things in the world than dividing the year between two of Herod's palaces.'

'We learnt about him at school. He was a crook.'

'He built nice things. I think we've got the most beautiful administrative residences in the Empire.'

Antony shrugged. It was clear he wanted to keep playing with his car.

Damn Jerusalem, he thought. Every year, this happens. My children go to the Roman school here for a month and treat the whole exercise as a holiday. Get miles behind with their schoolwork. Play up something fierce. In Caesarea, the Procurator's children went to a serious Roman school, with proper discipline. Mix with Romans and educated Syrians and Greeks. Learn to be good citizens.

And yet.

Pilate remembered his arrival in Judaea. Antony was eight. Camilla was fifteen. They had loved Caesarea, the children, and Camilla had also loved the young officer who led the official welcoming party on the end of Caesarea's pleasure pier. Claudia appreciated that Strabo & Strabo had offices in Caesarea; she wrote copy for them from time to time and visited her ad-land friends. Pilate began to feel easy in his mind about his appointment, less concerned about wrenching his children out of school and away from their friends and peers.

Then, at first on short trips outside the polished bubble of Caesarea, later in Jerusalem, came the children's questions.

He and Claudia and Marius had to explain why pieces of that man's face were missing, or that women went to the well because there were no taps in their houses. Then, there was Camilla's casual comment that she was taller than the local men.

'Sometimes I think they think *I'm* a man, despite the long hair, the boobs, and the *even taller* Roman officer hanging off my arm.'

For a moment, Pilate despaired at the sheltered lives his children led.

'That's malnutrition, Camilla,' Claudia told her. 'Dana says the sinks here break her back when she's washing up, too.'

'Why?'

'Built for a lower average height. They don't starve—no one in the Empire starves now, we've seen to that—but they don't eat enough protein to grow tall and strong.'

They saw tiny farms with skinny flyblown sheep inhabited by bent people among whom it was impossible to tell male from female were it not for the concealing black robes the women wore. He'd explained that the women covered themselves for reasons of modesty.

'What, the dirt isn't enough?'

'Don't be nasty,' he said.

He remembered that first time smelling Jerusalem long before seeing it, then seeing the horrified expressions on his children's faces as they made the same connection he did. Camilla asked if this was why Marius always insisted—whenever he visited them from Jerusalem—on washing and changing at the barracks in Caesarea before he set foot in the residence. Pilate had nodded. Later, he overheard Camilla gently and patiently telling Marius that she would clean him and his uniform with her own hands next time he came from Jerusalem. He had seen Marius do the mental arithmetic in his keen bright eye and *smile*.

'Should I ask your father if I might have the honour of sharing your coming of age?'

'Yes, Marius, you should.'

That first Passover, Claudia had taken herself off to Caesarea after only two days, complaining about the stench, the flies, the noise and not being able to leave the house. Pilate spent the rest of the month like a couple of his bachelor father friends—men who'd contracted for custody at marriage and then wound up divorced—talking to his daughter about the trials he presided over and no doubt boring both her and Marius rigid. Then Antony spent the best part of a week laid low with some waterborne gastrointestinal bug (the soldiers called it 'Joshua's Revenge'). The medic from X *Fretensis* had given the boy a shot and prepared rehydration salts. Antony sat in the kitchen in Dana's arms and drank from a stainless steel mug while she stroked the hair off his sweaty forehead. The medic turned to Pilate.

'You have to do something about the drainage in this city, Procurator. What Antony's caught kills countless children every year. It's like something from before the War against Hannibal.'

This was easier said than done, of course. Part of the problem stemmed from the Sanhedrin's control over much of Jerusalem's municipal development—a concession Gratus had made, perhaps unwisely—coupled with the cost of the project. Pilate tried persuasion, cajoling and pleading by turns, complete with a bright-eyed, bushy-tailed army *architectus* and his coloured flipcharts showing 'before' and 'after' statistics for various cities around the Empire; *and now here is the data for Londinium... here is the data for Moguntiacum...*

After six months of haggling and pilot studies and engineering drawings, he came to the conclusion that the local aristocracy's grasp of the concept of priority was up to shit. After all, *they* had running water and septic systems and gardens full of flowering shrubs to hide the smell. He used his grant of *Imperium* from the Senate ('always remember, Pontius, that *Imperium* is a broadsword, not a scalpel') and appropriated the necessary funds from the *corban,* the Temple pension fund. Jerusalem spent a year looking like a building site, the Sanhedrin hated him, and there were repeated incidents where urchins and Zealots rained rocks and broken tiles on the heads of soldiers and construction workers below. During the course of the year, eleven men were killed. At the end of that time, however, Jerusalem was fully sewered, with a dedicated aqueduct, baths, water pumps and toilets in every street, and underground fire hydrants. Maybe thirty people were prosecuted for tossing slops out the window after construction was complete. Pilate had repeat offenders flogged in front of Antonia. The slop tossing stopped.

From time to time he played a mental game, trying to put a pin between the two residences, Jerusalem and Caesarea. The latter was more modern and sophisticated, tricked out with the latest technology, but he suspected that the former was more beautiful. When he'd first been appointed, he and Camilla—both of them had something of a taste for architecture—had wandered through it, their mouths open in wonder. He'd thought of replacing the gaslight still in use through much of the structure, but Camilla dissuaded him, and he listened to her.

'The gaslight is lovely,' she said, 'softer and calmer, and now perfectly safe. You're more likely to get an electrical short in Caesarea—that place draws a lot of power. The only way this place would burn down is if someone set it on fire.'

About the only irritation in Jerusalem was Herod's rather conservative taste in interior design. The frescoes and mosaics were lovely, but showed only vegetation or scenery. Pilate knew this had been forced on the King by the local religious authorities. Pilate's predecessor as procurator had redecorated the bedrooms he and his family used with ornate erotic marquetry but left the rest of the residence untouched. Claudia considered it overdone (*walls and ceiling?*), but was forced to admit that after a few glasses of wine, it did become rather alluring.

Pilate had the rest of the small living area the family used refitted to suit Roman tastes, with an emphasis on polished marble and granite finishes and a proper household shrine. Claudia brought some of her extensive art collection from Caesarea, inserting painted statues into various newly cut niches. Her single act of destruction was the removal and—later—burning of the marital bed. She'd been shocked to discover that Gratus had never seen fit to replace Herod's furniture in the Jerusalem residence. 'I am not,' she told her friends, 'making love to my husband in the bed where Herod murdered his wives.'

There was a loud splash from the *frigidarium*; Pilate heard Marius bellow and Camilla giggling at him. Pilate looked up, watching the two of them flick water at each other, using their palms to push sheets of it into the air. Camilla swam at him in the teeth of a determined soaking; he stopped, stroking back her hair and kissing her.

Pilate sat, channel changer in hand, twiddling the little brass dial with his thumb. Nero was tucked into his side, his head resting across his lap.

'I don't think you should be up here,' he said. 'You shed.'

Nero's tail thumped up and down; Pilate was sure he could see black hairs flying around. *The animal should be bald, by rights. Never seen so much spare hair.*

The Jerusalem station was full of not-so-subtle Roman propaganda and religious crap. He struggled with the local language, even though they often used Greek subtitles. *Weirdest grammar I've ever seen.* Pilate paused when Caiaphas, serene, grey-bearded, came on screen.

> **Caiaphas:** We're most concerned with keeping the Jewish community united this Passover—
>
> **JTN:** There've been a number of serious disturbances in the city, like the Temple Riot.
>
> **Caiaphas:** Not as serious as you've been led to—

Pilate changed channel; he picked up *Communicatio Roma* and settled down to watch some real news in his own language.

> —confirmed today that the current trade talks with Serica were amicable, but are likely to remain unresolved at this point, particularly as the leadership situation there is obscure. Among other things, it is believed that the Serican regime has developed a 'terror weapon', capable of leaving the atmosphere and exploding hundreds of miles away.
>
> **Senator Caius Lucius** (*O–Latium*): As people should be well aware, much of what we say about Serica and its internal policies amounts to little more than idle speculation. Serica does not trade in a way we'd recognise. They do not appear to have developed

> medicine as such. Of course, the Han leadership is skilled and powerful; they've just made very different decisions about governance from the judgements Romans make as a matter of course.
>
> In other news, negotiations with Germany's Hermann III for the return of the final captured legionary Standard have progressed rapidly, in large part due to the weakened state of the Germanic Confederation. The Emperor issued a statement from Capreae this morning confirming that discussions were well—

Pilate turned the dial again, pressing his thumb forward. The Emperor, dressed in full robes of State, stared down a packed press conference, his stern face illuminated by glaring flashbulbs. *Poor old Tiberius Caesar, just not a media performer.* Pilate was old enough to remember the original German military fiasco—one borne of a failure to grasp asymmetric warfare—the one where the Standards were lost. It led to the comedic spectacle of a noted Roman *Legatus* telling the Empire 'we do deserts, not forests.'

He stumbled into the kitchen and collected a third beer. Claudia was pouring mineral water into a chilled glass beside the stovetop. She turned around, wiping her eyes with one hand.

'Sorry. I went to sleep. I've got two textbooks to proof in a week and I don't know where to start.'

Pilate shrugged. 'What's for supper, hon?'

'Marius and Camilla ordered pizza.'

'Pizza in Jerusalem tastes vile. You know that. Where's Avivah?'

'I let her go for the month. All her relatives are in Jerusalem for Passover; of course she wants to be with them.'

'And you didn't bring a cook and a couple of enlisted men across from Antonia? That's what you usually do. And where's Dana? Antony likes her.'

'I don't feel well.'

Pilate grunted at this, scratching behind his ear. He found Claudia's solicitude towards household servants and junior soldiers irritating.

'Has anyone fed the dog?'

'Maybe the children have.'

Nero approached the kitchen, alert at the mention of food. Pilate grunted again and balled his tunic to wrench the top off the bottle. She watched him tear the cloth and then methodically find a new spot. He looked at her.

'Great. So we get to eat pizza à la Jerusalem. It's times like this I wish slavery were still legal. I'd buy us a decent cook.'

Claudia rolled her eyes. 'It's not as though the family funding kitty isn't fat enough to stretch to a Greek replacement for the month.'

'Too much fucking around.'

'So's slavery. Personally, I got over little fingers in my dresser drawers when I was about five.'

'Fair point. I heard about the number of bottles that went missing with that old houseboy the folks used to have. He liked rosé, apparently.'

'I'll hire some servants for the next month, and borrow Dana from Caesarea.'

'I'll feed the dog.'

Nero came to heel and started drooling on his foot. Antony trotted into the kitchen and stopped short beside the sink.

Claudia hugged Antony to her chest.

'My baby lion,' she whispered. 'You're getting so tall.'

She messed his hair and tweaked his ears. The screen burred in the background. One of their guards knocked at the tradesman's entrance. Pilate saw that it was the smiling soldier; the one Camilla called *the man with the flip-top head*. The pizza man stood behind him: a Greek teenager, he dropped his eyes with respect when he saw Claudia Procula walking towards him, a five *denarii* note in her hand.

'*Domina*, I don't think I have enough change for that.'

Pilate washed the remains of the pizza off his hands, splashed his face and collected another beer. *That was better than I expected, proper base and cheese.* He examined his greying hair in the mirror behind the herb shelf, touching the dark circles under his eyes with gentle fingers. *Getting a bit thin on top, old man.* He ran his hands down his torso, settling them on his hips. *No love handles. Have to watch the beer, though. Don't deserve such a beautiful woman, you know. She still gives me stiff ones, just like that.* He wiped away a water spill with one of Claudia's fancy embroidered S.P.Q.R. tea towels and sat before the fat folder on the table in his study. *And to think I once looked forward to heading home.* He untied the dark pink tape binding it shut. Camilla and Marius meandered down the stairs, hand in hand, Marius in dress uniform and reeking of aftershave, Camilla dressed for a night on the town, a close-fitting silk shift bringing out her figure, a long dark gown with silver buttons draped over her arm. Her hair was curled and bound with silver bands, framing her face. Marius saluted him through the open door. *Still not used to that, really not.* While he watched, Marius helped her into her gown, stepping gracefully around her and doing up three of the buttons, his fingers deft. Nero tucked himself around Marius's legs.

First up, there was a long epistle from Caiaphas on Sanhedrin letterhead. Pilate sighed, gathered up the file and walked out onto the terrace. Orange light gleamed and shimmered on the domes and towers of the city below. He gazed over the

Upper City, where the Romans had their Quarter; he noted the white buildings and irrigated green playing fields of Jerusalem Academy; the impoverished Lower City where Jews—with exceptions—lived their lives; the restrained allure of the Greek Quarter, the city's chief supplier of sexual and gaming services; the vast square before Antonia, picked out by roving floodlights mounted on the fortress. Even from here, he could see children flying imported Serican kites in the great expanse. On the other side of the city was Central Station, the spine of its great railway shed glittering in the sun. Streets already in darkness divided each quarter from the other. He cursed himself for leaving decisions about transport infrastructure to the Sanhedrin.

The city needs a metro, but they won't let anyone put a stop under their precious Temple.

A molasses sun set behind him. Over the balustrade, downstairs in the courtyard, Marius and Camilla danced. They'd taken both Camilla's polished wooden radio and the dog with them; he watched her pause and fiddle with the valve on top of it. Driving Roman music spilled over the city, while Nero ran up and down alongside the wall, chasing imaginary game. Guards posted at each corner ignored the young officer and his woman, although Pilate suspected a few of them meditated on Marius's luck. He'd had the good fortune to cover himself in glory during a border skirmish with the Persians just before the Pilates arrived in Judaea. He'd then danced attendance on Camilla and swept the schoolgirl off her feet. Pilate was a modern father; he respected his daughter's choice of man but wondered at her firmness.

'It isn't the last days of the Republic any more,' he'd told her. 'These are modern times. It's all right to try a few first, see if you like them. You're a very good catch. Aim high.'

She shook her head.

'I only want Marius. I'm fed up with him inhabiting my dreams.'

He smiled.

'So you want him inhabiting your bed, yes?'

She nodded. Camilla had always been blunt.

Pilate turned his attention back to the letter from Caiaphas.

> From Caiaphas, Kohen Gadol of Jerusalem, to Pontius Pilate, Procurator of Judaea, Greetings!
>
> Please accept my best wishes for your continued good health and good governance—and also allow me to extend my regards to Claudia, Antony and Camilla—may your Gods and my God smile warmly on your family.
>
> The purpose of this letter is to acquaint you with some background information on the forthcoming trial of Yeshua Ben Yusuf. Of course, my interest in this case is hardly academic. I believe that Yeshua Ben Yusuf represents the most serious threat to the internal security of this province seen during your procuratorship.
>
> Ben Yusuf, as you are no doubt aware, is an itinerant preacher with a natural eloquence capable of winning him large numbers of adherents. He makes good use of the Empire's excellent railway infrastructure, spending his nights with friends in each town. He spouts the most ridiculous nonsense, and were it not for the fact that he is such a gifted speaker, his beliefs would be of no concern either to you or the Sanhedrin. Among other things, he claims to be God's representative on earth and the Messiah. It is unclear whether he seeks to usurp Roman rule based on these statements; none of them are blasphemous in Jewish tradition, but the

way he couches them is alarming to say the least. One of his followers, Mary Magdalena, has worked for a number of years with JTN. She has secured him numerous screen and radio appearances through her industry contacts.

I am aware that this does not constitute any crime under Roman law, and one could argue that the so-called 'news' media are there to be exploited. It is, nonetheless, gravely offensive to our traditions, and many people have been deeply hurt by Ben Yusuf's portentous (and inaccurate) pronouncements on the meaning of scripture and the observance of religious law.

Matters have been exacerbated of late. Ben Yusuf was almost entirely responsible for the Temple riot last week, which caused considerable damage to Temple property. Two people are in Æsculapion, one critically injured. Worse, numerous individuals participated in what amounted to the wholesale pillaging of a religious centre. It was only with some difficulty that my Temple Guard arrested him after the riot.

Finally, I feel bound to inform you that Andreius Linnaeus, your distinguished colleague, is representing Ben Yusuf. I know that Linnaeus's pro bono legal work is highly regarded throughout the Empire, and I regret that I am opposed to such an outstanding individual in this—

Pilate saw there was more, shoved the letter aside and paged through the file. Photocopies of Jewish religious code. Ben Yusuf's carpentry papers. Evidence photos of the wrecked Temple precinct after rioting. Transcripts of interviews. A handwritten note from Linnaeus on Cato & Cato stationery.

He scratched his chin and looked out at the smudges of orange fading into indigo night over the city. Marius and Camilla clattered up the stairs, complaining about mosquitoes. Nero followed at Marius's heels, his tail wagging, as Marius tucked Camilla's radio under his arm. Pilate looked at Caiaphas's letter, puzzling over things.

Hmm. Be good to catch up with Andreius.

Pilate and Linnaeus were rivals at *Collegia Roma*, in both politics and scholarship. They had also competed for Claudia's hand, and Pilate sometimes wondered why she chose him over the rising northern industrialist's son. That Linnaeus's mother was a freed slave—Angel Linnaeus bought Monica from one of his business associates not long before abolition—would put many high born Romans off, but not Claudia. She came from a long line of abolitionists. Pilate shrugged. Claudia was his; that was all that mattered.

'Pontius, you coming in?'

Barefoot and wrapped in a Greek *chiton*, Claudia stepped onto the terrace, pungent with insect repellent, a glass of wine in hand. She looked happier, more composed.

'Or you going to let the mosquitoes pick you up and carry you away?'

Pilate shuffled inside, tripping over the threshold. He dropped his paperwork and it scattered. Marius scooped it up from the floor by the handful, sorting things, then alphabetising the documents in neat piles on the nearest table. Nero stood guard beside him, stock still, watching, not getting in his way. Pilate was transfixed at Marius's beautiful Roman efficiency. *I was once like that, you know.* Camilla watched him from the kitchen, her eyes shining. Claudia watched Camilla watching Marius do the work.

Marius handed Pilate the reordered file and saluted.

'Thank you, Marius,' he answered, at once clipped and formal. 'I'm curious. You're heading out—as one does during *Festa*—but there seems to be a little more planning than usual attached to matters this evening. Where are you taking my daughter?'

Marius neither flushed nor missed a beat.

'We are going on the... Rite, Procurator.'

Pilate roared laughing.

'The merit of candour, at least.'

Claudia giggled along with her husband.

Camilla was flame red now. Marius stood stock still, at attention. Nero looked up at him, adoring.

'You appreciate that there is a degree of danger attached to following our rites in public in Jerusalem.'

'That's half the fun, and it is *Festa*.'

'It's coming up to Passover,' Claudia said, an edge in her voice. 'Pleasure is good. Worship is good. Unnecessary risks are not.'

'We're staying in the Roman Quarter,' Marius said, exuding professional calm. 'We're all First Cohort. We're all armed.' He gripped his forearm. 'We're all blood brothers.' Claudia could see the shadow of a machine pistol strapped beneath his arm.

'Ratio?' Pilate asked, raising an eyebrow.

'Three women, four men.'

'The ladies are in for a good night.'

Andreius Linnaeus saw them as the railway porter loaded his taxi, weaving along the Roman Quarter's cardo, Antonia and the Temple looming in the background. Distracted by the women's fitted clothes and the buff brawniness of the men, he handed the porter a five *denarii* note.

'*Domine*, this is far too much.'

Linnaeus looked at the banknote in his hand.

'So it is.' He paused. 'Honesty should be rewarded, my friend. Keep it.'

No Roman had ever addressed him so politely or tipped so generously. The porter held his hands up in front of his face, starting to bow.

'Don't do that,' said Linnaeus, drawing his eyebrows together.

'I'm sorry, *Domine*, but you are very generous.'

The porter watched him gaze towards the young people again, licking his lips, his appreciation frank. He curled his lean frame into the taxi. The porter watched him go.

Linnaeus saw the Procurator's daughter, her jet-black, purple-tipped hair travelling ahead of her, roiling in the wind. Then there was the *Optio* of the 1st Century, 1st Cohort, bristle headed, muscular, lean and brown. They were among friends. Two of the women—one black, one white—tongue kissed while the men looked on, grabbing their crotches. The loudest shouting came from a tall ginger dancing awkwardly, almost in the middle of the road. Camilla applauded then groped at the *Optio*'s chest (*damn, what's his name again?*). They joined hands now, Camilla in the lead, their movements rehearsed, like Maenads dancing around a Greek drinking vessel. They were on their way to the Fleet Fox (*a fine establishment*); Linnaeus knew the way well. He leaned forward in his seat, tapping the glass behind the driver's head.

'I want to arrive at about the same time as that group.' He pointed towards the knot of young people. Camilla was in her man's arms now; he lifted her and buried his hatchet face between her breasts.

The cabbie was Jewish; he looked back at Linnaeus, his eyes mournful.

'It be near Passover,' he said in broken Latin. 'The Fleet Fox be bad place. They be bad people. It be Sabbath already, and I have to work.'

He shook his head at the young people as they mauled each other, or laughed, or shouted vulgarities into the street. Two of the soldiers were kissing now, hands clasped around each other's bristly heads. Linnaeus repressed his ingrained Roman habit of correcting bad grammar. (*It's the verb of existence—how hard is that to get right?*)

'They're young and enjoying their bodies, and it's *Feria* for us, too,' he said in Greek, flapping his hands. It was an odd gesture, starting with his fingers pointing inwards at his ears, the backs of his hands forward. It finished with both palms facing the heavens. The cabbie's eyes widened at his perfect, unaccented Greek.

Rich Roman, then.

'Just go, please,' rich Roman said. 'There'll be a big tip at the end of it all for you.'

Linnaeus knew they were getting close when he heard driving music with a characteristic high female vocal spilling through the front of the establishment. *Ah yes, the song of the Rite, the closest there is to a cyclone in musical form.* She sang in Latin, not Syriac or Greek—unusual, this, a recent development.

The language was new, but the convention was rigid: she told of her aloneness since the Goddess went below, of her mother telling her how to bring the Goddess back, of the spell conjuring up a man who could join her in the summoning. Which by convention involved a coruscating vocal climb; there were women with a four octave range who sang for Cybele.

More upmarket than he remembered from previous visits, there was more green and purple and white. The foyer with its expensive glass frontage was now all marble, pale green and pink added to the other colours. A pair of moonlighting legionaries—in braces and black trousers, their upper bodies bare save for sculpted armour over the chest and back—stood on either side of the door, arms folded, stun guns on their hips, pistols tucked under armpits. Some wag had painted circles in the building's signature colours around its Priapus statue's oversized penis. The stone fox at Priapus's feet had also been painted—and with some care and attention to accurate detail, he noted. The fox looked up at the statue with knowing blue eyes. A sign behind the statuary read *Private Property: Keep Out*. Another sign over the entrance read *Members Only*. Linnaeus knew that in the entrance hall there was a giant ceiling painting of the Goddess with her arms above her head, a snake in each hand, her breasts exposed.

The building itself was some three storeys high, honeycombed with private rooms, bars in an assortment of styles, and a great central dining hall. Lights bloomed and faded on different floors, showing up a dance floor here, a bar there, a private room below. He saw the senior priestess who ran the place backlit with silver light on the top floor, recognisable even in silhouette thanks to her *polos* headdress, a crown of towers like a walled city's battlements.

He rolled down the window. The pungent scent of skunkweed mixed with aftershave, perfume, and fresh pizza flooded the cab. A pizza vendor sold his slices across the street: *Genuine Italian Pizza: I come from Neapolis—no second-rate Jerusalem shit here!* his sign boasted. The correctness of the sign's grammar led Linnaeus to suspect he was telling the truth.

Bright young things crowded around, stretching cheese away from their mouths as they ate. The cabbie covered the bottom half of his face with one hand, blocking his nose. He could hear the music too, and tried to curb an almost involuntary urge to tap the steering wheel. *How do they do that? And sing like a cat having its tail pulled at the same time?* Camilla and her entourage arrived; Fleet Fox staff emerged with magical suddenness, bearing wine in decorative cups. The group crowded around, laughing in their glittering voices. Linnaeus waited for his moment and let out a piercing wolf-whistle, his fingers to his lips. Camilla looked up, perplexed; then she recognised him and broke into a dazzling smile. She dragged her soldier towards his cab by the hand.

'Andreius Linnaeus, the man from *Picenum*, the most famous lawyer in the Empire,' she yelled, breathless. The young man at her side looked peeved at the delay. He saluted, smiled, then curled his arm around her waist.

'And you'd be?'

'Marius Macro, *Optio* of the First Century, First Cohort, *Legio* X *Fretensis*. Of *Campania*.'

'Ah, yes, I remember. Want to make a good night a great one?'

Marius appraised him coolly, one eye on the driver—a young ear-locked Jew simultaneously staring at and looking away from the Fleet Fox's entrance and its denizens.

'How so?'

Linnaeus fished in his briefcase, handing over a small tin. Marius flipped the lid up: rainbow tablets with smiley faces stared up at him. People were dancing on the footpath now, all in time, imitating a dance from a recent popular film.

'Very nice quality,' Marius said. The rest of them gathered around the lead pair, craning to see what Marius was holding. 'Woo hoo,' breathed the Legion's *Aquilifer*, a giant ginger with a British accent. 'You have classy taste.'

'The very best,' said Andreius. 'I was in Caesarea today, and took the time to do a little shopping.'

The cab driver's head was in his hands. He rocked back

and forth. And this is how they worship their filthy gods. Not supposed to have temples here, but they do it anyway. Do it by playing clever games with their laws. The singer had reached the midpoint of her soaring run. A short blonde woman—her arm linked with that of the taller, more robust black woman Mirella someone or other he'd seen her kissing—reached around the ginger and pinched one of the pills with delicate fingers. It sat on the tip of her tongue for an instant.

'Drugs are quick,' she hissed, raising her eyebrows. Linnaeus snapped his fingers, a sound at once loud and dismissive, then flicked the hair on the side of his head with two fingers: a salute of sorts, amused, even sarcastic. He pointed the two fingers at Camilla, grinning.

'Have a great rite, my friends.'

SOME HISTORY

Antony couldn't remember his first visit to Jerusalem, but could remember he liked it. It was nice to go from being in the middle of the class to somewhere close to the top. Caesarea Academy was the best school in Judaea, and he wasn't his sister, who'd carried off an Empire-wide mathematics prize the previous year. *My sister can do numbers.* The Jerusalem Academy was good, of course, but more 'cosmopolitan'. It was a Stoic word, *cosmopolitan*, and he didn't really grasp its meaning. He liked its effects, though.

He enjoyed the dedicated classes on everybody's different festivals, the way Jews gave themselves a day off each week (lazy, Romans always said), and children bringing food from home. He had fancy sweets from Caesarea for *Megalesia*, the Festival of the *Magna Mater*, while Jewish children brought their lamb, bread and herbs. He liked their Passover lamb, and would make himself popular by trading the Goddess's marzipan and crystalline fruit in the playground for chunks of lamb and funny flat bread.

'We're not supposed to eat these, but it do taste good,' one Jewish boy told him.

'My Mama says they rot your teeth,' Antony said. This was true; Claudia often said that, and told him in no uncertain terms that she expected him to share. He had no trouble complying. He didn't have a sweet tooth, and liked the savoury Jewish food.

He also liked the school's extensive playing fields, adjacent to Antonia and so often shared with young men from *Legio*

X *Fretensis*. The girls in the Senior School—well, the Roman and Greek girls, anyway—flirted with the soldiers, who whistled and blew kisses in their turn. One of his best memories of Jerusalem involved an hour tearing up the cross-country course on a quad bike ridden by a Capuan legionary out to impress one of the Senior School girls. It was dangerous but exhilarating, the young man swearing and showing off, the girl squealing, Antony clinging to the soldier and his girl in turn, hair whipping around his ears. When he came home covered in mud, Claudia raised an eyebrow, but didn't say a word.

Anti-Roman Jews would stand on the other side of the razor wire and watchtowers surrounding the school and abuse Jewish and Roman students on the inside in the most extreme terms. The guards in the watchtowers only intervened if one of the abusers stooped to pick up a stone. Often the abuse was in Hebrew and Aramaic, which Antony couldn't understand. For Romans, abuse had little effect. It was Jews that found it most stinging. He'd befriended Hillel Bar Kayafa—the High Priest's son—after finding him curled up under a tree near the perimeter fence, crying his eyes out. He'd always liked Hillel, even when he hadn't been introduced. Hillel was smart and kind and thoughtful, and spoke good Latin, better than a lot of Roman native speakers.

'Don't let the bastards grind you down.'

'Easy for you to say.'

Antony knew not to ask what the ragtag urchins outside had been yelling.

'All the hating on my family goes to Pater. It sort of misses me.'

'Lucky you.'

The words were grumpy, but Hillel's sobs were subsiding. He pushed a shock of shiny black curls out of his eyes and stood up. A few strands stuck to his forehead. Antony touched his forearm lightly, just the once.

'I've got a remote-controlled racer. Got it Saturnalia last. It's really good.'

Hillel played with Antony's toy car, buzzing it around the terrace until Pilate—weighed down with work he couldn't get through at the office—yelled at them to stop the racket. Antony obeyed his father with a swiftness that made Hillel's head spin and walked towards the *lararia*; Hillel followed him.

Hillel stood behind Antony as the latter lit his incense, admiring the small metal statues of what looked like exceedingly commonplace people as Antony moved his hands to a pattern. At one point he opened a set of wooden doors underneath the shrine, taking out a glass jar of unguent and pouring it into a shallow dish beside the burning incense. Antony held his hands open, palms up, and chanted. Hillel waited until he had finished.

'Who are they?'

Antony turned to look at him, perplexed. 'That's the Emperor and his *familia*,' he said.

'I know that, dummy. Who are these?' he pointed.

'Some are *lares*,' he indicated one pair. 'They protect this house.'

'Yes.'

'These are *penates*. They make us prosperous.'

'Yes.'

'This is my paternal Grandmother. She died last year. The others are some of my family's ancestors.'

'You keep statues of your dead relatives in your *house*?'

A shadow crossed Antony's face, which shocked Hillel. Antony had a sunny disposition, which Hillel liked immensely.

'Don't speak like that. It's impious.'

Antony came to the Dead Sea with Hillel and his family the next week and floated on his back while pretending to read the newspaper. He watched *Gveret* Kayafa light candles on Friday evening, while *Kohen Gadol* Kayafa prayed. He liked the candle lighting and the praying, watching silently and knowingly.

This is what their God wants.

He enjoyed the quiet of the Jewish Quarter on the Sabbath, eating cold food the cook prepared the day before. He liked listening to *Kohen Gadol* Kayafa pray in his musical voice. Like most Romans, Antony was a natural early riser, often encountering High Priest Kayafa in the kitchen as the sun rose. He watched him pray, saying nothing.

'What's that prayer your papa says every morning? I can just about say it, you know.' He began to recite the Hebrew. He was musical and his accent was good. Hillel looked down, fidgeting and turning red.

'Blessed are You for not making me a Gentile. Blessed are You for not making me a woman. Blessed are You for not making me a slave.'

Hillel rubbed the back of one hand across his face, a nervous gesture. 'I'm sorry,' he said. 'It doesn't mean we hate you.'

Antony shrugged.

'It's all right. I like being Roman. I wouldn't want to be anything else. I'm glad I'm a boy. And no one would want to be a slave, which is why we abolished it.'

Hillel looked relieved.

'I was worried you'd think we were being nasty.'

Antony waggled his head from shoulder to shoulder.

'Our soldiers call Jews sheep shaggers and sand fuckers,' he said. 'I wouldn't worry.'

At first Antony thought Hillel's house was bare and uninteresting, but he came, over time, to appreciate its pale apricot walls, seeing details in the sandstone for the first time. At home in Caesarea, Claudia's impressive art collection—sculpture, paintings, carvings—covered most of the house, and where there wasn't art, there was a riot of painted colour or decorative marbles.

'He's a lovely little boy,' Caiaphas said later, after Antony had gone home to Caesarea. 'Roman children always seem so loud and spoilt, but he's an exception.'

'His parents are nice but weird,' Antony told his parents that night at supper.

'How so?'

'*Gveret* Kayafa always does what *Kohen Gadol* Kayafa says, even when he's wrong. And she doesn't have no nice clothes.'

'Any,' Claudia corrected. '*Any* nice clothes.'

'And she's much younger and much prettier than him.'

'Well, quite.'

THE VISIT

Hillel was waiting as usual when one of Pilate's bodyguards dropped Antony outside the school. Even though it was *très* cool to be dropped off in an MRAP, the soldier—perhaps forgetting his charge was older now—made Antony outline his safety plan line by line, counting off the boy's answers on his fingers.

Hillel fell into step beside him. 'It's been bad here lately. The security. The Romans hardly leave their Quarter these days, or if they do, they've got about three guns each. Only whores go to the *cardo*, and they're always with heavily armed men.'

'That's not sex workers—that's only people on the Rite,' he said firmly. 'Sex workers are in the Greek Quarter.'

Hillel shrugged his shoulders. 'Papa says I'll have go to school with you soon.'

'Bad idea,' said Antony. 'The terrorists could get the Procurator's son and the High Priest's son in one hit that way. We have to come separately, and by different routes.'

'You're such a Roman, Ant.'

At lunch, Hillel told how his father had invited Antony to visit the Temple on Friday. He beamed when announcing the invitation, pushing his hair away from his forehead in such a way that the usual curly mess became curlier and messier.

'I didn't think followers of our rites could go in there.'

'Papa really likes you. He says you're the nicest Roman child he's ever met.'

Antony laughed. 'Am I the only Roman child he's ever met?'

Getting an invitation was one thing; the logistics of a safe visit was another. In the end it was decided he would go—once again in an MRAP—with Cornelius the Ginger and several fairly senior legionary officers. It wasn't ideal, because it wasn't discreet—you could hear the rotary engine whine streets away—but it seemed safer than any of the alternatives. Unfortunately, Jews in the vicinity would inevitably know their Temple had an important gentile visitor, and at least some of them wouldn't be happy.

Antony changed out of his school uniform in the Compound and stood just inside the door, waiting for Cornelius. The big man strode across the school grounds, machine pistol slung across his chest. He stopped and looked down at the boy. Antony craned his neck. Cornelius was huge, a man mountain.

'Hey, *Aquilifer* Getorex.'

'Cornelius's fine, Antony.'

'How tall are you?'

'Six foot seven, Antony.' He smiled. 'You've been asking me that for—what is it now—three years.'

'You wouldn't tell me.'

Cornelius grinned and ruffled Antony's hair. 'Fair enough. Now you know.'

Cornelius seemed to fold himself into the vehicle, while Antony sat in between two of Cornelius's inferiors. The MRAP was like a womb, and Antony felt himself starting to doze off. It was only when he heard what sounded like static (*not gunfire, surely?*) that he startled. *It's Cornelius's radio.* He listened as the legionary spoke into it in his low, calm voice.

The men around Antony waited, watching, coiled, ready to spring. The boy looked at them, at their concentration and calm and attention to detail and was glad, in a way he could not quite fathom, that they were his people. He could hear horses' hooves and sirens and shouting outside, could hear Cornelius's pithy account of events as they unfolded. The men were unperturbed; all their focus—he realised with sudden clarity—was on protecting him.

'I think you can take a look, now.'

It was Cornelius's voice. He touched Antony's shoulder and hoisted him up on one knee so he could see. The air was pungent with smoke and horseshit. Fire billowed from within one of the Temple courtyards, although the *vigiles* doused it soon enough. Soldiers and the Temple Guard fanned out, collecting rioters and spectators both, separating them and booking the former.

Antony had always found his namesake fortress, Antonia, impressive, but because he seldom left the Roman Quarter, he hadn't realised the extent to which the Temple dwarfed it. What the Temple lacked in height—Antonia enjoyed commanding views of the whole city—it more than made up for in sheer scale. The sun gleamed on its towers and courtyards, unadorned by comparison with a Roman temple, but beautiful in the same way the apricot stone in Hillel's house was beautiful. He was sorry to see it when two of its great courtyards were strewn with rubbish—food scraps, blood, cages of panicked birds, horseshit, sheep shit, trinkets and overturned stalls. Half-a-dozen scruffy looking rioters were thrown into a *Fretensis* paddy wagon. A JTN crew materialised. A crowd assembled to watch the fun. One of Cornelius's inferiors—a short, dark man with broad shoulders—popped up and stood on the vehicle's roof, his rifle perched on his hip.

'Look at this, sir,' he said. Antony detected a thick Spartan accent. 'Those fat arses in the Temple Guard are chasing some dumb fucker through the Court of the Israelites.'

Cornelius joined him, still holding Antony in his arms.

Antony did not complain—the view at Cornelius's head height was a good one.

'You want that street sign, kid? Jewish street signs look pretty interesting, I reckon.' Without waiting for Antony's answer, the legionary bounded down from the roof and retrieved it.

'Dunno what it says.'

'Caesarea, via Bezetha,' said Cornelius.

'How do you know that, sir?'

'Did that language course they offered a couple of years back. Which I recommend, by the way, although I didn't get out of it what I wanted to get out of it.'

'Which was?'

'Chat-up lines.'

'You made the mistake of thinking Judaea was a normal province.'

'Yep.'

'They don't wash often enough for me,' said the Spartan.

'Nothing that a trip to the baths won't fix,' said Cornelius.

'The fundamental problem is a refusal to open their legs,' said the street-sign thief. 'When you've figured out a way round that one, let me know.'

The rioters—it turned out there were still four at large—were skinny and fit, while members of the Temple Guard were anything but. Finally, the Romans waiting below in the Court of the Gentiles were drafted in. Antony could see Caiaphas standing off to one side, his face twisted into a wholly unfamiliar mask of rage. He waved his arms despairingly, looking all around him.

'I feel sorry for High Priest Kayafa,' he said to Cornelius's ear. 'I'm friends with his son,' he added, to no one in particular. Half-a-dozen Roman legionaries climbed the steps to the Temple proper. Cornelius observed through a set of binoculars.

'They've got Marcus Lonuobo on the job.'

'Who's that?' Antony asked.

'*Fretensis* sprint champion. Runs the Olympic qualifying time in the stade every morning before breakfast.'

Antony watched the Romans confer among themselves, then split up. He saw a sturdy black figure gain impossibly quickly on one rioter, then tackle him around the ankles. The next rioter was brought down by a blond legionary and pinned to the ground with a knee in the back. The blond handcuffed him.

Lonuobo somehow managed to corner the final two rioters, simultaneously. Both rioters kept running from the sprinter. He king hit one on the fly, knocking him out.

The final one turned to fight, launching what looked like a roundhouse kick at his pursuer. Lonuobo drew his machine pistol and stepped back, but gave no sign that he intended to fire. The rioter screamed a serious of epithets, so loud that even though Cornelius and his colleagues could not understand what they were, there was no doubt as to their offensiveness. Lonuobo's Latin response was both loud enough and clear enough to understand, even from this distance.

'I've fucking had you people!'

Lonuobo set his pistol to single shot and fired into the rioter's right kneecap.

'Hmm,' said the Spartan. 'Wonder what the little prick said. Marcus is pretty reasonable as a rule.'

The gunshot echoed around the Temple precinct, cutting through the hubbub. Cornelius climbed down from the roof, Antony still in his arms.

'Ah, *Aquilifer* Getorex.' (*Gotta get his attention somehow.*) 'You can put me down now.'

'Sorry, Antony, not thinking. And the name's Cornelius.'

Antony trotted behind the giant as he made his way towards Caiaphas and Hillel. The latter stood behind his father. The two—soldier and boy—climbed the steps to the Court of the Gentiles, dodging shit and pools of what Antony suspected was blood.

'I'm sorry, Hillel,' Antony blurted out. 'I hope it wasn't me. I was really looking forward to seeing the inside.'

'It's not you, Antony,' said Caiaphas, his voice thin and flat. 'Not at all.'

Antony looked at him. High Priest Kayafa wasn't like Papa; Caiaphas didn't address children directly unless he *had* to.

'I was hoping to show you around,' Hillel mumbled, 'it's beautiful inside.' Antony moved closer to him, patting his shoulder awkwardly. If Hillel were Roman he'd have wrapped his arms around him, but then Romans were touchy-feely people. He'd never seen Caiaphas touch his son—not even a pat on the head. Hillel fidgeted and stared at the ground.

Caiaphas approached Cornelius.

'It's Yeshua Ben Yusuf,' he said crossly. 'He's been building up to this for months, and now it's come to, to...' he trailed off. 'I think he wants to bring down the government.'

'That'll be a bit difficult,' Cornelius said, matter of fact. 'We're the government.'

Cornelius indicated the trashed courtyard with a wave of his hand.

'Your people are supposed to keep a lid on this crap, and they've utterly failed.'

'I'm sorry, *Aquilifer*.'

'Bit late for that now. You arm-twisted Procurator Pilate to get Roman troops out of the Temple precinct, and now you can't even stop criminal damage. What happens if it's terrorists next time?'

Caiaphas looked down.

Romans are the worst people in the world when they're right. They just won't leave it alone.

'Tell you what. Despite the moral hazard involved, I'll detail some of my men to clean this up. I'll leave you to think of a way to reward them for sorting out your mess.'

Caiaphas—his Latin was weaker than his son's—looked at Hillel.

'Moral hazard?'

Hillel had never had his father lean on him for language before, although his mother did it all the time. Even her Greek was sometimes spotty. He felt his face flush.

'It happens when you help people too much, Papa. They stop helping themselves.'

The short Spartan and his sign-stealing sidekick clattered up the steps towards Cornelius.

'Request permission to report, sir.'

'Permission granted, Tsamakis.'

'The ringleader appears to have made a getaway, although two of the captured rioters are associates, and one of them is currently assisting us with our enquiries.'

'Where is he?'

'According to the associate, he's in Gethsemane Public Park on the Jericho Road. The associate says he'll take members of the Temple Guard there to identify him.'

Saul drew deeply on his cigar and blew smoke down the bar. He watched the barman wipe a tumbler with a filthy rag and plant it in front of him. Apart from a pair of regulars at the back sharing bread, olives, and Celtiberian cerveza, he had what he suspected was the Greek Quarter's grimmest dive to himself. Half buried, and only accessible down a narrow, winding stair, Saul guessed that its proprietor, a Corinthian called Konstantinos, made relatively little from selling food and drink.

Saul peered through the smoke haze as one of the regulars stood to greet a sweaty man in heavy Persian robes. The two sat to transact some business; Saul saw the grey glint of gunmetal as what he knew to be a silencer changed hands.

'Want to try some Caledonian firewater?'

Konstantinos held the smeary tumbler under Saul's nose. The smell of peat rose from the brown liquid in the glass, making Saul's eyes water. He took it wordlessly, drinking slowly, trying not to gag. There were Romans, he knew, who were aficionados of the Caledonian 'Water of Life', as they called it. Saul cared only for the effect. The Caledonian liquor flowed into his memory, dislodging something long buried.

When he was a small boy, ten or so, his father had taken him to Rome on one of his business trips. The city awed and terrified him. He thought he was going to die when the little man at a scrambler intersection near the Forum turned green and streams of people seemed to flow into each other. Copying the Roman children around him, he reached out for his father but instead found himself hand in hand with a member of the Vigiles. Saul couldn't see his father and panicked, turning against the flow of pedestrians and trying to search the crowd. The little man had started to flash red–green–red–green–red and the Romans on the other side of the road stopped trying to cross. The policeman seized both his hands and lifted him over the kerb and onto the footpath.

'When the robot is red,' he said, 'you must not cross.'

(Romans scowled if you crossed when the robot was coloured red. It was wondrous, this, that the rulers of Europe obeyed the robot when the little man was red.)

Saul's father swam up out of the crowd and reclaimed him; the policeman smiled and the two men shook hands. Minutes later, he saw the same policeman spot fine a tourist for littering, and watched a group of outlandishly dressed women commandeer most of a trolley car. The driver rang his bell many more times than usual.

'Why did he do that?'

His father pointed to a woman dressed in brilliant saffron and red with glitter in her hair.

'She is getting married soon.'

He noticed that vendors and hawkers could leave their goods unattended on the footpath and nothing would disappear, not even fruit from greengrocers' boxes. He saw small children licking penis-shaped iced lollies and watched Romans his own age give up their seats in the Metro to pregnant women and crippled veterans. At one point during their trip—although it came to nought in the end—the Senate ordered a general mobilisation. The streets filled with armed young men walking to the recruiting stations.

'Where did they get their guns?'

'Every male Roman citizen has a gun at home. He is taught to use it at school.'

One day his father took him to Julian's house on the Palatine and went into the city. Julian was a business associate, and he left Saul largely to his own devices. Saul got a servant to massage him and then he washed in the baths, noticing that the Roman children went naked. When he dropped his shorts he wondered why they—boys and girls both—laughed at him. The servant who'd massaged him shook his head.

'You're naked.'

'So are you.'

'Part of your cock is missing,' he said, pointing at Saul's glans. 'You're only to show that part when you're about to have sex with someone, and you're too young yet for sex.'

Saul realised—albeit slowly—that they were mocking his circumcision.

'You have a weird definition of naked.'

'So do you.'

He dragged up his shorts and fled, leaving wet footprints in the corridor. He wanted to find Julian's office, and he slowed as he neared it. On the wall outside was an elaborate mural of two women kissing, their limbs entwined. Julian stepped out from behind his desk and came to the door.

'Why don't Romans ever steal anything?' Saul asked.

'That would bring shame,' Julian answered.

'But what's on your wall?' Saul said, pointing at the mural. 'That doesn't bring shame?'

Julian waggled his head, uncomprehending.

'No, of course not. It's not as though they're stealing anything.'

When he returned, Julian spoke to Saul's father, who then thrashed Saul for being impertinent. Roman parents did this. Rude children, they said, shouldn't be able to sit down afterwards.

'We are guests in Julian's house,' he said.

'But it's two women!'

'They don't care about that.'

'But it's not natural!'

Saul cried hot tears; his backside was sore and his father seemed to be looking straight through him. Julian appeared in the doorway, a tumbler of Caledonian firewater in hand: Saul could smell the peat.

'Am I interrupting something?'

Saul ran across the room, pointing at Julian's face.

'You're weird, all of you. There's something wrong with you!'

Julian stepped backwards, looking at Saul's father over the boy's head.

'I think you need to bring your son under control.'

'You haven't finished your drink,' Konstantinos said. 'You should. It's good.'

Saul threw it back, feeling the burn. He could stomach Julian's favoured drink, even if Julian were too much for him. Konstantinos raised one eyebrow and reclaimed his tumbler: it was cleaner where the liquor had flowed over the glass.

'Also, I think your Samaritan contact will be here soon.'

THE EMPIRE

'The Empire Hotel,' Linnaeus instructed the cabbie, tapping the glass behind the driver's head again. The latter slowly uncurled and gripped the steering wheel with white-knuckled hands. He saw the young people in his rear-view mirror; the soldiers and their women disappeared into the Fleet Fox, laughing. He realised that the woman with black and purple hair was highborn. Not a whore. The men were all officers; he could see their ranks. He found himself admiring their uniforms, the blood-red jackets, black piping, black trousers and high black collars. The very tall ginger wore the scales of justice on his collar, opposite the X *Fretensis* wild boar; the tanned one beside the woman with black and purple hair was wearing a black cloak lined with red. As he watched, the soldier flung it back over one shoulder, revealing the calf-length robe that officers sometimes wore as an alternative to trousers. Whenever he saw Roman soldiers in dress uniform, he always had the same struggle to prevent himself from admiring them. When they were in the streets wearing their desert battle dress and coalscuttle helmets and heavy boots, one could despise them—the body armour even made them look non-human—but not when they were preening like peacocks and charming the women who wished to reward the Empire's warriors for their protective efforts.

'It's probably better if you stop looking at them.'

He looked at his passenger instead—a lean, crow-like man with straight dark hair, now greying at the temples. A gold band around his head sat just above his ears, marking the fine hair, which was cut almost as short as a soldier's. He was wearing an expensive dark-blue robe with shoulder-to-ankle organ pleating, a gold ring on the little finger of his right hand, an ornate gold watch—cut in such a way that the mechanism showed—on a chain around his neck. A diamond sparkled in his left ear.

As he drove further away from the Fleet Fox, the cabbie felt himself start to thaw even though he was still well in the Roman Quarter, with its gracious porphyry-fronted homes, clipped lawns, and gardens adorned with marble sculpture.

'And you might want to let me open the window again. It smells like armpit in here.'

He drew up in front of the Empire, parking in the spot the valet indicated. Linnaeus handed him precisely three times the metered fare.

'Thank you, rich Roman,' he said, stumbling over his Latin again.

'Greek is fine,' Linnaeus said in Greek. He paused and looked the cabbie in the eye. His expression softened. 'I know that was hard for you.'

The cabbie looked down at his shoes. The crow-man was making an attempt at sympathy, rare in any Roman of his experience. He spoke in Greek now, far more secure than his Latin, although very far from Linnaeus's Attic perfection.

'Rich Roman, tell me this—why do you let your children, your *daughters*, act like that?'

Linnaeus laughed and flapped his hands, reverting to Roman type. '*Let* doesn't come into it. They're all free, citizens, and over sixteen. And it's *Festa*, when we remember how Cybele saved the city.'

The cabbie nodded without understanding.

'Now, I've got a bit on while I'm here, and a driver would

be handy. I'll pay triple your average daily takings to have you on call for the next week, with a bonus at the end for a job well done.'

The cabbie brightened. Romans were good to do business with, of this there was no doubt.

'I can do that.'

'Good. I expect a clean interior, though, and to have control over my own window. I suggest a scrub for both you and the seats.' The cabbie flinched.

If only these Romans knew how filthy they are!

'I'd like you here at zero eight thirty hours tomorrow. I have a residence in the Jewish Quarter to attend first, then to the Vinculum to see a client.'

He paused and extended his hand. 'Andreius Linnaeus, Advocate-at-Law.'

The cabbie accepted it, tentatively. 'I am David Ben David. Easy to remember.' He smiled. 'I even have a card.' He bent over and rummaged around in the glove box, producing a dog-eared business card.

ARIMATHEA

Joseph knew the Roman love of punctuality, yet still did not expect the lawyer to attend precisely at 0845 hours. He startled when he heard a car engine cut out in the street below and began to sweat when footfalls sounded on his front steps. *He came. He actually fronted. A big-shot Roman lawyer turns up for a non-citizen.* His inner eye—long prone to seeing all sides of every question—supplied a cynical rejoinder: *He showed because you've got the money to pay him, Joseph, let's not get ahead of ourselves here.*

Although he's not charging very much, to be fair, going on about pro bono publico and what have you.

Three sharp raps followed; the lawyer did not use the doorbell.

Joseph lived in one of the best parts of town: high, light, with commanding views of the countryside beyond the city limits. All the houses in the street—including, at the highest point, the High Priest's residence—were well set back and hewn from apricot stone. Joseph's house was faced with the local pink marble. His clipped lawn and elegant topiary marked him out as insufferably modish, even an aper of Roman fashion. He'd long ago given up explaining to his neighbours that he actually liked gardening, and that the clever trimming and cutting was a product not of hired Roman tradesmen but of his own hands.

Linnaeus looked at the man who stood before him—snowy bearded, short and ruddy, fleshy faced, green-eyed, bald, in a long white gown. He was uncannily like the paintings of Saturn he'd once seen as a teenager on the walls in the local temple. *And uncannily like one of Saturn's priests, too.*

His mother had taken him to see the *haruspex* to determine whether he should study law or medicine (*the liver was whole, and did not need curing, so law it was*). He'd fidgeted throughout the whole ritual, flinched when the Priest flicked his head with sheep's blood and compelled him to drink a cup of wine rendered bitter with strange herbs. The altar room with its dismembered sheep was dark, gloomy and more than a bit frightening for a clever boy raised in the sunlit uplands of the best school in the district. He found himself appalled not only by the bloodiness of the diviner's robes, but also by the fact his mother had paid money for the ritual and taken the outcome seriously.

'She's Sardi, and doesn't know any better,' Angel had said. 'Humour her.'

'Don Linnaeus, are you all right? Have you rushed to get here? I did not expect you so soon.'

Linnaeus snapped into the present, shaking his head. He flapped his hands.

'I am sorry, Rabbi Arithem—' he corrected himself, 'Arimathea. You reminded me of someone else, someone I haven't seen for a long time, and had long forgotten.'

'And hoped to forget, perhaps?' said Joseph.

'Yes, that too.'

Linnaeus extended his hand. Joseph took it, hesitantly.

'Would you like coffee?'

'A double espresso, if you've got it to hand. I'm afraid I've made the mistake of arriving uncaffeinated.'

'Please take a seat, Don Linnaeus.'

Joseph disappeared; Linnaeus heard the rising hiss of

a coffee machine. He sat at what he presumed was Joseph's dining room table, opened his briefcase, and began removing documents.

'You will have to rely on my Greek houseboy,' said Joseph from the kitchen. 'My cook is Jewish, and today is the Sabbath.'

'I'm happy to go down the street and buy coffee if preparing it for me will cause you to break your rite.'

'You don't need to be my *Shabbat goy*, Don Linnaeus. The boy will cope.'

Linnaeus looked up, not understanding, smiling uneasily.

'I did not think you would come, Don Linnaeus. You are only the second Roman adult to set foot in this street willingly.' His Latin was technically correct, but laboured.

Linnaeus leant forward. 'I'll speak Greek if you prefer.'

Joseph did not pause.

'I do not count the soldiers who patrol every day in their armoured cars,' he continued. 'I do not think they are here willingly.'

'There are better provinces,' Linnaeus agreed. 'Less dangerous. More fun.'

'Ah, yes. You and your pleasures, you Romans. That is rather your thing, isn't it?'

Linnaeus ignored the small barb. The boy set two tiny cups down on the table and bowed.

'Thank you, Kyril,' Joseph said, patting his head. The child flinched, just a little. *You're not supposed to pat Greeks on the head, Rabbi.* 'He's a good boy. Sends money home to his mother in Cyprus.'

Linnaeus watched the boy withdraw, his hands clasped, waiting for directions.

'Well, I came, Rabbi Arimathea, in spite of your fears. I've read the Yeshua Ben Yusuf dossier. I've made some enquiries of my own. I will see Ben Yusuf this afternoon. I've formed a preliminary view of various matters, and I'm sure you have some good information to share.'

Joseph looked at the lawyer. 'Yeshua Ben Yusuf is the most remarkable man I have ever met, Don Linnaeus. He is a scholar and a teacher, and he has a heart overflowing with compassion. Today I appear before you in "civvies", as your soldiers put it, but I am a member of Jerusalem's Sanhedrin—a Jewish priest, as it were.' He paused. 'The High Priest is furiously angry with Yeshua over the Temple riot, and there have been harsh words between us this past week. I have to convince him that he is mistaken.'

'That riot was special, Rabbi. I've got the *Fretensis* evidence photographs here.'

Linnaeus placed an envelope of 10" by 8" images before Joseph, who leafed through them slowly.

'Apart from that, there are two men still in Æsculapion, one in a deep coma. He may die, which will make Ben Yusuf's case more difficult. The State will make a case for murder *dolus indirectus* or *dolus eventualis*, and with good reason.'

Joseph's Latin finally failed him. '*Dolus ev*... I'm sorry, this I don't understand. I do not get to practise my Latin very often.'

Linnaeus switched smoothly to Greek. 'Broadly, they deal with a death that comes about when a person is in the midst of committing another crime, as a *consequence* of that person committing that crime, and allege that the person *knew* the consequence was likely.'

'Another coffee?'

'Please.'

Linnaeus continued over the hiss of the coffee machine.

'At present, the case against Ben Yusuf for breach of the peace, malicious mischief and aggravated assault is insurmountably strong. If he gets away with just breach of the peace and malicious mischief convictions and a few assaults,

Pilate will have him imprisoned—I'm thinking maybe seven to eight years—but that's likely to be it. Civilian administrators tend to prefer imprisonment to corporal punishment. Some of them also avoid the dreaded condemnation to the arena for capital crimes, although this is spottier. Many Romans of all backgrounds enjoy watching that for its own sake. If, however, the malicious mischief conviction is *in addition* to a capital conviction, then Pilate will revert to the traditional Roman method.'

'A flogging first?'

'Yes. We don't do it as much as we used to, and never to citizens, of course, but we still do it. Older Romans don't believe prison deters, even though there is plenty of evidence that it does. A reasonable compromise lets the floggers have their fun before a death sentence is carried out.'

Joseph nodded.

'Unfortunately, there's also a strong whiff of terrorism. One of the rioters apprehended—Yehuda Escariot—I don't think I've said that properly—came up as a DNA match for the IED bombing outside the Dea Tacita Centre last year. He'll be tried separately, of course.'

Joseph shuddered visibly, almost dropping his coffee. 'The abortion clinic?'

'Three legionaries died in that attack, including a doctor working in the Dea Tacita Centre as an emergency *locum* for *another* doctor the terrorists had knocked off earlier. Needless to say, the *Fretensis* people aren't best pleased that—' he struggled with the name.

'It's pronounced Iscariot.'

'—Aren't best pleased that Iscariot seems to be trying to cut himself some sort of deal by handing Ben Yusuf over to the authorities. If Tullius Capito has anything to do with it, they'll both have to spend a fair bit of time with their heads below their feet ingesting water through washcloths.'

Joseph gasped as the boy set Andreius's second coffee before him and then sat down, clutching the front of his shirt.

'So they will torture, then?'

'Only non-citizens, and only on application. These days it's all recorded for posterity and tendered as evidence, which stops the worst of what used to go on. Pilate has also forbidden electricity in Judaea. At a pinch, he can still send a suspect to Syria for electricity—everything's still allowed up there—but that requires the prosecutor to make a formal application in open court, and Pilate has to provide the Syrian provincial administration appropriate compensation. As they say, all regulated.'

'So every province is different?'

'A Roman never saw a market he didn't like, Rabbi. We've created an internal market in torture, with Britannia at one end—no torture for anyone—and Syria—everything permitted—at the other. The British methods are pretty good. Half the suspects in northern Gaul are interrogated in Londinium. Britannia does very well out of it.'

This time it was Linnaeus who *did* drop his coffee when the *vocale* in the entrance hall chimed. The boy answered it and then stepped into the kitchen.

'The *vocale* is for Don Linnaeus, Rabbi.'

Linnaeus stood and followed him, passing him a few coppers as he did so. The boy smiled and patted down his hair.

Joseph hurried away to fetch paper towels and clean up. He watched Linnaeus take the shiny metal and wood thing from the wall hook and push the little brass lever across to the side marked *receive*.

'I'm taking instructions right now. I did say hold all calls.'

'Oh, shit. I see.'

'Who's handling the State's case?'

'Is he good? Sounds British.'

'He'll at least keep the interrogation team under control.'

'I'll have to review the CCTV footage before I know what the new charges will be, won't I?'

'I'm going this afternoon.'

The boy wrung out a cloth and used it to wipe the table dry while Joseph watched. Linnaeus sat stoically, arms pinned to his sides, hands resting on the edge. Joseph looked at him. Linnaeus took a long time to speak.

'Well, now we do have a problem. They switched off life support an hour ago. There's a pile of CCTV footage, including a good whack of Ben Yusuf. The State prosecutor is a young chap by the name of Cornelius Getorex, who is apparently very bright.'

'I know Cornelius Getorex,' said Joseph. 'He's impossible to miss.' He indicated height with one hand, and rubbed his own bald scalp with the other.

Linnaeus felt a warm stab of recognition. 'Ah, yes, I have met him briefly. He'll be a most unhappy man right now, because I know what he did last night.'

David Ben David found himself a shady spot underneath one of Joseph Arimathea's cypresses, stretching his legs out in front of him. He reached out and pressed his fingers against the springy grass where he sat, admiring the way it bounced up again after a few seconds or so. He made vague plans around what to do with the triple takings he'd have by the end of the week, always scotching them in favour of something else that seemed more sensible or worthwhile. He watched a Roman MRAP whine up the street, two young legionaries sitting casually on its roof, rifles across their knees. One of them waved at him. He did not think the gesture was friendly, and did not respond.

No danger for them in better-off parts of town.

They'd bunker down in other places, though, to avoid the hordes of urchins who followed behind flinging stones. He'd seen their young faces gazing out as rocks pinged against the windows, unblinking and unperturbed. Romans in general disturbed him, but their legionaries had a depraved and sensuous cruelty that made him ill. Once he'd seen one pop up out of the roof and catch one of the rocks as casually as a normal person plucks an apple, then in one smooth, coordinated motion fling it back at the child who'd thrown it at him. And he didn't miss, either. The urchin's head split open—not fatally, but there was a great deal of blood. His young friends dropped their rocks and crowded around him. The legionary with the good throwing arm threw his head back and laughed.

Eventually thirst got the better of him. He brushed stray blades of grass from the clean linen shirt he'd donned first thing that morning, stood up and knocked on Joseph's front door.

'What I have to do,' Linnaeus was saying, 'is detach Ben Yusuf's behaviour in the Temple from anything Iscariot or his confreres may have done. He's got no priors—'

Ben David used the doorbell: both men inside startled.

'I'm thirsty, *Domine* Linnaeus. Could I have a glass of water?'

Joseph bounced up. 'Great god, who is that?'

'I'm sorry, that's my driver.'

'Why didn't you bring him in with you?'

The reproachful tone in Joseph's voice was unmissable. He bustled across the room, invited Ben David into his kitchen and fetched him a glass and pitcher of cold water. Linnaeus watched as he drank thirstily, his dark eyes blinking above the rim of the glass.

'Your driver is allowed inside, you know.'

Linnaeus scratched the back of his neck, self-conscious. In Rome, servants waited outside. He thought they did in Judaea, too, although perhaps not in Arimathea's house.

'The crucial thing to remember is that Ben Yusuf needs to be as candid as possible with me. If, as you say, he's always been pacifist in his outlook, then I can construct the temple riot as an aberration. I'm hoping the CCTV footage shows the fatality coming about thanks to something Iscariot or one of his lackeys did.'

'The Temple precinct shouldn't be a market,' Joseph said. 'That's what Yeshua was trying to say. It hurts the poor. The moneychangers who Yeshua confronted are among the most personally corrupt human beings I've ever seen. I've had this conversation over and over with Caiaphas, but he won't see reason. He's been using the profits to pay for upkeep, which makes it moral for him.'

Linnaeus flapped his hands. 'Convincing Pilate that there shouldn't be a market somewhere is going to be nigh on impossible, Rabbi. Caiaphas has, so I understand, been a competent High Priest. Your Temple is famous all over the Empire in part due to his efforts.'

'That's not what it's *for*, Don Linnaeus.'

'If Yeshua Ben Yusuf has issues with the administration of the Temple Precinct, then wrecking the place in the company of a known terrorist is probably not the best way to make his point.'

'Yeshua never made enquiries about his followers' backgrounds, Don Linnaeus. He took people as they are, forgave them their sins and told them not to sin again.'

Linnaeus failed to slap down his native cynicism.

'When did Iscariot join this happy little band? If he joined after abandoning his career as a bomber of abortion clinics then that's one thing. If he hit the Dea Tacita Centre after taking up with Ben Yusuf, however, then it's difficult to avoid the imputation that Ben Yusuf was in on it somehow.'

Joseph dropped his head and stroked his beard, a gesture that in many people would seem sinister but for him seemed nervous and distracted. 'You sound like my daughter,' he said softly. 'She has become Roman too, although the transformation is not yet complete.'

Joseph gathered his thoughts. 'In this statement I have to do, you say I have to write everything I know about Ben Yusuf?'

'Yes. But not what other people have told you about him, Mary Magdalena or Petros Bar Yonah and so on. It has to be what you know and saw, and what you'd be prepared to attest to under oath before the Procurator.'

PART II

MR BENNETT: Yes, precisely, Your Honour. The second element is paragraph (b) of the definition which is that: the action is done or the threat is made with the intention of advancing a political, religious or ideological cause; and (c) the action is done or the threat is made with the intention of: (i) coercing, or influencing by intimidation, the government of the Commonwealth or a State, Territory or foreign country, or of part of a State, Territory or foreign country; or (ii) intimidating the public or a section of the public. Now, that definition can be very loosely—I do not suggest accurately—but very loosely summarised as ideologically motivated violence designed to intimidate.

GLEESON CJ: It is loose. Was whipping the moneychangers in the temple an act of terrorism?

MR BENNETT: Your Honour, it might depend on a number of matters. The question of whether paragraph (c) would have been satisfied might have been involved there. Whether it is down to coerce or influence by intimidation, government, or whether to...

KIRBY J: It is intimidating a section of the public. It was certainly intimidating a few moneychangers. They would not have liked it at all.

—*Thomas v Mowbray & Ors* [2007] High Court of Australia Trans 76 (20 February 2007).

The parchment Yehuda referred to still holds pride of place on Saul's wall.

He can remember his father—rewarded for filling Legio III Gallica's field kit requirements—stepping up before the Legatus in the Temple of the Divine Julius in Antioch. Saul stood behind his parents, cringing as they took the Citizen's Oath and the Governor shook their hands, thanking Saul's father for his excellent tents and mess kits and service to the Empire. Saul was old enough to feel terrified as well as humiliated; his father had insisted on enrolling him in one of Antioch's biggest Roman schools. His parents didn't keep kosher and dressed and lived like Romans—his father even had a concubine for a three-year contract at one point—but Saul still had to bring notes to school asking to be excused for festivals no one had ever heard of. His parents attended synagogue on the High Holy Days, for appearances' sake.

'I'm Jewish,' he told his teachers. 'I have to go.'

'But you eat pork. I've seen you eat it in the dining hall.'

'I like pork,' he said.

They shrugged at this, and took to treating him as a special project, to be pitied.

'You watch brutality,' he told some of them once, when they'd invited him to a cage fight in the city, the big one beside the stock exchange. 'You listen to noise, not music. You only care about things, what you own, what you can show off—'

'We get it, Saul. You don't want to come. That's fine.'

'You're lucky to be at such a fine school,' his teachers told him. 'You should study hard and bring honour to your family.' He heard about eight-hour practice sessions in music or martial arts, saw a boy he slightly knew chained to the kitchen table until he'd finished his homework.

In the meantime his father groomed him to take over the family business and asked when he'd bring home a nice woman so in future there'd be a few grandchildren. Saul always found himself despairing at this. He didn't like women and he didn't want anything to do with them. He hated the way the Roman women students dressed, and he loathed the animal way all of them—male and female—entertained themselves.

The last straw came when he'd walked into a Roman barber and the man had cut his hair to look like a soldier's. He looked at himself in the mirror at home and when his mother told him there was only a week between a good haircut and a bad haircut, he began to sob.

Then there'd been the huge argument with his father when he wanted to go to Jerusalem alone for Passover.

'Judaea's dangerous,' his father said. 'That's why we don't live there.'

In the end his mother's sister in Caesarea came to the rescue, and he was allowed to go on condition that he spend most of his time with her family. She'd married a Spartan, and Saul found himself making continual social gaffes around his uncle. He'd refused to go to the palaestra *to exercise and when his uncle asked if he'd found a good* erastes, *Saul thought the older man was about to proposition him.*

'I, ah, kind of like him,' he had admitted to his aunt.

'He can't take you as his eromenos,*' she said.*

'Why?'

'You're related, even though only through marriage. If that's what you want, you need to go to the men's palaestra with him. You'll meet someone there. That's why he asked if you wanted to go; that way he can vet them for you.'

'Um, you're not supposed to be encouraging me to be a shirt-lifter.'

She shrugged and pointed her fingers at the ceiling, her hands open. 'De gustibus non est disputandum,' she said.

Saul fled to Jerusalem the next day, furious that he had to learn the appropriate ritual behaviour out of a book and despairing as he watched Jewish families who knew what they were doing with a beautiful, natural ease. At his wits' end, he climbed the great internal staircase and sat in the upper floor of Herod's colonnade, listening to the sages expound the law. He curled his hands around his knees, feeling the kiss of cool air on his cheek.

On his second afternoon in the colonnade, a young man sat beside him, introduced himself and picked up the book on Jewish law that Saul was using as a crib.

'It's a shame so many of us need things like this, now.'

THE PROSECUTOR

'Now that's a beautiful thing,' Camilla said.

Cornelius and Mirella had made spoons, her dark chocolate form curled inside his milk one. His arm was draped over her; she dozed lightly, and—perhaps partly consciously—snuggled into him. His eyelids flicked and twitched.

'He's dead to the world,' Marius said. 'But I think she wants some more.'

'They'll be serving our breakfast soon,' Rhianna said, making a nest with the abundant cushions around her and drawing her knees into her chest. 'I could eat about six eggs after that.'

Marius pulled something out of his teeth, holding it up in front of his eyes and examining it closely.

'What have you got there?' Rhianna asked.

'A blonde pubic hair.'

She giggled, then luxuriated on her back, looking up at him. 'You're the only natural blonde in here.'

Marius crawled towards her and rested his head in her lap, turning onto his back. She stroked his bristles.

'I think we can all agree that was a roaring success,' he said to no one in particular. 'Best bloc I've had in I don't know how long.'

There was a discreet knock at one of the sliding panels on the other side of the room; one of the Fleet Fox staff. 'Breakfast is served in the dining hall. You are invited to join us.' Her voice—transferred through the speaker—was coolly metallic.

Camilla gazed sadly at Cornelius and Mirella. 'We're gonna

have to wake them up.'

'They do look stunning together. Like an advertisement for an arty photographic exhibit or something.'

'I love her braids.'

'They'd make gorgeous babies.'

'They should get together permanently,' Camilla said. 'They always go well at *Festa*.'

Marius crouched next to the sleeping couple, lifting one of Cornelius's flicking eyelids and placing cool fingers on Mirella's neck. 'Food's up, people. Rise and shine.'

Cornelius was onto his third helping of bacon and eggs, ladling food into his mouth with one hand while he wrapped the other around Mirella's waist. Sometimes he fed her as well.

'You've got the biggest cock I've ever seen on a white boy,' she said with her mouth full. 'I suspect it's the biggest cock I've ever seen.'

Their bloc was scattered around the long table, eating for the most part in silence. There were three blocs beside their own, one all male, the others a blend of genders. The dining hall was vast and cavernous, its walls of polished wood hung with gilt-edged antique paintings. A portrait of the Emperor gazed sternly down on matters from above the main entrance. A dozen sticks of incense burnt down sweetly on a shelf in front of him.

'I've never seen someone eat so much food all in one sitting,' Marius said.

A Fleet Fox priestess—the woman with the oddly metallic voice, it seemed she talked like that all the time—touched Cornelius lightly on the shoulder.

'There is a messenger boy for you at the entrance counter, *Aquilifer* Getorex. Normally we wouldn't disturb a devotee at this point, but apparently it's very urgent.'

Cornelius disentangled his arm gently from around Mirella's waist, made excuses to the others and strode naked across the hall.

The boy was waiting under the portico, his hair slicked down, wearing cadet's uniform. He looked about twelve or thirteen. Cornelius had a fair idea who had sent him. The boy was careful to stand well back from the temple entrance, knowing his path was barred until he was older and an initiate. Cornelius was forced to step into the light. He squinted, conscious of his nakedness. *Do I have a lipstick ring around my cock, I wonder?*

'*Aquilifer* Getorex?'

'That's me, young pal.'

The boy handed him a note, his eyes glittering with the flat sheen of hero worship.

There are two urgent pending legal matters that need to be addressed before Passover, and Lucretius Viera is in Rome, the note began, without salutation. *Report to me in Antonia in 30 minutes.* Cornelius wondered, for a moment, why the paper had not combusted of its own volition. *Make yourself unavailable like this again and I'll put you on a charge.*

Cornelius—normally among the most soft-spoken of men—swore once, loud enough for his voice to echo through the whole complex. He stopped himself then, remembering that he had to tip the messenger boy. He looked down, relieved at the absence of lipstick in embarrassing places but also noting the lack of anything resembling pockets or money.

'I take it you'll be needing some of this?'

The priestess with the strange voice held up a twenty *sesterce* piece. It was an absurdly large sum for an errand boy. Cornelius took it and handed it to the child, who was now goggle-eyed with wonder. Cornelius turned to the smirking *gallus*.

'Add it to the bill, please, *Sacra Mater*.'

'I already have.'

Mirella followed him as he collected his clothing and wallet on his way to the baths.

'Work shit,' he said, kissing her on the forehead. 'And I've pissed Capito off. If he's feeling ugly, he'll make me piss in the bottle and I'll be up for a flogging.'

She watched as he drank three large mugs of water, one after the other. She joined him under the shower, oiling his back.

'Don't overdo it, lovely one,' he rocked his head back. 'Or I'll just want more and really finish up in a world of pain.'

He was surprised to feel her turning him to face her. He watched the water running in between her cornrows and cascading down her face. She clasped her hands around the back of his head. For a moment it seemed she wanted to say something; he waited but nothing was forthcoming. He pulled her to him and kissed her.

'I do want more,' he said, 'but I have to go.'

Enormously grateful that he'd brought his uniform jacket with him, he fumbled with his collar and swore at his clumsiness. He rubbed his chin, looking into the mirror.

'The joys of Celticness. Beards that fail to show.'

'You still gave me beard burn.'

THE HELP

Claudia stood at the entrance to Antony's den, knowing what must be done—to a place cluttered with objects of peculiar uselessness, to a twelve-year-old boy's second home. She pointed at the young Greek woman who had applied for the role of nanny for the next month.

'Clean it up,' she said.

After being burnt with poorly chosen domestic staff in Caesarea thanks to relying on agency recommendations, her policy was now to ask for half-a-dozen candidates that she would interview and put through their paces. She'd found her cook readily enough; a handsome, curly-headed young man called Aristocles. He prepared a selection of Greek, Italian, and Roman dishes for her under time pressure—and she hired him on the spot.

The nanny was proving a tougher nut to crack, however. This was not because the young women the agency sent her were incompetent with children, but because their accents were atrocious.

'One of the reasons I want a nanny is to force my son to speak Greek. I'm not, however, going to have him speaking something that sounds like it could have emerged from a Corinthian sewer. I'm quite happy to pay extra for a better accent.'

'Yes, Ma'am. We'll send you a different girl tomorrow, an Athenian.'

As Claudia watched, the Greek girl—*she's a pretty little thing*—started organising, discarding and filing. She hung

Antony's model gladiators from the ceiling and drove his remote-controlled racer into the cupboard. She had no ideas for the street sign, and turned to Claudia.

'*Domina*, this is a very unusual decoration!'

Claudia startled at the form of address.

'He probably wanted it for the pretty Hebraic script. I hope he didn't steal it, but you never know. Just prop it against the wall for the moment.'

The Athenian girl did have a good accent, what seemed to be a lively awareness of literature and art and—an unexpected bonus—she could dance. When she told Claudia she was saving money in order to pay for tuition at one of the better teacher training *collegia* at home in Athens, that closed the deal. Claudia called the agency, gave the names of her hires—the girl was called Zoë—and made arrangements for background security checks and payment.

'Zoë is an excellent choice, Ma'am,' said the woman at the agency. 'Her last employer was most impressed with her.'

She called the two of them to her and had them sit at the kitchen table.

'You are no doubt used to great lists of rules from Roman employers, breach of any of which is a sacking offence, yes?'

They both nodded.

'I have very few rules, but I *will* dismiss you if you break them. The first is that you will call me *Kyria* and my husband *Procurator*. I will not have the words *dominus* and *domina* used in this household. Some Romans find it attractive to pretend that they can still own slaves. My husband and I do not. Do you understand?'

Both of them had huge eyes at this, and they nodded gravely.

'Next, I will not have household goods sourced from

companies with significant overseas slaveholdings or trading interests, either in Terra Nova or elsewhere. To make this easier, I've prepared a detailed list for you.'

She handed both of them a printed sheet. Aristocles in particular studied it with great care, mentally checking lists of ingredients.

'Sometimes it can be hard to source things without buying slave-made goods, Kyria,' he said. 'This especially applies to sweets, to *chocolatl*.'

'If it seems to be proving impossible, tell me. My father was Lucius Aennius, and he expended much of his wealth in the campaign to end slavery. He died young, and I would like to honour his memory.'

Even Aristocles had heard the name. Greeks honoured the Stoic abolitionists of Rome, people who had to fight their own culture—with its rapacity and aggression—to free the inventors of civil government.

'You are to speak Greek at all times, even when addressed in Latin. Antony in particular will be resistant to this, at least at the beginning, but his Greek is really quite good. It is, however, in need of polishing.'

'What should I do if he says he can't understand something, *Kyria*?'

'Tell him to use the dictionary, Zoë.'

She nodded.

'As you've probably guessed, this residence was once a palace. There are half-a-dozen rooms you can each choose from. If at any point you decide you like one another, you have my permission to move into a room together.'

Each looked at the other, reddening but also smiling.

'You are to cooperate in keeping your living and working areas clean, but no more. General maintenance and hygiene is handled by the garrison.'

The relief on Zoë's face in particular was clear.

'As you are no doubt aware, the security situation in Jerusalem at present is not the best. If you form a relationship with anyone other than a member of X *Fretensis* or each other, I will have to be told before he or she sets foot in here.'

They both nodded.

'I have not scheduled any official days off for the month,' Claudia said, 'but if you approach me in advance, I will do my best to accommodate you.'

'That's very kind of you, *Kyria*.'

'In any case, the actual Passover period—from Thursday to Sunday—will be quiet for the most part. There will be one banquet during the course of the month, at which Zoë will have to dance, although I will notify you in advance once I have fixed the date.'

Zoë smiled. 'I am a good dancer, *Kyria*. I can dance the main themes from all major Roscius's films, the Woman's Pattern for the bloc, as well as traditional Greek dances.'

Claudia smiled at this. In the days of the slave market, Zoë would have commanded a high price.

'If you impress me, I will also contract you to work for us in Caesarea, which I think both of you are likely to enjoy.'

There were two vigorous nods at this. Most local Greeks were always trying to find jobs outside Jerusalem. Only *hetaerae* preferred the city to other places; they enjoyed the lack of competition.

'My husband will also supervise the Rite for Cybele on Sunday, which you are welcome to join.'

Claudia sat back in her chair.

'Questions?'

Aristocles held his fingers in front of his lips, reddening again and looking down.

'Will the *paterfamilias*, ah...' his voice trailed off.

Claudia read him the moment he used the Latin word.

'Like sexual services, Aristocles?'

'Yes, *Kyria*.'

'No, he won't. Of course, it is likely we will have guests over the *Megalesia* period who are less discriminating. The extent to which you accommodate their requests is up to you.'

Cornelius likes the Law Room; he feels at home among its banks of screens, boards covered in mathematical squiggles, stacks of legal documents, textbooks and glittering engines. He also likes the thought of having it to himself: Viera's a dry old stick, fond of form over substance and notorious for the petty exercise of authority, as well as a certain sly laziness that's seen Cornelius bear a fair bit of the load that should rightfully be Viera's alone.

The three enlisted men—one editing footage from the Court of the Gentiles, another examining footage from the Court of the Israelites, the third reviewing external footage—register some surprise when they see *Aquilifer* Getorex alone, without Viera. Cornelius dumps the two files—marked *Iscariot: URGENT MATTER* and *Ben Yusuf: URGENT MATTER*—on the desk with the dark-green leather inlay marked *Fretensis Advocati* in one corner. True to its usual inhabitant, it's impossibly neat. Viera has lined his fountain pens up along the edge in colour gradations, as though he'd just bought them from the store. Cornelius opens the top drawer; Viera has also clearly been stockpiling stationery and chewing gum. He grabs a wad of the latter and sticks it in his mouth.

Capito appears in the doorway; the three rankers stand and salute. After a moment's delay—and despite having just spent twenty minutes in Capito's office copping a thorough dressing-down—Cornelius joins them.

'At ease. *Advocatus* Viera is in Rome. Your supervising

advocate for the Iscariot and Ben Yusuf matters is to be *Aquilifer* Getorex. You'll afford all the assistance to him that you would normally afford *Advocatus* Viera.'

'Yes, sir!'

'*Aquilifer* Getorex, if you need any further backup, you may obtain it in my name. I realise I've called you back in the midst of leave and left you without an experienced supervisor, on top of expecting you to do a month's work in a week. But I'm sure it's nothing you can't handle.'

He smiles broadly.

At least he didn't make me piss in the bottle. Still, the delegation of authority's handy. I'll need Lonuobo and Crispus for a start, and a medic.

Cornelius stands fiercely at attention.

'At your service and at the Empire's, sir.'

The rankers—two techies, one paralegal—are Rufus Vero, Aristotle Eugenides and Cyler Lucullus. Rufus is youngest and most serious, with an early-stage bald spot. Cyler is tall and lanky and very dark, with snaggle teeth and a five-o'clock shadow. Aristotle is blond and handsome, with a strong Macedonian accent.

'It's not as though they were trying to hide anything, is it?'

Aristotle has managed—for the most part—to sequence the CCTV footage so that it starts with a long shot of Ben Yusuf and his confreres approaching the Court of the Gentiles from the Jewish Quarter and ends with Marcus Lonuobo kneecapping Iscariot in a far corner of the Court of the Israelites.

'Look at this,' he says. 'I've got a feed going into the display.' This last is a giant screen hung with brass clasps from the ceiling behind Viera's desk. Often given over to racing and gaming broadcasts, it now shows Ben Yusuf leading twelve heavily bearded men in single file up the steps. 'They seem pretty determined, don't you think?'

'If anything, Iscariot's the only one who doesn't look convinced, like he's trying to hide,' Cornelius says. 'Step it back a dozen frames or so. See his left hand? His head's down, he's half covered his face there... and it's still covered... now go forward thirty frames... at this point, when they head up the front steps and we pick them up in the Court of the Gentiles.'

'Camera two now,' says Aristotle. 'Iscariot's face is still covered. That must be, what is it, nearly a minute.'

'It's the most deliberate malicious mischief I've ever seen,' says Cornelius. 'No pushing and shoving, no arguments. Look how they fan out.' He indicates with one hand.

Three head towards the souvenir stalls and then split up. Five—including Ben Yusuf—head for the moneychangers' section. It's here that they observe the first punch. A man identified as Petros Bar Yonah flattens one of the moneychangers, while Ben Yusuf hooks his hands under the edge of the table and flips it.

'Where's Iscariot?'

'At this stage, he's beating up an old lady selling doves,' says Cyler.

'Camera six.'

The freed doves make feeble attempts to get clear, getting as far as the top of those tables still undisturbed. The old woman sits beside her broken birdcage, rocking back and forth, weeping, trying to shield her head as the rioting becomes more general.

'Probably everything she owns,' Cyler continues. 'I hope she can make a claim on the Temple insurance policy.'

'There's probably some stupid rule that says women can't claim,' says Rufus. 'They treat women like shit in this country.'

'Look at this,' says Aristotle.

Iscariot is slapping various animals—goats and sheep for

the most part—on the rump, encouraging them to stampede down the Temple steps and into the street. People are knocked out of the way, smashing into walls and stalls.

'It's like that thing they do with bulls at *ludi* in Hispania. That can go really wrong, you know.'

'There seems to be a bit of a gap in the sequence there,' Cornelius butts in.

'I've probably just stuck something in the wrong spot, sir,' Aristotle says. 'All the cameras were working, and Caiaphas is a stickler for the nicest equipment. That's how we were able to put this together so quickly.'

'Good stuff,' says Cornelius.

'Camera seven now,' Rufus breaks in. 'Somehow Ben Yusuf's armed himself in that interval. It's a stick or a whip or something.'

'Can you zoom that up any closer, Eugenides?'

Aristotle draws a box with his stylus on the tablet before him and waits for the image to render on the screen. 'Looks like a whip, sir. A stick or cane would be harder to conceal. He probably had it with him, hidden in his clothes.'

'Have we got any shots of his hands earlier in the sequence?'

'We have,' says Aristotle. He steps the footage back: Ben Yusuf puts the moneychanger's table down and scoots backwards across the Court of the Gentiles towards the steps. Cornelius leans over Aristotle and pauses the playback.

'There it is.'

Aristotle draws another box and waits again. A series of irregular black lines are clearly visible around Ben Yusuf's left fist.

'Wrapped it around his hand, the little shit.'

'Can you spell *dolus*, anyone?' asks Cornelius.

'Maybe we've got this wrong, sir,' says Cyler, trying to use the half-completed law degree the Roman Army's currently paying for. 'Maybe Ben Yusuf is the ringleader, and Iscariot's just a hanger-on.'

'Iscariot's got all the priors, though, and now you've got to add in the Dea Tacita Centre bombing.'

'I've got the paperwork and evidence baggie from forensics for that,' Aristotle says to the group in general. 'Just so's you know.'

'Bring it up to the beginning of the attack on the moneychangers again, Eugenides.'

'Yes, sir.'

It's at this point that things get more difficult to follow. Ben Yusuf moves along the line of stalls methodically, upending each table in turn. Petros Bar Yonah hits two more moneychangers—hard, too, he's clearly a big man—and money flies everywhere. Suddenly there's a mass of people scrabbling about on all fours or leaping into the air as money blows upwards and rolls downwards.

'Made flat to stack and round to go round.'

'Nothing like free money,' says Cornelius. 'I saw a bit of this stuff long distance when I was leading a protection detail for Antony Pilate. Kid was supposed to visit the Temple that afternoon. Hillel Bar Kayafa convinced his old man that one of Cybele's lads should get a proper Temple tour.'

'Did we pick up this Petros character?' asks Cyler. 'He's a bully.'

'Wait for the sequel,' says Aristotle.

Even Petros is stunned—his surprise clearly visible once magnified—when Ben Yusuf starts belabouring several of the moneychangers with his whip, drawing a fair bit of blood. Iscariot appears, pushes the shocked Petros to one side and grabs a moneychanger by his shirt collar, taking his legs out from under him with a neat foot movement. The whip really draws blood now—a man's cheek is opened up.

'No sign of the Temple Guard at this point, I note.'

'There may be more useless security formations in the Empire,' says Cornelius, 'but I can't think of many.'

A moneychanger gives as good as he gets, headbutting one of Ben Yusuf's unidentified followers, then punching Petros in the gut. The Temple Guard finally appear and two of them haul Petros off. A fleeing woman slips over, barrelling into another rioter's legs. He trips over her, hitting his head on a piece of jutting masonry as he goes. Now there's a lot of blood.

'Is that the dead one?'

'No, he's in Æsculapion still, but he'll come through all right. He was lucky the main body of the riot moved away from him, probably to avoid the blood.'

'What is it with moneychangers?' Rufus wants to know.

'They can't use Roman currency in the Temple precinct,' says Cyler. 'The Temple has its own *scrip* currency, and it's *only* available in the Temple. They can set any exchange rate they like.'

'We should do something about that,' Rufus says.

'They don't have many indigenous market mechanisms. They don't need us regulating one of the few they've got.'

Meanwhile, Iscariot has his hands around the headbutting moneychanger's throat and Ben Yusuf is struggling with a souvenir seller who's somehow contrived to grab the other end of his whip. Iscariot kicks the moneychanger in the balls, and then falls on top of him. Somehow, the moneychanger wriggles out from underneath, and the two wrestle fiercely.

'Give that moneychanger a medal,' says Cyler. 'He's got *coleones*.'

'Sore *coleones*, by now,' says Rufus.

The centre of the courtyard has now degenerated into a general all-in brawl, with members of the Temple Guard, bystanders and Ben Yusuf's acolytes picking up chairs and breaking them over each other's backs. Petros snaps the leg off one of the overturned moneychanger's tables and belts a member of the Temple Guard around the head with it, ripping his helmet off. The guard subsides to the ground almost gracefully, twirling on the spot. Someone draws a knife and lunges at a souvenir seller; a wide but shallow slash appears across his chest. More blood. More slipping.

'Whoever laid those slabs didn't test them for blood.'

'Not the sort of people who grew up watching gladiators and cage fights.'

The incident leading to the death is at once sudden and not particularly interesting. In successfully pulling his whip out of the souvenir seller's hands, Ben Yusuf causes the man to fly backwards and slam into a portly member of the Temple Guard. The guard falls, grabbing at the souvenir seller's clothing for support. The souvenir seller—perhaps because he's so desperate to resume fighting with Ben Yusuf—loses his balance and pitches forward down the stairs, head first. There isn't any blood, just a man lying still with his neck angled wrongly.

'I'll argue *dolus indirectus* and *dolus eventualis* in the alternative for Ben Yusuf,' Cornelius whispers, thinking out loud. Cyler smiles; he'd thought that, too.

'And *dolus directus* for Iscariot.'

Men of the 2nd Cohort appear now, hauling Iscariot off the moneychanger and biffing several of Ben Yusuf's associates into submission. The moneychanger springs up and hugs the legionary who rescues him. The moment is beautifully spontaneous, but as Aristotle magnifies it, the four of them laugh when they see the expression on the soldier's face.

'That didn't smell good,' says Rufus. 'Get a load of his nose.'

'Eau d'Armpit, I'd say.'

'That's when Iscariot bolted,' Cornelius says.

'He must've thought we couldn't follow him into the Court of the Israelites,' says Aristotle, puzzled. 'Otherwise why would you go up, rather than just blending into the mêlée and sloping out the front gate?' He zooms out. 'Look how many people there are, and the Second Cohort not fully in position at that point.'

'I think Iscariot has quite a bit of explaining to do, Eugenides.' He smiles a small, crafty smile. 'You know what happened after Lonuobo plinked him, don't you?'

'He turned state's evidence, sir, didn't he?'

'He offered to help us locate Ben Yusuf from the back of the ambulance within five minutes of being shot.'

'He knew his goose was cooked?'

'The Dea Tacita Centre attack's been unresolved for a year. And there's a long gap between Iscariot's last prior before that. We didn't take DNA swabs for routine convictions back then. We had a beautiful set of DNA for the grenade he rolled into the waiting room, but the only way we'd get a match was by catching him again.'

'Mind you, he wasn't to know he'd left DNA all over that grenade pin.'

'True. Hard to know what's going on there.'

'None of Iscariot's priors are super serious, either,' Cyler muses. 'He's a hairball, a rotten apple, a bum... he'd be a pain to have in your neighbourhood, but until Dea Tacita, there's no real terrorism. Hates us, of course, but it's mainly just minor property crime, a few piddly assaults—'

'The paramedics thought Iscariot was delusional and brought him into Antonia for treatment, but he kept making the same offer over and over again. Eventually *Optio* Marius Macro ordered he be given a massive painkilling injection and strapped up, just to see whether he'd come good on his offer.'

'Which he did.'

'Apart from insisting on travelling with the Temple Guard, yes, which I still can't work out. It gets better, though.' Cornelius rummages though the file Capito gave him and pulls out a single sheet of paper. 'It's from the Prefect of the Temple Guard.'

Rufus grows bug-eyed as he reads.

'He *kissed* him? Hobbled up to him on one leg and *kissed* him? These people are fourteen-storey fuckups.'

'Kissed who?' Cyler reaches out to take the statement from Rufus—who hands it to him as though it's road kill he's just cleaned out of a tank track. Aristotle leaves his engine screen for the first time and stands over Cyler.

'He kissed Ben Yusuf. Just walked up to him and kissed him. So they knew who to arrest.'

'Bullshit,' says Aristotle. 'This Ben Yusuf character's been on telly around here. I've seen him interviewed on JTN, usually during my pitiful attempts to learn some Aramaic. They knew who to arrest, no kiss required.'

Cornelius looks at the three men, at their perplexed and irritated faces. Cyler hands him the Temple Guard's statement, also holding it as though it's toxic waste.

'There's a lot I don't understand either, and much of it depends on what we can get out of Iscariot.'

'What we can get out of Iscariot with *extreme* fucking prejudice,' says Rufus. There's a real edge to his voice; Cornelius can hear it.

Here we go again: Roman legionaries who can't wait to bolt into the Camera, forgetting that once you've gone in there, you never leave. Or if you do, you don't leave by the way you came in.

'Have you ever done *Camera* duty, Vero?'

'No, sir.'

'Thought not.' He pauses. 'I want the three of you to do

three things for me. First, I want Eugenides to bring me a selection of cold meats and a double espresso from the Officer's Mess. Don't worry, I'll write you a pass. Next, I want Vero to take a written order to *Advocatus* Gaius Crispus telling him to report to me in sixty minutes. Finally, I want Cyler Lucullus to take a similar order to *Centurio* Marcus Lonuobo of the Second and to *Medicus* Darius Saleh of the Third to report to me here at zero six hundred hours tomorrow. After you've completed those duties, you're free to attend to other tasks until fifteen hundred hours, when you'll return here and package this CCTV footage in a form suitable for tendering before the Procurator in *Praetorium*.'

He rummages in his borrowed desk's second drawer, pulling out a yellow legal pad and Viera's senior advocate's stamp. He rotates the letter tracks so it now spells his name, then writes out his orders in the flowing Celtic script he was taught at school in Camulodunum. He notices the three men admiring his handwriting out of the corner of his eye. *One of the nice bits of Celticness, that.*

He stands, hands the paperwork over and salutes.

When he's sure they're truly out of earshot, he makes his way stiffly to the wooden racks of pigeonholes holding stacks of printed forms. He counts along until he locates the one he wants and takes two. He has trouble picking them up at first, a combination of his shaking hands and the tendency for Roman Army forms in long storage to stick together. *Shit, Cornelius, what are you? Not getting any easier, is it?*

Imperial Roman Army—*Legio* X *Fretensis*—Province of Iudaea—Form XXIII

APPLICATION FOR USE OF TORTURE

Nota bene: This form can only be completed by the senior legionary legal officer, and must be countersigned by ~~Legate,~~ Procurator, Primus Pilus, ~~Senator~~ in order to be legally valid.

Date:

Name of suspect (include all known names and aliases; attach criminal record in *ALL* cases):

Facts: (attach a separate sheet):

Relevant legislation/Code provision (attach a separate sheet if necessary):

Methods requested (mark as necessary): restraint, dogs, light, sound, water, ~~electricity~~.

Reasons torture requested (attach a separate sheet):

Name and stamp of Senior Legal Officer, *Legio* X *Fretensis*

Name and stamp of ~~Legate,~~ Primus Pilus, Procurator, ~~Senator~~

Senatus Populusque Romanus

Fellow officers blame Cornelius's interrogation scruples on his Britishness, on his basic reasonableness, on his sense of fair play. When he was promoted to *Advocatus* in Syria (which carried with it—among other perks—a business card) people saw the *licentia ad practicandum, Lond.* after his name and simply assumed that he'd be the Legion's legal conscience. In reality, he has no idea why he reacts the way he does, only that it's getting worse every time he's detailed to the *Camera*. And today—for obvious reasons of responsibility—is worse than all the previous shitty times combined, including the session in Antioch when he'd had to restrain an overeager young ranker with the habit of waving his electrode around his head and shrieking with laughter before applying it where Cornelius told him to.

He's eaten his lunch and almost finished rough drafts of the two applications on Viera's legal pad—his pen flowing easily over the yellow lined paper—when Gaius Crispus appears at the door. A rangy man with a pinched, aristocratic face and fine blond hair, Crispus is no more than three years out of law school, well-born and well-bred. *Finish up Legate one day, or doing Pilate's job. Father in the Senate, mother a consultant neurologist, born on a vast estate in Latium. Born to rule.* Perhaps not fully aware that Cornelius is now his superior, Gaius fails to salute, instead standing outside in the corridor with a mug of coffee in one hand and another yellow legal pad in the other. His mug bears the words:

> Sometimes I think
> —life would be easier—
> if I weren't so sexy.

Cornelius stands and salutes. Gaius hastily plonks his mug and papers on a nearby table and responds in kind.

'This better be good, Cornelius, I'm up to my ears in work.'

'You and me both.'

Cornelius hands him the draft application; Gaius smears his thin fair hair away from his forehead with his palm as he sits and reads. Cornelius watches his face for any change in expression as he comes to the nub of the argument. There is none.

'I suppose you'll need me in reserve for both interrogations.'

'Ideally, yes. You don't need to be there throughout.'

'Thank Jove,' he says.

I didn't know there were Romans anywhere who thanked Jove anymore. 'What do you think?'

'Of what?'

'The applications. Are they reasonable?'

'By Jove, yes,' he enthuses. 'Though if I were making the application I'd leave myself the option of going to the *Legatus* in Syria. Iscariot in particular should be made to wriggle about on the *parrilla*. Not telling you how to run your own case, of course, but the attack on the Dea Tacita Centre was particularly vicious. It's worth knowing if there's any more where that came from.'

'A Form 28 as well then?'

'No need to send it off, of course; it's just a useful thing to have in reserve if circumstances dictate.'

'Thank you for that, Gaius. I'd best let you get back to your frauds and petty thefts.'

Cornelius closes the door behind him, fires up the engine Aristotle was using and types out his Form 23 supporting documentation, rejigging his prose as he transfers it across. The act of writing is oddly calming, and by the time he's written up both sets of submissions and applied his sloping Celtic script to the covering pages, stamped them and sealed them up he's stopped shaking. Rufus is the first of his three rankers to return at 1500 hours, and is duly dispatched to Pilate's *Praetorium* with two envelopes.

'You can probably safely wait for his response,' Cornelius tells him. 'I'll be here.'

Pilate's office in Antonia—redolent of the office in his days at the firm—is a corner one, all wood panelling, giant fish tank populated with shark pups, nestled in the south-east tower. His ivory shark sculpture—*From the Partners and Senior Associates, Valens Advocates & Notaries*—has pride of place on one corner of his desk. It's probably not that safe; Antonia is properly a fortress, and the architects had to knock out a section of wall on two sides in order to give him his beautiful glass frontage.

Nonetheless, the view over the Temple precinct and Antonia's own parade ground is a commanding one, and Pilate admires it regularly. He has a soft spot for martial music that goes back to his childhood, in part because it sounds so very different from Roman popular music. A piercing air on half-a-dozen fifes reaches his ears, bulletproof glass notwithstanding. Since being appointed Procurator he's come to recognise the various tunes, apart from *Patria, Patria*, which he's always known. *Ah yes*, he'll think, *that's When Marcus Comes Marching Home* or—sometimes—one of the more risqué ones composed especially for a famous general's military triumph. *Julius Caesar* is a perennial favourite: *Romans, welcome home your brave whoremonger!*

Pilate is smoking a quality cigar, having earlier stood on his desk to disable the fire alarm. It's difficult to do much about the alarms in common areas—one can make a safety argument for them—but he refuses to be told what to do in his own bloody office, thank you very much.

His law clerk knocks on the door. 'Procurator?'

'Yes, Horace?'

'Two Form 23 applications, Procurator.'

Pilate raises an eyebrow. *Could only be from Getorex... Viera's in Rome on some sort of leave...*

'Let me see them.' He holds out his hand.

'The legionary who brought them tells me he has been instructed to wait, Procurator.'

'Hmmm.' He smiles bitterly. 'Getorex is getting cocky with his new rank.'

He sits behind his desk, still smoking steadily as he reads.

> ...In sum: it is my considered view that Iscariot did not act alone in the Dea Tacita Centre attack [Ref. Ex. 1] and we also now have conclusive evidence that the Temple riot was a coordinated, planned attack, perhaps designed to undermine Caiaphas's authority as High Priest [Ref. Ex. 2]. It is also clear that Ben Yusuf and Iscariot are long-time associates, and there is the distinct possibility that it is Ben Yusuf who 'turned' Iscariot, and not the other way around [Ref. Ex. 3]. The current levels of 'chatter' are similar to those before the Dea Tacita Centre attack [Ref. Ex. 4]. He is the sort of individual vulnerable to torture. His psychological assessment [Ref. Ex. 5] indicates the presence of narcissism and an allied belief in the rightness of imposing his personal moral code on others.
>
> The high degree of deliberation in both attacks leads me to believe that there are likely to be more where they came from, that they are getting closer together, and that there is a concomitant increase in risk. Twenty people have died and 278 have been injured in the last twelve months as a result of the combined activities of these two men [...]
>
> This is not an action I take lightly, as my history as a military lawyer in this fine Legion indicates. I respectfully request, Procurator, that you accede to my applications.

Pilate buzzes for his clerk.

'Convene the *Praetorium*, Horace. Call Getorex in from the Law Room and get Andreius Linnaeus to appear by *vocale*. Ben Yusuf is represented.'

Rufus does the first part of Pilate's bidding, clattering downstairs and fishing Cornelius out of the Law Room. He's sitting with his back to the door, his long legs propped up on the central desk, laughing in his amiable way. He's admiring the smooth technical skills on display as Aristotle and Cyler construct the video evidence package. He stands up when he hears Rufus at the door.

'I'll be back shortly, gentlemen. Vero, you stop here with them and help get this sorted. The sooner the better.'

By the time Cornelius has sprinted up the stairs three at a time—*sometimes long legs come in handy*—Horace has unlocked the *Praetorium* (the lit sign over the entrance reads *Matter in Session*) and obtained a notary from the State Reporting Bureau. The *Praetorium* is oddly shaped, occupying part of the long connecting wall in between the south-east and south-west towers. It's high and light as courtrooms go, although to Cornelius's eye, the ceiling slopes the wrong way.

The notary is an attractive young woman with long, roiling hair coiled into something like rope down her back, smart in Air Force dress uniform. A woman who isn't a wife, lover or sex worker in Antonia is still something of an event. *She must be on rotation from Damascus*. She sets up what looks vaguely like a typewriter, except it's taller, thinner and seems to have only eight keys. She sits behind it, adjusting the height of her chair. He pauses to admire the fine, almost Celtic spools and whorls of silver on one side of her face, looking for the indented spot in the temple she uses to communicate with the *strix*.

He walks towards her. She stands to attention.

'At ease, soldier. You'll be required to read two Applications into the official transcript. Here are copies for your records.'

Horace throws the switch behind the elevated bench. The letters S.P.Q.R. are picked out on the wall in backlit crystal, flanked on either side by the *fasces*, bundles of rods bound together and concealing an axe with a projecting blade. He pulls Pilate's chair out slightly, lays a selection of stationery across the blotter on the benchtop and fills a glass with water. There's something of a kerfuffle as he's unable to reach Andreius Linnaeus, instead broadcasting his secretary in Rome over the *Praetorium vocale*.

'Andreius Linnaeus's rooms, Inheritance and Family Division, this is Naira speaking.'

There's something noisy going on at Cato & Cato; her voice is indistinct above a hubbub of chatter and music.

'I'm sorry about the racket,' she says. 'The office is about to close for *Megalesia*. In any case, Don Linnaeus is in Judaea handling a criminal matter. He won't be back for at least a week.'

'That's where we're calling from. Sorry for disturbing you.'

Horace hangs up and looks at Cornelius, temporarily undecided at what to do.

'I can think of places I'd much rather be than Judaea right now,' he says.

'Can't we all,' says Cornelius.

'It may be worth calling the prison, sir,' the notary says. 'He's probably in the Vinculum "Cone of Silence".'

Cornelius smiles at her turn of phrase. Linnaeus is eventually located.

'Thanks a lot, my learned friend,' he snaps when he hears Cornelius speak. His voice is tinny and hollow over the—undoubtedly wiretapped—line from the Vinculum. 'Is Pilate there? Tell him from me to tell the prison governor out here to unbunch his panties. I've been fucking around for an hour trying to sort out a client interview in a non-bugged room. Even non-citizens get that much.'

Horace sniggers.

The young woman intercedes again. 'You're on a public *vocale* line coming into the *Praetorium*, Don Linnaeus. Everything is being recorded, even if I don't put it into the final transcript.'

His tone changes abruptly. 'My apologies, *Notaria*. I respectfully request that my earlier comments be deleted from the record.'

Clerk: All rise, the *Praetorium* is now in session.

Pilate: Thank you, please be seated. May I have appearances, please? The State?

Getorex: Cornelius Getorex, *Aquilifer* and Acting Senior Legal Officer, *Legio* X *Fretensis.*

Pilate: The Suspect?

Linnaeus: Andreius Linnaeus, Advocate-at-Law, Cato & Cato, Rome and Neapolis.

Pilate: Cause?

Notary: SPQR *versus* Yehuda Iscariot; SPQR *versus* Yeshua Ben Yusuf.

Linnaeus: I'm only acting for Ben Yusuf, Procurator.

Pilate: Iscariot is unrepresented. Duly noted in the record.

Linnaeus: I'll intervene on his behalf where necessary, Procurator.

Pilate: Duly noted in the record, Don Linnaeus. Yes, *Aquilifer* Getorex?

Getorex: I make two Form 23 applications, pursuant to *senatus consultum de re publica defendenda* number 44: terrorism.

Pilate: Please read the Applications into the record.

Notary: [...] Applications read into the record at the Procurator's request.

Pilate: Don Linnaeus?

Linnaeus: I wish to object in the strongest terms to the timing of this request. I have failed to secure an interview with my client at this stage.

Pilate: Why is that?

Linnaeus: I've had difficulties with the prison, Procurator. It appears that all the interview rooms are wiretapped.

Pilate: [Laughs]. If you make a bench application for Ben Yusuf to be removed to Antonia for interview, I'll grant it. Two rooms here, as I understand it, are unwired.

Linnaeus: Consider the application made, Procurator.

Pilate: Good. Do you object to the substance of the State's Applications?

Linnaeus: Yes I do, Procurator. My preliminary researches indicate that Ben Yusuf is not to be equated with Iscariot. He has no prior convictions. He has been gainfully employed for the last ten years—

Pilate: As what?

Linnaeus: He's a trained carpenter, Procurator.

Pilate: Ah, yes. I remember seeing his trade papers in the dossier.

Linnaeus: He's also appeared on Provincial screen and—once—Imperial screen to put his religious and philosophical arguments. I have had cause to view all of his screen appearances. While undoubtedly a deeply religious man—and religious in a way that seems strange to Romans—there is nothing to indicate any really violent proclivities.

Pilate: Do you have any procedural objections to the State's Applications?

Linnaeus: Yes, Procurator. Both men should be given the opportunity to answer the questions directed at them before the reflex reach for Form 23 that has become all too common across the Empire. It is quite possible that they will answer inquiries in the course of normal questioning without any further, uh, assistance.

Pilate: *Aquilifer* Getorex, what do you say to that?

Getorex: I voluntarily give an undertaking to the *Praetorium* that both men will be questioned *ex Camera* before any *in Camera* questioning takes place. I will also ensure that this first stage of questioning takes place in a different room, although I reserve the right to use the appearance of the *Camera* itself to frighten both men into truthfulness. If no further questioning is required, the interrogation will be terminated.

Pilate: Are you happy with that, Don Linnaeus?

Linnaeus: Not entirely, Procurator. I'd also like some recognition that I've been unable to interview my client as yet, at least when it comes to the order in which the two men are questioned.

Pilate: That's probably telling the State how to conduct its case, Don Linnaeus. What do you say, *Aquilifer* Getorex?

Getorex: The State always intended that the Iscariot interrogation would be conducted first, Procurator. The man has an obscene amount of blood on his hands.

Pilate: That reminds me. Have you lodged that DNA evidence, *Aquilifer* Getorex?

Getorex: I do so now.

Pilate: Good. Duly received and marked 'Exhibit 1 for identification'. I'd also like to know the substance of the charges against both men, just for the record.

Getorex: There are some minor matters to be added, but I've drawn up a *libellus conventionis* for murder *dolus directus* for Iscariot with respect to the Dea Tacita Centre attack, and murder *dolus indirectus* for Ben Yusuf with respect to the Temple riot.

Pilate: That's probably putting it a bit high, *Aquilifer* Getorex.

Getorex: I'll be arguing murder *dolus eventualis* in the alternative, Procurator. There's also some assault and criminal damage charges for both men. There may be a failure to warn for Ben Yusuf. I should also point out that the *Kohen Gadol* is pushing for a sedition charge—

Pilate: Yes, I saw that in the dossier, and find it frankly perplexing. Even the Zealots' political wing is smart enough to avoid campaigning in the name of a Jewish king.

Getorex: The State can leave the sedition matter in your hands as examining magistrate, Procurator, if that is what you prefer.

Pilate: I think that's appropriate in all the circumstances, *Aquilifer* Getorex. I'll lay the sedition charge on the table and make the results of my investigations available to counsel.

Linnaeus: Procurator, while I do not wish to be seen to be giving evidence or opinion from the bar table, my suspicion is that the sedition allegations represent an attempt to get Jewish blasphemy laws recognised under Roman Law.

Pilate: This is only an application, Don Linnaeus, and in any case your suspicion accords with mine. The nub of the matter is the death and destruction in the Temple, and Ben Yusuf's associations with Iscariot. Everything else is secondary. The thought of blasphemy laws creeping into our system fills me with dread, and you can rest assured I am sensitive enough both to detect their presence and to root them out with alacrity. That said, the High Priest insists that a Messianic claim is not blasphemous under Jewish religious law, although obviously enough it is something the Sanhedrin wishes to police to some degree. It is complicated.

Linnaeus: Yes, Procurator. I do look forward to seeing

the results of your researches.

Pilate: Good. Is there anything else, *Aquilifer* Getorex?

Getorex: No, Procurator.

Pilate: Don Linnaeus?

Linnaeus: No, Procurator—although I'd like to see those *libelli* as soon as possible.

Getorex: I'll have a set waiting for you when you get back from the Vinculum, along with an evidence package.

Pilate: I'll make my ruling, then. I *grant* the Form 23 Applications made under the hand of *Aquilifer* Getorex, Acting Senior Legal Officer, *Legio* X *Fretensis*. I *order* that Yeshua Ben Yusuf be removed to Antonia for interview in an appropriately private and secure room. I *note* that the State undertakes to conduct preliminary questioning *ex Camera* with a view to avoiding the unnecessary use of torture. I also *note* that the State undertakes to question Iscariot first as a concession to Don Linnaeus's difficulties with securing an appropriate interview facility for his client. Given under my sign and seal: Procurator of Judaea, this day the *Nones* of April in the year seven hundred and eighty-four *ab urbe condita*.

Cornelius stops by the Officer's Mess for a glass of wine. He drinks it too quickly, orders another, and then another. He returns to the Law Room with the beginnings of a lowering headache. Aristotle notices him sipping as he walks through the door.

The three men stand and salute.

'At ease, and listen up. You'll report to me here at zero six hundred hours tomorrow. Eugenides, you are to prepare the *Camera* in accordance with this Application—' he hands him a copy of Iscariot's Form 23. 'You've got a trade, yes?'

'Yes, sir. I'm a fitter, but this is pretty basic carpentry, sir.'

'Vero, you are to prepare the room opposite for an *ex Camera* interrogation.'

'Yes, sir.'

'Lucullus, you're to ensure that Iscariot remains awake tonight. I'm told you have some experience in these things.'

'Yes, sir.' Cyler smiles. 'Creatively erotic experience, mainly.'

'What's this?' Rufus wants to know.

Cornelius laughs. His head's buzzing, and even though part of him wants to *run away, fast*, there's no doubt Cyler's decision to play multiple erotic films end on end to a particularly stubborn terrorist two years ago tickled the legion's collective funny bone. Among other things, it led to the man implicating a dozen confreres in the midst of four hours of sexually charged and weirdly hallucinatory confessions.

'Sorry, before your time.' Cyler outlines the background. 'Then I just chained him to the cell wall and left one hand free. He stayed awake for forty-eight hours and gave himself a massive hand cramp—needed a cortisone shot after we'd finished with him. Watching him stare at the screen—he was pop-eyed, like a fish. It's fish that can't blink, right? I don't think he'd ever seen a naked woman before.'

'Interesting definition of torture,' says Rufus.

'If they were all like that I'd be a very happy man,' Cornelius agrees.

'I could try the erotica trick with Iscariot, sir. He's the type it might work on.'

'Up to you, Lucullus. I'm not particularly imaginative when it comes to that sort of thing. Make them stand up in bright light while playing loud music is about my limit.'

'*Deborah does Damascus* is my pick,' Cyler says, half to himself. 'Very good Jewish girl goes very bad. And in the R & R capital of the Roman Empire.'

Cornelius can almost see the wheels turning in Cyler's head.

'Whatever you do, the key is silliness and fun. Even if you have to chuck buckets of ice water over him to stop him snoozing off, apologise first.'

Cyler laughs. 'I get to be *Domine* Sarcasm. I see. Happens in every interrogation.'

THE MIDWIFE

Cornelius sat in the Law Room, alone. He was at Viera's desk, in a pool of yellow light. He spun one of Viera's nib pens around his fingers. He'd once had a theory that the faster you could send a pen skittering around your hand, the faster you were able to think. He remembered trying to prove his theory in high school alchemy, eons ago, and flicking his pen across the room. The reservoir split and ink spattered across three desks and the far wall. *Hehehe*, his teacher chortled. *The champion pen flicker comes unstuck.*

The desk lamp threw shadows up against the walls, but he made no move to turn on the big circle of lights overhead.

Why are you remembering this shit, Cornelius?

Because it's when you made your choice, some other part of his mind answered. *Wanted that law licentia, and couldn't afford to pay the tuition fees. That's about the strength of it.* He looked around the room—palms pressed flat into the desktop now—half expecting a Sibyl straight out of the stories he'd read as a child to coalesce in the shadows.

Asked for eternal life, I did, but forgot to ask for eternal youth. And now I want to die. He debated calling Mirella, whom he'd abandoned so abruptly that morning.

Is she still interested?

Of course she is, said the same dry, amused voice. *She's been interested for three years; all the while you've been out playing the redhead and fucking around just because you can.*

He chewed on his right knuckle and caught himself rocking gently back and forth. The three glasses of wine had worn off and only the Sibyl seemed to have any time for him.

Mirella spent most of the day at work bending her friends' ears about the fabulous man she'd enjoyed the previous evening, a lawyer who could double as an erotic movie star if he felt like it.

And he's a gorgeous ginger, too!

'I seem to recall a similar story this time last year,' one woman said. 'You should do something about that.'

Apart from that, she helped deliver five babies and was now onto her sixth.

'We're having a regular baby boom round here,' she heard one of the Roman obstetricians—a bouncy Calabrian woman with a huge honeycomb of hair—say a couple of times. 'Look at all these lovely babies just popping out everywhere.'

Her current patient—a *primiparae* woman with a damp tangle of black curls—was into stage two labour. Mirella sent the *doula* to fetch a birthing seat and took over massaging the woman's lower back when a nurse stuck her head around the door to the labour ward.

'Mirella Tanita?'

'That's me.'

'There's a call for you. Sounds urgent.'

Shit. Doesn't everyone know that I'm off limits when I'm in the labour ward?

The woman's man, a large, placid legionary in civvies—she could see his metal identity disc—crouched outside in the corridor. Mirella waited until the *doula* returned and then went and stood over him.

'You need to go to the men's room,' she said. 'This is women's business now. Offer up some wine and bread to Juno and wait there. There are beds for you; you can sleep if you need to. This can take a long time; this is the woman's battle. You're a soldier; you understand battle. She will need you soon enough.'

'I'm sorry,' he said.

She tried to place his accent. Sicilian, perhaps. Definitely very southern.

'I'm just glad it's coming now, not next week, when all our leave's cancelled.'

The mother-to-be dug her nails into the *doula's* hand and forearm. The man wiped tears away with one hand as he stood and watched from the door.

'I go now,' he said.

'We'll call you when the baby is about to come,' she said. 'Now go and wait in the men's place; you've been in the women's place for too long.'

She watched him walk away slowly, looking over his shoulder a couple of times. He was still crying.

He'll find some lads to play bocce with outside on the grass and all will be well.

The Calabrian ob-gyn joined her as she returned to the expecting mother's side. The latter was making small pleased noises as the *doula* massaged her back.

'Man hanging around?'

'Yes. I've sent him away now.'

Mirella gazed around the labour ward, by convention the most beautifully appointed part of any Roman Æsculapion. With walls of polished, pale-grey stone, a high vaulted ceiling, colourful tiled floor and soft light—bright light was only used if absolutely necessary, on mobile fittings mounted beside each bed—it was designed to reassure and delight those women who did not give birth at home. On one end wall was a great cut relief of a woman preparing to breastfeed her child—a copy of a similar piece on the Ara Pacis in Rome. Out of the corner of her eye, Mirella saw two midwives returning from a call-out. *I'm just going to the baths, Sophia,* she heard one of them say. *That got a bit messy, baby wanted to stay inside mama's tummy*.

'It really does sound urgent, Mirella. He's a Cornelius something hard to pronounce.'

Mirella started at the name.

'You'd better go,' said the ob-gyn, seeing the expression on her face. 'That's your man with the big dick, by the looks.' Mirella flushed and gave thanks for black skin, but she could hear her patient giggling, too.

'Shoo,' said the ob-gyn. 'I'll call you.'

Mirella followed the nurse into the reception area.

It was Cornelius all right, but he sounded like he'd buried himself down a deep dark hole somewhere.

'I know you said not to call you in the labour ward, and I'm sorry,' he blurted out. 'But I need to see you. I need you now.' There was a horrible, strangled edge to his voice she didn't recognise, and it frightened her.

'I'm about to catch a baby. Literally. I've got a new mama in stage two labour.'

'How soon can you get here?'

'Where's here?'

'Antonia.'

'Only after my patient's delivered safely. I've got the *doula* watching her now, who's lovely and kind and very good, but I need to be there.'

'Call at security when you get here,' he said. 'Please.' The strangled sound was getting worse.

'Baby coming through,' she heard the ob-gyn shout, followed by a burst of swearing in a language she knew to be Aramaic.

She walked briskly across the big square in front of Antonia, debating with herself when she should go about telling him she'd arrived. She'd never been inside Antonia—it always seemed a bastion of extreme maleness—and she admitted to herself that she still had no particular desire to go inside. She stopped in front of its grand entrance, gazing up at the stairs and two of the four squat towers, overlooking the Temple on one side and the city on the other. Cornelius was nowhere to be seen. Men with guns locked into their shoulders stood at the entrance, curly wires tucked behind their ears and into their helmets. She shivered, her sky-blue midwifery unit shirt and light robe no protection against a cold wind from the desert. *He'd better have a nice place to go. That's why the gods gave us hotels.*

Of course, her plan melted when she saw him, his hair somehow silvery in the floodlights crisscrossing the square and the entrance. He met her halfway down the steps and stretched out both his hands to her.

'Thank you,' he said. 'You had every right to tell me to fuck off, and you didn't.'

She stood on the step above him, so the top of her head came roughly to his eyes. He angled his head down and they kissed. He was a beautiful kisser. He touched her braids with his long, gentle fingers, curling stray bits of frizz around them. She noticed his cheeks were wet.

People milled around them, coming and going into Antonia's gaping mouth. Legionaries and their women. An older ranker with a heavy thatch of salt-and-pepper hair. A man standing on the front steps to have his photograph taken. Seeing them somehow made her feel better.

'Thank you,' he said again, pulling her closer, his hands on her backside.

'Talk to me, Cornelius,' she said, staunching his tears with her fingers. 'You sounded dreadful. You still sound dreadful.' She traced a line under one of his eyes. 'Look at these dark rings.'

'I think I've done something I'll regret.'

'When you rang me on the ward I thought you were having a coronary. Then I remembered fit thirty-four-year-old legionaries don't have coronaries.'

He smiled. 'Do you mind coming up to my quarters? It's nice and private. And I've got an ensuite.' She saw his eyes flash and came close to crying with relief. *The real Cornelius is still in there somewhere. He's just a bit lost right now.*

He took her hand and she willingly followed him into Antonia's maw, looking up, open mouthed, at the elaborately vaulted ceiling of its entrance hall, decorated with gold stars on a lapis lazuli field. *That must be a hundred and fifty feet high.* She watched as a member of the security detail adjusted an iris reader for Cornelius's height. Flashing patterns of red lines chased each other down his face. The guard waved him through. Even the security equipment seemed to be cut from the same polished black-and-white stone as the floor.

How did they manage that?

It was her turn.

'Papers, please, Ma'am, as this is your first visit. This will not be necessary in future, as we now have a biometric record.'

'I'm sorry.' She dug in her handbag, pulling out a folder of identifying documents, including her Æsculapion pass and identity card. The latter's purple background indicated a Roman Citizen. 'It's very beautiful here. I didn't know.'

He smiled at her, comparing images and punching her details into his engine. The woman on the Æsculapion pass had a small afro; the one before him and on the identity card wore cornrows.

'We make beautiful things, Ma'am. And you need to get

that photograph updated. Now please put your handbag in the tray and walk slowly through the backscatter machine.'

I've heard about these things; they turn them up so high you're naked.

The soldier manning the machine looked sidelong at Cornelius as she passed under the stone arch.

'Hot,' he mouthed. Cornelius gave him the finger, but he was smiling, too.

Paths and tunnels branched off from the hall in all directions; the place was simply vast. She was soon lost.

Well, if I want to escape now, I'm fucked. Just like the Cretan Labyrinth, only I've forgotten my string.

They passed a roomful of young men working out with free weights, and she was certain she recognised Marius Macro. At one point—and with a sharp stab of recognition—she spotted an operating theatre with its polished stone walls. *If you can see your face in it*, she remembered from her apprenticeship, *you know it's clean*. She suspected they'd climbed a long way—maybe halfway up one of the towers—when he finally stopped to unlock his door, motioning her inside and ducking in after her.

As she'd half expected, his quarters were immaculate, even austere. One wall was covered with his law textbooks, while the others played host to a selection of photographic prints, obviously carefully selected to match each other. She scanned a few titles at random: *The Law of Property*; *Delict*; *Carius on Contract*; *Forms, Precedents and Pleadings*. He'd arranged the books alphabetically by author. His bed with its cotton print covers was vastly oversized, but then, so was he. She also saw—for the first time—the physical evidence of his rank. Set in an elaborately hewn niche in the wall was what she knew to be the Standard of *Legio* X *Fretensis*. She stopped in front of it, admiring, reaching out.

'It's very beautiful. I've never seen one up close before. Only on parades.'

He was behind her now, one arm around her waist, pulling her away from it.

'Don't touch it. Bad luck if anyone other than the *Aquilifer* touches it.'

She drew her hands back with a swift, exaggerated motion.

'Especially if they're female, right?'

'Yes,' he said. 'Good guess. It's men's business.'

He spread his fingers around the edge of one of the smaller gold discs, chanting under his breath, his head down. She stood back, watching him raise his head as he sang; his voice was high and clear.

'Why is it in your quarters?' she asked when he'd finished singing and lighting incense before it. 'The garrison in Carthage had all their standards and *vexilla* on public display in the barracks. You could go and look at them. My sister and I went after school once.'

'Not allowed in Jerusalem,' he said. 'It's something to do with their religion.'

'What, there's some rule against a Roman Standard in public?'

'Yep.'

'You're kidding me.'

He shook his head. 'This is a true thing I'm telling you, Mirella. It's something to do with the pictures on it.' He pointed at the wild boar on one disc, and the prow of an ironclad on another. 'We used to keep them in Caesarea, but there's only ever about six hundred men stationed in Caesarea at any one time, and Standards are supposed to live with their Cohort and, in this case, with the main body of the legion.'

'Didn't know that,' she said.

'Well, when Pilate was appointed Procurator, he was pretty annoyed when he found out, so he ordered me and some picked men from the *Cohors Prima Augusta*—that's the official name for the First Cohort in *Fretensis*—to convey them to Jerusalem.'

'I think I remember there was some problem...'

'You're not wrong. Of course yours truly did it properly—formal military rail transport, Celtic pipers, honour guard—the whole bit. Pilate set them up in Antonia in the Entrance Hall, like you're supposed to.'

'And there was a riot. I remember now.'

'There was a riot. There was a *major* riot. People got killed because a Roman Legion wanted to have its Standard where it was stationed.'

'So Pilate ordered you to keep them in your quarters?'

'Yes.'

'Cornelius, who rules Judaea?'

'We do, Mirella.'

'Did it not occur to you to tell the people of Jerusalem to, ah, perch and rotate?'

She waved her middle finger in the direction of the Temple.

'It did,' he said, 'but in the end Pilate said it wasn't worth fighting over. At least they're in the right place, now, and we can use them for passing out parades in Antonia.'

He rummaged around in the small kitchen, putting wine under the freezer and setting the plate of olives, cheeses and sausage on the bench.

'Don't let me forget that wine,' he said.

'I don't intend to,' she said. 'I plan to help you drink it.'

He grinned at this, although she noticed that the smiles still weren't properly touching his eyes. He rubbed his chin. 'I really think I should shave. I already gave you beard burn last night.'

She poked her head into his ensuite bathroom. 'That looks like a rather nice bath.'

'It is,' he said. 'Would you like to share it?'

'Yes, I would like that very much.'

He flicked the taps on, pouring something sweet from a glass bottle with a stopper into the water. 'Hop in, lovely one, while I do something about my prickly face.'

Men aren't usually given to displays of public grooming, Cornelius the clever. This had better be good. As she stripped off and stepped into his bath, she watched him shave. He was a grooming show-off, of course, wielding a cut-throat razor with a steady and expert hand. She held her breath, not daring to speak, remembering how her own father would nick his face trying to use one of the things properly, trying to copy the clean-shaven Roman fashion. He hung his uniform carefully, putting the shirt in the laundry and then stepping in to join her. She sank under the water as he oiled his skin. She waited until he was comfortably settled, his long legs bent up on either side of her.

'What happened today, Cornelius?'

He gazed levelly at her, his eyes brilliant and grey.

'I applied to the Procurator for permission to torture two prisoners, starting tomorrow. That permission was granted, in part because I argued for it persuasively.'

'I see,' she said. She waited for a good couple of minutes, gathering her thoughts. He continued to look at her, unmoving, although she could see a small muscle in his right temple flicker. Finally, she spoke again.

'What made these two prisoners particularly, erm, torturable... worthy of torture?'

With deft verbal brushstrokes he painted in detail for her. She waited quietly until he'd finished, not interrupting or seeking further clarification or disagreeing. At one point during his exposition he gently moved his fingers along one of his impossibly fair eyebrows, as though searching for something. When he'd finished outlining and explaining, he simply stopped and went back to looking at her.

'Cornelius,' she said. Her voice was gentle. 'I want you to go and get that wine and food and bring it in here. I want you to pour us both a glass. And then I want you to listen to me. I'm asking you this because I'm very comfortable right now, and I don't want to move. So humour me.'

He hauled himself out of the bath immediately, suds all over his back and legs, and padded out of the room. She heard him in the kitchen, rummaging in the drawer for a corkscrew, opening the wine, fetching food and a pair of glasses. He paused to bring his coffee table next to the bath, setting the platter down on it, along with the wine and glasses. Then he stepped back into the bath, pausing to run some more hot water. She picked up her glass of wine and indicated that he should do likewise. He did not speak.

'When my great-great grandmother was a little girl, the Romans came to Carthage and conquered it for their very own. You probably know the story. The final battle was very fierce.'

He nodded, almost imperceptibly.

'Like me, my great-great grandmother was *Mauri*, and at that time not more than two years old. Now, before the Romans came to our city, every four years it was the custom of the city fathers to take a selection of two-year-old girls and sacrifice them to the Goddess Tanit. For some reason, the girls taken were nearly always *Mauri*. Our rulers in Carthage came from over the sea, and while dark like us, looked very different from my great-great grandmother. Yet, supposedly, the sacrificial subjects were chosen by lot. That the system was rigged in some way is indicated by my family name, *Tanita*. We belonged to Tanit.'

She could see the skin on the top part of his chest mottling, possibly with anger, possibly with lust, possibly with both. She'd never had a ginger for her very own before—even though the thought of one in her bed had often arisen unbidden in her dreams—and his pale skin was mysterious.

He swallowed a large mouthful of wine.

'The Romans forbade this tradition, and the City Fathers complained that the new law was destroying their culture and customs. The response of the Roman Governor at the time was to say that Romans, too, had customs and traditions. Their custom in this case was that every time the city fathers sacrificed a girl to Tanit, the Romans would build a gallows beside the Temple and hang the city father responsible by the neck until he died. Soon, no more little girls were sacrificed to Tanit, and so I am before you today.'

He looked at her face carefully, at her blazing black eyes. Her skin was too dark to redden properly, but where it was stretched tight between her cornrows, he could see how flushed it was. Her features—strong and defined—seemed to sharpen in the shadows. He sipped from his glass.

'Carthaginians remember the time before Rome came as the time of sacrifice, the time of ignorance. Not only were *Mauri* girls sacrificed. All girls of all peoples were forbidden from attending school. The city fathers sought to preserve this rule, too, in the name of El, our city God. El wanted the girls to be mothers only. The Roman Governor said this was wicked and wrong, and issued an edict ordering compulsory education for all children between the ages of six and ten. New schools with Roman-trained teachers were opened. Carthaginians—with few exceptions—ignored his edict. So the Roman Governor ordered the Imperial Navy to bombard the Temple of El while El's Priests were holding a vigil for the city. There was nothing left of the Temple, or of El's Priesthood, afterward. They were the first victims of your gunpowder and cannon and accurate range finding. Roman legionaries then went through the city at dawn, dragging children out of nearly every house in Carthage and marching them off to school. Some particularly obnoxious parents were beheaded as examples, their bodies exposed in the Central Square. Their children were given away to Roman families.'

He nodded, smiling faintly but still not speaking. He reached for an olive. So did she. Their fingers brushed.

'You know, I presume, the old saying that men fear women because you think we will laugh at you, while women fear men because we think you will kill us. I have felt this too. The last time I felt it was tonight. Had you not been with me, I would never have set foot in Antonia. I have never wanted to, and I have had soldier lovers before you. Here is a place that is home to three and a half thousand mostly young, virile men. It is something calculated to strike fear into any woman's heart. You even have little rituals that forbid women from touching your military symbols.'

He found it in himself to smile at her.

'There are no men in women's medicine,' he said, 'except for the odd abortionist.'

She smiled back at him. It was a fair point, the *healthworker*, *harmworker* division and all that went with it. Sometimes she was shocked, walking out of the maternity wing, to see other parts of the Æsculapion where the sexes of medics and nurses were mixed.

She continued. 'I will grant you those, however, as long as you do not terrorise the women of this city. And you do not. Everyone knows that the woman-bashers and rapists are seldom found within Antonia's walls. I have worked in A & E often enough to understand it personally. Nurses soon learn who beats, and who is beaten. The more cynical among us call the regularly beaten "women with houses who hate them", because they blame the door or the stairs for their wounds, but never their men.'

He laughed at that, putting his wine down and slicing some sausage. He passed some to her, then slid his hands over his back and chest, rinsing off the day. She mimicked him.

She refilled both their glasses, then pointed the neck of the bottle at him.

'You have a good system, one that has made you rich as Croesus compared to even your own ancestors. All in just two hundred years, or so. I don't understand how it happened, but you abolished slavery when my mother was a girl and it's been possible to watch the money pile up all over the Empire since.'

'That's just good economic policies.'

She shrugged. 'I don't understand that part, just the wealth. Long may you conquer.'

She paused, ready for the final burst.

'I do not have any illusions about what you must do to protect the world you have made for people like me. I know that to build schools for Carthaginian girls Rome had to bombard the city and destroy its most famous landmark. I also know that good people like me sleep peacefully in our beds at night only because rough men like you stand ready to do violence on our behalf. I was taught that saying at school in Carthage, a city that is now rich beyond its old city fathers' wildest imaginings. I have never forgotten it.'

She drained her glass. His was already empty.

'And now, Cornelius Getorex, I want you to fuck my brains out.'

'With pleasure,' he said, delighted and aroused all at once. His hands shot under the water, catching her hips and then pulling her towards him.

SPQR

PART III

'How beautiful are the works of this nation (the Romans). They have established markets, they have built bridges, they have opened bathing houses.' R. Jose said nothing, but R. Simeon b. Johai said: 'All these things they have instituted for their own sake. Their markets are gathering places for harlots; they have built baths for the purpose of indulging themselves in their comforts; they have built bridges to collect tolls from those who cross them.'

—The Babylonian Talmud, Shabbat 33

It took him the best part of Passover week to realise that he was being recruited. They started by lending him books that he read on the train between Jerusalem and Caesarea. Printed on cheap newsprint stock in uneven lines—as though the printer had been disturbed in the midst of setting type—and covered in brown paper, he read impassioned accounts of the hatred for the Roman occupiers and their 'filthy' culture and habits, and how the Greeks were their willing tools. There was also Philo's attempt to harmonise Greek philosophy with Judaism, although Saul noticed that the book fell open at the pages condemning the Greek vice, and that these had been heavily underlined. The rest of it was untouched.

They fired him up, these books, and more than once he felt his skin flushing and his heart beat fast as he sat in his seat. Once he stood up, his fists clenched, so agitated had he become. He made a decision to leave his first-class compartment and sit in second class. Then he tried to muster up the courage to sit in third, but its bare boards, scooting chickens, and people perched on the roof put him off. He passed the guard as the latter stepped out of his carriage, and looked at the people in third, mostly Jews mixed with a few Greeks and Persian refugees. They smelt of urine. He turned back, deciding at that moment to stay in second for as long as he could stand it, stepping over a sleeping man and dodging around a Greek woman breastfeeding her baby. The man beside her was smoking cannabis.

'Go back to first,' said the guard. 'Otherwise you'll never get the smell of smoke out of that good cape.'

Saul looked down at himself, then around at the people sitting in second class, noticing for the first time that he was being stared at, or at least his clothes were. He made his way slowly back to first, realising that he had left a pile of brown-wrapped Zealot literature and his wallet on the seat. Neither the elegant Roman woman opposite him nor the tall Corinthian beside him had touched either, although the latter raised his eyebrows as Saul sat down.

'This isn't Rome,' said the Corinthian. 'The locals in this province are thieves.'

Saul nodded, wanting to be angry but unable to bring any real irritation to the surface.

He arrived in Caesarea, and walked through the city streets rather than using the metro. He enjoyed taking in the fragrant night air until he reached his aunt's house. Dilios and Hannah had gone to bed and Saul took care not to make too much noise. He could see paperwork sitting on their kitchen table, material from Caesarea's Association of Spartiates. Dilios would often go to the men's meeting and it seemed that Hannah had been invited to join the women's meeting. One of the documents was partly filled in; he recognised Dilios's handwriting and Hannah's name and antecedents transliterated into Greek.

So she's officially becoming one of them, he thought.

He did not turn on the light, sitting in the dark at the polished wooden table, piling up his brown Zealot books beside the loose sheets of printed paper. He sat there for a long time, eventually getting thirsty. He stood and poured himself a glass of water. It was surprisingly loud.

'Saul, are you all right?'

It was Hannah, standing in a short tunic in the doorway. The dim light served to bring out her lean, whippy, muscular shape. She'd adopted her husband's people's customs with some enthusiasm. Saul noticed that their youngest son was standing behind her, rubbing his eyes.

'Go back to bed, Eurytos,' she said, bending and kissing the top of his head. 'It's late.'

The little boy nodded and padded away.

She walked into the kitchen, turning on the light and seeing the brown-wrapped books. She started to smile, and went to pick one up.

'Are you reading Milesian Tales, Saul?' she asked, teasingly.

Saul snatched the book out of her hand and gathered all of them together in a pile, holding them close to his chest.

'No, I'm not. I don't read Roman filth.'

Ben David follows the prison van with the blacked out windows across the desert towards Jerusalem. The sun is high now, and the sting of the approaching summer is already present in its pointed yellow fingers. He winds down his own window, cocking his left elbow outside and whistling under his breath. He looks in his rear-view mirror. Andreius Linnaeus is stretched out across the back seat, slack jawed and fast asleep. His briefcase is on the floor of the cab; one hand rests on it. Ben David is glad there's very little traffic on the road, and that the new Roman road—cutting through low hills and bounding over saltpans—is so unfailingly straight that there are no corners where sudden motion could wake *Domine* Linnaeus. *Yes, Domine Linnaeus now, and not just to his face. In my head, too.*

He's reasonably sure that Linnaeus is the first Roman for whom he's ever felt anything approaching affection, and the feeling is confusing and contradictory. Images from their meeting last night—the dissolute goy sharing drugs with his younger countrymen and women outside the Fleet Fox—bleed into the sharp-tongued lawyer upbraiding Joseph Arimathea this morning, which in their turn clash with what Ben David will forever call *The Incident At The Prison*.

He'd heard stories about Roman rages before, but had never actually seen one until Cyclone Andreius hit the Vinculum at approximately 11.00 in the morning. The proximate cause was the prison's failure to provide an unbugged client interviewing room, but on reflection Ben David recognises that this was merely the capstone to events that had gone before.

They'd left Arimathea's place in the mid-morning, Andreius pleased with progress and reviewing paperwork in his briefcase, making an occasional comment to himself.

Eventually they cleared the crowds and congestion of Jerusalem; Linnaeus looked up and made small talk with Ben David from the back of the cab, asking him about this landmark or that mountain. Soon afterwards, the Vinculum's central observation tower loomed up on the horizon, followed by its watchtowers and electrified fencing. Problems emerged when Ben David drove up to the boom gate at the main entrance. The sentry in the gate box was dressed in an unfamiliar green and black uniform with the letters CCM stitched over his left breast pocket. Just as the man lowered his head to look in through the window, Ben David asked Linnaeus—loudly enough for the guard to hear—'Where are the legionaries?'

Linnaeus leant forward and showed some paperwork to the guard, who scrutinised it with a sour expression on his face. He went into his sentry box with the documents in his hand and seemed to stay there for a long time. Eventually he sauntered back outside and barked a series of instructions at Ben David in staccato Latin.

'I'm sorry, could you please repeat?' Ben David asked; it was simply too fast, and perhaps partly in dialect.

'Don't worry, David.' Linnaeus's voice flowed soothingly into the front of the cab. 'He wants us to drive through the gate, around to the right and then down to the third building on the left. There's a shady place to park there.'

Clearly miffed that there wouldn't be a second chance to yell at the stupid Jewish taxi-driver, the guard stabbed at the button controlling the boom gate. It lifted slowly. Linnaeus waited until they were well out of earshot before speaking.

'This is not likely to go well.'

'Did I do something stupid?' Ben David asked instinctively, worried at the lawyer's harried expression.

'When we arrived, you asked where the legionaries were. You asked in Greek, which our grumpy guard—as you no doubt realised—understood perfectly well, despite the terrific peasant Apulian act he put on later. This is a private prison. There are no legionaries here, only prison guards employed by Capital Correctional Management.'

'Those letters were on his uniform.'

'Yes. The *Legatus* in Syria will not give Pilate any more troops, and Pilate needs a full legion just to keep Judaea governable. This means he contracted out the Vinculum to a private provider about three years ago.'

'So, this Capital Corrections, they run a prison for profit?'

'Yes. Among other things, it gives them an incentive to cut corners.'

The downward spiral continued when they discovered Ben Yusuf shackled to the floor of his cell in a puddle of urine and dressed in a prison jumpsuit. Permitted to accompany his employer after the to-do at Arimathea's, Ben David watched as Linnaeus rounded on the prison governor, another sullen-faced man in green and black.

'Unchain him at once and get him his day clothes, Don Governor. What sort of an establishment are you purporting to run here?'

'A prison, not a school, Don Linnaeus. He's up on terrorism charges.'

'He's not been charged with anything, unless you know something I don't. And if I recall correctly there's another two days to run before he has to be charged or released.'

Ben Yusuf looked up from the bottom of his cage, his eyes huge, dark, and sad. Heavily bearded, his head was shaven—although now there was a week's growth on it, it no longer shone. He smiled cautiously at Ben David, showing a recently blackened front tooth. Ben David pointed discreetly at Andreius.

'He's good,' he said in Aramaic.

The prison governor shifted uneasily from one foot to the other as an underling went to fetch Ben Yusuf's civilian clothing. He threw the clothes through the bars.

'You'll have to unchain him first.'

'He's a terrorist. I ain't going in there.' His accent—like that of the guard on the gate—was strongly Apulian.

'If you won't go in there, Don Governor, I will. Give me the keys.' He held out his hand.

Shamed now, the prison governor ordered a subordinate into the cell. The underling wrinkled his nose and turned his head away as he fumbled with the chains around Ben Yusuf's ankles and feet. The latter rubbed his wrists with obvious pleasure as the chains fell to the floor. He stood awkwardly, looking down, his clothes clutched in his hands. His shyness at undressing in front of these strange men was palpable.

'He stinks of piss. Has he washed?'

'He's a Jew. They don't wash.'

'Yes, but you do, Roman, and a *clean environment* is a *pleasant environment*.'

'You sound like an Imperial Public Service Announcement,' the Prison Governor said, testy.

'Oh, it's worse than that,' Linnaeus hissed. 'I sound like your *mother*. If she were here, I have no doubt she'd kick your arse.'

Ben David missed quite a bit of the nuance, but he watched the argument—all conducted in a low and civil tone—transfixed. He'd never seen Romans go at each other like this, and it was breathtaking.

'He's to be taken to the baths and given the opportunity to wash.'

The subordinate unlocked the cell again. 'Bath,' he barked in Aramaic.

Ben Yusuf shook his head.

'See,' the prison governor growled, almost triumphant. 'He's a non-washing Jew.'

Linnaeus looked directly at Ben Yusuf and spoke slowly in Greek.

'Is it because they can all see you?'

Ben Yusuf nodded.

'He's not Roman, Don Governor. We've all been brought up to take joy in our bodies. Not everyone is so *wonderfully* enlightened.'

Ben David's Latin wasn't secure enough to know whether Linnaeus was being serious or not.

'If you think I'm going to toss my men out of the baths for one prisoner, you've got another thing coming.'

'Not at all. And he's a suspect, not a prisoner. Take him to one of the booths in the *caldarium* so he can scrub up.'

The underling wrinkled his nose, drew his pistol, took Ben Yusuf by the arm and led him towards the prison baths. Linnaeus and Ben David followed, sitting next to the big *frigidarium* pool to wait. A couple of off-duty guards were swimming laps in it, while three or four others wandered around the edge, chattering in their strong Apulian dialect. Linnaeus noticed that Ben David, too, had dropped his head and turned away. He was scarlet under his beard.

Ben Yusuf eventually emerged from the baths dressed in clean but faded trousers, workboots and a heavy cotton shirt. He smiled at both of them, and there was real gratitude in the expression. Linnaeus appraised him with care: dark like one with Mauretanian ancestry, his beard was tightly curled and Linnaeus suspected that his hair—should he let it grow—would be similar. His background in the trades was obvious enough, too. His shoulders were broad and his forearms heavy. He caught Linnaeus by surprise when he extended his hand—like a Roman—towards him.

'I am Yeshua Ben Yusuf,' he said in clear but accented Greek. 'Thank you for helping me.'

'I am Andreius Linnaeus, your lawyer.' Ben Yusuf seemed puzzled at this. 'I represent your case in court. Today, I'm here to talk to you, and to make sure you're treated properly. What happened to your mouth?'

'They hit me when I first came.'

'Who?'

'The one who threw my clothes at me, and also one of his friends.' He pointed at one of the swimmers in the cold bath.

Linnaeus listened carefully, noting how Ben Yusuf's Greek grammar seemed to improve with every sentence he spoke.

The prison governor was waiting outside the baths when they emerged; his junior stood to one side, his pistol still trained on Ben Yusuf. He took a moment to handcuff him.

'I take it you're satisfied with things now?'

'A distinct improvement, Don Governor. Now all I need is a room where I can talk to my client.'

The marginal uptick in circumstances occasioned by the presence of a clean and sweet-smelling Ben Yusuf rapidly unspun as it became clear that every interview room in the prison was watched over by looming CCTV with a live feed going back to the Prison Governor's office.

'I can switch the feed off,' the prison's technical officer assured him, only to discover that he couldn't. Then the call from the *Praetorium* came through and Linnaeus lost the torture point. After this, Ben David watched as Linnaeus proceeded to take several strips out of his countrymen's collective hide.

Linnaeus turned on the group of guards—including the prison governor—who'd gathered at the back of the Vinculum's communications room to listen to the Form 23 application. He whipped his earpiece off, staring at them.

'This establishment is a disgrace to the Empire,' he announced. 'You do realise that, don't you?' He took a couple of big strides towards them, jabbing his finger in their faces as he spoke. Ben David found himself backing away. He had no desire—even accidentally—to be in the path of Linnaeus's rage.

'Does the phrase *ei incumbit probatio, qui dicit, non qui negat; cum per rerum naturam factum negantis probatio nulla sit* mean nothing to you? Do you even know what it means? Do any of you know where you might find it? Well?'

None of them answered him, although several of the younger guards were looking at the floor like naughty schoolchildren. Ben David suspected they knew what he meant, Apulian peasants notwithstanding. Ben David turned the words over in his own head and—by the time Linnaeus had finished his piece—he knew what they meant, too.

'I come here this morning and discover that—despite good facilities and plenty of space—no attempt has been made to separate convicted criminals from suspects. I find my client chained to the floor in his own piss and shit like a dog. I also note that some of you seem to like beating people up to keep yourselves amused,' he paused, his breathing ragged. 'Any idea where I'll find that phrase, yet?'

One of the guards slowly raised his hand, regressing to childhood under the verbal barrage.

Linnaeus wriggled his eyebrows. 'Yes?'

'In the *Constitution*, sir.'

Linnaeus laughed: a loud, horsy laugh. 'Congratulations. You get a gold star for that effort. Something any Roman ten-year-old should know as well as he knows his mother's face.'

He stopped to draw breath, plonking his briefcase down on the table behind him so he could gesticulate more freely.

'In case you haven't noticed, we run a fair bit of this planet. You've noticed that? Good. That's something.' Linnaeus was warming to his theme now. He flapped his hands again, the gesture more expansive than usual. 'We rule what we do because, on the whole, we're actually pretty good at what we do. Smarter. Better organised. We've got the rule of law.'

His voice became much louder. Ben David flinched; the prison governor looked like he'd been hit.

'Which is why if you forget what that means we may as well tear up the Constitution and chuck it in the fucking Tiber!'

Ben David waited until the Vinculum was behind them before offering his translation.

'*Domine* Linnaeus, that part from your Constitution, it means that the person who makes an accusation, he has to prove it, doesn't it?'

'Yes, David. There is a bit more to it, but that's the important part.'

'I think the next part says that it is hard for someone to prove that something *didn't* happen.'

'That's right. It's called "proving a negative" in law, and it is hard.'

'I didn't know it was a Roman thing, *Domine* Linnaeus.'

'For a long time, David, it was *only* Roman. It set us apart from other peoples. We were an example to the world.'

Ben David looked at Linnaeus's lean face: somehow, it had become less crow-like, less beaky. The eyes, while still very dark, were less closed off, the smile more genuine.

And I will go to my grave remembering a single, unarmed man upbraiding a room full of bullying thugs.

Linnaeus yawned massively now, rubbing his face with both hands. 'I'm sorry, David, I'm really fading here. Wake me up when you need papers for Antonia. I'm tired, angry and quite a few other things as well. I need to sleep.'

THE BANQUET

Caiaphas sat in his office in the Temple and worried. He had no idea what to do. *This is what happens, my friend, when you play both ends against the middle.* He looked out over the Court of the Gentiles and Court of the Israelites. He was waiting for the Prefect of the Temple Guard and Joseph Arimathea to put in appearances. If three heads really were better than one, he hoped for something good from the other two.

True to form, men of the 2nd Cohort had happily scrubbed both places so that—as the Cohort's leading Centurion cheerfully informed him afterwards—'you could eat off the floor.' Letting them into the Court of the Israelites was, in retrospect, a mistake. Even fellow members of the Sanhedrin grumbled about *kufer* despoiling a sacred place with their strange tools. They appreciated the brilliant white stone, though, and, as Joseph Arimathea pointed out in his usual sad and ironic way, there was no way the Temple Guard could have done *that*.

Caiaphas knew there was trouble coming as soon as the Romans shot Iscariot, especially that particular Roman, and in that particular way. He understood the vileness of the insult Iscariot had directed against Lonuobo, and he also knew Lonuobo's troubled history. It was also only a matter of time before Pilate—and his torturing underlings—broke Iscariot and started to establish patterns. *They love pattern, these Romans. See it everywhere. Organise the world around it.* Iscariot was such a *putz*, though, just had to go get himself wrapped up in a riot and then get shot. And shot in such a way as to be in so much pain his brain had simply vacated.

Too bad, really. Once upon a time, he was actually kind of useful.

Iscariot and Caiaphas came into each other's sphere of influence years ago—after Caiaphas had managed to get into a bruising argument with Pilate. It was not an argument he'd wanted, either—at that stage Pilate was still a new Procurator and Caiaphas liked him.

The argument was over the policy of Romanisation. Unlike his older, more traditional, predecessor—*Valerius Gratus, may his bones rot*—who applied Romanisation with real rigour, Pilate was not disposed to pointless conflict over matters of principle. He'd been headhunted by the Senate and was as much a businessman as a bearer of Roman *auctoritas*.

Gratus had threatened to reverse the old prohibition on the construction of Roman and Greek Temples in Jerusalem. 'My troops shouldn't have to practise their rites in secret,' he said once. 'At the moment they're being treated as though they're doing something shameful.' Pilate, by contrast, was content with the longstanding arrangements. Roman and Greek rites in Jerusalem were observed with discretion; by careful application of planning regulations everyone was kept mostly happy.

Caiaphas struggled to grasp Roman religious practices at the best of times, and was surprised at Pilate's insouciance on this point. The first time he'd visited the Procurator in Caesarea he was shocked to see that one of the smaller halls had been set aside for a life-size statue of Cybele, and that priestesses and *galli* who served her used it to hold musical recitals at Pilate's request. Caiaphas tried to avoid looking at the statue. Idolatry upset him, and to have it so brazen and bold—even though Caesarea was a Roman cesspit—in Judaea made him nauseous. It was one thing to see a small silver and lapis charm of Cybele hanging from a taxidriver's rear-view mirror, another to be confronted by a gilded idol with gems for eyes and brilliant blue skin. She looked fierce, not kind, and the lions seated on either side of her throne seemed to glare at him.

'Some Romans think we're a bit odd, too,' Pilate explained. 'As long as you Jews confine your oddities to Jerusalem, everyone will get along fine.'

As was so often the case, the disagreement between Caiaphas and Pilate had its origins in a banquet.

On the anniversary of his appointment as Procurator, Pilate invited Caiaphas and Esther and a selection of friends to a small party at his official residence in Caesarea. The anniversary was twinned with his daughter's coming-of-age celebration. The tone and structure of the invitation was such that Caiaphas knew the meal would consist in large part of the peculiar Roman custom of eating lying down, followed by a night of wild drinking. He'd done that once before, years ago. Apart from getting head-buzzingly drunk—the prone state seemed to make it much worse—it gave him a terrific dose of indigestion: he was pale and ill for forty-eight hours afterwards.

'What's this *coming-of-age* business?' Esther asked.

'She's turned sixteen, and can now appear in public in the company of adults.'

'That's a nice thought,' she said.

'That's not all it means, Esther,' he said, but did not elaborate.

Their prone banqueting was also very undignified for any woman who didn't have Roman sexual habits, which is why he was surprised when Esther—after he'd explained what the evening would likely involve—readily decided to join him.

'If you are to convince Pilate to abandon Romanisation, or at least the very bad parts, you have to meet him part way.'

Caiaphas agreed. Pilate had been excellent on religious issues; fair recompense would probably involve one Roman banquet and the subsequent dose of indigestion for both of them.

'It means we'll be staying overnight. People don't leave until about midday the next day.'

'That's not an imposition on them?'

'Oh no, not at all. That's their way. If a Roman decides to write the night off, he means the next day as well.'

Esther reddened and looked down.

'Will they, ah, ahem...?' Her voice trailed off.

'No, not with us there. There'll be some smutty talk, and Camilla will dance with her betrothed, but that's all. Pilate's not too bad, as Romans go. He doesn't use his servants and he doesn't have a concubine.'

'Remember, I need to be back in time to prepare for Shabbat.'

On the way to Caesarea, Caiaphas recalled Gratus's 'hard' version of Romanisation.

It had started with the posters of a smiling, tanned young legionary with his right hand extended and the Aramaic tagline *Rome is truly your friend* that went up everywhere almost as soon as Gratus appointed Caiaphas High Priest. Underneath the tagline—in smaller writing, but still clearly visible—were listed the benefits of long-term concubinage with a Roman soldier: health insurance; generous education vouchers for any children; free Latin language classes; movement to the top of the *colonia* housing queue; Roman citizenship (conditional on the birth of three children). When he first saw the posters and queried Gratus—in abject horror—the grey-haired old Procurator blew him off.

'It's the same policy all over the Empire, Caiaphas. Long

term, it reduces the scale of our military commitment. Men who join the legions must be unmarried. If they're married, enlistment is treated as automatic divorce. They find their woman or boy in the provinces. There's a reason we do that.'

Caiaphas had no idea how this worked in practice; after the smiling soldier appeared, there was a notable uptick in violence all over Judaea. Not only were the posters regularly torn down or otherwise defaced, women seen to be spending too much time in the wrong company were often attacked. In Jerusalem, this tended to mean a shaven head and a thrashing. In more remote areas, there were stonings and honour killings. As was the Roman way, when they caught them, the stoners and honour killers were dragged into the street and shot in the back of the head. The bodies were left naked and exposed with signs hung around their necks. The signs said things like 'barbarian' or 'uncivilised'. The nightly news became almost impossibly bloody.

There were other things to Romanisation, as well. An abortion clinic appeared at the back of the Jerusalem Æsculapion. And then, to cap it all, Gratus re-installed Herod the Great's golden Roman Eagle, Caesar's personal symbol, in the Court of the Gentiles. For a while there it was cut down every night; the detail from X *Fretensis* tasked with restoring the Emperor's damaged dignity shared the stories of what had been done to it with their comrades. The stories got around.

'Shit in the beak today.'

'One wing gone altogether.'

'Wreath bent into a cock every day this week.'

'Head wrenched off and shoved up its own arse.'

Caiaphas explained to Gratus that the Emperor's Eagle was considered a graven image. Gratus countered that major temples to any other god or goddess everywhere else in the Empire got Caesar's statue as well as his Eagle.

'There's no way that Eagle is idolatrous. Your problem is images of people, yes? Get over yourselves. I'm tired of this whole Jewish special snowflake routine, really I am.'

After a while, the damage stopped being funny to the men of X *Fretensis*. A group led by an athletically gifted young soldier called Marcus Lonuobo—known throughout the Empire because he'd won an Olympic championship and then opted to join the Legions—determined to do something about the persistent disrespect.

Caiaphas remembered seeing Lonuobo and his young friends from his Temple office as they were 'sticking up for Caesar and sound values'. The story grew—at first on JTN, where perplexed Jewish viewers were treated to the spectacle of a glossy black legionary explaining his values to them in irritatingly perfect Aramaic. Soon Syrian, Greek, and Italian regional networks put in an appearance. Then Lonuobo got a prime-time interview slot on *Communicatio Roma*, the state-owned Imperial broadcaster.

Within a week of the CR interview, he'd been promoted. Gratus and *Primus Pilus* Capito knew they'd unearthed a rare talent. For his part, Caiaphas knew a public relations disaster when he saw one. He put the word out that Caesar's Eagle had to stay. He got his own back, though—Caiaphas could work canny when he had to—eventually winning Pilate's agreement to leave security entirely in the hands of the Temple Guard.

Partly thanks to his high profile, partly because he was charming and easy on the eye, partly because he was now an officer, Marcus Lonuobo also contributed to the next stage of the Romanisation programme. Shortly after the CR interview, he acquired a Jewish woman. From an educated, respectable family—daughter of a doctor and a teacher—she was literate and photogenic. Other men in Antonia were no doubt doing something similar, but none of the pairs were quite as striking as Marcus and Zipporah. The smiling soldier posters suddenly disappeared, to be replaced by tasteful black and whites of the happy couple flogging the same inducements or—as Caiaphas noticed the Romans called them, 'incentives'. By now the rest of the Sanhedrin backed him into a corner, demanding that he talk to the new Procurator about the posters. 'They mean to turn Judaea into a Roman whorehouse,' one old Rabbi complained. 'It's disgusting.'

Caiaphas and Esther arrived at Pilate's Caesarea residence, stunned by the lack of security compared to Jerusalem. The coastal city—purpose built to taste—represented the Romans in their native environment. A young legionary parked their official car for them, while a servant guided them past immaculately trimmed topiary and marble statuary, up a sweeping flight of stairs, around a sunken entertainment room (Caiaphas could see Antony, Pilate's youngest, parked in front of the screen with the family's nanny and black retriever) then up two flights of stairs onto a tiled mezzanine overlooking both the *frigidarium* and—on the other side of a curved wall made entirely of one-way glass—Caesarea's famed harbour and marina. Pilate and Claudia approached them, hands outstretched.

'Welcome to you both.'

'So pleased you could make it.'

Caiaphas knew most of Pilate's other guests by sight at least. To Pilate and Claudia's right there was Primus Pilus Capito and his (considerably younger) lover, the administrator at the Dea Tacita Centre. The medic—fine boned, lean, physically Capito's polar opposite—had a long Egyptian name, which he shortened to Remus. Caiaphas wanted to hate him, but he had a tinkling, musical laugh and a winning sense of humour.

Even so, Esther jabbed her husband in the ribs when Capito lay down next to him to dine.

'Is that what I think it is?'

'Don't say anything. They'll get really pissy if you do.'

Camilla's presence at table—beside a bristle-headed young officer, and to her father's left—was, of course, new. Her hair was blonde today, and piled up on top of her head. She somehow contrived to look older than the man beside her, who must have had the best part of ten years on her. When they'd arrived, she'd given Caiaphas a cautious smile while Marius took Esther's hand and then bowed his head. This flustered Esther momentarily—she told Caiaphas later—but she did find it flattering.

Making up the group was one of Pilate's old law school friends, a man Caiaphas hadn't met, Andreius Linnaeus, and his woman, Philippa, the principal of an architects' firm in Rome. She looked like an older version of Camilla. Caiaphas took an instant dislike to both of them, even allowing for the fact that he'd managed to finish up cheek by jowl with an abortionist practitioner of the Greek vice. Both had the needling, arch wit common among upper-class Romans, which Caiaphas found most irritating.

'You're in the god business, then?' Linnaeus remarked when Pilate introduced them.

The military men, of course, were in uniform, while Remus had opted for trendy black silk and a high Serican collar. Pilate—as host and Procurator—was forced to wear a traditional toga over his robe. He shed it as soon as he'd dealt with formalities. Caiaphas noticed that he wasn't completely certain of how to remove it; one of the household servants unwound it while he held his hands out to the sides, taking care to avoid draping it on the floor. The women had gone for various diaphanous and strappy dresses apparently designed for banqueting. Esther pointed out the huge splits up the sides.

'I don't see myself in one of those, I'm afraid.'

She was sensibly and soberly dressed in a long dark skirt and a cotton overshirt.

Caiaphas and Esther finished up directly opposite Pilate and Claudia, for which they were grateful. The man was extraordinarily socially adept, facilitating introductions and telling amusing little anecdotes about how he'd come to meet everyone at the table. He even managed to keep the bulk of the conversation in Greek—he'd intuited that Esther's Latin was confined to pleasantries. Claudia was chic, as always. Well dressed and well groomed, she was one of the few women who could let her hair go completely silver and look better for it. Her lustrous shoulder-length mane curved under her ears and shone in the setting sun that streamed in through the one-way glass.

Esther leant close to her husband, discovering something useful about Roman dining habits. 'She's a very attractive woman,' she was able to point out, discreetly.

'Pilate's still in lust with his wife, he's told me so himself.' He paused when he saw the shock on her face. 'Romans love sharing that sort of detail with just about anyone, Esther. You get used to it.'

Strangely enough—as Caiaphas realised later—the meal had gone very well for the most part. The seesawing nausea he expected from eating and drinking while prone held off, his toast to good relations between the Procurator and the Temple went down well, and he found Capito and Remus engaging interlocutors. Capito—with his steel-grey flat-top and obviously broken nose—explained the concept of fall in constructing aqueducts and drains to Caiaphas and Esther, who both watched him with genuine interest as he drew deft cutaway diagrams of pipes and masonry on the back of a stray envelope. Then, inexplicably, the evening started to go badly. There'd been a brief lull in the conversation when everyone seemed to draw breath, leaving Camilla speaking into the void.

'We've had to do analysis of material drawn from our recent culture,' she was saying to Philippa, 'which is a bit radical, I suppose.'

'As long as you're still reading Virgil,' Philippa responded.

Linnaeus laughed at this, waving his glass at the servant in charge of refills.

'Having some awareness of contemporary issues is surely useful,' Claudia broke in.

'That's not hard to achieve,' Capito said. 'Watch the screen. Read the papers. I don't think it needs to be taught in school.'

'I suppose some of it's interesting enough,' Linnaeus said, looking directly at Camilla. 'Even if it's not what you want to do with the rest of your life.'

'Sometimes. My Latin teacher really liked my essay on *Drowning Slowly*. First and only time I've ever got an A for anything in Latin. And off Licinia, too.'

'A notoriously hard marker,' Claudia explained to Caiaphas and Esther.

'This is at the Academy here?' Caiaphas asked.

Pilate nodded. 'That song was a phenomenon last year, though,' he added. 'I've lost touch with lots of contemporary cultural stuff, but *Drowning Slowly* was pretty hard to ignore.'

'Apart from the fact that it's a real earworm,' Claudia pointed out. 'Always good in a popular song.'

'The visuals were apparently very evocative; he went to the trouble of having a sequence shot especially,' said Linnaeus. 'Although I've only ever seen outtakes on the news.'

Caiaphas had the awful bottoming-out feeling he often got when Romans started talking about their music.

'I'm sorry, I don't think I've heard it,' he said.

'Don't worry, High Priest. I've got it here. I'll show it to you. I think I must have watched it about a million times while I was writing that essay.'

Camilla stood up and disappeared around the corner to fiddle with something in the next room. Caiaphas and Esther watched a set of panels slide apart as a long rectangle on the wall illuminated. She resumed her place beside Marius, who gave her a sharp buss on the forehead.

Caiaphas had heard it, after all, but never paid attention to the words or context, except to note that it did not sound at all like most Roman music of his acquaintance.

'It's Gallic music,' Camilla said, apparently reading his mind. 'Roman music is modal; theirs is tonal. It's a very different sound.'

Caiaphas watched, now, as a dark young man sang a direct and simple account of taking his woman to an abortion clinic shortly after the Saturnalia. Visually, the story he told played out behind his head using what looked like handheld footage—except for a coruscating series of aerial shots showing a stereotypical Roman planned colony, all grid patterns and intersections. A camera tracked the couple's metro journey through it, picking out landmarks as they went: central station, the Forum, the baths. At one point the camera paused on the girl's face; she was crying.

Presumably the singer was actually a Gaul, not just using their music. In the song, he told how he'd taken his girl to the clinic when her parents were away in another large Gallic town. Only the chorus was in any way symbolic; this was the 'drowning slowly' of the title. It showed the musicians—he'd added a drummer and a man playing an unfamiliar (to Caiaphas, anyway) stringed instrument—in a studio as it filled with water.

It was extraordinarily affecting and compassionate, devoid of either cant or sentiment. Caiaphas found himself in tears by the end. He felt Esther clasp his shoulder; even with her weak Latin, she'd picked up the gist of it.

'I'm sorry, High Priest,' he could hear Camilla saying from what seemed like the other end of a long, hollow drain. She was standing over him, her face filled with concern. 'I didn't mean to upset you.'

'I've never seen that all the way through either,' he could hear Pilate saying to Linnaeus. 'What a bombshell.'

Capito put the tips of his fingers together in front of his face. 'It's become a rite of passage, I suppose.'

'I didn't think you Romans had the capacity to be that honest with yourselves,' Caiaphas said. 'I'm amazed.' He felt Esther touch his shoulder again, felt her radiating concern, but it was probably too late. *Oh well, hung for a sheep as for a lamb.*

'I wrote about it as a rite of passage,' Camilla said softly, rejoining Marius and looking at Capito. 'I'm glad it's not just me who saw that.'

'There are worse rites of passage,' Marius said, also looking at Capito. His hair seemed even spikier than normal.

'It's just a sad song,' Philippa volunteered. 'All things pass. Both love and mankind are grass.'

'Spoken like a true Roman,' Caiaphas said to her.

'Well, yes, she is Roman,' Linnaeus said archly. 'We have largely common values.'

'A young man in Gaul seems not to agree,' Caiaphas countered. 'He seems to understand that much of your lifestyle is built on death.'

He looked at Remus, but the medic's head was turned away as he got a refill.

'Victor Gerius is a Gaul, yes,' Camilla said. 'He was a musician in *Legio* XXI *Rapax*. He left the legion without re-enlisting for a second stint in order to start his music career.'

'Well, since the Roman military has a remarkable talent for draining compassion out of people, the fact that he could write a song like that after sixteen years of being taught *not to care* is remarkable.'

'I suspect we need to steer this conversation into calmer waters.' Claudia looked hopefully at her husband, but for once Pilate's enviable social skills had deserted him. He was staring at Caiaphas, his mouth open.

'I don't think I've heard a more baseless slur directed at the Imperial Roman Army in my life,' he said.

Capito looked at Caiaphas, then across the room at his Commander. He had not expected the civilian to intervene with such emphasis. 'Thank you, Procurator.'

'You don't want to address what you do, do you?' Caiaphas knew that everything coming out of his mouth was propelled by alcohol, but as he spoke, it was as though a dam had overspilled. 'Your military is the anvil, Romanisation your hammer, my people the workpiece you seek to shape. You wish to rebuild the world in your image, yes?'

'We have been doing that for a long time, Caiaphas,' Pilate said evenly. 'You aren't the first. You won't be the last. We know what works and we can prove it.'

'Has it not occurred to you that some people do not wish to be Romanised, Procurator?'

'Regularly, Caiaphas.'

'Can you at least spare us the propaganda that encourages your legionaries to steal our women?'

'I think you'll find the process is usually the other way around,' Marius said. 'That is rather the idea.'

Linnaeus laughed and flapped his hands. 'Newsflash: people respond to incentives.'

'At least, change the law so that the men may marry. At

the moment our women live in the *vicus* beside Antonia like whores.'

'Good luck with convincing the Roman military to change a hundred and fifty-year-old policy,' said Capito. 'Anyway, it's only enlisted men who can't marry.'

'There are more of them, and they are predatory.'

Pilate's eyes had narrowed to slits. 'Caiaphas, Romanisation is a centrally developed program. You could always take it up with the Senate.'

It was Caiaphas's turn to snort, half in amusement and half in derision. 'I don't think so. It doesn't seem to work very well for you in Judaea, at any rate.'

'On the contrary,' said Marius, his eyes—usually a lovely sea green—now the colour of flint. 'Syncretia is partly about increasing the future pool of available citizens from which the military may recruit. That's going well—we're in the midst of an unprecedented baby boom, with a plurality of births in the last two years the result of unions between X *Fretensis* personnel and non-citizen Jews. It contributes to cultural assimilation and improvements in peace, order, and good governance. We're particularly pleased with rising female attendance numbers at school, and there's been a decent drop in rates of interpersonal violent crime, too.'

He made neat, incisive movements with his hands as he spoke, the statistics rolling out of his head at will.

Caiaphas stared at him.

'You must be the most calculating people ever to walk the earth.'

'No, actually, we're not. It's just that tying down an entire legion in one small province is very costly, as you'd appreciate. School vouchers and public–private health insurance arrangements are much cheaper long term than men-at-arms.'

Caiaphas let his head flop forward onto the heels of both

hands in mock despair, leaving his fingers pointing at the ceiling. Surprised, he heard titters and giggles from various people around the room. Pilate was one of them. Perhaps aware that he was being laughed at, Marius declined to join in, pursing his lips slightly.

'I do believe we have punched through offensive and come out the other side,' Remus observed.

'You kept rather quiet for all of that,' said Claudia. 'Shrewdly done, my friend.'

Caiaphas looked at the medic, waiting to be dismissed as an imbecile or something similar. Romans had a good line in nasty put-downs, and having just insulted his host, he expected the rest of them to lay down a decent artillery barrage.

Instead, Remus smiled a beatific smile.

'I will say one thing only, and I will not be drawn on anything else.' He paused, presumably for effect. 'Abortion is a medical procedure, and there are two ways to perform medical procedures. Those two ways are *well*, or *badly*. I prefer well, myself. I now return you to your scheduled programming.'

Pilate's laughter this time was full throated, and he even found it in himself to smile somewhat crookedly at Caiaphas and Esther. Philippa and Linnaeus, however, looked positively thunderous.

'Now Marius and Camilla have a little something to share with us for Camilla's coming of age', Pilate offered, his good graces back in evidence. 'Take it away, those still young enough to pull this off.'

Marius and Camilla, their enthusiasm restored, bounded up and cleared themselves a performing area underneath the screen. Once again Camilla fiddled in the room next door, re-emerging once more.

'Count us in, Papa.'

Esther looked at Caiaphas, perplexed.

'The fun part of the evening,' he explained in Aramaic. 'They'll sing, dance and get outrageously drunk.'

Pilate rapped his knuckles on one of the tables in front of him for the count, while the two young people posed for the start of a dance. Camilla's hands were in the traditional starting position—one open in front of her eyes, one open behind her head, her elbows out to the side.

Marius stood bolt upright behind her, his feet apart, his hands on his hips.

'We're going to be treated to something from Roman cinema,' Caiaphas whispered to Esther.

Esther had heard—always second hand—about Rome's musical cinema, with its historic origins in their musical theatre. She'd even caught snatches of it as she walked down the street; the pulsating rhythms and duelling vocals would leak out of top-floor windows or through workplace doors, even in the Jewish Quarter. Sometimes children would dance to it on street corners, and if the legionaries were in a good mood, and felt safe enough, they would play it through the speakers in their armoured vehicles. Loathed by many Jewish parents—chiefly because it was so infectious and distracting, especially for children—she'd made a point of avoiding it.

And yet, now she found herself transfixed by the sheer joyousness of what she saw.

Marius and Camilla whirled and spun, laughing and smiling, their steps smoothly coordinated. At one point he threw her in the air and somehow contrived to catch her, all in effortless time. Esther had heard Caiaphas write Roman dance off as the vertical expression of a horizontal desire, but this was only tangentially sexual. Most of it was a celebration of timing, balance and skill.

'They're beautiful,' she said, loud enough for Caiaphas to hear. 'It's beautiful.'

The rest of the diners were clapping along, while Linnaeus and Capito periodically let off high-pitched verbal trills. Caiaphas watched his wife cheerfully nod her head in time with the beat. Camilla and Marius turned each other about once more, then finished the way they'd started. Both were breathing heavily; their faces shone under the droplights in the ceiling.

'That was fabulous, you two. One of the loveliest things I've ever seen.'

Marius and Camilla registered astonishment, followed by her parents, followed by the rest of the party. It was Esther who had spoken.

'Have you seen the film?' Marius wanted to know. 'You should. We think we're as good as Quintus Roscius and Magilla Macer.'

'Whoa, that's a big call,' said Capito. 'Remember they sing a lot of their own stuff, too.'

'But not at the same time,' Camilla pointed out. 'They use playback singers.'

'Was that their voices on the music you played?'

'Yes. From *Who am I to You*? Just about my favourite film ever. I'll lend you my copy if you haven't seen it.'

Esther looked at her husband, who was making odd noises in the back of his throat.

'I don't think this is wise, Esther,' he said in Aramaic. 'Hillel already has an unhealthy obsession with Roman cinema.'

'I wouldn't let that worry you, *Kohen Gadol,'* Capito broke in, also in Aramaic. 'Most Roman cinema is quite chaste. We already know what we do in our spare time.'

'And there's always a happy ending, followed by a terrific song,' Marius went on.

Caiaphas had walked past Roman schools in Caesarea—and even Jerusalem Academy—and seen hordes of schoolchildren in the grounds practising the big brassy dance numbers they'd seen at the pictures. It always looked harmless enough, just lots of kids having a bunch of fun.

'There are worse things to take from Rome,' Esther said. 'Subject to my vetting, Hillel can listen to their cinema music.'

Caiaphas got the distinct impression he'd been overruled.

The rest of the evening—spent in an agreeable alcoholic haze—revolved around Capito and Pilate attempting to teach him to dance, while Claudia and Philippa worked with Esther. Marius and Camilla disappeared, while Remus and Linnaeus—who'd both drunk more alcohol than anyone else—sat on the floor watching the tableaux before them.

Esther opened her eyes and waited for the ceiling to come into focus. This took some time, and involved concentrating on the woman's face cut in profile into the crystal light fitting. An aquiline and aristocratic face, it was not so much beautiful as handsome, even severe.

Livia Augusta; the Emperor's mother.

She noticed that she'd managed to find her way to their allocated guest room, remove her clothing, bathe and flop into bed. So had Caiaphas. He was on his side, snoring very gently. Their clothes—very damp—were strewn all over the floor, and she could see pools of water on the bathroom tiles. *We appear to have created a floordrobe.* She debated trying to move, procrastinated for several minutes, then finally pushed the sheets aside and sat upright, taking care not to wake her sleeping husband. *My bones are made of glass. My head is full of treacle. I cannot feel my feet. God, I am never doing that again.* The room was still very dark, shuttered against what she knew would be brilliant morning light. *Although it's facing west, so maybe not too terrible. How do I know that? Pieces of my mind have gone missing.* She stood very slowly and carefully, and immediately knelt down on the Persian rug with her back to the bed. *Not so fast, honey child.* She waited for another minute or two, on her hands and knees, and then tried standing again, this time without mishap.

She padded across the tiles in her bare feet, taking in their blue and green highlights and the sea creatures painted onto them. She stopped at the bathroom door, leaning against the jamb. There was a great deal of spilled water on the floor; it was clear that she and Caiaphas had bathed together. The bath was generously proportioned, as one would expect in any Roman residence. She edged around the bidet and sat on the loo; there was a sharp sting as she urinated. *And we did that thing too. Figures, I suppose.* She could see her overnight bag in the corner; her brain slowly registered the fact that there would be a clean set of clothes in there, practical and comfortable. *And toothpaste.*

Linnaeus was sitting next to the *frigidarium* in trews eating scrambled egg when she made her way downstairs. He'd thoughtfully made the glass facing the harbour rather opaque—this was apparently adjustable—although it was still very bright. She could make out the outlines of yachts and smaller pleasure craft in the marina. She squinted.

'I can black that out completely, if you like,' Linnaeus offered.

'We have to drive back to Jerusalem at some point; the sooner my eyes adjust, the better.'

'Did you catch a good sleep?'

'I can't remember bits of last night.'

'You had a good time.'

'I'm sure I did. I do remember dancing quite a bit. Just not what happened next.'

'We all came down here and got completely shit-faced. Caiaphas jumped in with all his clothes on, and Capito had to fish him out.' He pointed. 'It's easy to drown when you're drunk.'

She registered some shock at this.

'I don't remember.'

'Lack of practice at drinking, that's all. We were all in there at various points. You too. With Capito playing lifeguard. I don't think it's possible to get that man drunk. He's got a reinforced liver.'

A young servant emerged from a room sequestered under the stairs leading to the mezzanine with a tray in his hands.

'One of the Jews you are?'

Esther laughed at his Aramaic.

'I speak Greek, it's all right.'

The relief on his face was palpable. 'I have some of your special food, Ma'am. On the Procurator's orders.'

She sat at the table opposite Linnaeus, surprised at how hungry she was. She ate in silence. Linnaeus watched her with detachment.

Slowly, the rest of the group—save Marius and Camilla—emerged to greet and eat. Capito dived into the water and swam a dozen lengths before hauling himself out and inhaling a considerable quantity of bacon and egg. The servant with bad Aramaic brought out tiny cups of strong Roman coffee. Remus blundered out of his room in the altogether and remembered there were Jews present only when he was halfway down the stairs. Esther had her back turned, but Pilate and Claudia both noticed and laughed as he sprinted back up the stairs.

'We're missing your other half,' Philippa said to Esther.

'He'll emerge in due course,' Pilate offered. 'He's older than the rest of us.'

'Even me,' Capito said drily.

Philippa also dived in to swim lengths. She moved through

the water more smoothly than Capito had done. Nero followed Philippa, trying to keep up with her, and then gave up. He hauled himself out, trotted over and sat next to Pilate, then shook himself, soaking the Procurator and anyone else nearby. Esther winced, but the Romans seemed to find the dog and everything about him funny.

'The young people are missing,' Esther looked up the stairs. 'They danced so beautifully.'

'Busy doing dancing of a different sort, I'd say.' Remus reached across her for a coffee. 'At sixteen, we let them go. They usually seize the opportunity with some gusto.'

She looked at him, slowly grasping his meaning.

'So a Roman child must remain chaste until sixteen?'

'That is the custom,' Claudia explained. 'Our culture is based on milestones and rites of passage. Coming of age is sixteen, although that number has varied both up and down historically. Majority—including suffrage and enlistment—is at eighteen; full power to contract comes at twenty-one.'

'Joining the army involves a contract, surely?'

'Traditionally, their father signs on their behalf,' Linnaeus said. 'Mothers can sign now, but under the old law, it was only the father. Part of his job as *paterfamilias*.'

'The traditional system's breaking down these days,' Claudia went on, 'but our reputation isn't fair. It was only at festival time in days gone by. Back before the war against Hannibal, we were straighter than you Jews.'

Esther found this hard to believe, and said so.

Claudia's voice was fey.

'During festa, there is misrule; when *festa* is over, we go back to do the work.'

Esther looked at her. At that moment, beautiful, civilised Claudia seemed alien. She'd heard the legionaries say that, both when they killed and when they built.

Do the work! Do the work!

She looked up towards the stairs, cautious. There was no sign of Caiaphas.

'I'm sorry about my husband's outburst.'

'I think he's angrier about Romanisation than just the posters,' Pilate pointed out. 'Other subject peoples dislike Romanisation.'

'I know you can't change your law just for us,' she dropped her eyes. 'But the posters are very galling.'

Pilate nodded, smiling. 'Perhaps you should be *Kohen Gadol, Gveret* Kayafa.'

'I was just thinking that,' said Linnaeus.

THE ZEALOT

Yehuda Iscariot was filling tanks and minding the store at the Golden Fleece service station on the Caesarea–Jerusalem road when a man he recognised as the High Priest pulled up in his long black official car. The roof was not retracted. Yehuda wiped his hands on an oil rag and walked out to see what was wanted, whether he'd come into the store or just need fuel. When the High Priest stepped stiffly from the passenger side, Yehuda understood *why* the roof was up: he looked ripped, as did his wife. Both had dark circles under their eyes, while Caiaphas's long grey beard badly needed brushing. The fact that his wife—a much younger woman—was driving told Yehuda all he needed to know. Yehuda unhooked the fuel nozzle.

'Large night last night, Rabbi?' he asked cheerfully in Aramaic.

Caiaphas nodded mutely.

Yehuda watched Caiaphas walk into the store and browse the cigars and painkillers and antacids on sale above the magazine stands. Esther stood beside him as he fished first a cigar in its metal tube, then a pouch of cannabis, off the shelf. He'd never tried the latter, probably because it was popular among Romans.

'You're not thinking of starting that filthy habit?' Yehuda heard Esther say.

'It's tempting. Means I'll die faster.'

Yehuda watched the High Priest contemplating what Zealots had come to call *Roman Relief*, holding the cannabis in one hand as he read the officially mandated information on the packet.

'You know, that sounds like something I could do with right now.'

'If you want anything stronger, you'll have to go back into Caesarea, to an apothecary,' Yehuda said.

'Oh no, this will do nicely.'

The Golden Fleece was a good spot for Yehuda's purposes: plenty of powerful types turned up as of necessity, and the depot at the rear of the store was popular with drivers from all over the Empire and beyond. He'd become skilled at not only siphoning information from people but also sorting the useful bits out and sending them on to where they were needed. He kept listening to Caiaphas and Esther from behind the counter: sorting, filing, compartmentalising.

'I hope I haven't burnt my bridges with Pilate.'

'I'm sure they understand that the drink talks quite a bit at their things.'

'They're generally not good with insulting the hosts, though.'

'You didn't insult Pilate and Claudia. You insulted Capito and Marius. Different story. Marius was busy thinking with his little head while Capito is big and ugly enough for most things not to worry him.'

Caiaphas laughed. 'I hope you're right.'

She paused to collect a Greek-language newspaper. 'I think the revolting propaganda will go.'

'That doesn't really change things.'

'It'll stop Judaea looking like a Roman whorehouse.'

'Form over substance.'

Her voiced tightened. 'What do you suggest, then? Trying to throw them out? These people live for the fight, that much is clear. Try to fight them, and you're playing by their rules.'

Yehuda busied himself behind the counter, listening intently. He reached down slowly, pretending to retrieve something he'd dropped. He unplugged the cable leading to the store's CCTV; silently, the camera winked out.

'Some of us want them gone, Rabbi.'

Caiaphas looked up, abruptly.

'One of them stole my sister. Then he shot my brother when we tried to get her back.'

The young man in the blue mechanic's overalls had real pain in his eyes. Esther put her hands over her mouth.

'Shot me, too, but I lived.' He flipped his bib down, then turned and pulled up his shirt. There was a livid scar on his back, above his right kidney.

'He was drunk, so not very careful.'

'For this, the Lord brought us out of Egypt,' Caiaphas said softly. Esther still had her hands over her mouth. She shook her head slowly.

'So, some of us fight.'

Caiaphas paid for the fuel, newspaper, cannabis and painkillers, handing over his Temple expenses card. When Yehuda returned the card and his receipt there was a small strip of paper curled around it.

'Only from a public *vocale*,' he said.

Esther did not see the paper change hands. She watched out of the corner of her eye as her husband used his inexpert fingers to roll a fat joint while she drove. *Fat because he doesn't know what he's doing, just following the instructions on the packet like that.*

He rolled down the window and smoked it, shaking his head when she went to retract the roof. It was one of the strong hydroponic varieties, and from time to time—despite his best efforts—she wore a faceful. Afterwards, he dozed off. She spent the whole trip seeing the service station attendant's scar in her mind's eye.

...and healing and redemption and forgiveness and atonement for us and for all His people Israel...

The *vocale* number stayed hidden in Caiaphas's wallet for a month, tucked behind his identity card. He looked at it daily, debating whether to throw it away. He felt Roman eyes drawn towards it every time he opened his wallet to pay for something. He particularly noticed its special weight when he had lunch with Pilate in Caesarea. *I have a terrorist's contact details in my pocket*, he wanted to shout. *Really!* The impulse to caper like a small child shocked him; *maybe I do not bear secrets very well.*

Over the same month, the Romanisation propaganda disappeared: Caiaphas was genuinely surprised, Esther less so. Other posters—normal ones spruiking businesses, new films, construction firms, factory jobs in Syria, restaurants, imported beer—appeared in their place. He did not know when this removal took place. *Here today, gone tomorrow, and good riddance.*

It was this removal—for which he made a point of thanking Pilate personally, during one of their oddly strained lunches—that decided him. That evening, he threw the slip of paper into the kitchen bin. He felt better straight away.

Two days later, he was watching the news; it was *Communicatio Roma*, to which he'd frankly become addicted, though it pushed his Latin to breaking point. The main evening news bulletin managed to combine straight news coverage with the specialist commentary of the best magazine programmes. Even better, the presentation was arch and witty—something he'd come to appreciate as his Latin improved. CR was an

Imperial mouthpiece, but it was a self-aware and literate one, unafraid to combine mockery with praise.

Tonight he was annoyed that he'd missed more than half of the bulletin. Severus Agrippa, the anchorman—he of the loud socks, bouffant hair, and vertiginously superior sneer—was talking to a veteran in a dark-blue toga. The man still wore his military haircut, and his scalp glistened under the studio lights.

> **Agrippa:** So your movements are completely unimpeded? Back to normal?
>
> **Gaius Favius:** Better than normal, Severus. If anything, I can move more freely now than I did before the attack.

Caiaphas leaned forward as a montage showing Favius played. Here is Favius just after he's lost the use of his legs thanks to a Zealot IED in the Galilee. Then there is surgery and radical stem cell therapy; he is cocooned in a research laboratory with tubes coming out of his arms and legs. Now he's in the Servicemen's Æsculapion learning how to walk again, grasping a set of parallel bars. He sweats and swears as a medica coaxes him towards her. 'You can do it, soldier!' she shouts. He swims. Now he rides a horse. Now he strides through fields in boots and cap and coat, shotgun broken over one arm, a curly-coated black dog at his heels. Ducks fly overhead and he stoops to shoot. Swelling music, heavy on the percussion and marching feet, plays in the background.

Caiaphas felt something catch in his throat, and his hand went to his mouth. He hated the way Roman propaganda could manipulate his emotions like that. CR always abandoned any pretence at detachment or wit when it reported on the Roman military, but that didn't mean its sentimentality was any less skilful. He felt drawn to Favius, to his beaming, suntanned face and hearty laugh. He loved, in spite of his ambivalence towards Romans and their morality, the fact that science meant Favius could walk and dance and make love to his concubine and play with his children and complete his duty.

> **Agrippa:** So your duty is very important to you?
>
> **Favius:** Nothing is more important to me.
>
> **Agrippa:** I think you may consider this person as important to you as your duty to the Empire, Gaius.

Caiaphas watched, unable to breathe, as an attractive woman—she looked to be in her early thirties, but it was difficult to tell, Romans being fond of both genetic manipulation and cosmetic surgery—emerged from behind the newsdesk and sat beside Favius. She was his embryonic donor, Agrippa explained. Her abortion had, quite literally, given him his legs. He beamed at her and kissed each of her cheeks. Unable to locate the channel changer, Caiaphas launched himself across the room to turn it off, but he was too late. He staggered to one side, vomiting into the waste paper basket. *And most of that landed on the floor, Kayafa. Well played, good sir, well played.*

Esther was kashering the kitchen—it hadn't been done for a while, and they'd had a fair few gentile guests of late—when she spotted someone's backside and legs hanging out of the big industrial bin in their street.

She poured the jug of boiling water she had to hand down the sink. The rising steam temporarily obscured her view, so she opened the window to get a closer look. *What's in our bin?* She leaned out to shout.

'Whoever you are, do you mind getting out of our bin? I can assure you that there's nothing in there worth having!'

The figure began wriggling backwards. One hand was holding a bag of her kitchen rubbish. It finally landed on its feet and then turned to face her. Although his hair and beard were skew-whiff and he had one of the outer leaves from a cabbage stuck to the side of his head, she could still recognise her husband.

'Bar Kayafa! What *are* you doing?'

'I threw something important away by mistake.'

Joseph Arimathea did not expect the High Priest to turn up on his doorstep just before he was due to roll himself into bed. He was in his nightshirt, brandy nightcap in hand, and had just had a long and awkward conversation with his daughter. She was insisting on going to Rome for a Hotel School reunion. He was not happy, and was even less happy when there was a loud and imperious series of bangs on his front door.

He stomped to the door and swung it open. Caiaphas was on the other side, ashen-faced, his breathing laboured.

'What's wrong, *Kohen Gadol*?'

'Everything.'

'Come in. Can I get you something to drink?'

'Whatever you're having.'

Joseph poured his superior a double nip and waved him towards the sofa.

'Do you watch *CR*?'

'What on *CR*?'

'The news. Tonight's news.'

'Yes I do, and I did.'

'Did you see the abortion segment?'

'You mean the paraplegic legionary segment?'

Caiaphas was having difficulty speaking. '"Help for

Heroes," they call it. She ticked a box when she went to the clinic.'

'They require consent from citizen women. With non-citizens, consent is presumed.'

'Shameless. She was... shameless. And Agrippa, with that *knowing* look... the soldier, just gormless... goofy smile. Romans are... *shameless*.'

Arimathea guided Caiaphas's glass towards his lips, made sure he took a decent mouthful and then pressed firmly on both of the high priest's shoulders. Arimathea's gaze was steady; he had to make an important point in a short space of time.

'Romans are many things, *Kohen*, but shameless is not one of them. They feel the most acute shame at things *they* find shaming. Cowardice on the battlefield. Lack of filial piety. Stupid or lazy children.'

Caiaphas was showing signs of distress, mouth-breathing and sweating. Joseph put down his brandy and reached out to grasp his forearm. They sat in silence as Caiaphas slowly brought himself under control.

'Last month, after an appalling piss-up at Pilate's residence in Caesarea—I feel guilty about participating—I met a young man who I am reasonably certain has ties to the Zealots, maybe even the *Sicarii*. At first I wanted none of it, but... that abortion story...'

Joseph could feel the blood draining out of his face.

'Rabbi, it is your role as *Kohen Gadol* to try to create a bridge between Judaea and Rome. And if participating in Pilate's piss-up contributed to the removal of that revolting "screw a soldier, here are the side benefits" propaganda, then your sore head was a small price to pay.'

'My wife says something similar.'

'What do you propose we do with this Zealot? Give him

money from the Temple treasury? Provide moral support? You realise the Zealots hate you and me as much—if not more—than they hate the *Romoi*. We should know better, that's their logic.'

'I want something done about the Dea Tacita Centre.'

Joseph looked into his brandy balloon, swirling its contents gently around the bowl.

'He gave me a *vocale* number. JER 2476. He said I should call it from a public *vocale*.'

'It'll be a dead drop. Someone will collect the messages it receives and get in contact with you. And believe me, they will get in contact with you. Nothing would warm a Zealot's heart more than a compromised High Priest.'

'Maybe I can steer them away from attacking Jewish civilians.'

'Ah, here we see the great delusion; the man of reason who thinks he can influence men of unreason.'

Joseph stood up, indicating that the conversation was over.

'*Kohen Gadol*, whatever you do, understand that you do it on your own account. This discussion—as far as I'm concerned—did not take place.'

Caiaphas waited for the lunch hour before changing out of his vestments into a pair of nondescript trousers, long-sleeved flannel shirt and overcoat. It was cold outside; two days previously Jerusalem had experienced one of its rare snowfalls. He folded the scrap of paper and tucked it—once again—behind his identity card. He looked around his office once, carefully, before stepping out into the bitter, brilliant sunshine, picking his way through the crowds of people in both the Court of the Israelites and the Court of the Gentiles. As he'd expected, no one paid a middle-aged Jewish man with a big beard in ordinary clothes any particular heed.

He made his way across the square in front of Antonia towards the row of *vocale* boxes. Half-a-dozen legionaries and their women rehearsed dance steps. Women with small children gathered on the other side to gossip and watch their older children play. A pizza vendor used his Antonia licence to good advantage, selling slices for considerably more than they were worth. Two businessmen in sharp robes walked in front of him, deep in discussion.

Even though there were several *vocale* boxes on the other side of the square, most of them were in use, or had chewing gum stuck in the coin slot. The final one featured a young Samaritan woman arguing in her oddly accented Aramaic. He waited until she stormed off, leaving the handset hanging before—fumble-fingered and terrified—he made his call.

'Leave your details,' a prerecorded, neutral voice said in technically correct but accented Hebrew on the other end. There was nothing more.

Caiaphas had prepared his words carefully. 'I met a young man in the Golden Fleece a month ago. I'd like to meet him again.'

Will that be enough? It'll have to do, won't it?

Still shaking, he hung up.

Nothing happened for a week, and he assumed that he'd not given them enough information, or that they'd lost interest.

Maybe that was just the fellow outside Caesarea getting excited. Saw the High Priest and decided to have words. Oh well.

He was preparing to leave for home the following Wednesday afternoon when he noticed his car had a flat tyre. It was parked in his designated spot in the Temple's underground facility. He made his way back up to his office and called the Automobile Association, his mood tetchy. Caiaphas was completely unmechanical, and hated admitting that not only could he not change a tyre, he couldn't even check the water and oil in his official car. He sat down to wait for their mechanic, a Greek-language newspaper to hand. He'd completed most of its cryptic by the time a member of the Temple Guard arrived to let him know a mechanic was waiting outside to be let in. He made his way downstairs.

'Rabbi Kayafa?'

'Yes, that's me. I presume it's got a puncture.'

'Should be easy to fix.'

'I'm sorry to call you out for such a trivial thing, it's just...' his voice trailed off.

'Plenty of smart people can't change a tyre,' the mechanic said amiably.

The mechanic pumped the tyre first, advising him to buy a new one sooner rather than later. Caiaphas then watched him—smoothly and without any fuss—change it for the spare. He stood and presented the insurance forms to Caiaphas for signature; attached to the top copy was a note bearing the words 'Wednesday, 5 pm, vocale 71, Jewish Quarter'.

Nothing showed on the mechanic's face. Caiaphas pocketed the note, thanked him, signed the forms and drove home. Once again, he stored the note behind his identity card. Two days later he had cause to retrieve some paperwork from the front passenger seat and noticed that the tyre in front of the door had not gone flat, which meant someone had let it down deliberately. He felt a sinking, nauseating sensation wash over him.

You're being watched, my friend. Better start watching out for yourself.

Caiaphas was worried that finding public *vocale* number 71 in the Jewish Quarter would be difficult, but he soon realised that public *vocale* boxes—and other amenities—radiated out from wealthier areas or a market in roughly concentric circles. *Good old Romans and their town planning, so very predictable, yes.* He realised that exposing his distinctive Sanhedrin car and government-issue licence plates would be dangerous, and made his way from the Temple by bicycle. The trip rattled his teeth and made him appreciate why people in Jerusalem disliked riding outside the Roman Quarter, which had new and smooth concrete streets. Dust swirled around him, getting in his eyes and mouth. A camel took a shine to him while he was waiting at a level crossing for a goods train from Caesarea to pass through, attempting to eat some of his hair. It stank, and he swatted its nose away.

Vocale 71 was distinguished by its location in what was obviously a very poor street. He chained his bicycle to a streetlight and strode up the hill until he spotted the telltale purple painted box with its golden *Tib. Imp* on the fascia. Many of the houses had broken windows, some of which were boarded up. Washing hung on lines of string between them, while any intact walls were daubed with anti-Roman graffiti. A woman with the sort of pinched face only long privation can produce eyed him suspiciously from behind one of the boarded-up windows. *I suppose I look well fed, like I've been on easy street too long.* He looked away from her, deliberately, noticing every streetlight was broken, apparently a long time ago. One house sported a giant—and well-executed—mural of two Zealot fighters, blue and white bandannas wrapped around their heads, rifles pointed at the sky. Three goats grazed on a patch of open ground in between two of the boarded-up houses.

While he was waiting, he heard rather than saw a Roman MRAP make its way into the cobbled street, followed by a cloud of urchins with rocks. Instinctively, he moved inside the *vocale* box, taking what refuge he could. The urchins kept up a steady fusillade of rocks, broken bits of cobble and what he suspected were handfuls of their own shit. For a while the soldiers just sat there, although the driver gunned the rotary engine; its characteristic scream radiated outwards. One of the legionaries had a round, crafty face, and it was this man that Caiaphas saw lean across the driver and flick a switch inside the MRAP.

The entire street was now treated—at high volume—to the main theme from what was probably the most popular recent Roman cinema release. Like all their music, it was infectious and distracting. The urchins were clearly conflicted, because some of them started to bounce up and down in time with the music, while others kept throwing broken pieces of cobble. The round-faced legionary was also bopping his head up and down in time, looking at the children and smiling. Caiaphas shook his head sadly, glad that the box gave him some protection from what was a considerable amount of noise and stench. Slowly, the armoured vehicle—complete with dancing, fighting retinue of children—moved out of earshot, and Caiaphas relaxed against the glass, watching as his breath condensed on it.

The *vocale* chimed, startling him. He hesitated for a few seconds or so and then picked up, feeling foolish.

'Hello?'

As he answered, he felt strong arms and hands around his face and chest, and something pungent and moist was shoved under his nose. He lost consciousness.

'He's coming up now.'

Caiaphas heard voices. There were several of them, one quite close—his breath smelt bad. He opened his eyes, although his eyelids seemed gummed together. The man from the Golden Fleece was standing over him, a water pitcher in hand. He poured a little into Caiaphas's eyes; the latter shook his head vigorously and rubbed his face, trying to see.

'Say something.'

'Something.'

'Very funny.'

Caiaphas was not trying to be funny, it's just that whatever they'd hit him with was making his thought processes rather literal.

Well, I suppose I'm for the hop.

He doubted the Romans would negotiate for his release, although to be fair they'd never been tested on that point. The man seemed to read his mind.

'You're not being held hostage. After you've talked to us, you'll be free to go.'

His tone was not hostile.

Caiaphas felt hands under his armpits, dragging him upright. The world greyed out momentarily as blood rushed from his head, and he closed his eyes again. One of the men braced his legs against Caiaphas's back; it kept him seated upright, but he could feel knees in the back of his neck. They hurt. Slowly the world came back into focus.

He was in a room somewhere; it was entirely nondescript. *A warehouse? A shipping container?* There was not a single item of decoration or identification. A low-power light bulb hung from the ceiling, illuminating half-a-dozen young and earnest faces in chiaroscuro. A chair stood in the middle of the room; the man from the Golden Fleece sat on it.

'I am Yehuda. You wanted to speak to me again.'

This caught Caiaphas unawares, and he groped for words.

'I got the impression you wanted to speak to me, too.'

Yehuda laughed. 'Yes, we did, but we're not sure whether anything will come of it. You're a collaborator. When I met you you'd just enjoyed an evening of decadent Roman hospitality.'

'They throw a good party.'

Caiaphas suspected he wasn't helping his own cause, but the muck flowing through his veins was impossible to repress. It seemed to be speaking for him. The young men laughed.

'As long as you forget what's underneath their drinking, fucking, and looting, I suppose they do throw a good party.'

It was a thoughtful and literate voice, not remotely like the Zealots who periodically turned up in Roman captivity on the news, all appalling grammar and bad teeth. He wondered if the Romans gave them drugs, too.

Just for effect, you know.

'Since it's unlikely that any member of the Sanhedrin is going to be genuinely in favour of liberation from Rome, we'd like to know why you're here.'

Caiaphas bit his lip, and then took the plunge.

'The Romans have a ruling *method,* applied without variation wherever they conquer. I've heard Pilate call it *a beautiful set of numbers*. Low crime rates, low infant mortality, efficient markets, good public health, and high rates of literacy... for both men and women. Most other peoples have not yet worked out how to achieve these things by themselves. And if you are honest with yourselves, you will know that all those numbers have improved since Rome has ruled Judaea. Everything else follows from these.'

There was an abrupt movement at the back of the room; Yehuda was forced to restrain one of his confreres from launching an attack on Caiaphas. He pulled him backwards.

'Get down, idiot. He's right.'

Yehuda looked up at Caiaphas, breathing hard. 'What you're saying is very hard to hear when *Romoi* have killed half your family and raped your sisters.'

'The Romans only care about numbers in the aggregate,' Caiaphas continued, watching the wild-eyed young man in

Yehuda's arms closely. 'As long as things are getting better on the whole, the fact that a few individuals have suffered badly is of no import to them. They think they've figured out the sum of human happiness.'

Yehuda nodded. 'This is the philosophy they teach in their *collegia*, no?'

'I've met many Roman *collegia* graduates, but no Roman philosophers. I presume they have them, but pay them no heed. Philosophy is seen as a Greek affectation. The people they listen to are lawyers, generals, engineers, and economists.'

'The makers and doers, as they say in their recruitment advertisements for the legions.'

Caiaphas smiled at this. 'Yes, the makers and doers; that's a useful way of putting it, a very Roman way.' He hugged his knees to his chest. The room was cold. 'I do not think it is possible to defeat them, to drive them away. I do think, however, that it is possible to force them to change their method.'

Yehuda's expression was carefully neutral. 'This defeatism is perhaps understandable.'

Caiaphas ignored the comment.

'There are some numbers Romans love that all of us—from the weakest collaborator to the strongest Zealot—rightly hate.' He paused. 'I want something done about the Dea Tacita Centre, Yehuda. It makes me sick at heart. These people will massacre the innocent to get their beautiful set of numbers, and it is wrong.'

Yehuda nodded again, as did one or two of the other men in the room.

'You're talking about targets the whole country can agree on?'

'I suppose so, yes. Killing Jewish civilians you consider "collaborators" is not winning you many friends at the moment.'

'We'll keep talking, Rabbi. We'll be in contact.'

If anything were likely to make Roman rule popular in Judaea, it was the Jerusalem Æsculapion. Built within the first five years of occupation, it was large, modern, and state of the art: a tangible reward for paying Roman taxes. It was also—like everything the Romans built—of striking beauty. There were sections that made it look like a traditional Grecian Æsculapion—even a lovely garden Temple to the God of Health where recuperating patients could sit and take the air—but the focus was on healing the sick and on training new medical staff, in line with new medical discoveries.

Many people also still recalled the ramshackle monstrosity it replaced, with its persistent outbreaks of bacterial infections, unaccountable infant deaths, and botched surgery. The Romans had simply scraped the old Æsculapion off the surface of the earth and replaced it with what they considered a 'proper' Æsculapion. Even the most traditional families—those who thoroughly rejected the Roman baths, the Roman mania for physical exercise and Roman schooling—brought their babies to the Æsculapion to be vaccinated, weighed, and checked by kindly nurses and efficient *medicii*.

Yehuda had often stood outside the main gate—with its attractive, trilingual signage and gracious colonnaded entrance—and wondered bitterly why his people had not been able to run an Æsculapion and yet the conqueror could. He knew that an attack on it—or any part of it—would need to be managed with the utmost care.

About the only consolation was the fact that the Dea Tacita Centre was a self-contained structure, separated from the main complex by a narrow access way. Any attack would have to come from the Æsculapion side, not the clinic side. If the Zealots damaged the Æsculapion, he suspected it would be the end of their movement, at least in Jerusalem.

One advantage of this plan was his ability to use the

rooftop gardens to observe comings and goings between the main complex and the low-slung building backing onto it: who worked where, who rotated through different units and wards, who stayed in one place.

He established that nursing staff turned over rapidly, often coming and going fortnightly. Dea Tacita had no nurses of its own. Doctors, by contrast, rotated less frequently, and there was a hard core of baby killers who never shifted. One was a fine-boned man who always dressed in black; he appeared to have some authority. Another was a muscular blonde woman who drove a red sports car, *very rich that one, to have her own car.* Another, again, was an older black man with military bearing and a limp. He walked with the aid of a silver-topped cane.

The blonde woman was the easiest to follow, thanks to her distinctive car and a habit of always leaving it in the same spot. It didn't take long for Yehuda to establish where she lived (top floor of a swank apartment block overlooking the Fleet Fox in the Roman Quarter), what she enjoyed doing in her spare time (regular trips to Caesarea and Antioch for the latest theatre) and who her lover was (a mechanical engineer and military contractor in Caesarea). It only remained for Yehuda to choose his gun and plan a way out.

He realised with some regret that the only way he was going to make good his escape was by abandoning the gun on the roof. The Zealots weren't that flush, and leaving equipment forfeit was not good for the treasury. *Still.* He sourced his weapon through a Persian small arms dealer on his way out of the Empire. The Persian gave Yehuda the full tour of his shed, offering pithy suggestions and stripped-down commentary. After some dickering over the price and ammunition Yehuda chose a Capua 28-4, a sniper rifle.

'Good weapon, that,' said the Persian. 'Handles well, light kick, easy to disassemble. You must be into hunting in a big way.'

'I believe in taking one shot.'

He spent the next week getting it onto the Æsculapion's rooftop garden in pieces, concerned particularly about keeping the stock hidden. At one stage he was nearly swept up in an antenatal class, making the mistake of tagging along behind a large group of very pregnant women. The midwife running the class—a tall and efficient black woman—looked at him quizzically, said a loud 'no men allowed' and began searching through some paperwork she had tucked under her arm—before he ducked into a nearby toilet to hide.

On the appointed day, he arrived early, made his way onto the roof and hid in the fire escape while he assembled the rifle with latex-gloved hands, cleaning it of prints as he went. He heard people—voices, laughter—as the nightshift made its way home and the dayshift arrived.

His moment came at 0740 hours. He hooked the gun under one arm and stretched himself out along the ground beside a large marble planter box overflowing with rosemary. He positioned the barrel through a gap in the railing; it gave him a good line of sight over the Dea Tacita Centre rooftop. The blonde medic in her shiny red car always arrived between 0750 and 0805, parking identically and then making her way around to the main entrance and out of his sight. He felt oddly warm towards her now, almost as though he knew her personally.

He had maybe twenty seconds to make his kill.

Remus was standing in the reception area with one of his visiting doctors when the shot came. As he told the investigator sent from X *Fretensis* later in the morning, it sounded like a firecracker going off or a car backfiring, and had he not been looking through the clinic's glass frontage at the time, it was entirely possible that he would not have looked up at all. But he was looking up, and he saw Victoria Valentina prop, spin and collapse. Both of them—not thinking for a moment that they could also be targets—sprinted to her aid, but the bullet had taken most of her head off. The visiting doctor dropped to his knees, as much from shock as from any desire to render assistance. Remus looked up, whirling on the spot as he stared all around him. His anguished cry was loud enough for people making their way over to Maternity and Burns to hear clearly.

> **JTN:** In news just to hand the Zealots have claimed responsibility for the death of Md Victoria Valentina, as well as for a leaflet distributed throughout the Jewish Quarter detailing Dea Tacita Centre staff home addresses. This brings to five the number of terrorist attacks over the last twelve months, and is the first attack on a Jerusalem target since the Jerusalem Academy bombing four years ago. As a general rule, the Zealots have confined themselves to IEDs directed at the Roman military—usually in remote areas—although several deaths of prominent Jews linked to the Roman administration remain unresolved. The Zealots attached the following statement to their claim:
>
> 'We reject the Roman ideology of death, and will not rest until we have driven you and your corruption from our land. We and thousands like us are forsaking everything for what we believe. Our drive and motivation doesn't come from tangible commodities that your world has to offer.'

> *Primus Pilus, Legio* X *Fretensis*, Tullius Capito has undertaken to provide a military medical officer to the Dea Tacita Centre.
>
> [Cut to shot of Capito, Entrance Hall, Antonia]
>
> **Capito**: We won't be cowed by terror, and as part of our mandate to protect the Empire and defend her citizens and subjects, we will provide a replacement medic for Victoria Valentina starting tomorrow.

The following morning, Caiaphas looked at the front page of the Judaean edition of *Tempus*. There was a detailed obituary for Valentina, alongside a photograph of the legionary to be her replacement—a clear-skinned, high-cheekboned young man with a *caduceus* on his collar.

This is going to end badly.

PART IV

This is no different than what happens at the Skull and Bones initiation and we're going to ruin people's lives over it and we're going to hamper our military effort, and then we are going to really hammer them because they had a good time. You know, these people are being fired at every day. I'm talking about people having a good time, these people, you ever heard of emotional release? You ever heard of emotional release?

—Rush Limbaugh

The Governor knew he could no more imprison [Fabrigas] for a twelvemonth, than that he could inflict the torture; yet the torture, as well as banishment, was the old law of Minorca, which fell of course when it came into our possession. Every English governor knew he could not inflict the torture; the Constitution of this country put an end to that idea.

—Lord de Grey CJ, *Fabrigas v Mostyn* (1774) 20 St Tr 82 (KB).

'No,' Saul had to tell them the first time they asked for his advice. 'Apply for a permit. I'll buy the fertiliser in Damascus and bring it to your property in Samaria.'

'They'll know,' Kelil said.

'If they know, they won't suspect. You're supposed to be running an agricultural college, teaching young Judaeans the latest in Roman farming techniques and overcoming the traditional enmity between Jews and Samaritans.'

Kelil was a young man, his beard still fine and light, his olive skin unlined. Saul could see his chin through the hair. He looked dubious.

'Look, I'm supposed to be part owner,' Saul went on. 'My name's all over the incorporation paperwork. I know how Romans think. They'll think someone like me bringing in fertiliser is entirely right and proper. There may even be government grants available for it, if I know Romans.'

He watched Kelil and Yehuda as they struggled with the concept. He didn't explain that having his name on the college's corporate paperwork gave him near perfect plausible deniability. Saul was impressed that the local Zealots had the wit to dream up the idea. It meant they didn't have to engage in too much actual farming (which was hard work), could enrol Zealots as 'students' and bring quantities of ammonium nitrate into Judaea even though first Gratus and now Pilate had banned its sale within the province.

'So we'll apply for the permit, you'll buy it and bring it in from Syria?'

'Yes, while waving this around,' Saul said, holding his identity card between his fingers. He could see Kelil's eyes tracking the words ROMAN CITIZEN *as he moved his hand. Kelil pushed the hair that hung over his forehead back. Saul could see him sweating.*

'We thought you were a Roman plant, you know.'

'I know that.'

'We couldn't work you out,' Yehuda added. 'We knew you weren't born Roman. We checked.'

Kelil leaned forward. 'We do have friends in the Archives and Registry Office, you know.'

Yehuda turned on the young man and flicked his ear. Kelil

winced. 'Shut your lip,' Yehuda said.

'Sorry,' Kelil said, rubbing his ear.

'Turned out that one of the brothers knew your father,' Yehuda said. 'This brother, he was a sail maker who worked as a pattern cutter in the Antioch plant. He vouched for you, although he didn't think much of your father.'

'My father isn't observant.'

'We know. He used to fuck his Greek secretary on the desk in his office.'

'She was his concubine,' Saul said.

'You're thinking like a Roman again, Saul,' said Yehuda. 'That's porneia.'

BEN YUSUF

Linnaeus watches as Ben Yusuf is brought up out of his Antonia cell and walked to the interview room. His feet and wrists are shackled to each other, but the young legionary doing the supervising looks at Linnaeus, asking with his eyes—which are large and violet—whether releasing him is permitted.

'Let his hands go free, soldier, thanks.'

The legionary nods, taking a key from his belt and unclipping the padlock. He drapes the chain over his arm and looks at Linnaeus.

'There's a panic button under your desk,' he says in Latin. 'I don't think he's as bad as the other one, but he's still considered dangerous.'

'Thanks, soldier. May I trouble you for some water for both of us, and a coffee for me?'

Linnaeus—in a way he'd never imagined possible—finds himself grateful for Antonia and the Roman military. Ben Yusuf's cell is spartan but spotless, the soldiers thereabouts professionally neutral. The interview room is usefully furnished. Someone has even left him a block of yellow legal pad. Linnaeus sits down, opens his briefcase and takes out papers, pens and other bits and pieces. Ben Yusuf sits opposite him, watching the stationery ritual with some interest.

'It's much better here,' he says in Greek.

'Even so, do not expect the legionaries to be your friends,' Linnaeus says, rehearsing his standard warning on the police and military. 'Do, however, expect them to be well trained and disciplined. They will not take sides until told to do so.'

'They are a good advertisement for your Empire.'

Linnaeus looks directly at Ben Yusuf, uncomfortable.

'I am your legal representative. It is my job to defend you against the charges the State has brought against you in this *libellus conventionis.*' He holds up a set of typed sheets. 'Normally, as a non-citizen of limited means, you would be unrepresented, and would simply have to answer any questions the Procurator asks of you directly. However, you have good friends, and one of them has engaged me on your behalf.'

'Joseph is a good man.'

'I formed that view as well.'

Linnaeus pulls out the card with the prosecution's CCTV evidence on it, a series of photographs of the Temple Courtyards after the riot, and a heavy, plaited whip sealed up in an evidence baggie. He feeds the card into his portable calculation engine. Ben Yusuf watches this process with a special kind of awe.

'I've never seen one of those before.'

'I had this one made for me.'

'Does it do everything that the big ones do?'

'No. But it does what I need, and it lets me work wherever I like. I just have to remember to recharge the battery.'

Ben Yusuf reaches out to touch it, running his fingers along the edge of its wooden housing and pausing at the little metal feet—shaped like lion's paws—holding it above the surface of the desk. Every time Linnaeus does something, tiny mechanisms in the lid whirr and spin.

'When I was learning my trade, my father would buy Roman tools whenever he could afford them, they were so beautifully made.'

'That is the Roman way. Things should be useful, hardwearing, and beautiful. We do not like to throw things away, or to make things that wear out easily.'

Ben Yusuf nods, his tradesman's eye still transfixed by the machine.

'Now, there are some things you ought to know,' says Linnaeus. 'First, the State has successfully applied for you to be put to the torture.' Ben Yusuf's eyes widen at this. 'Yes, torture. And I can assure you that as polite and reasonable as the young men in this building may seem, they are expert at extracting information from people with closed lips. Do not even think about lying to them.'

'I will tell the truth.'

'Good. If you are truthful, you will never see their vicious side.'

'What do I have to do for you?'

'You need to answer my questions as truthfully as possible, too, just as you will for the State. These charges are serious, one of them capital; it could see you executed. Caiaphas is also trying to hang a *sedition* placard around your neck. This province is not the most stable in the Empire. The Procurator will not hesitate to execute the sort of troublemakers that in other places would be flogged and released, or given a stint behind bars.'

'You seem to be doing the same job as the State, then.'

'I use the information you give me to put your case at its best. Cornelius Getorex, the lawyer for the State, will use that same information to put your case at its worst.'

'All the same information?'

'Yes. That's what lawyers have to work with.'

The violet-eyed legionary knocks on the door, tray in hand. He puts it down to Linnaeus's left. Linnaeus sees that he is called Cassius, and notices—almost incidentally—that the water pitcher and 'glasses' are made of some sort of light non-shattering material, so they can't be thrown or broken or used as a weapon. *Think of everything, these people.* He also notices that—perhaps through inadvertence, or even generosity—the soldier has brought two coffee cups and a large cafetière. He looks at Ben Yusuf.

'Would you like some coffee? It'll be good coffee; Romans won't drink any other sort.'

Linnaeus notices that Ben Yusuf holds his cup with his little finger extended. Instinctively, he reaches across the table and curls the finger in.

'Don't do that.'

'I see you plan to give me a nice set of Roman manners, too.'

Linnaeus laughs. 'I suppose so. It always goes down well in court, especially when one is being tried by Romans.'

'What is the capital charge?'

Linnaeus realises now why Ben Yusuf's face has been so blank.

'Has no one told you? The man you fought with over your whip—' He holds up the evidence baggie—'pitched down the stairs in the Court of the Gentiles and broke his C3 vertebra. He died this morning, and you've been charged with felony murder.'

Ben Yusuf pushes himself away from the edge of the table, his face ashen. 'I never meant to kill anyone...' he breathes. 'I'm so sorry. This is terrible.'

Linnaeus is a lawyerly cynic, but even he recognises real remorse when he sees it.

'Your situation is made worse because the death occurred while you and your confreres were busily committing another crime—or, rather, multiple crimes. At one point someone was wielding a knife. Petros Bar Yonah, one of your followers, must have assaulted a dozen people. He'll be rounded up in due course.'

'This is a very bad thing.'

'The State will come at you for two reasons in particular, Yeshua. The first concerns just what you and your twelve friends were trying to achieve in the Jerusalem Temple on the day of the riot. The second—and which I haven't mentioned yet—is whether you knew about Yehuda Iscariot's terrorist activities at any point after he took up with you, but before he carried them out. If you did, you have failed to warn against an act of terror.'

Ben Yusuf's coffee cup clatters into its saucer.

Linnaeus plays him the CCTV footage; he watches it carefully, his hazel eyes narrowed in concentration.

'This is the basis of the felony murder charge. We're dealing with *dolus indirectus* or, in the alternative, *dolus eventualis*. These two phrases describe the quality of your intent. In the first, the State will argue that you realised that the negative consequence would *inevitably* ensue. In the second, the State will argue that you realised the negative consequence would *probably* ensue.'

Ben Yusuf nods. Linnaeus pulls an old edition of *Tempus* from his briefcase. It shows the destroyed front of the Dea Tacita Centre after Iscariot's combination IED and grenade attack last year. As is usual with Roman news coverage, it does not spare the reader. There is a picture of two paramedics shoving a woman missing an arm and part of her head into a body bag in front of a section of collapsed masonry.

Linnaeus reads the first few paragraphs of the story, pausing to translate Latin terms he suspects Ben Yusuf may struggle to understand.

'I can answer the second question most easily, sir.'

'Please address me by name. You will have to display exaggerated politeness towards many other people in the course of the next week. There is no need to replicate the behaviour with me.'

'When Yehuda first came to me, we spoke at length about Rome's occupation of Judaea, and his desire to expel the Romans from our country. He admitted to me that it was he who shot the woman medic, the one who liked theatre.' He pauses, gathering his thoughts, while Linnaeus writes furiously, his nib pen skittering over the lined yellow paper. 'I forgave him this sin, and told him that he must go and sin no more.'

'Joseph Arimathea described this forgiveness business to me this morning, and I must admit I'm struggling to grasp what it means. How can you forgive someone when they haven't been punished or admitted their error?'

'Of course it is better to admit wrongdoing, but forgiveness is most important for the forgiver, not the forgiven.'

'That still leaves punishment. Where I come from, you must repay your debt to society before any of this, uh, forgiveness comes about.'

'People can set themselves on the right path after forgiveness, especially when they examine their conscience.'

Linnaeus shrugs, letting the foreign concept sail over his head.

'Did he give you any inkling that he was planning another attack?'

'He talked constantly of his hatred for Rome, Andreius. His sister had taken up with one of the *Romoi*, a man called Andrus, and Iscariot desperately wanted her to leave him.'

Linnaeus's brow creases and his eyes narrow. 'So he could kill her for shaming the family honour, no doubt.'

'Andrus shot Iscariot's brother dead, Linneaus, and shot Iscariot, too, but not fatally. I suspect that, yes; there was a matter of family honour involved. It seems the brothers surprised the couple in the midst of the sex act.'

'I see,' Linnaeus says.

'Until her brothers appeared, I have no doubt she was consenting—this is the thing that matters to you, yes? But after she had seen her brothers shot, she was not consenting any more. Like a dog going back to its vomit, Andrus decided to finish what he'd started.'

'She still chose to stay with him, though?'

'He has other redeeming features.'

'What sordid little lives,' Linnaeus says.

'It became difficult to take Iscariot seriously, so regular were his anti-Roman tirades. I stopped listening to him after a while, although I did make a point of locating the soldier and Soraya—that is her name now—and telling them that Iscariot wanted them both dead. His sister's circumstances seemed to make him angrier than everything else. Soraya clung to her Roman; she had made her choice. She lives in a much nicer house than would otherwise be the case.'

'Where is Soraya now? Where did this happen? I may need to call her and Andrus as witnesses.'

'This is all in Nazareth, in Galilee, where I was born. I forgot to tell you that. Andrus is quite senior in the garrison in Galilee. He took her to Sepphoris—she can live with him in the barracks there, he has permission. It's the only town in Judaea where Jews and Romans and Greeks live together.' He pauses, clearly struggling to convey his thoughts. 'I mean to say, there are no quarters.'

'People of different backgrounds in the one street?'

'Yes; a Jewish house beside a Roman house beside a Greek house.'

'That is what the rest of the Empire is like, Yeshua, especially in the West.'

Ben Yusuf shakes his head, marvelling.

'Well, that's where they live. Soraya told me he's canny with money. I do not know what rank he is, sorry—I don't understand Roman ranks. His first name is Irie.'

'That's a nickname. His full name will be Irenaeus.'

'Irie did not seem to care about the threat very much. He was content to love her in his Roman way, buying her clothing and jewellery and nice food, and taking her to the baths in Sepphoris. He said if Iscariot tried to come after him, he'd finish that job as well. He told me he thought he'd earned the right to her, that he wanted to have something nice to look at. She's beautiful in a way that Roman men seem to like.'

He does not elaborate on this point.

Linnaeus snorts. 'He sounds like a bloody *Calabrese* peasant.'

Ben Yusuf shrugs. 'Your soldiers are mostly well behaved, Linnaeus, but they are also supervised more closely here in Jerusalem. In the Galilee and elsewhere, they discover women so grateful for a few kind words that they are soon corrupted by it. There is nothing to stop them taking advantage.'

Linnaeus pours both of them another coffee, looking hard at his client. *That was shrewdly observed, my friend.*

'You speak much better Greek than you let on.'

'I speak Latin, too.'

Linnaeus starts at this, particularly the strong Apulian accent.

'You speak *Puglie* dialect. You picked that up in the prison. Don't go calling it Latin around anyone other than me.'

'Maybe I should speak like you, then. *There's a panic button under your desk.*'

It's his own voice he hears talking back at him, followed by the legionary jailer's voice, neatly divided into two sentences.

'Fuck!'

He hits the panic button, summoning the violet-eyed soldier, and then steps away and backwards, spilling scalding coffee on his hand. He slowly dabs the burn with a silk handkerchief, staring at Ben Yusuf the whole time.

'How did you do that?'

'I'm sorry I frightened you,' Ben Yusuf says. 'Sometimes I can't help it.'

'Shackle his hands, soldier, and then tell me where I can smoke.'

The soldier locks Ben Yusuf in the interview room and takes Linnaeus into the room diagonally opposite. There's a large, sloping table in the middle of it, which he leans against, smiling crookedly.

'Enjoy. No fire alarm in here. Never has been.'

Linnaeus laughs at this. 'I take it the smoke alarms aren't universally popular.'

'Gratus installed them. He had a thing about smoking. Pilate doesn't care. And as I say, there's never been one in here.' He shrugs amiably. 'I'm in the room at the end of the corridor when you need to go back in.'

Linnaeus pops his cigar out of its tube, cuts it, and lights up, his hands shaking.

This room is also spotless, larger than the interview room, and painted pale green. A single window—covered in wire mesh and set high in the wall—is the only natural light source. The day is bright outside, but very little light gets into the cells under Antonia. Linnaeus turns on the overhead lights, watching them as they blink on one after the other, set into stone fittings in an attractive circular pattern.

He then realises where he is.

The sloping table has restraints on each corner, and a rack and pinion mechanism on the side to allow its angle to be made more severe. A large watering-can, decorated incongruously with painted poppies, hangs from a hook on the wall, as do several washcloths and cotton towels, and a set of manacles. There is a small sink to one side. Someone with a lovely Capuan hand has painted S.P.Q.R. on the far wall, with the tagline *took their wages and are dead* underneath. As with the writing, so with the rack and pinion gearing; it is beautifully made, the brass fittings polished. *We make beautiful things.* A fat electrical lead trails across the floor, leading first to a control box with dials and then dividing into a pair of electrodes with wooden handles. The control box itself is plugged into an oversized electrical socket, obviously capable of delivering more power than a standard outlet. Linnaeus puts one hand over his mouth, exhaling cigar smoke through his fingers.

What lovely people we are, when we don't get our own way.

Ben David waited loyally for Linnaeus outside Antonia. He leaned against the driver's side door, his hands in his pockets. The evening was cool and fragrant, such that he didn't mind waiting. He'd enjoyed watching kite-flying children and their promenading parents, and even joined one group of adolescents in eating at the *gelateria* near the entrance to Antonia. Most fascinating of all were the trysts between soldiers and their women on the steps of Antonia. He was so distracted by one pair—a giant redheaded man and a black woman who deliberately stood on a higher step so the redhead could kiss her comfortably—that he didn't notice Linnaeus behind him.

'My opposite number,' Linnaeus said, startling him.

Ben David snapped out of his reverie. 'I'm sorry, I didn't know you were there.'

'*Aquilifer* Getorex obviously has a fine evening's entertainment planned.'

He noticed that the black woman was high and heavy around the backside. The redhead rested his hands on her haunches. Even from this far it was possible to see that he particularly liked this part of her.

'You may recall him from last night. The big redhead.'

Ben David nodded slowly. 'Yes, I do. He was with that girl, and...' he struggled to finish the sentence '...and another girl, also.'

Ben David thought that Linnaeus was at his most crow-like just now, his eyes almost closed to the world. He spoke as much to himself as to Ben David.

'I've had shoddier days in my legal career than today, but I'm struggling to think of many. A man could do worse than try to wipe out the after effects with a decent fuck.'

The redheaded man took the black woman by the hand and led her into Antonia.

Ben David flushed. 'I can take you to the Greek Quarter, if you like.'

Linnaeus laughed at this—a genuine laugh—and his closed, black eyes opened and sparkled with warmth. 'You really do possess hidden depths, David. No, take me back to the Empire. If nothing else, it's a full service establishment.'

Cynara—that is what she called herself now, Romans being incompetent at pronouncing Rivkah—saw the famous lawyer talking intently to the concierge. His hands moved precisely from side to side, describing an image in the air. She'd been managing the Empire for five years now, and she was fairly sure of the substance of his request. The concierge nodded and smiled, then made a call. The lawyer waited, propped against the desk, looking pensive. The concierge handed him a card; the lawyer thanked him and then made his way towards the ground floor bar.

'He wanted a *hetaera*, yes?'

The concierge—one of her best staff—was an appealing

Helvetian with high cheekbones and a curly, receding hairline.

'He's had a bad day at the office. Says he could get a bit rough.' He stopped.

'I'm amazed we've got any to spare, what with that *Indoi* trade delegation in this week.'

'The *Indoi* boys are busy sleeping with the Roman girls. Women are not free in their country, so it's a big thrill for both sides.'

Cynara chuckled at this. 'I suspect the Roman women drive a hard bargain, too.'

'I don't doubt it for a moment.'

He flicked through some paperwork stored under his desk.

'You should introduce yourself to Don Linnaeus. He's quite the success story, the kind of person we want singing our praises when he goes back to Rome.'

'His mind may be elsewhere right now.'

'A Roman mixes business and pleasure with considerable skill, and until he goes off with his *hetaera* he will happily pass the time with you. You know this.'

'Thank you, Armin. When it comes to teaching people how to suck eggs, you're the expert.' She winked.

Armin laughed.

Linnaeus was sitting at the bar with a glass of wine when she introduced herself. Clearly pleased to be the object of her attention, he ordered her a drink and—surprise, surprise—turned on the charm.

Cynara was dark and shapely, with thick black hair swept back from her face and held with tortoiseshell combs. She felt his gaze rest appreciatively on her eyes, her lips, her breasts and then her hips. He returned to her eyes, looking into them. They passed the time with chitchat about *collegia* attended, friends in common (there were three) and places visited. He expressed surprise when she told him she'd gone to the Hotel School rather than *Collegia Roma*.

'I won a scholarship to the Hotel School,' she said. '*Collegia Roma* only offered a place. In rhetoric.'

He pulled a face at this and at first she thought he was moving onto the next phase of what would no doubt be a most pleasant seduction—should she let him have his way—but he veered off.

'This is going to seem strange, but I think I met your father today.'

He held her business card up to his face, scrutinising the name. 'Cynara is a common Roman girl's name, but Arimathea most certainly is not.'

'He's on the Jerusalem Sanhedrin. If that's who you met, then yes, that's my father.' It was her turn to look at him intently. 'This is in connection with the Ben Yusuf matter?'

'Yes. I'm not really at liberty to discuss it any further with you. Your father is an important witness—among other things.'

'I know the background. Papa is paying for you. He told me. He said he'd hired a famous lawyer. I didn't realise how famous.'

'You flatter me.' He leaned towards her, brushing his fingers against the inside of her wrist. 'Until I looked properly at your card, I assumed you were Roman. And I've spent the last twenty minutes trying to place your accent.'

She smiled at him, and she suspected he was beginning to regret making other plans for the evening. She'd met a good number of Roman men like him in her time: mercurial, witty, skilled at pleasing women. This one radiated a slight but thrilling air of danger.

'My opinion of your father was already high, but where did he get the courage to send you away to Rome for further study?'

This tack surprised her, and she knew that she would have to wriggle free of him before he went to the concierge and said he'd changed his mind about the *hetaera*.

'He thought he could combine the best of Rome and the best of Judaea in his children's education, Andreius.'

'You went to high school in Caesarea, then?'

She was impressed that he'd worked this out, and nodded.

'That must have been a hard trial, for a Rabbi's daughter.'

You don't know the half of it, charming Roman lawyer boy. You really don't.

SCHOOLDAYS

Cynara had visited Caesarea before, but never as a student at its most illustrious school. She and her father had taken the train from Jerusalem's vaulted Central Station with its polished grey stone and iron beams, its riotous, coloured interior and glass clerestory. A man in a grey uniform helped them find their seats in first class, carrying her trunk and calling her 'young mistress'. She said 'thank you' repeatedly and then remembered that you were supposed to give them money.

'They're nearly all the children and grandchildren of slaves,' her father told her, 'Greeks who the Romans hauled off at sword and gunpoint.'

She took a one *denarius* note from her pocket and watched the man's eyes widen with wonder.

'Young mistress, this is more than a day's wages.'

She took to gazing out the window, watching the countryside slide past. Farm children in tattered clothes ran beside the train, waving. The track was die-straight save where it curved around the base of a range of hills and vaulted a watercourse. She turned to watch the second- and third-class carriages cross the railway bridge with its arches of iron. She liked the iron bridges even more than the stone ones: they seemed to be made of light and air. She pushed her face against the glass to keep it in view for as long as possible. Her father put his arm around her shoulders.

'You'll be all right,' he said.

Her father didn't like to visit *Caesarea Maritima*,

Caesarea-on-Sea. Jews were outnumbered there; the city was defiantly Roman, Syrian and Greek. There was even a Temple of Rome and Augustus with its characteristic clock tower at the highest point. She admired its tree-lined streets and glittering public buildings as the train pulled into the station. Clumps of eleven-year-olds with similar trunks thronged the platform. Many of them, she noticed, were alone. One little boy was crying. The man in the grey uniform manhandled her trunk onto the platform and her father hailed a taxi.

Her hair blew back off her forehead as the *kufer* city assaulted her senses: savoury food smells from outdoor cafés and restaurants; the sharp tang of the sea; elaborate percussive music from an open office window above a colonnaded market. At each intersection there was a glossy black stone statue with a square base of a man and woman joined together, standing back-to-back, the man with an erect penis, the woman beckoning with one hand. Intellectually, she knew they had no sexual meaning, and were there to invite commerce and prosperity into the city, but she was still shocked, and put her hand to her mouth.

On the other side of the Forum, she saw an aristocratic school that seemed to be made wholly of white marble set in vast playing fields. There was a sign with a large M in a circle next to the gate. Some of the students—most of these seemed older—looked at the taxi and her bearded father, smiling and curious. One girl waved at them. Their uniform was a dark-blue robe cut from a single piece of cloth; the girls' was longer and had gold embroidery in geometric patterns around the square neckline.

The sign in front read *Caesarea Academy: Scientia est potestas*.

Her father saw her into her rooms in Hall, talking to teachers, wardens and medical staff while she stood mute, listening to her new fellow students' rapid Latin.

'The skiing in Helvetia was rubbish this season.'

'We went to Teotihuacán on one of Pater's interminable business trips.'

'Did you hear about that avalanche in the Gallic Alps? Apparently Brutus Casci broke both his legs.'

'Although we did get to see a human sacrifice. They cut out the heart and chuck them down the stairs. Pater was most disturbed and asked them not to do it again, at least not on his account.'

'We only went to Corfu.'

No one spoke to Cynara. Her father put his arm around her shoulders again.

'You'll be all right,' he said.

One of the teachers looked down at her; the woman was tall, handsome and severe, with wire-rimmed spectacles. Her long straight hair was a mixture of black and grey.

'You must be Cynara Arimathea,' she said. 'I am *Mage* Daria Saleh, and your new Head of Year.'

Cynara watched her father look up and boggle. *Mage* Saleh was dressed in the beautiful and elaborate robes of a High Priestess of Cybele.

'You'll be all right.'

Caesarea Academy didn't run to kosher meat—Cynara was the only Jew in the school—so she found herself in the company of four Pythagoreans who ate no meat for entirely different reasons.

'The animals have a soul, too,' one of them told her. 'Your own soul could go into one of them when you die.'

The five of them collared one end of the longest dining table in Hall and stuck the wooden placeholders with PYTHAGOREAN DIET cut into them beside their plates. They sat together for the rest of term.

From time to time, her father had cause to wonder at the amount of lamb she consumed at Passover Seder during the holidays.

'You're not eating very many vegetables,' he said once.

'Trust me, Papa, I'm getting *plenty* of vegetables.'

He also had cause to wonder at the amount she slept when she came home.

'Do they keep you up all night?'

'No Papa, but they don't break for Shabbat. I haven't had a day off for the whole term. Romans think we're lazy, taking a day off every week.'

She made a very deliberate choice not to emulate her peers' sexual habits. At first this was easy enough; Roman parents kept their children in line until sixteen, often with some severity. She kept company with her four Pythagorean friends; things seemed to slide graciously off their backs if they did not care for them.

'You can choose,' said the girl who told her about the souls of animals. 'That is just their way.'

She also found the Academy's compulsory sex education classes fascinating, sometimes repellent, but always, well, instructive. She sat at the back with the Pythagoreans and tried not to blush scarlet in every class. She was grateful that they split the sexes, although one of the Pythagorean boys told her what transpired in their classes; it wasn't a secret.

In time, she befriended a Roman girl outside of her Pythagorean circle. Inara was bouncy and charming and sociable, a scholarship girl whose father was a Centurion based in the Galilee. She was too eccentric to be the most popular girl in school, but she was clever and respected, and she took Cynara under her wing.

'We can't have you spending all your time with those bean haters,' she said once. 'They're lovely people, but they're so serious and high-minded they must shit marble.'

Inara was on the school's organising committee for *Megalesia*, she directed a couple of theatre productions each year, and she edited the school yearbook. It was Inara who pulled the whole run after someone broke into the production room and wrote *Future Vestal Virgin* under Cynara's photograph just before the proofs were due to go to the printers, and it was Inara who took Cynara to see *Mage* Saleh when Marcellus Mara wouldn't take 'no' for an answer.

'He's not to follow you to your rooms,' Inara said. 'That's *iniuria*. You have to tell *Mage*; she'll make sure his name stinks all over the school.'

Mage Saleh looked over her wire-rimmed glasses as the two of them fidgeted in her book-lined office. Cynara tried not to look at the objects the priestess used for bookends: vividly painted sculptures of passionate lovers; a pair of matched bronze dildos; a Greek vase with two smiling men facing each other, their hands on each other's hips.

'Part of the problem is that you like him, yes?'

Cynara nodded and fiddled with the hem of her uniform.

'I want him, and then I don't. It's very confusing; I don't know what to do.'

The priestess rested a pen on her bottom lip, pensive.

'Leave Marcellus to me; there are more important things for you to worry about. You follow the Jewish rite, yes?'

'I'm Jewish, if that's what you mean.'

Mage Saleh stood up and ran her fingers along the spines of a dozen books just behind her until she found what she wanted. It took Cynara a moment to recognise the Hebrew typeface on the cover. *Mage* Saleh adjusted her glasses and read for a moment before looking up.

'Is anything that God made bad, Cynara?'

'No, *Mage*, of course not. God's creation is good.'

'That means sex is good, yes?'

'Yes, *Mage*. Sex is good, because the Lord made it.'

'In our rite, we say that sex is a gift from the Goddess. You should enjoy it.'

Marcellus stopped pursuing her—indeed, he stopped speaking to her—and Inara invited her to join the *Megalesia* organising committee. She hesitated at first, but Inara was very persuasive.

'Nothing God made is bad, remember.'

Cynara made a buzzing noise.

'Romans made *Megalesia*, not God, Inara.'

'It's good, though. Come on. We could do with your financial planning skills. Last year's committee went four hundred *denarii* over budget.'

Cynara gave in to this flattery. Part of her wanted to condemn it, but the streets full of dancers and ornate floats, the percussion and singing, the sheer ecstasy of the young people who volunteered to garland the Goddess's statues and carry them through the city and throw saffron and turmeric over each other and into the air overwhelmed her doubts. The cross-dressing in particular fascinated her. Romans had strong views that men should dress like men, and women like women, so seeing soldiers in banqueting dresses while their women wore borrowed fatigues and oversized helmets was at once shocking and hilarious. 'Madness is permitted once a year,' *Mage* Saleh told her.

Cynara and half-a-dozen girls from her year worked on the Temple of Cybele's float alongside the priestesses and *galli*. It was fun, getting covered in paint and plaster every day for a week, especially as the temple staff did the fine work, painting the statue and preparing the art that would decorate the base. Cynara watched as a priestess climbed a set of steps and painted black eyebrows on the Goddess's sky-blue skin. Not thinking, Cynara stepped back, kicking over a pot of paint. She swore, and then hurried to right it, kicking it again. An expanding pool of blue paint found a passage across the paint rags and onto the tiled floor. She grabbed a handful of rags and a pot of turps, trying to clean it up. At that point, she noticed a dark, curly-haired boy—maybe five years younger than her in age—peering at her from behind a pillar. He was very still.

'Well, don't just stand there,' she yelled at him, irritated at his stare, wiping her blue fingers with a cleaning rag. 'Help me clean it up.'

'Not allowed,' he said.

Cynara blew a raspberry at him, conscious that there was now blue paint in the ends of her hair. 'Why not?' she asked, a hard edge to her voice.

'I'm a boy.'

Cynara pulled up short, feeling even crosser.

'Well, why are you here, then?'

'He's here because he's my son.'

Cynara turned towards *Mage* Saleh's voice, aware that she had gone scarlet. The High Priestess was standing at the edge of the float preparation area, arm in arm with a man. The man wore a cream toga with a Senator's wide purple band at the edge. He had the same dark curly hair as the boy. Cynara watched as the boy ran around the edge of the preparation area, avoiding crossing over into it at any point.

'Daddy!'

'Darius!'

The man swept him up in his arms, while *Mage* Saleh made her way towards Cynara, bending down and helping her clean up.

'I'm sorry I yelled at your son,' Cynara said, feeling sheepish.

The High Priestess smiled. 'It's all right; he's not supposed to be calling anyone "daddy" in here, either.'

Cynara looked at the boy and the man, with their identical hair and skin. 'They look alike.'

'Yes, they do.'

Mage Saleh stood and called out to the man. 'My patron is in Corinth this week, so if you want to take Darius to the rifle range for the afternoon and then meet me here for supper, I am available to you.'

The man—he held Darius's hand now—nodded and smiled. The boy looked like he was about to start dancing at any moment, he was so pleased with himself.

'I'll take you up on that offer.' He had a cut-glass accent, like the announcers on CR.

Cynara blushed again. She understood, perhaps for the first time, at least some of what the Priestesses of Cybele did in their beautiful temple on Caesarea's *cardo*.

Megalesia also contrasted with other Roman festivities in ways she appreciated. Caesar's birthday, for example, or Armed Forces Day, always filled her with fear, with their serried ranks of troops marching down the *cardo*. Their steps were quick and in perfect time, and they sang. After the soldiers always came a selection of weapons, sometimes with demonstration crews. If she were honest with herself, it was this aspect she found most frightening, partly because her Roman friends took such unalloyed delight in displays of military might, climbing onto roofs and cheering themselves hoarse, and partly thanks to the brilliant science and engineering they invested in inventing things that killed. *These are not*, she thought, *people given to beating their swords into ploughshares*.

Four months after *Megalesia*, Inara was absent for a week and returned to school pale and ill.

'Inara! Where did you get to?' Cynara asked that morning, in the dining hall, sitting opposite her.

'Caesarea Æsculapion,' she said.

'Are you all right? What's the matter?'

Inara shook her head from side to side—a common Roman movement Cynara did not quite understand—patting her shoulder and looking perplexed.

'It was only an abortion. I got sick because it was a bit late.'

Cynara tried to stifle an audible gasp, but failed. Inara did not seem to notice.

'I didn't know I was pregnant. It's a bit of a shit when you keep getting your period, or something that looks like a period.'

'But how did you...?'

'Cynara, you're such an innocent flower, you really are. I had sex, didn't I?' She pointed. 'With him.'

Cynara recognised the boy by sight, but could not, for the moment, recall his name. He was in the year above them.

'Did you tell him?'

'No. It's women's business.'

The following afternoon, Cynara followed Inara to the Temple of Dea Tacita, located behind a row of shops on one side of the Forum. Cynara watched as her friend bought a small stone sculpture of the Goddess cut to look like a baby seated with her legs crossed. Inara sat in an alcove to one side of the main shrine and wrote something out on the piece of coloured paper that came with the statue. Cynara watched her tie the paper around the statue's neck, clasp it to her chest with both hands and approach the cella with its large statue of the Goddess. Cynara drew back: this, she knew, was the most sacred part of one of their temples.

If I go in there, that's idolatry.

She watched Inara disappear into the gloom.

'Are you lost, dear?'

Cynara nearly leapt out of her skin. The priestess touched her arm; her expression was solicitous and gentle.

'I'm waiting for my friend,' she said, pointing at Inara.

By this stage, her eyes had adjusted to the contrast such that she could see that there were hundreds—perhaps even thousands—of the little stone sculptures gathered around the walls. She watched Inara ladle water from the still pool at the Goddess's feet and pour it over her little statue's head. The movements were rehearsed and—in their own way—beautiful.

'Are they all for aborted babies?' she asked, a dawning realisation striking her.

'Many of them. Some are for stillbirths and miscarriages, too.'

'Does this mean they feel guilty?' she asked.

The priestess looked at her, perplexed.

'This Goddess helps the babies find their soul and go across the Styx, or find a better place to be born,' she said. 'They do not need to be afraid.'

'What do the pieces of paper say?'

The priestess fiddled in her robes and handed her a printed one.

'This is the correct form of words.'

Precious soul, I thank you for wanting to be my child. But this is not the right time, and this is not the right place. I am not meant to be your mother. Go, precious soul, and find the right time and place.

Linnaeus waved his hand in front of her face.

'Earth to Cynara, come in Cynara.'

She shook her head, coming up slowly.

'I'm sorry, I was wool-gathering.'

'I noticed. Would you like another glass of wine?'

She looked past his shoulder as he spoke. 'Your *hetaera* is here.'

Linnaeus turned to see one of the hotel's pageboys pointing a *caffe con latte* young woman in his direction. He raised his eyebrows at Cynara, inclining his head.

'Would you care to join us?'

She inhaled, her eyes widening, taking a moment to compose her expression into one of regret.

'I'm working, Andreius. Another time, perhaps.'

She watched him cross the terrazzo; he took the young woman's hand and—within moments—she laughed at something. Cynara could see the little muscles underneath her eyes creasing, and watched Linnaeus touch her cheek with his fingers.

Oh, he is good, that one. Charm the birds out of the trees.

Later that night, Cynara had cause to go downstairs and speak to the staff on the night desk. It seemed one of the Hotel's *Indoi* guests was inexperienced with red wine and port and needed some medical attention. He sat next to the concierge's desk, his head resting on his arms and knees. She waited for the ambulance and made sure he was good to go, sending a Greek-speaking member of staff with him to the Æsculapion.

She was about to go back upstairs to her rooms when Andreius Linnaeus and his *hetaera* tangoed out of the lift. Both sang at the top of their lungs, and then danced around the Empire's marble lobby. She did not try to stop them; the girl was in transports of delight. Cynara suspected—as skilled as the Empire Hotel's women and boys for hire were, all of them recruited under the auspices of the Guild of Sex Workers—the opportunity to take real enjoyment from their work was perhaps not so common. He bent her over one arm, spun her around and then drew her into his chest.

'That was a good thing, Fotini,' he breathed in Greek, his voice husky. 'We can get on with a bit more now.'

Cyler Lucullus handed *Aquilifer* Getorex's order to report for the next day to *Centurio* Marcus Lonuobo with some trepidation. The latter could be unpredictable when Zipporah's name came up in dispatches, especially official ones, ones attached to S.P.Q.R. letterhead, or with *Legio* X *Fretensis* stamps on them.

This time, however, Lonuobo simply read through the Form 23 and Cornelius's supporting documentation with an expression that registered nothing at all. Cyler only realised there'd been any effect when Lonuobo opened his mouth; the man could hardly make a sound. Then he reached out, clasping Cyler's shoulder and crying, his head dropping, the paperwork trembling as his hand shook. He shielded his eyes with it; the tears flowed fast now—Cyler could see spotting on the legal forms. He stood still, indecisive for a moment, then decided that despite Lonuobo's seniority and fearsome reputation, the man needed comfort. He wrapped his arms around him.

'At least we caught him, sir.'

'Thank you, Lucullus.'

'You can really hurt him now, sir. That's only fair.'

'Yes. Yes I can.'

Lonuobo finally stepped away, his eyes bleary and red.

Marcus Lonuobo and Zipporah were known among the men of *Legio* X *Fretensis*, with good reason, as 'The Perfects'. This perfection ran the gamut from movie-star good looks to ridiculous amounts of talent to a backstory that could have been written by the Imperial Propaganda Office.

Lonuobo met Zipporah and charmed her—as seemed to be his people's special skill—but he disdained the sort of underhandedness that often characterised relationships between Roman soldiers and Judaean women.

'I am not,' he said at one point, 'going to be doing furtive stand-ups in an alley somewhere.'

He went around to her parents' house in the better part of the Jewish Quarter and asked for their daughter's hand in marriage, along with the offer—in these enlightened times, *in lieu* of bride price—to pay for the wedding. And they said yes, which was even more staggering in its way. The story was so remarkable it made not only JTN, but also turned up as the 'human interest' piece that often featured at the tail end of the *Communicatio Roma Newshour*.

'How the fuck are you going to pay for a full *coemptio* wedding?' Cornelius—at that point a rather green *Advocatus* just posted from Syria—had asked. 'You're looking at fifty thousand *sesterces*. You'll have to pawn some of that Olympic silverware, kiddo. I can register you for a *sine manu* marriage, you know, like the rest of the Empire does. Won't cost you a *denarius*, but you'll have to cohabit for a year, *first*. Find out if you love her.'

'You're suffering from a deficit in imagination, sir. As far as they're concerned, I can't fuck their daughter *until* I've done the whole box-and-dice ritual.'

In one of those stories that is calculated both to warm the heart and to make gloriously saccharine screen time, the men of *Legio* X *Fretensis* raised the money and hosted the ceremony. This last included an exercise in mass catering that involved Zipporah's mother arriving with five of her friends to kasher one of Antonia's kitchens.

'If that woman ever comes here again,' one legionary cook

was heard to say afterwards, 'I'm falling on my sword.'

Cornelius and his Celtic friends turned their talents to preparing the parade ground for a wedding. Lonuobo's aunt decorated Zipporah's hands and feet with henna, while the *Legatus's* wife loaned her a proper Roman wedding gown, all saffron veil and orange silk. Zipporah remembered standing in Marcus's quarters as two Roman women—Marcus's friends—parted her hair with a fine, sharp knife, according to Roman custom, and then braided it.

Her parents convinced a Rabbi to serve as the ceremony's religious witness and make the contract resemble a *ketubah* as much as possible. Then, despite his notorious grumpiness, Procurator Gratus came to the party, pulling strings so a famous playback singer provided the music. Lonuobo never received a bill for her performance; Gratus must have paid. A crew arrived from the Imperial Propaganda Office in Syria to do one of their standard 'Romanisation made good' documentaries.

'At least we'll have a good wedding video,' Lonuobo observed.

'When it comes to over the top, you Romans wrote the book,' she responded.

Zipporah's Jewish relatives all fronted; there were a *lot* of these, which pleased her parents no end. And they did appreciate the effort that had been made.

Not a Jewish boy, but a very good boy regardless.

There are perks attached, as some of his friends observed, to being the province's poster boy. And, by common consensus, the wedding went *off*.

Lonuobo kept kosher when he was with her, although he drew the line at getting any bits of his body cut off. They were the first couple to own property in the new military *colonia* built to extend the city. She lived there alone except when he was on leave, rolling around the vast new house. In time other women moved in to be her neighbours. The *colonia* was gated, ringed about with walls topped with electric wire, metal spikes and broken glass, and guarded by military contractors from Caesarea. Intended to be wholly self-contained and completely pedestrianised—with its own forum, baths, theatre, primary school and parks—when Pilate arrived he made it self-governing as well.

'Decisions ought to be made by those whom they most directly affect,' he said. Year on year the *colonia* registered a crime rate of nil.

Zipporah was elected to the *colonia* council and started training through the All-Empire *Collegium* as a teacher. This meant watching her lectures on screen and sending coursework through the post. A self-directed personality, she liked her life. Her only unhappiness centred on her parents' reluctance to visit. They seemed to turn up about once a year, and always complained that the *colonia* was not a 'community'.

'Why don't you live in Jerusalem proper, Tzipi? Even the Roman Quarter is better than this.'

'Err... this didn't cost us anything, Mama. That's a big part of it. And Jerusalem isn't very safe any more.'

She also shelled three peas in four years: three boys. The first somehow contrived to have her alabaster skin and green eyes, while the next two were lighter versions of their father.

'Ma'am, does the army pay you commission?' one of her Roman woman friends asked her, laughing. 'Three boys.'

She'd always planned to stop at six, a number that flummoxed most of her Roman neighbours.

'I'm from a big family,' she said.

Yet, when she fell pregnant with her fourth, she found herself unable to cope. *This is not morning sickness.* Not coping was a new thing. She'd dealt with the media fallout from her wedding with aplomb, even the *paparazzo* that insisted on trying to get photographs of them on their honeymoon. *My mother had eight kids and still worked. Not good enough, Tzipi.* She was especially furious because she had a live-in Persian housekeeper who helped a great deal, and who obviously adored the boys.

I am so bloody weak.

I am not my mother.

She realised that something was going to have to go: the council, perhaps, or even her teaching *licentia. Can't keep all the balls in the air anymore. Drop one, and you'll drop the lot.*

So she resigned from the council.

And still couldn't cope.

She told Marcus over a long and teary dinner, one that was supposed to celebrate their fifth wedding anniversary. He called the housekeeper and let her know that Zipporah would not be home that evening.

'Give her some good times, *Domine*,' she said. 'She needs it.'

He took Zipporah to his Antonia quarters. They made long, slow love and talked for a long time.

'You probably still think going to the *silphium* is wrong.'

Going to the silphium, that's how they say it... the pharmaceutical company's wordmark coming to stand in for all abortifacients.

'Yes I do. It's just right now I don't see any alternative.'

'You don't have to be your mother. Only Tzipi. I married Tzipi.'

She started to cry again.

'And things can be wrong but necessary.'

In the morning, he rang the Dea Tacita Centre.

The legionary medic chose his words with some care, his gestures small and precise.

'We ask men to leave so we can make sure that the *silphium* is the woman's choice. I'm sorry.'

She'd cried and clung to Marcus when they'd arrived, and when the *medicus* had asked him to step outside, she'd sworn at Dea Tacita Centre staff in three languages *seriatim*, waiting for something to have an effect. Women in the waiting room had stared at her, and the clinic's administrator—she knew him by sight, for some reason—had poked his head out of his office, but there was no anger at her outburst. The receptionist simply offered her a private room.

'Sometimes Roman men will railroad a Jewish woman into choosing the *silphium*. Not because they are bad men, but because it does not mean much to them.'

She nodded, wiping her nose again. The medic reached behind him and handed Zipporah another box of tissues.

'For the same reason, you cannot sign this consent form while I'm in the room. I will leave and only return when you knock on the door to my surgery.'

Lonuobo paced; at one point he stood on the far side of the Dea Tacita Centre facing the Æsculapion's rooftop garden. Another legionary—a ranker from the 1st Cohort—joined him, smoking a cigar.

'Morning, sir.'

'Morning, soldier.'

'The national ritual, sir.'

'I suppose so.'

Both men hit the ground and drew their side-arms at the sound of something in between an artillery barrage and a burst of fireworks from close to the Æsculapion's main entrance. People came to the door of the Dea Tacita Centre, looking for the source of the racket. Lonuobo crouched, looking down the driveway.

'Officer down!' someone was yelling. 'Officer down!'

Lonuobo and the ranker ran a crooked path, using buildings along the driveway as cover and covering each other. Both could see a vehicle with official markings overturned on its side. There was a large hole in the floor of the chassis. The driver was sprawled across the road face down, his legs missing. Most of one leg was now lodged in the Æsculapion's chain wire mesh fence. His passenger—an officer Lonuobo did not recognise at all—was on his side, clutching his stomach, gouts of blood running through his fingers. Smoke poured into the street in front of the Æsculapion.

He was close enough to note that the officer's flashes were Syrian—*Legio* III *Gallica*—as were the vehicle's plates—when there was a much larger blast behind him. He turned just in time to see the front of the Dea Tacita Centre crumple.

> **JTN:** Terror in Judaea took on a new form today. The attack on the Dea Tacita Centre—calculated to bring about maximum loss of life—achieved such deadly effect because it was preceded by an IED directed at the Legate's Tribune. This had the effect of drawing people into the clinic's congested waiting room and doorway and diverting military resources—soldiers nearby ran to their comrades' aid—such that a Zealot was able to roll a grenade into the waiting area and make a clean getaway. Prefect Lucius Sejanus of the Imperial Counter-Terrorism Agency has more.
>
> **Sejanus:** The crucial thing here is the attack outside the Jerusalem Æsculapion's main gates. This was not small, as can be seen from the footage you've just shown. It killed one man and seriously wounded

> another. The response of military personnel on the ground was entirely reasonable: they immediately sought to neutralise the danger, moving towards it. However, as we now know, the IED was only prefatory to an act designed to cause far greater carnage.
>
> **JTN:** Presumably the blast was worse due to the confined space...
>
> **Sejanus:** Undoubtedly. Most grenades have a relatively confined kill radius—only fifteen feet or so, although this one was at the higher end of that range. Any destruction is made greater by orders of magnitude in such a small area.
>
> **JTN:** We can confirm, however, that among the dead is Medicus Titus Verres of the Third Cohort, the young man—as viewers may recall—seconded to replace Medica Victoria Valentina after Zealots also assassinated her [...]

Marcus Lonuobo did three things after the Zealots killed his wife. First, he sent his sons to live in Caesarea with his aunt, taking care to ensure that they never visited Jerusalem or heard Hebrew or Aramaic spoken again. All three were enrolled—years in advance, as was becoming necessary—for Caesarea Academy. Second, he volunteered for *Legio* X *Fretensis's* new Counter-Terrorism Unit. Finally, he chose to be the sort of dissolute Roman that Judaean mothers warned their daughters about.

This meant a lot of time in Caesarea visiting his boys, and even more time spent patiently explaining the finer points of Hebrew and Aramaic grammar to his fellow legionaries, interpreting terrorist 'chatter' and skulking around the province pretending to be—variously—a wealthy Nubian businessman, a successful lanista, or an interpreter and broker for *CreditGallia*. He had a knack for deception and was capable of fooling senior officers and even erstwhile intimates into thinking he was someone else. Meanwhile, his fellow legionaries started laying bets on how many women Marcus Lonuobo could bed on a weekly basis. Those detailed to manage Antonia's security reported Lonuobo's doings to Cyler—who took an interest in this sort of thing—with a degree of stunned awe. Cyler quipped that he wished he could borrow Marcus Lonuobo's body for forty-eight hours.

There are two men I want to beat up and three women I want to fuck.

Pilate did not consider himself prone to hate, but something about this latest exercise in terrorism gave him the eerie sensation that he was standing at the edge of an abyss, looking down into the blackness.

'I've never encountered people like this.'

Claudia looked up from the manuscript she was editing and rested her sharpened blue pencil on her bottom lip, tucking a few strands of her silver hair behind one ear. He went on, almost to himself.

'Crooks, yes, mafia types, yes—all ruthless and destructive in their own way. But there was always, you know, a point.'

'They want to drive us out of Judaea, Pontius. That much is clear, surely.'

'And blowing up an abortion clinic is going to achieve that how? The IEDs in Galilee probably have more effect, although trucks *Fretensis* uses these days are so heavily armoured that Zealot IEDs haven't killed a legionary for three months.'

'That's why they went after Dea Tacita. They managed to kill two soldiers, and cripple the Legate's Tribune to boot. The civilians were just—what do you say—*collateral*.'

'I'll never get used to seeing that word used in that way.'

'I don't think collateral is something about which Zealots particularly care, to be honest.'

Pilate looked at her, reaching across the table and clasping her fingers. He noticed that Nero was under her chair, his head resting across her feet.

'They hate everything that's good and enjoyable, Claudia. It's a hatred of the human race. Not just obvious things like wine and sex, either—they seem to hate art, theatre, music, good food, trade. Have you seen the way Caiaphas carries on around Nero? They've even got an issue with dogs.'

'Not all of them, Pontius; the Zealots are quite mad. I'm sure if you spoke to the average Judaean, you'd find that most of them are scared spitless of the Zealots.'

'I'm not used to being hated for what I am,' Pilate said. 'Hate has to be earned.'

'Gratus made some poor administrative decisions, Pontius.'

'There's been more terrorism on my watch—a lot more. Maybe I've given too much ground. That's what Vitellius will say, anyway.'

'The Legate?'

'I've got an Eye conference with him and Capito tomorrow morning.'

She leant towards him, pushing her paperwork to one side and moving around the table. She stood over him; her hair fell forward and brushed his face. He felt her adroit fingers lifting his tunic.

'I love you for what you are.'

'Time is a fleeing merchantman,' he told Capito when the latter took a seat in his office, along with Advocatus Viera and *Optio* Marius Macro. Capito suspected the line was a quote from some famous poet. He did not know what Pilate meant, but the words *felt* true. He admired Pilate's shark pups as they wriggled their heads from side to side in his giant fish tank. *Work of art, that.*

Horace brought Vitellius's image up on the Eye, made sure the connection was secure and then made himself scarce. There were a lot of unhappy faces in that room. Even the Procurator—a serene man, or at least one not prone to showing much stress—had been short with him that morning. Vitellius was in dress uniform, his bullet head shaven so short on the sides the skin seemed to glow. Horace could see the Damascus skyline, complete with its famous Temple of Baal and Astarte and the East Empire Stock Exchange, outlined behind him. Pilate's view over Caesarea's harbour was certainly something, but the Syrian Governor had one to match it.

Horace pulled the door to behind him.

Vitellius was clearly unhappy.

'I understand my Tribune died this morning, Procurator.'

'Yes, *Legatus*. I'm sorry.'

'And you have no idea of the killer's identity?'

'The Zealots have claimed responsibility, *Legatus*.'

Vitellius pursed his lips. 'I'm aware of that fact.'

Capito addressed himself to Vitellius. '*Legatus*, request permission to speak.'

'*Primus Pilus* Capito, permission granted.'

'Your Tribune and his driver should not have been travelling in an open-topped, unarmoured vehicle. All troop movements in Jerusalem outside the Roman Quarter are conducted in secured vehicles as a matter of course. The worst that IED would have done to an appropriately fitted *Mars* class MRAP was—maybe—blown the tyres.'

This was news to Vitellius. 'What is going on down there?

Please dispense with formalities.'

Viera was the first to speak.

'I've had *Aquilifer* Cornelius Getorex prepare a detailed analysis of all the criminal matters we've handled in Jerusalem in the last twelve months, sir. A copy has been couriered to you, but until you read it, the findings can be summarised as follows: even criminal activity in Judaea has taken on a political cast.'

'How so?'

'Most fraud matters routinely involve money laundering, and fully seventy-three per cent of murders in Jerusalem in the last year—excluding domestic murders, which remain distressingly common—have been of Jews linked in some way with the Roman administration. We've lost teachers, magistrates, firemen, community police, nurses, sympathetic rabbis, and one medic.'

Pilate interrupted.

'Replacing them is also getting difficult, sir. Romans, Greeks and others take the positions readily enough, but the effect of this is that Judaea is increasingly becoming a province of Jews ruled over and administered by foreigners.'

It was Marius Macro's turn to chip in. 'It's difficult to read trends in such short-term data, but I'm willing to stick my head out and say that, if something isn't done, things will get worse on both the concubinage and education fronts over the next ten years. These people won't Romanise at all, it seems.'

'We could make some positions Jews only,' Viera suggested.

Pilate's face flushed. 'I draw the line at preferencing. It creates resentment.'

Vitellius shifted about in his seat. 'Procurator, I seem to recall you deliberately weakening the thrust of our Romanisation policy shortly after you were appointed.'

Before Pilate could answer, Capito came to his rescue again.

'We need to be careful not to get correlation and causation mixed up here. Proving a link between the Procurator's decision to remove some of the advertising and a drop off in concubinage rates would be like looking for the proverbial needle in the proverbial haystack.'

Vitellius looked at Marius.

'Macro, you could control for the relevant factors, surely?'

'I could try, sir.'

'Part of the problem may be direct Roman administration, sir,' Capito was saying. 'This terrorism didn't seem to exist when we had Herod in place.'

'You'll also find that the numbers stayed static, and poor, during nearly forty years of Herodian administration,' Marius said.

'I'd go further than that,' Pilate added. 'I think Herod ran Judaea into the ground. I used to think—and so did Gratus—that this was simple incompetence. Now I'm not so sure. Some of the decisions he made were perverse.'

Capito scratched his grey bristles, gazing out over the harbour. It was bathed in soft pink light, thanks to a rather pretty sun shower. The sea was blue, streaked with silver.

'Jewish culture has to change,' he said.

'Good luck with that,' Pilate said.

Vitellius now looked uncomfortable; he hadn't realised where Pilate was going. 'You're talking about the death of Marcus Lonuobo's wife, I take it.'

Pilate bit the inside of his lip; he could taste blood. 'I stand by my view that the Imperial Propaganda Office show on Marcus Lonuobo's circumstances was equal parts cheese and shitty production values, and made us look like amateurs.'

'On top of everything else,' Viera added, 'they expect men to mutilate themselves for sex.'

Vitellius was pop-eyed, visualising a Jewish version of the

Rite of Cybele.

'What do you mean, *mutilate*?'

Viera looked distinctly uncomfortable, and crossed his legs.

This left Pilate to explain.

'Jewish men have the foreskin of their penises removed, *Legatus*. It's normally done eight days after birth, and while not something any Roman in his right mind would tolerate—it makes going to the baths, well, *awkward*—it's harmless when done at that age.'

Vitellius's face was flushed as well as pop-eyed, now. Pilate continued.

'An adult non-Jew who marries a Jewish woman is meant to undergo the same procedure. Obviously, on an adult, it's far more serious. No sex for a month, not even masturbation, and a very ugly cock afterwards.'

Capito leaned forward in his chair. '*Centurio* Lonuobo refused to have it done, *Legatus*, although I understand his wife did ask him.'

Vitellius now looked as uncomfortable as Viera; it was clear from the angle of his shoulders that he, too, had crossed his legs.

'Procurator, I know you're trying to do the right thing down there, but these attitudes need to be stepped on.'

Capito's voice was very soft. 'Winning hearts and minds in Judaea is difficult, *Legatus*. Documentaries showing one of their daughters with an uncircumcised man don't help.' Something seemed to catch in his throat. 'And now she's dead.'

'They seem to be immutable in their values,' Marius added. 'The rest of the Empire respects good governance. In Judaea, they want their own governance, regardless of quality. It's very sad.'

Vitellius detonated.

'Are you enabling their backwards, ignorant, and uncivilised religion? What sort of spineless and indecisive people have we got down there in Judaea?'

Pilate massaged the spot between his eyebrows with his middle finger.

'We all know they're culturally inferior, and that our civilisation is superior, *Legatus*. Unfortunately, they're also rather wedded to those culturally inferior values. Undermining the values may involve killing a lot of them.'

'You need to make a decision, Procurator. Rome fought three wars against Carthage, remember; sometimes killing is necessary.'

'I was trying to win their hearts and minds, at least for a bit longer.'

'If you get them by the balls, their hearts and minds will follow, Procurator.'

Or you'll have an awful lot of eunuchs.

Vitellius dismissed Capito, Viera and Marius; Pilate could see the three of them loitering with intent outside his office.

Vitellius's voice was gentle and menacing. 'Black the one-way glass, Procurator. This conversation is between you and me.'

The finger might have been a step too far.

'I detect a worrying softness in you, Procurator.'

'I'm sorry, *Legatus*. I'll try to harden my resolve.'

'This softness is common in civilian administrators, I grant you. It's just I'd always thought you were immune to the worst of it. Now it seems you've managed to infect your inferiors—even men like Capito.'

'What do you suggest, *Legatus*?'

'Reintroduce electricity. It's not as though we need it much here in Syria; I keep it mainly because Judaea is immediately to my south. Come up with a system of effective reprisals. Double salaries for new appointees to administrative roles, and where a Jew has equal qualifications and experience to a non-Jew, appoint the Jew.'

Pilate nodded, looking at the Damascene images behind Vitellius's head. A group of priestesses were rehearsing a dance in front of the Temple of Baal and Astarte, stopping and starting repeatedly in order get the complex pattern right. It was early; their audience—small, but appreciative—was made up of early traders standing in front of the Stock Exchange waiting for the bell to ring.

'It's your province, Procurator,' Vitellius went on. 'You don't have to do any of this, or you can do some of it, or do something else entirely. You do need to think about what you ought to do, however.'

'Yes, sir, I will.'

'And get a haircut. You look like an actor, not a Roman administrator.'

EVIDENCE

After a while, Cyler was forced to wear earmuffs against the racket he was generating in Iscariot's cell. *Condemnation to the arena for this fucking noise, Cyler. Can't produce this and then expect to live.* From time to time he looked up and gave thanks for three feet of lead-lined, reinforced concrete between the cells and what he suspected were eight-per-room dormitories above. As he'd suggested to Cornelius, he started using erotica with the volume set high but not to maximum. He was careful around Iscariot, too; *the little bugger bites.* He'd got the nurse who came in during the late afternoon to give him a painkilling shot in his knee. Iscariot somehow twisted downwards as the nurse withdrew the needle. The suddenness of the movement caught Cyler unawares: the nurse bounced back, screaming, holding his shoulder. Iscariot sniggered, blood flecking the corners of his mouth.

'Fucking shit bit me,' the nurse said in Latin. He peeled his fingers away from his scrubs; there was an expanding bloody patch on his shoulder and neck.

'Fuck, I'm pissing blood.'

'Did you get the shot in?'

'Yes sir, I did. Bastard waited until I stood up.'

'Right. That's the last shot he gets. I'll write you an infirmary pass. Fuck knows what diseases the little cunt's got. Get yourself cleaned up and then go to bed.'

'He'll be in severe pain if he doesn't get another shot in eight hours, sir.'

Cyler smiled lopsidedly, showing his snaggle teeth.

'Good,' he cooed.

Erotica worked for about seven hours, although it seemed to make Iscariot angry rather than horny. Cyler watched him from the monitor room screaming, gesturing and swearing at *Deborah does Damascus* on the cell's screen; it was funny in a twisted sort of way, and he found himself wishing he could understand Aramaic. *No accounting for taste, Cyler. Remember that.* Cyler caught Iscariot's head starting to droop after about seven and a half hours and fetched a pail of ice water from the infirmary down the corridor. He killed the lights in the cell, sidestepped silently and threw it over Iscariot's head.

'Sorry, sunshine. Can't have you getting snoozy on me. Need you bright and shiny for the boss in the morning.'

Iscariot spat on the floor. 'Filthy Roman motherfucker.'

'Oh yah, my mother fucks. And she enjoys it, too,' he said in Greek. He laughed amiably. 'You know, that's something you people could learn. All that pent-up sexual energy, no wonder you're fucked in the head.'

Iscariot spat again, this time at the spot in the dark where he thought his tormenter was standing. Cyler skipped away and flicked the switch. The aircraft landing lights he'd rigged up in the cell blinded him momentarily. Iscariot shielded his eyes with his free hand, screaming at the brilliant white.

Cyler went back to the monitor room, watching Iscariot abuse him in mixed Greek and Aramaic, shaking his hand at the CCTV. *Got to think of something a bit clever, Cyler.* He wandered down the corridor to the small library, fetching a collection of Roman cinema scores and—simply because they happened to be sitting there—a handful of children's shows. He wondered how they'd turned up in the interrogators' library. He shrugged, taking them back to the monitor room. He loaded up a stack of the cinema scores and *really* cranked the volume. This nearly blew *him* out of his chair, never mind Iscariot, who now stared at the CCTV as though there were a monster living inside it.

Once his ears adjusted to the volume, Cyler danced around the monitor room, his steps light and coordinated. Sometimes he stepped out into the corridor, twisting the monitor screen so he could watch Iscariot out of the corner of his eye. The music was much louder here, like he was at a live concert. Cyler found—as always seemed to be the case—that the high-pitched female vocal mixed with a driving beat worked best. He loaded up cards featuring all the best female playback singers he could find and watched Iscariot's wincing discomfort with amusement. *And we play that at a wedding or rite, while everyone dances or gets horizontal. No accounting for taste, Cyler.* Next up, he selected a set that was known all over the Empire as a bloc rite soundtrack; he skewed it to emphasise numbers popular with aficionados of the Greek vice.

This angered Iscariot in much the same way as the erotica had done, and he started swearing and gesturing at the CCTV again. Cyler killed the sound for a few seconds at one point and switched the transmitter across to two-way.

'You know, this is actually fun. Gets rid of all the bad mental stuff that makes you want to go out and kill innocent people. You should try it sometime.'

Iscariot screamed at the CCTV in Aramaic.

I am so going to have to get Lonuobo to translate this, it sounds mad, never mind what he's actually saying.

After a while even the music palled, and Cyler was forced to resort to ice water for the second time. On a whim, he threw the *Fun with Fractions* card into the narrowcast unit. The screen in Iscariot's cell winked back into life.

And here, we hit paydirt.

For whatever reason, men dancing around dressed in

multicoloured costumes teaching Roman preschoolers how to do sums infuriated Iscariot more than twenty bloc rite anthems back-to-back. Cyler danced a jig on the spot. *Oh, I don't just do erotica, I do educational telly! (Although you could call erotica educational, tee hee.)* He flicked the transmitter open again.

'Got a problem with counting, Iscariot?' His voice was cheery. 'Adult literacy and numeracy classes are free at your local Temple of Minerva.' He paused, putting on his best Roman propaganda voice: deep, trustworthy and filled with good intentions. 'This has been an Imperial Public Service Announcement, brought to you by *Legio* X *Fretensis*.'

Iscariot was barking now.

Now I know my ABCs.

He followed up with children's cartoons, children's musicals and children's science shows. He found an almost indescribably cheesy one featuring furry hand puppets that aired in a mixture of Aramaic and Latin on JTN. The music was excruciating, Samaritans trying to sing Roman style in Aramaic. It was at this point that he ran to the infirmary and availed himself of a set of construction worker's earmuffs.

If I never see anything furry again, it will be too soon.

Cyler went back to erotica momentarily, and almost immediately regretted the decision—even though the effect on his captive was good. Perhaps because he was tired and over-caffeinated himself, *Fun with Fractions* and *Deborah does Damascus* started to blur in his head.

Shouldn't have done that, Cyler, next time you whack off, it'll be in fractions. Three quarters plus two eighths plus the mass of the ass equals the angle of the dangle plus the sum of the cum.

Cyler killed the sound and opened the transmission channel again, struggling to control his own hysterical laughter.

'Hey, if this keeps up, you'll be able to do long division by next week.'

At that point, he noticed Iscariot had an impressive nosebleed, and trotted off to the infirmary to get him some medical attention.

The medic on duty was grouchy. 'I'm not sending any more of my men in there to get bitten, Lucullus.'

'Sir, I'll pull his bloody teeth out with pliers if he tries that again.'

'Or you could just put a bag over his head.'

The medic stood up and fetched a first aid kit and blood pressure cuff.

'And, by the way, your musical taste over the last four hours has left a great deal to be desired.'

Cyler grinned. 'That's why I had to add *Deborah does Damascus*, sir.'

Ben David pulled into his spot in front of the Empire to wait for Linnaeus. The last few days had made him familiar with Linnaeus's morning ritual. This involved multiple cups of espresso—usually at the hotel, but sometimes at a convenient Roman Quarter café. After the awkwardness at Arimathea's, Linnaeus made a point of inviting Ben David to join him, and he always paid. He spent the time they shared at table explaining how the coffee they were drinking came to taste like it did: where it was grown, how it shouldn't be bitter, how adding *chocolatl* made it mocha, how sweet it should be. It was fascinating in its own way. At one point he asked Linnaeus if he considered himself a coffee connoisseur.

'Of course not. Wine, maybe—I've always secretly nursed an ambition to retire to the Province in Gaul and run a boutique winery—but not coffee. I just like nice things. Good food, good wine, fine art, beautiful women, lovely young men, music, theatre. In my youth, there was a bit of politics, too; you know, the things that make life worthwhile.'

Ben David did not know, but he managed to balance admiration for the Roman's resolve and courage with distaste for the man's personal habits. There was a woman at the Empire, Ben David knew, a high-class whore: no need for someone of Linnaeus's stature to dally in the Greek Quarter. Linnaeus liked her and spoke well of her, taking her views seriously.

Ben David got out of his cab and leaned against the driver's side door. Linnaeus was a few minutes late—most unlike him. He made his way past the marble columns leading towards the Empire's reception. The big glass double doors slid apart. Ben David scanned the lobby. Linnaeus was standing to one side of the concierge's desk *mauling* his favoured young woman. There was no other word for it. He had a hand on each cheek of her backside; one of her legs was hooked around his hip. Ben David felt his skin flush and fought the urge to stare. Eventually the two of them approached the concierge, hand in hand. He handed them some paperwork, which they both signed. Linnaeus grinned his crow grin and headed towards the door.

'You have lipstick all over your face, *Domine* Linnaeus.'

'No doubt, David. I'll clean it up as we go. Sorry I'm late.'

'Only ten minutes, *Domine* Linnaeus.'

'We'll be going to the Roman Quarter this morning, then the Jewish Quarter this afternoon. I'll stop to buy us lunch. I think my Jewish Quarter witness is quite poor—judging from the address—and I don't want to impose.' Linnaeus handed over a slip of paper with the addresses written in Greek. Ben David saw the name Mary Magdalena at the top and felt a little shock of recognition. He searched around in his memory. *She's famous for something or other. Can't remember what.*

Linnaeus cleaned his face with an emollient cloth he had stashed in his briefcase.

'My, my, I have finished up with that everywhere. Just found a bit on the top of my ear.'

Ben David smiled. He could see Linnaeus angling his head so that he could get a clear line of sight into the rear-view mirror.

'You should let your Jewish witness give you something, *Domine* Linnaeus, or he will feel very rude.'

'Even to a Roman?'

'You are helping his friend, especially after the prison business.'

'What do you suggest?'

'A drink and some of the bread he'll have prepared for Passover, *Domine* Linnaeus. That would be my suggestion.'

By the time he'd pulled up before an ornate set of gates facing an elegant apartment complex on the border of the Greek and Roman Quarters, Ben David had remembered why he knew Mary Magdalena, at least by name. She was a newsreader on JTN. Not recently, though. A security guard on the gates admitted them once Linnaeus announced his presence and his business. He pointed Ben David to a parking space.

'Today is a new day,' Linnaeus announced to no one in particular as he pressed a button marked *Mary Magdalena & Nic Varro*.

A buzzer sounded deep within the building; the door swung open. He and Ben David climbed two floors to reach an open door facing onto a large terraced area. An outdoor pool sparkled below. A woman was waiting for them. She extended her hand.

'I'm Mary Magdalena.'

Linnaeus held the block of yellow legal pad he'd taken out of his briefcase in the cab in front of his crotch and—with as much calm as he could muster—put his briefcase down in order to shake her hand. *It's rude to point*. She was, bar none, the most beautiful woman he'd ever seen. He had a sudden sharp mental image of roistering with her somewhere nice—the baths, say, in his villa in Etruria—but there was something else, too. She had an air of authority, of command. He could imagine her telling him to do something ridiculous and complying without hesitation: streaking at the arena, say, or picking a fight with a six-foot six-inch legionary. He realised that part of her wonder was an unpickable ethnic ancestry. Her skin was mocha, with shining black hair hanging over her shoulders in loose tresses. Her eyes, however, were blue-grey, and her lips blood coloured.

She was wearing a fine linen tunic, not too long: her legs were brown and shapely. He could see her breasts pushing against the material.

Nic Varro, whoever you are, you are one lucky prick.

'I see we have a very Roman man here.'

Linnaeus smiled at that. 'You are a stunning woman,' he said in Latin. 'Please accept my apologies for staring at you like that.'

'That is the best of Rome,' she said. 'You do not pretend. Come in.'

Linnaeus and Ben David followed her into the dining room. She pointed Ben David into the kitchen alcove, pouring him a glass of water.

'Thank you for bringing him. Please wait here while we talk.'

She fetched Linnaeus coffee, olives and hot rolls and sat opposite him. He went through his briefcase—not speaking—pulling out various evidentiary items and statements. He was more than a little annoyed with himself. He'd spent the night and part of the morning slaking his appetites most agreeably and within an hour another beautiful woman had set him off.

Mary picked up the evidence photographs taken in the Temple and leafed through them.

'They made a mess, didn't they?'

He turned his portable calculation engine to face her, pointing out where she could pause and review the sequence.

'Whoever put that together knew what they were doing.'

'Cornelius Getorex and his friends in *Legio* X *Fretensis*, Mary. Getorex in particular is fearsomely competent.'

He outlined the substance of the case against Ben Yusuf, pointed out that the State had access to torture if it so wished—at this she blanched—and made his request for a statement. He handed her a proforma indicating the basic structure, but pointed out that he could edit when and where necessary. Finally, he came to the unsettling interview with his client. He recounted the incident where Ben Yusuf appeared to mirror his own voice and that of the young man detailed to guard him.

'I know that actors—good ones—can do the same trick, but it's as if he *were* me.'

'He sometimes shows himself in that way.'

'The further I've gone with this case, the more I've come to realise that I don't understand what I'm defending. I have no idea what you, Ben Yusuf, Arimathea, and Petros are trying to achieve. For many Romans, *religio* is just another name for notions of the "don't walk under ladders" variety. I suppose you'd call me one of those Romans. It's time to build a plausible case, and if I don't understand what you're trying to do, then I can't do that.'

She looked at him, her expression both curious and sad.

'Do you believe any of your gods are real?'

At first, he was taken aback, but the opportunity to observe her beauty—it was beyond sexual now, almost hypnotic—encouraged him to respond.

'It depends. There are places I go where I feel the spirits are very close. I have a villa in Etruria, and I always feel that it belongs to the *lares* more than it belongs to me.'

'Do they frighten you?'

'No. They guard the house. They let me know if I'm doing something I shouldn't be doing.'

'Such as?'

'Building something I shouldn't. This happened a couple of years ago. I wanted to build an extension on the baths. My woman at the time was an architect and drew up the plans. We'd got to the stage of looking at fittings—granite benchtops and taps and whatnot—and mosaics for the floor. Philippa noticed it first, but I'd felt uneasy for a while, too. The spirits weren't malicious, but they didn't want us building there. My tools went missing—I lost a new compound drop saw and a drill. All our tiles arrived broken. '

'It sounds like you do believe in your gods, then.'

Linnaeus felt awkward; he was used to asking the questions. 'Only the gods in that place.' He paused. 'They showed themselves to me, and to Philippa.'

'Do your gods love you, Andreius?'

He realised with a shock of recognition and respect that his cross-examination skills were matched by her interviewing skills.

'Why should they? Those spirits belong to the villa in Etruria. You should respect them, though. Otherwise it's like living in someone else's house without paying rent.'

'There are other gods, Andreius.'

She had control of him now.

Pity any poor bastard she interviewed who tried to lie to her.

'Sorry, I see what you mean. Cybele looks after the Roman people. I feel for Cybele.'

'There's a lot of sex and drugs at that festival, Andreius. You would expect a Roman boy to enjoy the Festival of the *Magna Mater*.'

'I've loved it since I was small, though, where sex and drugs and those things don't matter. In my hometown, the children lit paper lamps and floated them down the river, to remember the soldiers and the ancestors. I remember standing watching from the balcony of an apartment overlooking the Tiber with my mother when I was six or so. You know, the big annual re-enactment, from the war against Hannibal... of when she first came to Rome. Her priestesses and one of the Consuls brought her glossy stone up the river in an old-style Greek ship, one with the banks of oars, and the water was on fire. They had these slow-burning fires threading the length of the river—like fireworks but silent—and the whole city seemed to be holding hands on the bank, their faces lit.' His voice grew soft and distant. 'They brought the stone up to the Temple of Cybele, and we followed the priestesses. There was music; they play the drums very well, make you want to dance. Maybe I'm confusing two different years' festivals, because I'm with the Angel in that memory. We all held hands. The Consul gave Cybele's stone over to the priestesses and to the leading matrons of the city; they sang and danced.'

'The Angel?'

'What I've always called my father.'

'So you joined the Goddess and the people, then?'

'Yes, I think so. It's like everyone blends into everyone else. You can do that when you're young. When you're older, you need artificial help.'

'Hence the sex and drugs and booze.'

'I remember seeing the *gallus* emasculate himself,' he said, in real reverie now. 'The blood and the way he shrieked, a joyous shriek. He was taken up. The blood spread out over the forecourt. I was sitting on the Angel's shoulders, and I wanted to come down, I was afraid. The Angel said part of Cybele's spirit could come into him and let him do that, because his mind was open.'

'So she's a bigger goddess than the spirits in your Etrurian villa?'

'Yes, of course. She protects the whole Roman people.'

'What about a god that loves the whole world, Andreius? How would that be?'

Linnaeus looked at her and shook his head, half in wonderment and half in disbelief.

'That can't be. Cybele did not protect Carthage. She protected Rome. When she first came to Rome—at our invitation—Hannibal was running up and down Italy destroying Roman armies right and left, but we all know who won the war against Hannibal.'

'So gods support their favourite peoples and cities, then?'

'You Jews have a god that looks out for you...' his voice trailed off. 'Only, he doesn't seem to do it very well.'

'Ben Yusuf says it doesn't have to be like that any more. God loves all of us.'

Linnaeus felt his mind start to clear; this was all getting a bit weird for his taste. *You have to build a case, Andreius.*

He thought of the religious commune near his Tuscan villa. They were Pythagoreans or some such—vegetarian and pacifist and grave. They sold honey on the roadside in front of their property. Linnaeus always made a point of stopping and buying some when he went on holidays. It tasted good. Once he'd seen them building a farm building of some sort—a city boy, he had no idea what it was—all working together, helping each other. He sat in his car with the roof retracted, observing them for two or three hours, until they'd almost finished. They were painting their pentagram on the door by the time he drove away.

'So you're trying to found a new religion, a new religious movement?'

'We believe every man and woman can find their way to God, Andreius.'

'Why do you need a new religion? You have Judaism, and while that's strange to someone like me, at least it has an ancient pedigree.'

'We think we have something truer in our hands.'

His native cynicism resurfaced.

'So you're better people than the rest of us working stiffs?'

'I detect an Epicurean, Andreius.'

Linnaeus baulked at this.

'I'm not an anything, Mary, but your Ben Yusuf is going to be dead soon, unless he can come up with some very good reasons for trashing the Jerusalem Temple. Starting now. He tried to tell me he had some sort of higher authority when I saw him yesterday, but that won't fly in a Roman court. Even worse was the crap about businessmen and merchants not entering the house of the Lord. Pilate's just going to laugh.'

She looked hurt.

'It was information that Yeshua and his friends got from Niccy and me that, ah, encouraged them to act as they did.' She stood up to make more coffee and offer water to Ben David. 'You should get a statement from Niccy when he comes home from work. He's not one of Yeshua's followers, but he worked out what the Sanhedrin have been up to when it comes to collecting the Temple tax. He has the Roman head for figures.'

'I'm seeing Petros Bar Yonah this afternoon, Mary.'

'Nic will be back before midday. He does all his work in the morning these days.'

Linnaeus speared an olive with a toothpick and brought it

to his lips.

'You both work for JTN, yes?'

'I do. Niccy owns it.'

'I'm sorry. That would have been in the brief, which I've read. I must have forgotten.'

'It always manages to shock people, that Judaea's only Aramaic and Hebrew language screen station is owned by a Roman.'

Linnaeus flapped his hands. 'Only momentarily in my case—there's nothing like good old Roman know-how.'

'The Jerusalem Temple is a criminal enterprise, Andreius. There's no other way to put it. And if you're a Jew, there's nowhere else to go. Niccy's a journalist now, but he studied economics in Mediolanum as a young man. He told me that what they're doing would be illegal in Italy. Your regulator, I can't remember the name...'

'The Competition Council.'

'That's it. He said the Competition Council wouldn't permit it to operate.'

Linnaeus started scribbling furiously. If Nic Varro came good with a decent set of numbers, then—just maybe—things were looking up.

'First, there's the exchange rates they fix for converting Roman money into the Temple money. Nic calls this *scrip*, I'm not sure why...'

'*Scrip* means you can only spend it in the Temple, like the tokens at a fun fair.'

She nodded. 'We have to pay the Temple Tax—and buy anything within the Temple—using these.' She fumbled around in a little tray sitting on the windowsill and placed a sparkling silver coin on the table before him.

He picked it up, holding it before his eyes. 'There's a lot of silver in that. It's beautiful.'

'It's a Tyrian shekel. It's ninety-five per cent silver. Under Jewish law, only pure money is acceptable to pay for things in the Temple.'

Linnaeus admired the shining coin, watching it sparkle as he turned it over in his fingers. 'Roman money is independently worthless, although you can take it to the Central Bank and swap it for an equivalent value in gold. Well, that's the theory.'

He took a twenty *denarii* note out of his wallet and pointed to the writing beneath Scipio Africanus's head. 'See? *Will Pay to the Bearer on Demand*.'

She picked up the note, looked at the writing and nodded.'I'm not sure there's enough gold on the planet to cover every inhabitant of the Empire making a run on the Central Bank and asking for all their *denarii* to be converted into gold, though.'

'The thing is, the Temple sets the exchange rate in such a way that whenever they change Roman money into shekels, they make an enormous profit.'

'That's how currency trading works, though. You wouldn't bother, otherwise.'

'But the disparity is huge—four *denarii* to the shekel. Niccy says it should be about 1.4 to 1—that lets the moneychanger make a fair profit. And if you pay for something big with a whole shekel that requires change, you have to pay a separate fee to get your change.'

'Okay, that's crooked; it's like a truck system. Nic is right—they're illegal in Italy.'

'The worst part is that the fee to get your change is fixed—whether you're buying a whole ram or two doves, and since shekels only come in two denominations—one or a half—paying a fee is often unavoidable.'

'So you're penalising the poor—once with the exchange

rate, and then again with this "change fee" caper.'

'And traders fiddle their prices so that it's not worth asking for change. They keep the difference. It's fair to say that the Temple's moneychangers and merchants are hated the length and breadth of Judaea.'

'I wouldn't mind betting that the Temple is screwing the traders, too.'

She was taken aback. 'How so?'

'What's a license to trade in the Court of the Gentiles worth?' He grinned. 'Don't answer that. I'll call Caiaphas as a witness and ask him.'

'That's the kind of thing Nic notices. It's very Roman. I wish we were better at it.'

'Caiaphas is obviously brilliant at it, and if he's Roman, I'll eat my shoe.'

'This system is much older than Caiaphas, Andreius. It's been that way since Herod built the Temple. Caiaphas inherited it.'

'Getorex will argue that all of this is irrelevant, of course. I can hear him saying "objection, Procurator, relevance?" already.'

She looked down. 'It's hard when someone's died.'

'There's also the Roman attitude to markets, Mary. You know how seriously you Jews take your God? Well, that's how seriously Romans take the market. Markets have made us stupidly, stunningly rich in a very short time. You really don't want to go in there and be impious. Pilate and I went to the *Collegia* together. I don't think he believes in the concept of market failure.'

She laughed. 'You sound just like Niccy.'

'I'm looking forward to meeting him. What you've told me today is the first thing I've heard that's given me a sense that this case is about something other than young men with a sense of entitlement trying to remake the world in their image.'

Her smile was sly. 'That's what Rome does.'

Another delicious image of the two of them carousing in his Tuscan villa had crept unbidden to the surface of his mind.

'*Touché,*' he said.

Nic Varro arrived twenty minutes later; Linnaeus observed Mary watch him walk through security into the apartment complex's stairwell. She had tears in her eyes as she held the shutters to one side. He bounded up the stairs—Linnaeus could hear his footfalls. A tall Etruscan, he had the chiselled face and aquiline profile of his people; his curly black hair was very short, ruched back from his forehead and slick with pomade. Linnaeus noticed he wore heavy gold earrings and rings and a mass of gold jewellery around his neck and wrists; it was all of a piece with his collarless cream silk shirt and dark narrow trousers.

Before acknowledging Linnaeus, he strode over to where Mary was sitting, cupped one of her breasts in his hand and bent down to kiss her. She did not seem to respond, except perhaps to incline her head towards his. The movement was almost imperceptible.

He stood and introduced himself, then bolted to the bathroom.

'Need to use the facility.'

He was away for a long time.

There is something very strange going on here.

When Niccy re-emerged, his dark skin was flushed. Mary made eye contact with him for the first time.

'Andreius is here for the Ben Yusuf case. He needs to talk to you.'

Nic laughed; the sound was high and forced.

'Ah, the Dick Police's honourable defender.'

Linnaeus realised with some trepidation that Nic's view of Ben Yusuf was very different from Mary's.

'I haven't heard him called that before...' he paused, trying not to smile. 'But Mary has discussed the financial arrangements in the Temple you worked out, and I'd be very grateful to see your figures.'

'Oh, that. I'll get them.'

Mary stood up. 'I have some errands to run, so I'll leave the two of you to chat. You and your driver are welcome to stay for lunch.'

Linnaeus stood in the middle of the room, feeling rather awkward.

Nic returned in a different shirt—blue cotton this time, and unbuttoned a long way. He handed some papers to Linnaeus and sat down, resting one foot on the opposite knee.

'I hope the Procurator blows Yeshua Ben Yusuf's head off.'

Linnaeus flapped his hands. *This is a bit of a shock.*

'Well, it won't be Pilate personally, but men from *Legio X Fretensis*. And Roman executioners are generally dissuaded from shooting high. It makes a mess, quite apart from anything else.'

'Oh no, the messier the better. I want to see his brains on the ground.'

Linnaeus resisted the urge to move *far* away. Nic looked at him, the anger draining out of his face, to be replaced by an emotion Linnaeus couldn't identify. He propped forward, his elbows on his knees, his head in his hands.

'I'm sorry. I should explain properly. Another coffee?'

Nic stood over the coffee machine, working it like a real pro. The coffee he made was much better than Mary's, and topped off with a leaf pattern in the milk. Linnaeus admired it.

'You've done that before.'

'I worked as a barista to pay my way through *collegium*. I didn't get a scholarship.'

'Mary said you studied economics at Mediolanum. That's a good institution, with a strong economics division.'

'I fucked around in high school. Scraped in by the skin of my teeth and had to face up to the fact that I was at one of the best *collegia* in the Empire with no scholarship and no money from home. My parents were—and are—skint. So I made coffee and sucked cock to get through.'

He rummaged through his wallet and handed Linnaeus a card. As soon as Linnaeus saw the blue and yellow symbol he knew what it was. He started to laugh.

'Life member of the Guild of Sex Workers. I'm impressed.'

'I was their Mediolanum accountant for four years. I'd be drawing up accounts and giving blow jobs in between working my way through *Mathematics for Economists* or *Principles of Microeconomics*.'

'I take it you're not into the Greek?'

'No, but I can pretend like a champion, Greek for pay only.'

Linnaeus looked at him. He was agitated, crossing and uncrossing his arms. Linnaeus took the chance to repeat the observations on Ben Yusuf's case he'd made to Mary earlier, and sketched in some background. He requested a statement to explain the financial findings Nic had made.

'No, never. I won't stand in the way of Rome blowing his head off. He's right about their bent Temple, but wrong about everything else.'

Linnaeus couched his question with care. 'Ah, what's the problem with Ben Yusuf?'

'He stopped me fucking my wife.'

This time Linnaeus didn't laugh.

'How?'

'He's got this moral code. You're not supposed to screw around before marriage. It's like Rome in the days of the Twelve Tables. And there's no divorce allowed, either.'

'But you're married... how long have you been together?'

'For six years.'

'And neither of you have absented yourselves from the family home for three days consecutive each year?'

He shook his head.

'Roman marriage isn't good enough for Dick Police. You have to have a ceremony.'

'You mean convert to Judaism?'

'Gods no. They're deeply religious, but I wouldn't call them Jews. According to him, we're not married in the eyes of God.'

'Mary's a citizen? You have rights of *coniubium*?'

'Yes and yes.' His expression had become wistful and sad. 'Sometimes she even crosses out *sine manu* on the relationship status question on Imperial forms.'

'I take it this is a new thing, then?'

'Only since the Dick Police showed up. I'd been running JTN for two years when Mary turned up at interview for a secretary's job. She went to Jerusalem Academy and got good grades, but her parents wouldn't let her leave Judaea for further study. I hired her on the strength of her good looks and good language skills and trained her. She was my main newsreader for seven years.'

'What's your media background? You look a bit familiar, that's all.'

'I used to present *Communicatio Roma At Market*. Once a week, market wrap-up and analysis. It was me that started calling the Procurator of this fine province *Don SINDEX*, back when he was still at Valens.'

'I remember, now. You had long hair then, in a ponytail.'

He stood up and went into the kitchen. 'Want a joint? I grow a bit of my own. It's quite mild.'

Linnaeus shook his head. 'I've got cigars to get through, but if you're smoking one of yours, I'll join you in smoking one of mine.'

The two of them sat on the balcony overlooking the complex's gardens, their legs partly hidden by the green forest of Nic's cannabis plants.

'I've tried pointing out to Mary that her omniscient God probably knows we're married.'

Linnaeus had to think about this for a moment.

'Omniscient? You mean he knows everything?'

'Knows everything, watches everything, sees everything. He's supposed to be watching us all the time.'

'Even in the loo?'

'Yeah, even on the toilet. In the sack, too. Everywhere, in fact. He's a bloody nuisance.'

Linnaeus blew smoke rings, listening to Nic vent. He couldn't blame him, really.

'She was pretty annoyed with her parents over the study thing. She'd been accepted at Bononia, see. So she went Roman, and it was beautiful to watch. That I was the beneficiary was even sweeter.'

Linnaeus had no trouble visualising this process.

'Everything was going well. JTN started to turn a profit. I'd found a great market niche. I was married to the most beautiful woman in the Empire. She loved her job. She was brilliant at her job. Her parents decided they could be proud of the woman they watched on screen every night. We started to visit them from time to time. They even reciprocated. Peace was breaking out all over the place.'

'Then Ben Yusuf turned up?'

'She went to cover a story in Galilee. Ben Yusuf was

involved. Apparently people in Nazareth tried to chuck him off a cliff and he'd been rescued by men from the Roman garrison in Sepphoris. He'd claimed he could cure their sick kids or some such, and when he didn't come good, they reacted badly. There was definitely something funny going on.'

'Sounds nasty.'

'Parts of this province are pretty bloody primitive, Andreius. At least once a week some poor woman gets stoned to death because she went with the wrong man. It's got that way we don't cover it any more, except when the killers have laid hands on a legionary's woman and he gets trigger happy.'

'Those stories make the papers in Rome sometimes. I even saw a CR *Vista* documentary on it once. *Honour killing*, I think they called it.'

'Honour killing, my arse,' said Nic, 'it's the most barbaric thing you've ever seen. At least Ben Yusuf tried to stop them doing it.'

'Have you seen him do that? Or do you know anyone who has?'

'Ask around the Galilee garrison; get hold of one of the officers, they'll know. Apparently he stares the bastards down, which takes *coleones*.'

'He's got a magnetic personality. I learned that when I interviewed him.'

'I don't see it, unfortunately. He strikes me as a terrible ham. Mary loves him, though. She thinks he can set the Jewish people free.'

'From Roman rule?'

'Sometimes it sounds like that, Andreius. It really does; but then he skitters away and it somehow stops being "hating the Romans" hour.'

'Some of his followers are into hating the Romans.'

'You bet. I've had most of the boys in here at various times.

In the end I put my foot down and said that Iscariot and Simon, his greasy little sidekick, weren't welcome any more. Both of them clearly think people like me should just crawl away and die.'

Linnaeus admired the heads on one of Nic's plants, running his fingers through the leaves.

'Mary expects a *coemptio* marriage?'

'Yes, all fifty thousand *sesterces*' worth. And we haven't fucked for eighteen months.'

'Oh gods.'

'That's just what I haven't been saying, except from time to time in the Greek Quarter, when I feel like I'm going to bloody burst.'

Linnaeus did find this funny. He could imagine Nic doing a big Etruscan bravura performance, with swearing, stomping and slamming doors.

Where are you going?

To the Greek Quarter!

Linnaeus reached across the little wrought-iron table between them and clasped Nic's shoulder.

'I know I'm a stranger, but I'm going to give you a piece of advice.'

Nic drew the last from his joint and flicked the butt over the balcony. The lawyer's black almond eyes were lucid and open, boring into him.

'Go to the bank. Get a loan. Marry her.'

'But we're already bloody married!'

'Not as far as she's concerned, at least not any more.'

Nic looked down, grabbing the balcony rail. He was crying. *That wasn't far below the surface, Andreius. He's had this corked for a while.* Nic rubbed his eyes with one hand.

'Yes, it means swallowing your Roman pride and—even more—your Etruscan pride.'

Nic laughed at this.

'We were civilised while you lot were still pissing in the Tiber and sucking your own cocks.'

Linnaeus let this last float by.

'If she were mine, Nic, I'd have trouble doing my job. I'd get boners in court. I'd be spending every minute of every hour thinking about what I'd be doing that night.'

Nic was crying hard now, his sobs coming in big rasping gasps.

'I would crawl on my hands and knees over broken glass for a woman like that. I would mortgage my *mother* for her.'

Nic laughed through his tears.

'When she comes back from her errands, I want you to ask for her hand in marriage. Formally. Like in the pictures, just before they do the big song-and-dance finale.'

Mary let herself into the apartment to see Ben David pouring a glass of water for Nic, who was sitting at the kitchen table, his eyes raw and red-rimmed. Linnaeus was next to him, both arms around his shoulders. She heard the lawyer say, 'now you go' as she closed the door behind her.

Nic made his way towards her, skirting the table; he had always been swift and controlled in his movements.

'Put your shopping down,' he ordered; there was a tone of authority in his voice, something she'd always liked in him. She complied without thinking, resting the cardboard box to one side. He stopped in front of her and took both of her hands in his. His touch was so commanding she did not try to pull them back. What came next, however, made her eyes widen with a mixture of fear and wonder. He knelt before her and breathed in, holding her wrists in his hands.

'Mary Magdalena, will you marry me? Will you be my lawful wife?'

Linnaeus and Ben David watched as she drew him upright and then into her arms. 'I want to be your wife,' she said. 'I want to have your babies.' He began kissing her; she did not try to move away. His hands were buried in her hair. Her hands slid up under his shirt.

'Oh yes, I want to marry you.'

Linnaeus and Ben David both applauded.

When Cornelius went to open the Law Room at 0530 hours, Marcus Lonuobo was sitting outside in the passageway, eating a roll. He stood up and saluted.

'Come in, Lonuobo. We'll have coffee.'

'Yes, sir.'

The two of them put themselves to work in the small kitchen at the back of the room, complete with sign above the taps in Viera's spidery hand: *Your mother does not live here.* They prepared two large cafetières and waited for them to brew. Cornelius looked hard at Lonuobo; the latter seemed calm enough, not jittery or angry. *Still.*

'Lonuobo, are you here early because you're keen, or for some other reason? How long have you been waiting outside?'

'I've been waiting for half an hour, sir. I think I'm frightened of my own anger.'

'I can detail someone else if you're concerned about losing control. I've pencilled in a shadow for your role. Rufus Vero.'

'He's very young, sir.'

'That's what I thought.'

Cornelius poured coffee for both of them. 'I've seen two men finish up with serious mental problems after *Camera* duty, back when I was in Syria. Both of them were young, with something of a mean streak but no real reason to be mean. If you don't have reasons, you fuck up.'

Lonuobo's voice was soft. 'I have reasons, sir. Too many,

perhaps. And I've already hurt him.'

'What did Iscariot say to you in the Temple that day? I've got reasonable Aramaic, but I didn't catch it.'

'He told me I still hadn't learnt to keep my Roman cock out of Jewish cunt.'

Cornelius raised his eyebrows and exhaled. 'I'll have to step on you if you get out of line.'

There was a single knock at the door. Cornelius stood up.

'Come in.'

Medicus Darius Saleh stepped inside and saluted.

'Reporting for duty, sir.'

He looks about twelve. There should be a law against it.

Saleh's forehead was high and unmarked, his skin an even light brown, his curly hair restrained by the severe military haircut.

'I don't believe we've ever worked together before, Saleh.'

'No, sir. *Medicus* Titus Verres was my immediate superior. Your dealings would have been with him.'

Cornelius nodded. 'So you have an interest as well?'

'Yes, sir.'

'Hmmm.'

Cornelius led his team down to the cells, the curly-headed medic at his heels, Lonuobo bringing up the rear, Eugenides and Vero in the middle. They paused on the stairs when wake-up sounded, turning towards the sound and standing to attention.

'Hands off cocks and onto socks,' Cornelius said afterwards, to general mirth.

They heard the racket from outside the monitor room some distance before they arrived. Cyler emerged and saluted, a shiteating grin on his face. He led them inside and cut the worst of the volume. Iscariot was still swearing at Roman children's shows; he shook his head in surprise when the volume dropped.

Cornelius orders Cyler to 'water' Iscariot again and then takes them into the secondary room he's had Rufus Vero prepare. He orders them to sit, collects his thoughts and documents and speaks.

'Any State that tortures commits a wrong. Never forget that. I hope I don't have to remind anyone of this basic fact at any point over the next few days.'

Lonuobo and Vero—*surprise, surprise, next to each other*—are impassive. Cyler looks at his fingernails. Saleh stares, transfixed, his medical kit on his lap like a schoolboy's lunchbox. Aristotle has his chin perched on one fist, his back rigid.

'We only torture to avert a greater wrong. That's why there are rules.'

He hands a set of printed sheets to each man. 'I don't doubt you know the rules, but I'm providing the relevant pages from our Military Interrogation Code just to make sure. I'm going to stand here for five minutes while you read them through.'

The room is silent save the ticking of the wall clock and the small movements of the men as they concentrate their minds on what is before them. Cornelius watches the clock to ensure that five minutes pass.

'I have assigned each of you a role and set of core questions. Iscariot is a high-value asset. He will not respond to direct questioning except—possibly—under torture, although I will make an initial attempt. We need to be subtle and oblique. It is imperative that you retain the characteristics of your role throughout. Lucullus, as you know, you will be *Domine* Sarcasm. I hope you've been in character all night.'

'Yes, sir. He thinks I'm an oversexed imbecile.'

Cornelius laughs at this.

'Lonuobo, you are *Domine* Nasty. You and Vero will hood him and drag him by his hands to the *Camera*. You will then propel him with force into the flexible false wall Eugenides has prepared. I will remove the hood and speak to him about what will happen if he does not assist us with our enquiries. I am *Dominus* Legally Correct. The Code forbids me from touching him.'

'Yes, sir.'

'Eugenides, you are *Domine* Friendly. You are to be kind and sympathetic, and when Lucullus and Lonuobo disagree with each other—as they must appear to do so at various points—you are to take Lucullus's side, but without the sarcasm.'

'Yes, sir. I didn't realise I come across as friendly.'

Cornelius grins. 'You do.' He continues, his skin shining in what little light there is to share.

'Saleh, your role is medical supervision. I understand his knee is braced?'

'Yes, sir. I'm concerned that he hasn't had his shot.'

'He shouldn't bloody bite people, then,' says Lonuobo.

'We then bring him here—*ex Camera*—for initial interview. If we give him a big enough scare, then he may cough up the goods without anything further. After I speak to him, he is to remain hooded at all times. You are also to respond to my hand signals at all times. I do not want to use your names.'

Saleh is shocked by the contrast between Cornelius's low, calm instructions and their frenetic execution. Vero and Lonuobo are both muscular and fit; their combined strength as they drag Iscariot down the corridor and then fling him into the false wall in the rear of the *Camera* nearly leaves Saleh behind. He tucks his medical kit under his arm and sprints after them. Eugenides has done something odd when constructing the wall, because when Iscariot is thrown into it there's a bang like a shotgun going off and he rebounds into the two soldiers. They step into him, absorbing the force and steadying his head, preserving him from injury. The movement is oddly tender.

Cornelius holds up three fingers, and they wind up and launch Iscariot into it twice more. Saleh winces at the sound. Finally, Cornelius grabs the top of the hood and pulls on it as he is pinned upright. Iscariot is bug-eyed and winded. Rufus and Lonuobo pull his head backwards and then hold his chin so that he cannot move his head from side to side and see his captors. The other men turn their backs, rendering themselves unidentifiable. Cyler grabs Saleh's shoulder, dragging him around as well. Cornelius stands in front of him, looming. Saleh can hear him speak in his careful but limited Aramaic.

'I am going to ask you some questions, and I expect honest answers. If you do not give honest answers, we will hurt you. We don't want to hurt you, but we will if we have to. Look at what we have in this room.'

Saleh turns his neck just far enough to see Lonuobo use the power in his wrist to twist Iscariot's head towards the floor, so he can see the sloping table, the watering-can, the manacles and trailing electrical flex.

Cornelius pulls the hood back over his head and points towards the interview room opposite. Lonuobo and Vero drag him by the hands again, once more forcing Saleh to sprint in order to keep up with them.

Rufus wrinkles his nose. 'Someone's been smoking in there.'

Saleh shrugs. 'There's no smoke alarm. I'd say everyone on this floor has smoked in there at some point.'

'It stinks.'

Cornelius points towards a single chair in the middle of the room. Lonuobo and Rufus shackle Iscariot to it and step back.

Cornelius sits directly opposite him, behind what looks like a school desk. For some reason, there's a spare block of yellow legal pad on the seat. He hands it to Cyler, who—unsure of what to do—stashes it on top of a filing cabinet. Cornelius indicates with his hands that they should sit on either side of him. The seats are arranged in a horseshoe shape, facing Iscariot. Cornelius turns to face the room's CCTV. He speaks in Latin.

'This day is the first after the Nones of April in the year seven hundred and eighty-four *ab urbe condita.* This is a Form 23 interview pursuant to *senatus consultum de re publica defendenda* number 44: terrorism. The interview subject is Yehuda Iscariot, who is charged with murder *dolus directus* times nineteen for the Dea Tacita Centre attack, which took place two days after the *Kalends* of August in the year seven hundred and eighty three *ab urbe condita*. I, *Aquilifer* Cornelius Getorex, Acting Senior Legal Officer, *Legio* X *Fretensis*, take responsibility for this interview. It will be conducted in Greek and Aramaic.'

Cornelius folds his hands and rests his chin on them, looking across at the hooded figure seated with his back to the door.

'Why did you betray Ben Yusuf?'

Iscariot blows a raspberry. It's distorted by the hood, but still distinct.

'This isn't wise, Iscariot. You may think we're soft, but there's a reason we rule the world and you don't.'

He points at Lonuobo, and then Lucullus. Both nod in response. Lonuobo's voice is oily and sibilant; Cyler's dry and good-natured.

Lonuobo: I hear you've got a hot sister, Iscariot.

Iscariot: Fuck you.

Lucullus: Have you? Is she available?

Lonuobo: We'd have to talk to *Centurio* Irie Andrus of the Fourth Cohort and see. In Sepphoris, Galilee. Would you like that, Iscariot? We could all go up and see her.

Lucullus: We Romans like to share, you see.

Iscariot: You are sick people... from a sick fucking country.

Getorex: I understand you objected to your sister's choice of husband, Iscariot.

Iscariot: She's not married. She's whoring with him.

Lucullus: Whoring? No, no. You're wrong there. Whoring's a *community* service. She's only servicing *one* Roman.

Lonuobo [in Aramaic]: As I say, there's something we can do about that. If she's up for it.

Lucullus: What? Make a real whore out of her?

Iscariot: You people are *filthy*.

Lucullus: I'd be careful, flinging accusations like that around. You don't smell too flash yourself.

This goes on and around for a while, a dance of innuendo and shame and honour that involves Lonuobo attacking Iscariot's manhood and Lucullus sometimes endorsing his colleague's comments and sometimes pulling a face and saying things like *it can't be that bad*. It includes the luscious detail that when Iscariot and his brother caught their sister and Irie *he was giving it to her on the newspaper machine outside the Roman barracks*. Saleh can hear Iscariot's voice becoming more strained and angry as time passes; he keeps trying to curl his shackled hands up and away from the floor. Lonuobo scares Saleh, the way he pads around the room, moving close to Iscariot and yelling from within an inch of his ear without warning.

I'm glad he's on my side.

'You're not much use as a Zealot, you know. Couldn't even stop your sister fucking off with one of us,' Lonuobo says. Cyler grins and takes his opportunity.

'Followed, of course, by fucking one of us.'

Cornelius sails above the sneering, his voice low and even.

'What was your response to your sister leaving with Irie Andrus, Iscariot?'

'I tried to kill the fucking bastard.'

Lonuobo speaks in Aramaic; Saleh watches him spit the syllables across the room.

'Well, that didn't go very well. As I say, not much of a Zealot.'

Cyler giggles.

'Yah, looks like you're only capable of killing defenceless civilians—'

'I got the Legate's Tribune, you stupid fuckwit.'

Saleh sees Getorex smile and write CONFESSION 0838 hours across his notebook. Iscariot's head waggles back and forth inside his hood and his shackles clatter against the legs of the chair; Saleh wonders if he's angry that he's just implicated himself. He knows the Forensics unit were careful to prevent the details on the DNA they'd obtained from the grenade pin reaching the media.

Getorex holds his palm up in Cyler and Lonuobo's direction. He points at Aristotle.

'Tell me about your brother, Yehuda.'

Iscariot's head swivels about, searching for the source of this new and gentle voice.

'Who's this?'

'I'm Aristotle, Yehuda.'

Iscariot finds it within himself to laugh.

'That's not your real name.'

'Yeah it is mate. Tell me about your brother.'

'He helped me. He straightened me out.'

'How so?'

'I was turning into one of you—thieving and drinking and fucking.'

'That's pretty impressive. How did he convince you to go straight?'

'He helped me get a job. He taught me what Rome is doing to my country.'

'What job?'

'He got me work in a scrap yard. He wanted me to do an apprenticeship.'

'What as?'

'As a fitter. He's a fitter.'

'So am I. It's a good trade. Which scrap yard?'

'Kerioth's, in Sepphoris.'

Saleh sees Getorex write POSSIBLE ZEALOT FRONT—KERIOTH SCRAPWORKS, SEPPHORIS in his notebook. He notices that Iscariot's voice is almost wistful as he talks about his trade, his master and learning to work with his hands. Getorex takes down the names of associates and people who visit the scrapworks. Saleh watches as he covers a double page in his notebook with lines and boxes, drawing in names and relationships as Eugenides and Iscariot keep chatting away.

Iscariot's fatigue starts to show; he stumbles over things, and does not seem to notice when Getorex gently backtracks to ensure details are correct. Saleh props his chin in his hands and admires as Getorex colour codes and numbers the boxes. Three boxes are coloured green and marked with Z. Aristotle is smiling. Saleh is sure the smile is genuine, and that the two of them are actually talking.

That's quite a gift you've got there, Aristotle Eugenides.

Saleh is shocked when Getorex includes him in a three-way point that takes in Lonuobo and Rufus. Getorex crosses his hands in front of his chest and then mimes having his arms shackled at the elbow behind him. Rufus and Lonuobo vault their desks and are on Iscariot before he has any sense of the change in circumstances. They strip him naked, leaving only the hood. Once again Saleh is forced to trot in order to keep up with them as they drag Iscariot into the polished stone corridor and across into the *Camera*. Saleh notices for the first time that underneath the door into the *Camera* there's a rubber seal. They do not slow down when they drag his naked form across it, and for the first time, he cries out.

Saleh stands to one side as Rufus pins Iscariot's arms behind his back and threads a length of wood under his elbows. Lonuobo handcuffs his arms together and to the timber, and then adjusts the rack and pinion gear on the central table, making the slope notably more severe. The two men then lift Iscariot onto it. They join him and haul him upright.

'Stay,' Lonuobo orders in Aramaic.

He bounds down, light and graceful.

Rufus then makes a move towards the outsized power outlet on the wall. He throws the switch and twiddles the dial on the control box to maximum, producing a loud mains hum. For a terrifying moment Saleh thinks he's going to start prodding

Iscariot with the electrodes. Instead, he hands both to Lonuobo, who touches the ends together. They hiss and crackle. Saleh notices that Iscariot is struggling to keep his footing, a combination of knee pain and the table's steep slope.

Cornelius appears in the doorway.

'We're going to leave you for a while. You can think about telling us the truth while you're standing there. The floor is electrified, so if you slide off the end of that table, you'll dance like a madman until one of us notices and turns off the power. We can see you from where we are, but because you haven't been very helpful this morning, we may not be in any hurry.'

Saleh's mouth is drier than the Judaean desert, but he finds it in himself to speak. He speaks in Latin, hoping Iscariot has no sense of his desperation.

'Sir, he *has* to have a shot *now*.'

Cornelius raises a single eyebrow.

'Our medic wants to be kind to your knee, Iscariot.'

Lonuobo is shaking his head. Rufus looks at the floor. Cyler slouches against the S.P.Q.R. painted on the wall. Aristotle is behind Getorex, staring longingly up the corridor toward the toilets.

Saleh looks daggers at Lonuobo.

'*Primum non nocere,*' he hisses.

Getorex looks at the young physician's face. His skin is glazed over with a bronze sheen.

'Switch it off for the moment, Vero. Let him have his shot.'

Rufus makes a great production of stomping across the room and switching the power off. The hum dies away.

Saleh opens his medical kit and prepares a painkilling injection. His hands are shaking so much he can't draw it up at first. He stops, struggling to control his breath and tremor. Eventually—although not with the best technique—he gives the shot. Iscariot makes a small whining sound; Saleh can feel him trembling as he touches his skin. He closes his kit and steps back. He watches Rufus step towards the outlet again. The hum returns.

Cornelius stands beside the open door, pointing them all into the corridor. He closes it behind them.

Cyler sprints towards the monitor room.

'I break for coffee!' he yells.

Saleh tucks his medical kit under his arm. 'I've never needed to piss so bad in my life.'

Lonuobo joins Cyler in the monitor room. Within thirty seconds dance music flows down the corridor.

Cornelius arrives a few minutes later to see Lonuobo in charge of brewing coffee, Cyler sorting playback singers into orders of priority, Aristotle on his back on the floor stretching his thoracic spine, Vero taking orders for snacks. Cornelius writes him a pass to the Officer's Mess. Cyler is bouncing around the room. Soon everyone joins Cyler, and for five minutes or so Cornelius feasts his eyes on the discombobulating image of a post-interrogation party fuelled by nothing more than coffee and release.

Rufus returns with everyone's orders.

'Neat bit of bullshit about the electrified floor, sir,' he says.

Only Saleh is missing.

Cornelius pokes his head into the passageway. The medic is sitting on the floor outside, his head resting against the wall, his arms wrapped around his knees. One hand clasps the other's wrist. His medical kit is beside him. The eyes are shut, his unlined young face beautiful even under the artificial light. He seems to be mastering himself somehow.

'Saleh?'

He moves to stand. 'Sir?'

Cornelius holds his hand up and bends down before him,

sitting on his heels.

'I suspect that came as something of a shock.'

'Yes, sir, it did. I appreciate Lonuobo's distress but I'd appreciate it even more if he stopped telling me how to do my job.'

'I take it you're not from a military family?'

'My mother was High Priestess at the Temple of Cybele in Caesarea, sir. She was an inside woman for years, which meant an, ah, interesting childhood. I'm a temple child. I suspect I'm a bit unusual if you put together a profile.'

Cornelius extends his hand and pulls Saleh to his feet.

'So you had twenty mothers and no father?'

'All that, sir, yes. And learning to meditate while sweeping the temple steps as the sun rose, scraping the drunks and druggies up off the footpath and giving them a place to dry out overnight on Festival days, being seduced by a thirty-year-old initiate at sixteen.'

'A few men round here would be jealous of that story.'

'Don't worry, sir, they are.'

Cornelius guides him into the monitor room.

'If he needs medical care, I'll always override Lonuobo and Vero.'

'It didn't look like that at first, sir. I started to panic.'

'I'm trying to make Iscariot think that good treatment is conditional on good behaviour.'

'That's not the way medicine works, sir.'

'I know that. There's no electricity in that floor, either. It's the appearance that counts.'

Lonuobo welcomes them with a cafetière in his hand. Rufus is sitting on what had been Cyler's overnight table stuffing his face with bread and cheese. He hands some to Saleh. Cyler flicks through the various CCTV feeds, settling on the *Camera*. He brings Iscariot up on the main screen.

'How long are we going to leave him there, sir? If he falls off and nothing happens to him, we may lose any advantage we've gained.'

Cornelius joins Cyler behind his desk and watches Iscariot tremble on the screen, his fingers flicking behind his back as he struggles to retain his posture.

'Just half-an-hour; we've got a confession already, and I'm pretty sure I've got the beginnings of some good intel on Zealots in Galilee; Lonuobo thinks so, too. He's going to do some work on what we've got out of Iscariot so far and see where it leads. There's been a lot of chatter.'

Cyler is slicing sausage now. 'They *really* hate the Dea Tacita Centre.'

'If I can get to the bottom of the Ben Yusuf business with the water torture, I'll be very happy. I'll ask Pilate to defer the death sentence at trial so we can exploit him properly. Today is just the initial break.'

Cyler has a mouthful of sausage. 'They're really rushing these two matters through, sir.'

Cornelius puts his coffee down; 'Passover this Friday,' he says. 'There's some religious reason why Ben Yusuf in particular has to be tried before Passover. I have had it explained to me but it's over my head.'

'He tried to destroy their Temple, sir,' says Saleh. 'Passover is an important festival, and he made the sacred place unclean. Of course they want him dealt with before it begins. They can start their *festa* in good conscience, then.'

There is an authoritative tone in the medic's voice that catches Cornelius unawares.

'Of course,' he says. 'If you want to know about religion, ask someone religious. Thanks for that, Saleh.'

Saleh continues, smiling. 'They'll be out in force on Thursday buying all the bits for it, too—the lamb without blemish they have to sacrifice. The priests kill it, drain it and the family cooks it. It's about the only time they hit the piss—four glasses of wine each, men and women alike, and close together, too. It's a big deal.'

Rufus has never been in Jerusalem for Passover; all this is new to him. Saleh can hear the tone of admiration in his voice. 'Apparently there's going to be two and a half million people in Jerusalem by Tuesday. Normally there's five hundred thousand tops.'

'Why we've got no leave after then,' Cyler says mournfully.

Cornelius looks at the screen, and then at his watch.

'We go back inside in twenty minutes.'

Mirella woke with a start, a confused dream chasing itself away. Sun streamed through the slit window to one side of the bed and crossed her body like tiger stripes. She craned her neck so she could see his wall clock; it was just before ten in the morning. The room smelt strongly of sex mixed with his aftershave. *It's a good combination*, she thought. She leaned out of bed, collecting used condoms off the floor with one hand. The sunlight struck the gold and silver disks on the Standard now, bathing the room in crepuscular light.

She stood up, stretching, luxuriating in the light, watching it touch her skin and scatter; she turned slowly on the spot, in wonder. The Eagle on top of it seemed to be watching her; she made the fig sign at it: *stay away, nasty men's business.* She crouched down, opening one of his bedside drawers; her fingers flicked through undies and military issue vests until she found a faded cotton shirt at the bottom.

She binned the condoms and used his sink to wash her smalls, hanging them over the edge to dry. *Oh Cornelius, I'm making your quarters all girly.* His shirt—with its faint smell of him—came almost to her knees. She peeled it off and attended to herself, sitting in his bath and using his scented oil and bath tools to scrape herself clean of the night. All his grooming utensils were spotless, as though he'd bought them the day before. She determined to leave them the way she found them, and then dried his bathroom floor as well.

She went to his bookshelf, hoping for something other than law, some poetry or novels or *Milesian Tales*, perhaps. No luck. She did find an ancient physics textbook with pencilled annotations in the margins and a bilingual dictionary, *Latina–Cymraeg, Cymraeg–Latina.*

Do you actually, you know, read for pleasure, Cornelius?

She flicked through the dictionary, looking at the Celtic words and shaking her head. *There must be some system for pronouncing that.* At something of a loss and wanting him badly now, she went into his kitchen and raided the fridge. She was polishing off some ciabatta with oil and pesto and two of his fresh figs when she saw a fat photo album on the shelf where you'd normally expect to find cookbooks. She washed her hands and took it down. In the process, a large sheet of folded paper fell out onto the floor; she picked it up and opened it out on the benchtop.

It was a child's map of the Roman Empire—out of date now, they'd conquered more since it was issued—lovingly coloured in and its provinces labelled in a careful hand, by someone with beautiful handwriting. His name was in the top right hand corner, *Cornelius Getorex, Fourth Year*. A stamp at the bottom revealed he'd received a prize for handing in such a neat piece of work. His teacher's comments were in an adult version of the same gorgeous hand.

She felt intrusive, going through his things like this, but the little boy's map was touching in its own way, if only because he'd kept it for so long, and looking at his photographs was a fair substitute for looking at him.

She opened the photo album. The first half dozen pages were taken up with a series of black-and-white images of a Celtic chieftain in plaid. He was sitting or standing, very still, his hair stiffened with some sort of waxy fixative, his face and exposed shoulder covered in intricate spiral tattoos. Some of the images showed him with a staff in his hand. In three others, a curly-headed Roman soldier in the black frock coat with silver buttons worn in Julius Caesar's time stood next to the Celt, rifle musket and ramrod in one hand. The Roman was always smiling. She suspected the photographer was the soldier featured; the images that included him were often blurry, or showed the metal clamp behind the Celt's head. Someone with less skill was manipulating the shutter. She thought he was likely the Legion's official photographer to have access to such good film stock: the images of the chieftain by himself were startling, beautiful but also disturbing. The gaze behind the lens was not an affectionate one. The word *Brittunculus* was written in a Roman's spidery hand along the white margin of one image.

Not very nice, whoever wrote that.

Underneath the last photograph was a label in Cornelius's handwriting: 'My Great-Grandfather.'

She remembered her school history lessons. Roman guns cut down the Gauls. The bullets rifled—reputedly, Caesar developed this innovation himself—but were soft lead and blew huge holes in their targets. If a warrior survived the impact and did not bleed to death, the wound almost always got infected. The only effective treatment was amputation. She'd read stories of field Æsculapions filled with piles of legs and arms.

The Britons had watched their Gallic kindred defeated and enslaved, and they learnt. Thousands of screaming Celtic warriors would descend on the Roman enemy at full tilt and before the legionaries had time to reload, forcing them to scatter or besting them in hand-to-hand combat. She remembered black-and-white interview footage of an elderly Roman veteran of the British Conquest from high school.

'There are people who say they've heard the Celtic Cry and say they ain't been scared by it. Well, in that case I'm here to say they ain't heard a real one, because it made much braver men than me piss their pants.'

Caesar—as he always did—had an answer. Through force of will he trained his men to hold the line, their bayonets fixed. Instead of thrusting the blade straight ahead, they thrust it to the right, evading the Britons' shields and cutting them down. It took nerve—each man depended on his neighbour killing the Celt coming at *him*—but it worked. Caesar took Britannia, too.

She turned the page. After the chieftain, the album told her of Cornelius's life. She saw him in his school uniform in front of the Roman school in Camulodunum, with his parents and siblings. *One of four, Cornelius, big tribe you've got there.* There was a photograph of him as a grinning child—large gap in his teeth—holding the coloured-in map. There were ribbons for sporting achievement, a prize for marksmanship, various large and hairy dogs, a 10 × 8 of his passing-out parade and lots of Britannia's green fields. One picture showed him on the mouth of a winding, shimmering river with what looked like dock buildings in the background. Boats plied their trade to and fro across the river; the water was silver. She ran her fingers around the edge of the image.

How did your eyes ever adjust to the desert, Cornelius, after all that lovely green? Pinned to one page was his *licentia* testamur, to another his certificate of Roman citizenship, to another again his military oath with his flowing signature underneath. After that, there were several photographs of a very trim Cornelius in what looked like his great-grandfather's Celtic finery—the plaid was rich and dark, various lighter and darker-green squares—beside a young woman with curly black hair and the palest skin Mirella had ever seen. An older woman was tying their hands together with an embroidered scarf.

Handfast with Bella, a year and a day, he'd written underneath.

On the next page he was holding a ginger-haired baby girl in front of what looked like the Temple of the Divine Julius in Camulodunum, grinning hugely. *On the birth of my beautiful daughter, Ciara*, the note said. Mirella thought *maybe he joined up to divorce her, they can do that*, but then realised the images were out of sequence if so. It seemed Ciara was born while he was still studying, and long after he'd enlisted.

That 'year and a day' thing means something. Maybe she was his concubine, just with a short contract.

There were more shots—very recent ones, all in colour—of the little girl and the black-haired mother. It seemed the girl was about nine, now. There was an ornate wedding picture—a Roman wedding, with its orange silk gown—near the end. Bella was with a blond legionary in mess dress. Finally, there was a card from Ciara, written to her father.

Dear Pater, today at school we made sweets for Matres *and for* Magna Mater, *I was going to send you some except I ate them, when are you coming to visit us next?*

She ran her fingers across the card, marvelling at the child's grave beauty in the image on the opposite page.

I want this man, in my bed but also in my life.

She felt a sharp twinge in her belly and her fingers went to her crotch. She drew them up in front of her face. She was bleeding heavily; the sex had brought her on two days early.

Shit. I hope he doesn't mind a nice bloody one.

When Lonuobo and Rufus turn off the power, sweep Iscariot onto his back and then tilt the table rapidly in the opposite direction, their prisoner whimpers. Lonuobo grabs the bottom of the hood under his chin and snaps his head to one side.

'Real brave now, aren't we?' he spits, in Aramaic. Cornelius does not stop him; his face is impassive.

'Hook him up, Saleh, and read off his vital signs.'

'Yes, sir.'

Saleh clips a pulse oximeter to Iscariot's left forefinger and then attaches it to the portable medical monitor that Aristotle wheels in from the infirmary. He runs cables underneath the table and plugs them into the regular socket. This means crawling on his hands and knees for a moment; he hears Lonuobo snigger softly. He stands up as Vero tightens the restraints around Iscariot's wrists and ankles, pinning his arms above his head. Lonuobo fills the watering-can in the small sink on one side of the painted S.P.Q.R. on the wall. Cornelius is standing in the doorway, blocking the light from the corridor. His shadow falls across Iscariot. Saleh clutches his medical kit to his chest as Cornelius flicks a switch; the circle of light in the ceiling paints itself in. For the first time in his life, he feels shamed and shocked by the naked human form, splayed and pinned like this. He crouches down, realising that of necessity he will be beside Lonuobo.

The rest of the group assume their positions around the *Camera*. Cyler and Aristotle sit at two of the desks, while Lonuobo holds the floral watering-can and Rufus a heavy towel. Cornelius stands over Iscariot, his hands clasped behind his back. Once again, he turns to face the CCTV, announcing his business in Latin. This time it includes, after the language statement, the line *the method used will be the water torture.*

He looks at Saleh, then across at the medical monitor.

'For the record, his vitals, please.'

'Temperature normal; pulse 72; blood pressure 115 over 75; oxygen saturation 98 per cent.' He raises his voice. 'Get that last number below 85 and he's at risk of temporary asphyxiation. This will mean waiting for a few minutes while I bring him up again.'

Cornelius nods, looking hard at Saleh. The medic seems convinced, now, part of the process.

'We do fifteen on, then fifteen off, and if he isn't forthcoming after that, we do thirty on, thirty off.'

Lonuobo and Rufus both nod. Cornelius raps the end of the table three times, attracting Iscariot's attention. The hood twitches.

'What we are about to do to you is very unpleasant. No doubt, given your history, you have heard of it. You can avoid this by answering two simple questions for me. First, I want to know why you betrayed Ben Yusuf into Roman hands, and second, I want to know whether he has assisted you in any of your terrorist attacks. Just those two questions, Iscariot. Answer them for me, and you can go back to your cell and sleep.'

For all that he is trembling with pain and fear, Iscariot's answer is distinct.

'Fuck off, *Romoi.* Just fuck off.'

Rufus—once again with surpassing swiftness—pulls the hood up, clapping a large piece of cloth over Iscariot's mouth. He flicks the hood onto the floor. For a moment or so, they all see Iscariot's eyes. He blinks in the hard light. His expression is still one of defiance rather than abject terror. Rufus pulls the towel over his face. Lonuobo balances the watering-can in his hands, holding it about eighteen inches above.

'Enjoy the music, sunshine,' he says as he begins to pour.

Saleh wants to reach out and offer comfort as the ten-second point passes—Cornelius counts, watching the clock—and

Iscariot begins to struggle, his hands contorting.

'Oxygen saturation ninety per cent,' he says.

Cornelius holds his hand up; both torturers step back from their work, taking the towel with them. At this point, Saleh notices that there is a channel cut into the stone under the table to drain the water away.

They think of everything.

Iscariot's head bounces up and he takes in huge, gasping breaths.

'Why did you betray Ben Yusuf, Iscariot?'

Lonuobo looks towards his senior officer, the blue watering-can cradled in his hands like an infant. Cornelius counts down the fifteen seconds' relief.

'Oxygen saturation back to ninety-five per cent,' Saleh says.

'Put him under again.'

This time, Lonuobo deliberately floods the already saturated towel with a higher volume of water. Saleh watches him smile. At one point he tucks the watering-can under one arm and leans over the table as he pours so that he can grab his crotch with the other hand. Saleh suspects this detail has gone unnoticed by the others. Lonuobo's breath swirls around Saleh's head; he smells of peppermint and cocoa butter and aftershave.

'Oxygen saturation eighty-nine per cent.'

Iscariot tries to flick his body to one side; Vero uses his hands to hold him still, pinning the towel to the table on either side of his head as Lonuobo pours. This time Iscariot's distress is uncontrolled; his hands contort into claws.

'Oxygen saturation eighty-four per cent.'

Cornelius holds his hand up; once more the two men step back, allowing Iscariot to breathe. Great gouts of water bubble out of his mouth; it runs backwards over his cheeks and forehead. Saleh dries his left arm to prevent water getting into the medical equipment. For the briefest moment, he makes eye contact.

'You're too decent for this job, *Medice*,' Iscariot gasps.

Saleh looks at Lonuobo, who grins. His hand shoots across the table and grabs Iscariot's ear, twisting it. Iscariot screams with pain and shock.

'We'll stop this as soon as you answer our questions. There's only two. You choose.'

'I think he's trying to say something useful,' Aristotle says.

'I thought that too,' says Cyler from his spot by the painted lettering.

'Only a rude comment about our redoubtable medic,' says Lonuobo.

Rufus looks up at Cornelius, his fingers hooked under the towel, asking with his eyes whether the table should be righted and its prisoner released to answer further questions.

'Oxygen saturation back to ninety per cent,' Saleh says.

Cornelius purses his lips as the seconds pass, indecisive for a moment.

'Put him under again, gentlemen. Thirty seconds.'

Gaius Crispus trots along to the cells, mug and yellow legal pad in hand. Cornelius asked him yesterday to put in an appearance at 1100 hours; he doubts he'll be needed, but his curiosity is piqued by the thought that they've captured a serious, proper terrorist. He stops outside the *Camera*, draining the dregs of his coffee. He's been waiting for fifteen minutes or so when he hears the blurred sound of whoops and cheers from inside.

Supposed to be soundproof, that.

The door to the *Camera* flies open. He watches as two men sprint towards the infirmary pushing a medical monitor on wheels before them, while two others—with some ferocity—haul the prisoner by the hands up the corridor. He sees one man plant his foot in the middle of Iscariot's back, propelling him into his cell. Others clap their hands with childish glee, and he notices that Lonuobo's fly is unbuttoned. Everyone is wet to a greater or lesser degree, even Getorex; he's last out, with a smouldering grin on his face. Crispus watches as he throws his head back and lets fly with the weird banshee cry of the Celts. The noise rises and seems to fill the air, blocking out even the potential for any other sound.

He'd seen a documentary last year that reckoned—done properly—that was the loudest sound capable of production by the human vocal cords.

I can believe it.

Getorex turns to face him. Mercifully, he brings the wail to a halt.

'I do love a good conspiracy, Gaius,' he says.

He re-establishes a grip on his subordinates, stopping them from caroming around the cells and corridors and ordering them upstairs to the Law Room.

'You too, Gaius, you'll appreciate this.'

Crispus raises his eyebrows. He's never seen Getorex do anything remotely Celtic *in his life*... apart, of course, from parading around in red hair and tumbling Roman women into bed. *We do like our gingers.* In fact, he's never seen Getorex so much as raise his voice.

He follows the rest of them upstairs to the Law Room, his boots thumping on the stone.

Cornelius turns to face Crispus. The *Aquilifer* is standing in front of Viera's desk; the rest of the group are scattered around the room. Cyler Lucullus—who looks most drained of all of them—is propped against the wall underneath the shelves of forms and precedents, his legs stretched out in front of him.

Lonuobo has finally buttoned his fly.

'There's some sort of internal Zealot shit fight going on. Caiaphas paid Iscariot to betray Ben Yusuf to us,' says Getorex. 'Thirty Tyrian shekels for his trouble.'

'Temple money,' says Crispus, a look of wonder spreading over his face. 'That's their special Temple money.'

'The *scrip*, sir?' asks Cyler.

'Yes,' says Lonuobo.

Crispus is stunned. He looks at Cornelius with a degree of respect and then strides across the room to shake his hand.

'Well done. What a great piece of intel.'

'He inhaled most of the Antonia *frigidarium* before he was willing to share, mind you, but we think it was worth the wait.'

'What a prize little shit. Caiaphas financing terrorism. Who knew.'

'It gets better, too. Caiaphas contacted Iscariot and his Zealot chums before the Valentina assassination, suggesting the Dea Tacita Centre as a suitable target, one that, ah,' he pauses, looking through his notes and finding the right page, 'everyone in Judaea could agree on.'

'What about the big attack last year?'

Lonuobo stirs at this. 'He was adamant that was just him and his Zealot friends, without any help from Caiaphas.'

'You wouldn't need input from Caiaphas, though,' says Aristotle. 'That's the sort of advice you only need to hear once.'

Rufus shakes his head, looking at Cornelius. 'Why only thirty pieces, sir?'

Crispus fiddles around in the webbing at his waist, looking for something. 'There's a little more to it than that,' he says. Eventually he pulls a coin from his pocket, flicking it neatly towards Rufus and Aristotle, who are sitting next to each other. The former catches it, sweeping his fingers downwards. He holds it up in front of his eyes, watching it glitter.

'I take your point, sir. If you wanted to start defacing coins of the realm, this would be a serious temptation.' He hands the coin to Aristotle, who also admires it.

'Apart from that, the exchange rate in the Temple is four to one, thanks to some clever fixing. Melting them down will net you a slightly better return, but only slightly.'

'About four months' wages, then, for an unskilled enlisted man,' says Saleh. 'It still doesn't seem like very much money to me.'

'Stop thinking like a Roman and start thinking like a Judaean,' says Cornelius, wheeling out the commercial skills that are part and parcel of his job as *Aquilifer*. 'One of the few perks attached to service in this miserable bloody province is the purchasing power of the *denarius*. Everything's cheap here. Go to Southern Gaul or anywhere in Italy or—even worse, Rome—and you'll soon see how much your money doesn't buy.'

He looks at Cyler. 'I'm tempted to order you to get some sleep, Lucullus, but I suspect that would be futile. I imagine you'd like a night pass.'

Cyler nods, smiling his crooked-teeth smile.

'Yes, sir, very much so, sir.'

'You've earned it. You will need to report back by zero six hundred hours, however. If you go early... I'm sure I don't need to say any more.'

Cyler—despite his brain being fuzzy and slow—begins to think about Laia, a Greek Quarter woman he likes and tries to see every month or so. If he calls early, he'll get her for a good long stint.

'In the meantime, I'll report to Pilate. Crispus, once again, I'd appreciate your views.'

'Gladly given, *Aquilifer*.'

'We may yet see the first recorded instance of a Roman

Procurator making a Procurator-shaped hole in the ceiling.'

Crispus watches as Getorex catches Lonuobo's arm before he can leave the Law Room with the others.

'I want a word with you, Lonuobo.'

'Yes, sir.'

Getorex phrases his comments with care.

'You were aroused in there, yes?'

Lonuobo nods. If he were white, he'd be blushing. He looks down.

'May I remind you that all interviews, including Form 23 interrogations, are recorded, and that any Roman citizen with standing may view them while a matter is before the courts.'

'Yes, sir, I know.'

'That includes members of the press, many of whom are Roman citizens.'

'I'm sorry, sir.'

'I want the terrorism in Judaea to end as much as anyone, Lonuobo. I don't want any more innocent people to die like Zipporah died. And you can play a part in that, with your language skills.'

Lonuobo looks at him.

'For that to happen, we need to be better than the people we fight. Sticking your hand down your trousers while you're subjecting someone to the water torture is not the way to do it.'

'No, sir, I know. I'm sorry, sir.'

'There are people of both sexes and of indeterminate sex in the Greek Quarter who will do that sort of thing for you, if that's what you like. I'm sure you're aware of this fact.'

'Yes, sir, I am.'

'Who pays your wages, Lonuobo?'

'The Senate and People of Rome, sir.'

'Exactly. And remember your oath. You owe the Empire service with honour.'

Crispus watched Lonuobo leave, chastened. He marvelled at the easy way Cornelius bore the mantle of authority. Sending the ranker with the crooked smile to the Greek Quarter was a masterstroke, as was reproving the over-enthusiastic Centurion without charging him. He wished for that sort of respect on an almost daily basis; he was aware much of the respect that came *his* way did so only because in days gone by, senators' sons once formed the core of the senior officers in a legion. They could still leave after only three or four years and head into politics, just like the old days, but it wasn't quite the same.

The big Celt whose old man earned his citizenship as an auxiliary is a better Roman than I am.

He turned to Cornelius.

'There's more where that came from, surely?'

'We've not even scratched the surface of what he knows about Zealotry in this province.'

'Isn't it worth going at him again this afternoon? He'll be tired and weak.'

'He hasn't been tried yet, Gaius.'

'Yes, quite,' he paused. 'I do wonder what he knows, that's all.'

He'd collapsed onto his hands and good knee when one of them kicked him in the back, vomiting water and bile everywhere, then pissing himself. He'd screamed with pain for two or three minutes as his bad knee bent then straightened. He heard sneering laughter coming from the door. Now he was too tired and sore to move away from his own mess. At some point—after he'd shivered on the floor of his cell for twenty minutes or so—the medic and a nurse came to check his vitals. A third legionary joined the two medical men, pouring warm water over his naked form and mopping the floor with sharp-smelling disinfectant. He could hear the three of them conferring quietly in Latin, a language of which he spoke little. At one point, Saleh bent down and shone a torch into each of his eyes and pulled his mouth open, looking down his throat.

'There's a clean tunic on your bed,' he said. 'You should get on your bunk.'

Once again he was impressed at the gentleness of the medic's voice; he caught himself snivelling as Saleh's nimble fingers took his pulse and stroked his hair away from his forehead. Saleh stood up; Iscariot could hear the crisp snick of metal on metal as he stowed the torch in his medical kit.

The cleaner used the handle of his mop to turn Iscariot over, cleaning where he'd been lying. The strings flicked the side of his face. Saleh did not attempt to make him stand, instead draping a blanket over him where he lay; it was made of a strange, textured material.

Probably won't support my weight if I try to top myself with it.

They'd got a lot from him: his dealings with Caiaphas, the name of a close associate, the broad structure of Kerioth Scrapworks, a confession. He knew, now, that they would kill him, probably in the arena in Caesarea before a baying Roman crowd, possibly with something creative added. He found he didn't care very much about Caiaphas.

PART V

They renounce legal marriages and fill their populous institutions in cities and villages with celibate people, useless either for war or for any service to the State; but gradually growing from the time of Arcadius to the present day they have appropriated the greater part of the earth, and on the pretext of sharing all with the poor they have, so to speak, reduced all to poverty.

— Zosimus,
the last pagan historian of antiquity, AD 498.

Saul sees the Samaritan woman standing at the desk, waiting for the ancient porter-cum-innkeeper to retrieve her key. He takes it from the row of hooks behind him, slowly, painfully, handing it to her. The driver taps Saul on the shoulder from behind.

'We go now,' he says. 'You needs you rest.'

Saul ignores the old Samaritan, watching the woman sweep her messy hair up on top of her head and draw her scarf over it. She's still wearing the blue dress under her black gown, and her smeared make-up has gathered a layer of blond dust. She follows the two of them up the creaking stairs, key in hand.

'I get my things,' she says to the driver. 'We go to the baths, then.'

Saul stands in the doorway to the room he'll be sharing with the old man, watching her collect a small trunk bound with straps. She drags it behind her while Saul watches. He notices the uneven floorboards, how they're rotting in places, and wonders what will happen when he lies on the bed. The room is large enough, with a big green copper bath to one side, but the rug is threadbare and when he moves across to open the shutters he notices that the slats are caked with grime. Dust has blended with the filth and his fingers come away black. He looks into the bath. There's a dead rat in there, curled to one side as though sleeping. Ants are eating its tail and the bone is exposed.

The Samaritan woman looks at him from the doorway.

'Go to baths in the town,' she says. 'Don't wash here.'

She unbuckles her trunk and reaches into it, removing a glass bottle. She stands over the bed and shakes it before removing the stopper; Saul can smell concentrated cedar oil. It's at that moment he realises the bed is double.

'You need to wash,' Saul says, looking at the old man.

'I sleep on the floor,' he says.

As Saul watches, he unrolls a blanket and strips off his cloak. He bends with surprising suppleness and stretches out on the floor, his head on the bulkiest part of the cloak. Saul goes to pass him one of the pillows, but not before the woman has splashed it with the oil.

'Are the fleas here that bad?' Saul asks.

She looks at him.

'What you think, rich Jewboy? Course they bad. This place a hole, but not suspicious.'

Saul nods, watching her drag her trunk across the floorboards to the room next door. She hooks the big metal key around her wrist. Saul gathers up a change of clothes and a towel, following her downstairs. They stand outside the front entrance for a moment, and Saul runs his hand over the door's peeling paint. Before they set off for the baths, he chances to look over towards the inn's stables, seeing the two donkeys and the cart under the cool of the awning. He winces, thinking of what's under the driver's seat.

There's been a dust storm through the town in the last couple of days; everything is coated with fine ochre sand, even the Roman

MRAP parked in the middle of what passes for a square. Half-a-dozen little boys kick a ball around under the eyes of a legionary sitting in the turret, his hands crossed over a mounted 50-calibre machine gun. Saul notices that he's draped oilcloth across the belt feed to keep the sand out. At one point the ball floats into his field of vision; he catches it deftly and flicks it back at the boys.

'Romane, you come play with us?'

The boy has the ball tucked under his arm and is looking up at the soldier, who waggles his head slowly.

'What that mean?' the boy asks in broken Greek.

'It means he'd like to but can't,' says one of the other boys, in Aramaic.

Saul and the woman circle the MRAP and cross the square as the sun dips below the horizon, orange light crisscrossing the sky and illuminating the dark bases of clouds on the eastern border. Over there, he knows, is Persia, and refugees sit in makeshift tents beside Roman fortifications with their stone towers, electric wiring and anti-personnel mines. Sometimes people fleeing the instability cannot read the CURO! TERRA MINAE signs and blow their legs off attempting to cross illegally. He's seen the long queues as they wait to cross at official gates, watched as Roman soldiers send back the old and infirm and bring in the young—single, families, children—to be screened for contagious diseases, vaccinated, scrubbed within an inch of their lives and issued with non-citizen identity cards. Every now and again they shoot one they consider an infiltrator or spy. Many, he knows, are fugitive slaves. The Romans do not care, and despite repeated requests that escaped slaves be returned to their Persian owners, the Roman Senate's response has always been a flat 'no'. You do what you want on your property, they say, and we'll do what we want on ours. Beyond that initial burst of health and hygiene, the Roman state does nothing for them, but it doesn't stop them coming. They pour into the open maw of factories and mines; some of the good-looking ones turn to sex work, while others go 'in service'. Saul squints up at the towering purple clouds, expecting rain, wondering what colour the town is when it's sluiced free of dirt.

The baths are Roman, not Greek, and mixed. The different sections are undecorated but clean, kept in good working order. It's late, and they're nearly empty.

'You only got an hour,' says one of the attendants, 'then we have to chuck you out and clean up.'

Saul notices that his accent is Samaritan. There are quite a few soldiers inside still, chattering boisterously. They look slyly at the Samaritan woman, but she doesn't notice. Saul sets about cleaning the day's dust off his body and out of his hair, forgetting the woman for the moment.

It's when he goes into the frigidarium to cool off and swim for a bit that he sees her again, talking amiably to one of the soldiers. The man has a distinctive beaky face but it still takes Saul a moment or two—absent the uniform—to realise that it's Clodius from the checkpoint. He watches the woman pull herself out of the water and walk towards the changing rooms. Clodius follows her and says something to her. She spins and slaps him. Saul climbs up the stairs and drips his way across the tiles, expecting that he might have to go to her aid. He stops outside the changing rooms, hearing Clodius and the woman talking in Greek, their tone conversational. He waits a moment before joining them, pointedly dressing nearby. Clodius does not look at him.

'It was nice,' Clodius is saying. 'I'd like to do it again.'

She nods, letting him rest his hand on her neck and kiss her lips.

'I've got some leave coming up,' he adds. 'I was thinking of going to Cyprus or Malta. Be nice to have a woman with me. I'll pay for everything, of course.'

She nods again; his face is very close to hers. At one point Saul hears the words 'concubinage contract' and realises that Clodius is suggesting one of the myriad Roman legal arrangements designed to allow sexual activity while preserving the woman's honour.

When they leave, Clodius moves to follow them and she turns and slaps him again. Saul watches her spit on the ground at his feet. He waggles his head from side to side and grins at her. Saul waits for her and they walk up the cardo to the inn, Clodius following them. When they arrive, Clodius follows her into her room.

Saul steps around the sleeping old man and stretches out on the bed in his clean clothes, feeling the chill of the night settle on him as he stares at the ceiling and inhales cedar oil. There's a non-working ceiling fan, its blades blackened at the leading edge. The power fails at one point; he notices that the only light from outside comes from the Roman castrum, harsh and white, mounted on MRAPs or surrounding the barracks. He can hear Clodius and the woman speaking through the thin wall, their voices still conversational. He feels conflicted, wanting to go next door and protect her but also remembering how she held the door open for him and the way he smiled as she did so. It's like one of their plays, Saul thinks, the demanding man and the resisting woman, until her will is overborne. He begins to doze off and only wakes again when he hears her screaming. He leaps out of bed but his feet are asleep and he finishes up sprawled flat beside the tub with the dead rat in it. He braces his hands palm down against the floor, feeling grit beneath his fingers, still listening.

'Go back to bed, sonny,' says the old man. 'She all right.'

Saul turns his head to face the voice in the dark, seeing moonlight from the shutters crisscross the old man's wizened figure. One of the screams terminates in a high-pitched giggle, and he hears Clodius join in. He straightens up, sitting on the edge of the bed, looking towards the room next door. There's a long silence, followed by gentle conversation and more giggling, then low moans from both of them. Saul stretches out on his back and stares at the ceiling once more. Just before he drifts irrevocably into unconsciousness, he hears booted feet on the stairs outside in the hall followed by the crunch of gravel below his shuttered window.

A little later, it begins to rain.

Cyler trotted back down to the monitor room after he'd made arrangements for the afternoon; he needed to return the borrowed music and children's shows he'd used to the library. On a whim—as he walked past—he slid the hatch to Ben Yusuf's cell open and looked in on him. He was lying on his bunk, reading, one hand tucked under his head. Cyler squinted, but couldn't make out the title of the book. There were more books on the floor, along with a newspaper and an empty, upturned cardboard box.

Ben Yusuf looked up at Cyler, put the book he was reading to one side with some haste and stood up, like a soldier at morning inspection. His bunk was neatly made; the blanket pulled tight and tucked in.

Wonder if you can bounce a sestertius off it?

'Sir, would I be able to request some more reading material? I'm onto my last book.'

Cyler pressed his fob against the lock and stepped into the cell. It snapped into place behind him, echoing down the corridor. Ben Yusuf had spoken in Latin, which piqued his interest.

'What are you reading?'

Ben Yusuf held the book up in front of his face, so that Cyler could read the spine.

'*The Aeneid*. Is it in Latin?'

'It's a parallel edition. My Latin isn't good enough by itself, although it's getting better. Dido's just killed herself with his sword.'

Cyler smiled. 'Every Roman kid reads that book at school. You're kind of forced to. It's an act of rebellion *not* to read it. I didn't like it at school, but I read it after I joined the army and enjoyed it then.'

Ben Yusuf gathered up the books he'd already read and fetched the cardboard box, packing it and handing it to Cyler. There was poetry in both Latin and Greek, with the Latin in parallel editions; an anatomy textbook; several works of contemporary Greek fiction; a collection of salty *Milesian tales*.

Now this is a man with wide-ranging tastes.

'Some more, please. Books,' Ben Yusuf said in Greek. He mimed turning the pages.

Cyler snapped out of his reverie, looking hard at Ben Yusuf. 'I'll get you some books from the main library.'

Ben Yusuf watched him go; this was the one who'd spent most of last night playing loud music at some prisoner or another. So loud, in fact, that the edges of it had seeped into Ben Yusuf's cell. He suspected it would be his turn to encounter something similar from a different legionary tonight.

Probably the one with astonishing violet eyes, what's his name, Cassius, that's it.

Cassius had fetched him from his cell for his interview with the lawyer and returned him afterwards. He also took him to the baths each afternoon and stood over him while he cleaned himself. Ben Yusuf tried to control his shame; for them, he knew, this was social and natural. On his first visit, he'd fumbled around like a fool with the strange Roman bathing equipment.

'Do you want soap, like a Celt, or scented oil, like a Roman?' Cassius asked. 'Because you don't appear to know what you're doing.'

He'd then stepped forward and—in a series of swift, coordinated movements—showed Ben Yusuf how to manipulate the hooked scraper over his body and reach the difficult spots.

'This is a *strigil*. You clean it up afterwards like so.'

Ben Yusuf nodded, following the soldier's instructions and looking around at the men of the legion in their home environment, his skin reddening. He could not get used to their nudity or—now he understood some Latin—their foul language. The floating noun, verb, and adjective: 'fuck'.

'It's a barracks,' said Cassius by way of explanation, watching his discomfort, 'in a province where getting a fuck for love, not money, is hard, especially for enlisted men.'

He noticed that Cassius had not used words like *amor* or *eros*—their language drew fine distinctions when it came to the emotions—but *affectio*. Cassius's eyes narrowed. 'And enjoy this while it lasts, while you're still a suspect, and not a prisoner.'

After the first bath, Cassius had stood in the doorway to Ben Yusuf's cell looking at him with an openly lecherous expression on his face, licking his lips. Ben Yusuf backed away, his hands up in front of him.

'It's all right,' he'd said. 'I'm not going to do anything more than look at you. The Code forbids it.'

'Thank you, sir.'

'Even if you wanted it, I couldn't give it to you. But I do like to look at you.'

Cyler thumped upstairs, oddly invigorated. He emptied the contents of the cardboard box onto a trolley marked *shelving* and wandered up and down the stacks, pulling things off at random. He focused on Greek-language editions of Roman books or Greek fiction, taking care to replicate the previous box's omnivorous quality. He did make a point of selecting Sulpicia Calla's biography of Sarius Roscius, *The Man Who Took Us to the Movies: the Father of Roman Cinema.* It was in Latin, but richly illustrated.

He can figure it out.

Ben Yusuf took the cardboard box from Cyler with real gratitude, picking out the biography of the film director. On the cover was a selection of frames—all black and white; the film in question came out fifty-five years ago—from the most famous long take in Roman cinema. Two children—a preteen girl in a tatty robe and a smaller boy in a set of barbarian trews—ran through fields of grain as the railway came to their village for the first time. The children's heads poked up from within the long grass as the undercarriage roared past. Their eyes were enormous with wonder, delight and fear.

Ben Yusuf flicked through the pages. Roscius had a special talent for filming children, that much was clear: in another sequence, a laughing group ran through narrow streets, stopping to sluice themselves off under a public water pump and then sprinting along the banks of the Tiber, joining in a religious procession. They, too, had huge dark eyes—it seemed to be a recurring motif. Of course, there were the inevitable song-and-dance sequences, and as the book progressed, some of these were in colour. At first they were tailored to male tastes; women danced to music while men watched. As society changed, so did the dances. Men and women danced together. The settings became more opulent, the images more joyous.

In the last sequence in the book, a man sat outside in the sunshine on an elevated mound of earth, his hands clasped loosely around his knees, singing his heart out for a woman who had clearly just turned sixteen. She stood in front of him, a little distance away. Their relative positions meant they looked directly at each other.

Ben Yusuf held the page down, balancing the book in his other hand. 'I would like to hear what he's singing; some of your things are very lovely. It's always amazed me that your cinema is so, ah, modest.'

'Cinema has different conventions from poetry or fiction or art.'

'Have you ever wondered why that should be?'

'Things need rules, art as much as anything else,' he said.

Ben Yusuf nodded, watching the young soldier's face with interest as his enthusiasm for cinema filled it with light. He pointed his fingers out from his chest as he spoke, as if forgetting that Ben Yusuf was his prisoner.

'In his movies, everything is alive. It's like it's all going to burst through the screen and start happening next to you in the cinema aisle. Other directors try to achieve the same effect, but Roscius is the only one who did it in every film he ever made.'

There was a separate section on his Civil War still photographs.

'The Civil War gave him the money to start making all those movies,' Cyler said. 'They're how he made his name.'

Ben Yusuf turned the pages with slowly, his hands shaking. There was one terrible image of the Roman Forum—taken at the height of the conflict—showing a dozen dead bodies strewn casually over the brickwork. It was clear that most of them had been shot in the back of the head.

'The Proscriptions,' said Cyler. 'There's a nasty photograph over the page; it's very famous. Just a warning.'

Ben Yusuf drew back at a crisp and terrifying shot of a man's head and hands impaled on a stake in front of some sort of public monument. He covered his mouth; the man who took it had thought to alter his camera settings so as to enhance the contrast. Blood in Roscius's photography was an oily black.

'Who is that?'

'A famous politician and lawyer called Cicero. He did some very stupid things, but he didn't deserve that. It got worse, too. After Roscius took the picture, Mark Antony's ex stuck her hatpin through his tongue.'

'Heavenly Father, your people are cruel.'

'That photograph changed history. It made *Imperator Augustus* look so bad that he was forced to develop a proper system of representative government. He'd have set himself up as a tyrant otherwise, like Julius Caesar tried to do.'

Ben Yusuf turned the page; Cyler stopped speaking. This time men and one woman—scientists, presumably—stood in front of some sort of vast engine covered with banks of switches and relays. He noticed that one of the men had hair down to the middle of his back—very unusual for any Roman male in that period.

'What's that?'

'Minerva-I. The first mechanical–digital calculation engine, developed to break codes during the Civil War. People don't like to admit it, but there was a lot of scientific progress due to the Civil War.'

Ben Yusuf rummaged through the rest of the books.

'I see you've given me some essays by the Cicero fellow.'

Cyler shrugged. 'He was a good writer and speaker. That's why he made enemies. We study his speeches at law school, even though the legal system's changed a fair bit. The judge has a lot more power now.'

'You're looking forward to being a lawyer, then?'

'That's why I enlisted, so I could go to law school.'

'And because you're a patriot, I presume?'

Cyler was taken aback at this.

'I've had enough people try to kill me since I joined up to prove that.'

'And no doubt you've killed a few.'

'Oh yes. We're good at that, we Romans.'

Ben Yusuf smiled at this, at both its casualness and vigour. He watched as the soldier stowed the Roscius biography back in the box, his movements neat and sharp, his jaw with the determined set that seemed to be trained into all of them, his hair cut so short on the sides the scalp showed, his hands and forearms lean and brown.

'If you wanted to develop a good Latin accent, to whom would you listen?'

'People from Latium—but outside Rome itself—are supposed to have the best accents,' he said, puzzled at the question. 'That's the accent all presenters and announcers on CR have. In fact, you could just watch Severus Agrippa and Arminia Brenna every night and copy them.'

'They present the *Newshour*, don't they?'

'That's right. Of course, I'm from Latium, outside Rome, and my accent's atrocious.'

'Your family is poor, though.'

Cyler was starting to feel uncomfortable.

'That's true. My parents were on the corn dole for a while. People like me don't have perfect accents, even when we do well at school.'

'So Romans will help the poor?'

A look of incomprehension crossed Cyler's face. 'Only vouchers. You exchange them for food and cooking gas. You only get them if your employment's seasonal or spotty.'

'Perfect accent or not, your sister is very proud of you.'

Cyler's eyebrows shot up.

'Now that's a neat trick.' He poked his finger in Ben Yusuf's face, smiling crookedly. 'I may have been awake for thirty-six hours, but I know I didn't tell you I've got a sister.'

'I knew.'

'Or you guessed.'

'That's what you say.'

Cyler folded his arms and cocked his head to one side, examining his prisoner.

Ben Yusuf said nothing, but maintained eye contact.

'I've had to haul a can of paint to the top of an aqueduct to defend my sister's honour. Twice.'

'That was necessary, in these modern times, in your country?'

'Where I grew up, yes.'

Cyler remembered how the Centurion during his basic got that story out of him. He'd spent most of his training being called Waterboy; he was expected to answer to it. Every time he failed to respond, he had to drop and do fifty. He did a lot of push-ups during his basic.

'What are you doing now?'

'Me?' Cyler asked guilelessly. 'I've got a night pass. I'm going to the Greek Quarter to see a woman I want to fuck.'

'She's likely someone's sister, too.'

Cyler's clear eyes darkened.

'Leave respecting women to us, *Domine* Cliptip. We don't kill them just for wanting an enjoyable fuck with a man who doesn't beat the shit out of them.'

Ben Yusuf watched as Cyler turned on his heel, let himself out of the cell and then drove the metal hatch home, blurring some—but not all—of the sound from the corridor outside.

Lucullus: *If he's a terrorist, I'll shit in my boot and eat it.*

Ben Yusuf: *Is it possible to shout across such a vast gulf?*

Pilate spread the statements from members of the Galilee garrison across his desk, perplexed. He was no nearer to resolving the sedition or terrorism issues coalescing around Ben Yusuf than he had been when he'd arrived to see Horace waiting with a fat envelope in his hands.

'From Irie Andrus, Senior Centurion of the Fourth Cohort, Procurator.'

The Galilee *Advocatus* had gone to some trouble to collate

multiple statements; he'd clearly also been careful to avoid imposing his own view of events on what were sometimes poorly educated enlisted men. The soldiers' recollections amused and infuriated him by turns. There were times when Pilate began to wonder how many repressed comedians there were buried in the ranks of *Legio* X *Fretensis*.

He began the slow process of selecting the most relevant, eventually isolating six that seemed to cover a range of different perspectives on Ben Yusuf, from a man who intervened to prevent violence to one who openly advocated it.

The first was from a Centurion, and acute. Pilate starred the corner.

> Near Capernaum is a hill the locals call Carn Hattin. Ben Yusuf was in the habit of getting up there and declaiming to his followers and anyone else who happened to swing by. We were expecting some fireworks because the week before an IED went off in North Galilee and killed three men and crippled a fourth, and two weeks before that Ben Yusuf had been running around the place telling people to trade in their clothes for firearms. I have to say the gun-toting Ben Yusuf was not in evidence on this day. In order, this loon believes the following:
>
> I. People who do jack shit will inherit the earth.
>
> II. People who help people who have done jack shit will get helped in turn.
>
> III. People who are hungry and do jack shit about it will get fed anyway.
>
> IV. People who are upright will get into the Kingdom of Heaven. According to my woman this is their version

of Elysium.

V. People who are NOT morally upright but who 'repent' their evil ways and abase themselves before their God will get into the Kingdom of Heaven.

VI. All of this (especially IV) is conditional on believing in their God. That counts anybody Roman out, even Stoics and other good folks.

Those six aside, the most useful statement was undoubtedly that from Andrus himself. The man had an observant eye and an intuitive grasp of how to manage a region with the largest wealth gap between town and country that Pilate had ever seen. Andrus had been shrewd when he'd used private contractors as linesmen rather than relying on his own Cohort or Roman military contractors, for example. They were not seen as representative of the hated Roman enemy, and Zealot attempts to shoot them off the top of power poles dropped to zero almost overnight.

Even so, Andrus was not the most articulate reporter. Pilate was shocked such a senior officer could make so many written errors and got Horace to bring him his service record. He was unsurprised to find that it revealed a battlefield commission and a clutch of decorations for conspicuous valour, including the coveted *Corona*. The Roman Army practice of promoting very brave men come what may was still well and truly intact.

Who gives a shit if he doesn't know his ablatives from his datives?

And that's a very Roman thought right there.

He began to read Andrus's statement.

From Irenaeus Iulius Andrus, Senior Centurion, IVth Cohort *Legio* X *Fretensis* to Pontius Pilate, Procurator of Judaea, Greetings! [...]

There was a frantic series of knocks at his door. Pilate's head jerked up.

What the?

He pressed the buzzer under his desk. Horace had clearly been leaning against the door; when the latch gave way, he was flung into Pilate's office. He righted himself and apologised. Horace was an urbane young lawyer from Pilate's old Hall at *Collegia Roma* doing his first year in practice as a law clerk; seeing him red in the face and bug-eyed was rather unexpected.

'This better be good, Horace.'

'*Aquilifer* Getorex has uncovered a terrorist conspiracy.'

Pilate stood up, frowning.

'Send him in.'

Horace popped his head around the doorway, beckoning. He stood to one side as Cornelius ducked inside.

Cornelius saluted and handed Pilate a typewritten report.

'This probably explains this morning's findings more quickly than I can, Procurator.'

'This is the first of the Form 23s?'

'Yes, Procurator. Yehuda Iscariot's.'

Cornelius watched as expressions of incredulity and then rage crossed Pilate's face as he read.

Pilate jabbed at the buzzer on his desk, summoning Horace once more. The young man—becalmed after his earlier excitement—stood patiently behind Cornelius's chair.

'Send for Caiaphas, Horace. I want to see him. I want to see him *now*.'

'He may refuse to attend, Procurator. There's already been one member of the Sanhedrin who refused to enter Antonia this week. He feared being made unclean.'

Pilate's tone was icy. 'You have full military authority to compel his appearance. I am not in the mood to be trifled with, Horace.'

Once Horace had left, Pilate turned to Cornelius.

'I should congratulate you on a job well done.'

'Thank you, Procurator.'

'I suppose I'll have to start thinking about appointing a new High Priest, too.' He clasped his hands around the back of his head, staring at the ceiling. 'I really did want to avoid doing what Gratus did, going through High Priests like the Blues go through managers.'

'Seven High Priests in eleven years, Procurator.'

'Exactly. It's administratively disruptive and creates no end of resentment.'

'I'm not privy to your appointment policies, Procurator, but I'd consult with *Primus Pilus* Capito before doing anything precipitous.'

'Yes, that's a good thought. I'll do that. Wait there.'

Cornelius watched as Pilate spent ten minutes chasing Capito down, finally hauling him off the parade ground.

'I should have looked out the window first,' he said.

Cornelius stood and caught a glimpse of Capito's grey head disappearing under an arch.

Capito read through the report while Pilate and Cornelius watched in silence. He was already flushed from standing in the sun, so if he were as furious as Pilate it was difficult to tell. He looked up when he'd finished, handing the paperwork to Cornelius.

'Well, this is a turn up for the books, Procurator.'

'I'll say. I don't just want to fire him. I want to fire him with extreme force.'

'Out of a cannon, Procurator?'

'I was thinking a catapult, actually.'

'At the risk of attracting your entirely justified ire, may I suggest leaving him in place?'

Pilate stared at Capito, drumming his fingers on the table.

'Why?'

Cornelius leaned forward, attracting Pilate's attention with a small movement of one hand. Capito looked sidelong at the lawyer.

'Because you've got him over a barrel,' Cornelius said.

'How so?'

'As you know, Procurator, the High Priest is granted immunity from prosecution all the while he holds office.'

'Yes, I'm aware of that. I enjoy a similar privilege.'

'I can draft up an undated *libellus*—directing and financing terrorism, I should think—and leave it lie on the table. When and if you sack him it's instantly enlivened.'

Pilate smiled a crafty smile, looking hard at the young man.

'If you ever leave the legions, there's a job for you at my old firm.'

Cornelius smiled.

'Of course, there is a risk—the more time passes—that leaving a prosecution hanging over his head will look like an abuse of process.'

'That may be so, but the underlying substance of the charge is very strong. I could defend myself against allegations I've abused my position, I think.'

'The other issue is leaving someone who is seditious in place, Procurator,' said Capito. 'You'll have to make an assessment of whether he's just been compromised... or properly turned.'

'Well, quite.'

When Horace appeared at the office door, Caiaphas did not need to be told why. He stood and took leave of Arimathea and the Prefect of the Temple Guard.

'If you go into Antonia now you may be unclean for Passover,' said Arimathea.

'I'm not sure I'm being offered a choice, Joseph.'

Horace took him through the secret passage Herod had constructed. It connected the Temple to Antonia and allowed Roman troops to appear around the Temple precinct with intimidating swiftness. Tiled in pale green, lit by strips set into the tiles, it looked like a mortuary. There was a faint sound of dripping from somewhere above him and the concrete underfoot was damp. He ran his fingers through his beard, trying not to think about the men who had undoubtedly met their ends here, shorn of the need for anything so inconvenient as a trial. He looked at Horace and his soft curls, wondering if he were armed with a view to facilitating the disappearance of a meddlesome High Priest. The thought made him feel strangely light; once the bullet came he could float free of Judaea, the Temple and the Sanhedrin and its consuming concerns. It was only when his thoughts turned to Esther and Hillel and the four adult children from his first marriage that his resolve faltered. He stopped, clutching Horace's shoulder and then vomiting at his feet. Horace drew back, sneering.

'Just go,' he said, 'straight on.'

Horace turned his back and kept walking. Caiaphas heard him whistling cheerily from far ahead in the passage.

No arms, then. Just contempt.

Maybe Pilate wants to do it himself.

He hurried now, trying to catch Horace's distant footfalls. He startled when he realised that the young man had stopped and was waiting for him. The strip lighting along the walls flickered and distorted Horace's rather delicate features. There was, Caiaphas knew, a certain sort of mature Roman male who would find Horace very attractive.

Horace's face was quizzical, now, rather than contemptuous.

His hands were clasped behind his back.

'I do appreciate you bringing me this way, Horace,' he said. 'It's at least discreet.'

'Public humiliation is the least of your worries, High Priest. The Procurator would like an explanation. He would like an explanation so much that he gave me powers of arrest in order to compel your appearance, should you have tried any asinine religious excuses for refusing to enter Antonia.'

'I see. This way the people of Jerusalem do not see their High Priest entering a gentile barracks in Passover week.'

'Perhaps. The Procurator emphasised haste, not religion, in his order to me.'

Caiaphas looked at Horace, hearing in the voice of a twenty-three-year-old baby-faced collegium graduate Rome at its harshest, highest and fiercest.

These people are terrible enemies, Kayafa.

Perhaps their pleasant manners and bent morals let you forget that.

Caiaphas did not consider himself anti-Roman; he just didn't like some of the things they did. Finessing this, however, was going to take some doing. His mind ran like a rodent on a wheel as he tried to think how he was to explain himself to Pilate.

Pilate did not invite Caiaphas to sit, instead leaving him stranded in the middle of his office. Capito sat to one side and the big ginger lawyer to the other. Both the soldiers had turned their chairs so that they, too, faced him. Pilate rested his arms, palms down, fingers pointed, across the desktop. Capito looked thunderous. The ginger was smiling.

'You have been a guest in my house,' Pilate was saying. 'You have broken bread with my family. Your son and my son are all but inseparable. You were present at my daughter's coming-of-age celebration. You have also been a competent and careful High Priest; although, if any more of this sort of thing comes to light, I may have to revise my opinion on that score.'

He leaned forwards, folding his hands and resting his chin on them.

'Why?'

Caiaphas had not expected this. He had half wanted Pilate to be angry and patriotic, to produce the sort of explosive rage at which he knew Romans excelled when their Empire or its interests were threatened. Instead, the Procurator's tone was hurt, even confused.

'I am not anti-Rome, Procurator. Only a fool would oppose your rule, which has been wise and beneficent—'

Capito snorted.

'—I am, however, opposed to some of the things you do. In a moment of weakness—this I freely concede—I made my feelings known to the Zealots.'

Cornelius leaned forward in his seat.

'I understand you contacted the Zealots yourself.'

'No. One of them identified me when I stopped to refuel after Camilla's coming-of-age banquet and gave me a means of contacting him.'

'If you're interested in keeping your hide intact,' Capito growled, 'you'll share that information with us, *now*.'

Caiaphas wanted to point out that he, too, was a Roman citizen, and so the threat of torture cut no ice with him, but he thought better of it. He reached into his wallet and withdrew the *vocale* number and the note, glad in a perverse way that he'd kept both all this time. He then recounted the spare tyre story.

'Which means there's a rat in the Temple Guard,' said Cornelius.

'I'd be more surprised if there wasn't a rat in the Temple Guard,' Capito said, with some venom. 'They're worse than useless.'

'You do appreciate just what your moment of weakness has wrought, do you not?' Pilate's tone was bitter. 'Dead medical staff. Dead soldiers. Dead civilians—lots of dead civilians. I don't expect you to agree with the Roman view of abortion, but for Goddess's sake, no one's making you have one at gunpoint.'

'Our taxes still pay for it, Procurator.'

'No they don't. After the last attack I shifted a few columns in the annual budget around. Rest assured that abortion in this province is now centrally funded. Judaean taxpayers don't pay a *denarius* for it.'

'That doesn't stop it being murder, Procurator.'

Pilate brought his fist down on the desk with such force that his carved shark bounced into Cornelius's lap, while his inkwell spilled onto the leather inlay.

'I find talking about this disturbing, High Priest,' he said, his voice oddly throttled. 'It's women's business.'

He pressed the buzzer, summoning Horace.

Horace entered to see Cornelius standing in front of the fish tank, cradling Pilate's beautiful ivory shark in his hands. Pilate was attempting to soak up the pool of dark-blue ink that now occupied the middle of his desk. The Procurator's fingers were inky and he had a smudge on his chin. Caiaphas had retreated to the back of the room. Capito sat serenely in his chair, watching as Pilate handed the blotting paper to Horace.

'You'll need this,' he said.

Horace fetched water, sponges and a towel from the washroom at the back of Pilate's office. He paused to take in the large bath, what he suspected were solid gold fittings, and the intricately patterned tiles. Some of the motifs—rather than the usual flora and fauna—were intensely erotic, not of a type properly found in a workplace.

That'll be a Gratus touch, then.

He paused when he heard raised voices from the office.

'I fail to see how Ben Yusuf is more dangerous than the Zealots,' Pilate was saying.

'He's building a mass movement, Procurator. At the risk of being impertinent, have you been paying attention to what's been going on in the Galilee?'

Horace set down his bowl of water on the desk and began the clean-up. The four of them talked around him.

It was Capito's turn to sound icy.

'We are aware that some of the village elders up there have gone a bit, shall we say, free range. We have been monitoring the situation.'

'He had five thousand people at a public meeting outside Capernaum, Procurator.'

'People do have a right of assembly in the provinces,' Cornelius said. 'Gatherings like that will be monitored by our troops and only if there's a risk of criminal activity will we break them up.'

Caiaphas's tone was despairing.

'Did you not see what he did the day before the riot? He marched into Jerusalem *on a donkey*, and in *triumph*. There were tens of thousands of people cheering him.'

'I did read the report, yes. I don't get the donkey, though. Is he too poor to afford a horse? A ticket to Central? There is an express train from Sepphoris.'

'It's a prophesy, Procurator, hundreds of years old now, but dear to the hearts of many Jews—not just Zealots—that the Messiah will come in triumph to Jerusalem on a donkey. The donkey means he is appropriately humble; Judaism values humility. We are not given to Roman pomp and circumstance.'

Pilate's eyes grew wide.

'And the Messiah is meant to rule as a king?'

'Yes, Procurator. I know what Rome will do if the Zealots and their friends properly raise their hand against you. These men really do believe that a ragtag army of insurgents can defeat the greatest military power the world has ever seen. The result will be a bloodbath, you know that better than me.'

Pilate's voice was very soft.

'Yes. If only because I know who will lead the Roman forces.'

'Vitellius, sir?' asked Cornelius.

'Yes, Vitellius will take command. And that man is without mercy.'

'I find it disturbing that you went to a Zealot, despite your fears,' said Capito.

'If I could have found someone other than a Zealot to grass him up, I would have done so. Iscariot was all I had. It is only a matter of time before Ben Yusuf turns to violence. The fact that Ben Yusuf numbers people like that among his closest followers should tell you something.'

Pilate stirred from his introspection.

'The fact that you number people like that among your associates should tell *you* something, High Priest.'

'I spoke to him once, Procurator. *Once*.'

Caiaphas watched as Horace managed to saturate two hand towels with watery ink, finally revealing the green leather inlay in the top of Pilate's desk. Capito moved his head and shoulders out of the way as the young man wrung the towels out into his bowl. At one point the soldier touched the back of Horace's hand.

'You missed a bit,' he said, pointing.

Horace nodded, standing and facing him, smiling.

'Procurator, it was my people's Temple he tried to destroy. And that was just him and a dozen confreres.'

'One of whom was clearly faking,' Capito said, 'considering the sequel.'

'You've told yourself so many stories, High Priest, I don't think you know what you believe any more,' said Pilate. 'For what it's worth, I think you genuinely thought Ben Yusuf was going to go upscale when he felt he'd got the numbers to do so. I don't accept, however, that your contact with Iscariot and others of his ilk was as marginal as you make out. Someone had to get that shiny money from the Temple treasury to him.'

'It was marginal, Procurator. Check your own records. Call that number. If they're still using it as their dead drop I'll eat my shoe.'

'I'm impressed, High Priest,' said Cornelius. 'Not every priest or priestess is familiar with the terminology of espionage.'

'I do watch CR, *Aquilifer*, especially *Newshour*.'

Cornelius wriggled his eyebrows and smiled wryly. 'I hope, as a patriotic citizen, that you pay your licence fee.'

Capito sat up abruptly.

'He's a citizen?'

'One of the perks that goes with the High Priest's job.'

'I suppose I'm to be removed from office, Procurator.'

'Actually, no,' Pilate said, his voice mild. 'You're too useful where you are.'

Caiaphas felt the blood drain from his face. He wanted to be sick again and leaned against the wall. It was further away than he expected and it was all he could do to stop himself sliding down it.

Horace dumped the ink-stained towels and wads of blotting paper into his bowl. Caiaphas saw him touch Capito's shoulder with one inky hand before he disappeared into the washroom. Capito patted his fingers.

Cornelius explained the process whereby a criminal prosecution could be allowed to lie on the table, only to be enlivened on the dismissal of someone enjoying immunity from prosecution while in office.

Caiaphas stepped forward.

'You can't do that.'

'We can, and we intend to,' said Pilate. 'You're welcome to review the relevant articles of the Roman Criminal Code with *Aquilifer* Getorex after this meeting. I'm sure he'd also be happy to take you through a story our great lawyer Cicero once told, illustrating the principle admirably. See Damocles, sword of.'

He leaned back in his chair. His eyes narrowed to slits and he pursed his lips. For the first time, Caiaphas realised, he was seeing the driving corporate lawyer that Pilate had been in the time *before*. And he could see that lawyer dancing.

'I think I shall rather enjoy having the High Priest of Jerusalem bending over and taking it up the arse *from a Roman*.'

Capito leant forward and patted Caiaphas's arm much as he had patted Horace's fingers a moment earlier.

'Not literally, of course.'

When Horace returned from escorting Caiaphas to his Temple office, he noticed that Capito and Cornelius were still standing outside Pilate's office, chatting. Cornelius had his hands clasped behind his back and was laughing at something Capito had said. The latter folded his arms and scanned the corridor, his gaze pausing on Horace's closed office door. Horace noticed and pointedly moved into his line of sight, clicking his fob against the door, opening it. He dumped his paperwork on the desk and made his way towards the two soldiers, smiling. He looked up at Capito.

'Was that just play, sir?'

'That was deadly serious. The High Priest of Jerusalem is now the Procurator's bitch.' He paused, putting two fingers under Horace's chin and drawing his face towards his own. 'But don't worry, I'm far gentler with mine.'

Cornelius watched this byplay with amusement, shaking his head.

'I thought I'd been posted to Jerusalem, not Athens,' he said.

Capito stopped kissing Horace for a moment and shrugged amiably. Cornelius watched the young man rest his palms against Capito's chest.

Gentlemen, get a room.

'I'm going back to my *quarters*,' he continued, 'where I've got a beautiful *woman* waiting for me.'

'They're always in here,' the woman on the other end of the *vocale* was saying. 'Very quiet, never cause any trouble, and always take care to reshelve when they're finished. Most people leave books scattered everywhere for us to pick up.'

Lonuobo leaned back in his chair, stroking his chin. Cornelius's graceful network diagrams from the morning's interrogation were scattered across his desk.

'So you want us to come and look at what you've found?'

'I thought I ought to talk to someone, you know. Just doing my duty as a citizen.'

He punched her name and identification number into the calculation engine in front of him and waited. The machine spat out her profile and he tore it off.

Marcia Cirulla, Archivist, Agrippa Memorial Library, Jerusalem. Born in Syracuse, forty-eight years old, trained in Alexandria (*so she'll be good*), married twenty years to Lara Neria, a florist with business premises in the Greek Quarter. He read all the way down; apparently, Cirulla specialised in the preservation of rare books and ancient manuscripts. On a whim, he called up Lara Neria's profile as well; she was younger than her lover and also Sicilian. It seemed that she, too, had once been a librarian, but had inherited money and purchased the floristry with it.

Lonuobo waggled his fingers at one of the Counter-Terrorism Unit's rankers, attracting his attention. 'Trace this,' he wrote on a scrap of paper. The man nodded, moving across the room and disappearing behind a calculation engine that seemed to take up an entire wall.

'Although it's written in gibberish, from what I can see, or at least not in any language I recognise,' she went on.

Lonuobo smiled; it wasn't often that he got the chance to apply his talents to some old-style cipher. He doubted that it would be too hard to break. The clever part of the scheme was leaving messages concealed in the pages of books in a public library. Communication only required a signal indicating that a message had been left. It was simple, but ingenious.

And would have gone on indefinitely had some clueless ninny not stuck the book back on the wrong shelf.

She clearly hadn't expected her call to the provincial counter-terrorism unit to be treated with such interest. Lonuobo could hear the enthusiasm in her voice.

'I want you to take a copy of the message, put the original back in the book and reshelve the book where it's supposed to be.'

'I'll do that right now, officer.'

'Keep the copy safe, and wait for our man. In the meantime, watch to see if anyone comes to collect it.' He paused. 'Do you have CCTV there?'

'No, officer. This building is classified "public" under the Code.'

'Well, take a very careful note of his appearance, then—and not just obvious stuff like beard or height. I want eye colour, style of dress, any distinguishing marks.'

'Yes, officer, I'll do that, if anyone comes for it.'

'I'll send one of our people to talk with you. He's a forty-year-old black man. He'll be conservatively dressed and wearing a CreditGallia interpreter's pin on the left side of his collar. His name is Lucas.'

'Of course, officer. I'm so glad to be of service to the Empire.'

Lonuobo traded pleasantries and hung up. He scanned around for his subordinate.

'That call came from the library?'

'Yes, sir,' the man said, picking up Cirulla's profile and reading it. 'I expected it would. The likelihood of a Zealot impersonating a middle-aged Sicilian librarian strikes me as extremely remote.'

'It'll happen eventually, Krikos. Or they'll take one hostage and make a demand. Release ten Zealots or the librarian gets it.'

Krikos watched his superior gather up his paperwork, lock it away in secure storage at the back of the Surveillance Room and then pocket the key. For some reason, Lonuobo always managed to come up with worse scenarios than the terrorists before the terrorists did.

Lonuobo headed to his quarters to retrieve his alter ego, Lucas Rioni, sober and staid interpreter and broker for that paragon of Imperial probity, *CreditGallia*. He pulled out one of Lucas's dark grey robes and Lucas's Alexandria Academy collar and chain, taking care to ensure the pin was attached in the right spot. Lucas's briefcase was at the foot of his bed; he opened it and sorted through various booklets and papers outlining mortgages, house and contents insurance and business development loans. He looked at the identity card, turning it over in his hand. Lucas, he was reminded, had a wife in Caesarea and a concubine in Jerusalem, along with two daughters by the former and a son by the latter. With some reluctance, he stowed his machine pistol in the briefcase, too. This disguise did not permit him to hide the bulk of his weapon under his arm. He then stood in front of the mirror, running a generous leavening of silver colouring through his hair and massaging it in with his fingers.

He washed his hands, looking carefully at himself.

A handsome middle-aged banker looked back at him. Lonuobo was heavily muscled around the abdominals and the material in his robe—nipped in at the waist—pulled tight in spots, which made him look overweight. It was a useful effect. His knack for looking entirely unlike himself was such that people would simply presume he was visiting the barracks for business purposes. He collected his briefcase and made his way down to the cells and one of the discreet passages out of Antonia.

Marcia Cirulla recognised 'Lucas' as soon as he walked into the library, although she waited patiently while he wandered around the ground floor and pretended to orient himself. He paused before a bust of the Agrippa who'd superintended the construction of this library. *De Sua Pecunia Fecit* was cut into the plinth.

Eventually Lucas made his way over to the counter and introduced himself, shaking her hand. They made small talk and she slid him the copy she'd taken of the piece of notepaper she'd found by mistake earlier in the day.

'No one came for it,' she said casually. 'Maybe they missed it, because it was in the wrong place.'

'There's an ongoing problem with misplaced books in this

library,' he said. 'It's something we need to discuss.'

She directed a subordinate to mind the counter and took him into her office, locking the door.

'You did well there,' he said, sitting down opposite her in the proffered chair.

'I don't think I could have kept up the pretence for much longer, to be fair.'

She was a striking, matronly woman with large breasts, lustrous black hair and good skin and he thought momentarily of seducing her—but then he remembered her profile on the engine and suspected that she may not be interested in him.

'They come in here quite a bit,' she said. 'The beardy ones, I call them, although in the last couple of weeks a couple of them have started to shave.'

'Do they borrow anything?'

'No, but I've started to look at what they read. Lots of high school alchemy, along with books on ballistics. Once one of them tried to engage me in a conversation about guano.'

'With a view to blowing things up?'

'I have no idea. I had to look it up. I've been to a farm maybe three times in my life, and that was three times too many. I later learnt that you use guano in gunpowder, although I suspect that his interests weren't in gunpowder.'

Lonuobo laughed, opening the slip of folded paper. He recognised the cipher, although it wasn't one he could break without a calculation engine. He'd need to go back to Antonia and play with it for a while.

'They're up to something, aren't they?'

'Perhaps,' he said, looking again at the cipher. 'How many different ones have you seen?'

'Three,' she said. 'One of the shaven ones made a pass at a Roman high school student last week. He looked utterly crushed when she blew him off.'

Lonuobo laughed again.

'They really have no idea,' she added. 'They seem to think women are just up for it, without appreciating that effort and skill is required.'

Lonuobo liked this, and chortled appreciatively. On a whim, he thought he'd try his hand.

'On that note, I can't interest you in a pleasant evening with a man, can I?'

It was her turn to chuckle.

'You are lovely to look at, but I was cured of boys before I turned twenty, and in any case I am well and truly spoken for.'

Lonuobo smiled broadly at her; she winked at him in return. 'So we've got three beardy types reading alchemy textbooks and asking the librarian about guano,' he said. 'And someone leaving messages in cipher.'

'Yes,' she said. 'Exactly.'

'You've done very well, Ma'am,' he said.

'Marcia, please,' she said, standing to shake his hand. 'It all helps, as my father used to say. He was in Germania, and came home. He knew.'

Lonuobo nodded his head, acknowledging her familial sacrifice. The men who'd made their way back safely from the German fiasco twenty-odd years ago were breeds apart.

'If ever you change your mind about that pleasant evening...' he slid a *CreditGallia* business card across her desk. '... Do let me know.'

'I shall,' she said, smiling.

As he left her office, he saw a young man with shaving nicks all over his face enter the building. The young man's hair was short but not soldierly, layered up the sides and back and combed forward over his forehead. He wandered around the educational displays on the ground floor before making his way towards the spot where Lonuobo knew he would find a particular book. Lonuobo paused outside the main entrance, watching him and noting for the first time that the Imperial Postbox had been repeatedly marked with chalk, scored across the glossy purple paint. One of the chalk marks—directly over the *Tib. Imp.*—was very fresh. Lonuobo watched as the young man located the book he was chasing, opened it and retrieved the note. He didn't attempt to disguise his interests, scanning the message as he left, pausing only to sneer at the gracious colonnade leading to the library's main entrance.

Lonuobo hailed a taxi.

When he directed the cabbie to the guest spaces some distance from the barracks and then paid him—tipping generously as he did so—he noticed activity out of the corner of his eye. Both he and the cabbie stepped out of the vehicle and watched across the square as two young men hoisted a Zealot banner—the seven-branched candelabra, blue on a white field—up the pole where Caesar's Eagle was supposed to be. The Eagle itself was nowhere to be seen. The two men made no attempt to run away afterwards, standing on the roof of the colonnade that ran around the Court of the Gentiles and admiring their handiwork, arms folded. Two members of the Temple Guard came and remonstrated with them, but did not attempt to remove the symbol. It was only when several members of the Roman garrison appeared—one of whom pointed his weapon at the two men, making them lie face down with their hands pinned behind their heads—that something was done. Two legionaries handcuffed the prone men, while another shinnied neatly up the pole and tore the banner off the crossbar where the Eagle's feet had rested.

Lonuobo ran to his quarters to change, sticking his head under the tap and rinsing the worst of the silver out of it. He stored Lucas away and donned his uniform. He was consumed with a sense of mounting dread. The expression on the Zealot's face as he'd left the library kept surfacing unbidden in his mind's eye. He clattered downstairs to the surveillance room.

He pulled his portable radio out from under his desk and loaded several cards of soothing music into it. He'd occasionally been forced to work with *Centurio* Friere on cryptanalysis and had found himself nearly driven mad by the other man's preference for decrypting to loud music. Today, however, Lonuobo had the Surveillance Room to himself. He retrieved Hebrew and Aramaic letter frequency charts and a set of *tabula recta* from his bottom drawer and stuck them up on his engine's glass case, then punched the ciphertext into the machine. As he extracted the plaintext—it was a clever but not exceptional autoclave system, and the key was 'messiah'—he gave thanks for Marcia Cirulla's sharp eye.

When the whole message came clear, however, he put his hand over his mouth.

MESSIAHGOISRAISETHEBANNERTEMPLE3YEHUCENTRAL STATION 3:15PMGODISGREAT

'So you don't know who your father is?'

'No, Eugenides, that's sort of the point.'

Aristotle—a Macedonian country boy unfamiliar with much outside his home province—was impressed by this detail.

Saleh had joined Rufus and Aristotle in the enlisted men's mess, taking care to remove his officer's insignia before entering. His was an unfamiliar face, and several of Rufus and Aristotle's friends stopped to look at him. He took some ribbing about 'slumming it' with rankers, but he was a medic, not one of the dreaded Centurions, so their comments were gentle enough. The mess was vast and smelt of beer mixed with onions and garlic, its floor decorated with the same black-and-white geometric pattern as Antonia's entrance hall. He admired the unfinished walls, rubbing his hand over the rough brickwork. Perhaps due to growing up in one of Caesarea's most sumptuous buildings, he'd acquired a taste for rustic finishes. Rufus plied him with several large mugs of a strong, cloudy drink he'd not encountered before.

'From Britannia, from apples.'

Saleh's first instinct was to pull a face; it was sharp and pungent and made his eyes water.

'What is this stuff?'

'Cider. Now drink up, it'll put hairs on your chest.'

'I've already got hairs on my chest, thanks.'

After the second mug, however, he found himself habituated to it, and gave thanks that he had nothing pressing to attend to in the afternoon. There were some records to update and some paperwork to do, but no task requiring total clarity. Even so, he eyed the cloudy beverage before him with suspicion, taking care to eat well—the food was basic, plentiful and wholesome—in between each mug.

'Doesn't that annoy you?'

'What?'

'Not knowing who your father is?'

'Doesn't it annoy you, being named after a second-rate scientist?'

'That's not fair. He taught Alexander the Great.'

'I doubt he taught him much.'

Rufus watched the two men spar, bemused.

'Don't argue about philosophy, it's not worth your trouble.'

'I'm not arguing about philosophy,' said Saleh. 'I'm arguing about science. And Aristotle was a bad scientist. Exhibit number one, dissection. You have no idea how hard people from

Alexandria had to fight to get dissection accepted in Rome when the medical *collegium* was first founded. There was a period there where Alexandrines were nicking bodies after gladiatorial shows and public executions and selling them to the medical school.'

Saleh's voice had become loud; he'd pulled his Alexandria Academy chain from inside his uniform and was flicking it back and forth around his fingers to emphasise his points. People were starting to look at him.

'When a woman dedicates herself to Cybele, she can do one of two things. She can take a patron straight away, or she can entertain without one until she finds one she likes. If she takes a patron, she can still see other men if she wants. If her patron comes to her, though, any man with her must leave.'

Rufus sat drinking quietly. None of this was news to him; he'd seen it in Rome. Aristotle, however, was fascinated.

'It's like what they have in Corinth, in the Temple of Aphrodite.'

'I don't know what they have in Corinth.' He paused. 'In return for her services, the Temple or her patron—or both—pays for her to learn to sing and dance and write poetry, and to serve the Goddess outside the Temple. My mother trained as a teacher; her patron paid the tuition fees. These days an awful lot of the "service" seems to be planning festivals and managing investments. Two priestesses in Caesarea are merchant bankers.'

'And any children stay in the Temple,' Aristotle said. 'That's the rule in Corinth.'

'Yes, this is our rule, too. My mother had a patron, but also another man she liked very much. She thinks this other man may have been my father, but they didn't have paternity tests in those days, and in any case a man has no claim on any Temple children. Even if such a test had existed, neither man would have asked for it.'

For reasons he was never quite able to elucidate fully in later years, Saleh found himself enjoying both the cider and the two rankers' company more and more as time passed. The three of them finished up singing together at one point. As the afternoon wore on, he wound up confiding a mass of personal information. This process culminated in an invitation (from Aristotle) to the Mithraeum under the cells as an *observer*. He'd heard that such a structure existed in Jerusalem, but had never known that it was so close.

'You can't stay for all of it, of course, but you can establish, ah, if you like what you see.'

'I'm already initiated to Cybele,' he said.

'Oh no, that doesn't matter. Mithras will help you take your men's business in hand.'

'Aren't you bending the rules a bit, having it under Antonia?'

'The Fleet Fox is on the *cardo*, in plain sight.'

'Fair point. I even know the priestesses who manage it. That takes no small amount of skill, in a place like Jerusalem.'

'In any case, *Aquilifer* Getorex is our Pater. He runs things very well.'

That name alone both soothed and inspired. He'd decided earlier in the day that he'd die in a ditch for Getorex. He suspected there were worse places to die than in a ditch, but even so, he'd die in them, too.

He also wasn't sure how this conversation led to one of Aristotle's blood brothers using one of Saleh's own scalpels—stashed away in the webbing at his waist, for emergencies—to cut his inside forearm on both sides, then do the same—on one side only—to both Aristotle and Rufus. The three men stood, their arms and fingers pointed up and intertwined, and caught the blood in two kylixes, one on each side of Saleh. Aristotle's blood brother—Cassius of the violet eyes—poured some good red wine over the gore and bade them drink, Saleh first. Cassius held the drinking vessel high above his head, invoking the Gods and seeking their good offices.

'Blood brothers against the wind,' he said.

'Against the water,' said Aristotle.

'Against the earth,' said Rufus.

'Against man, his agents, his heirs, his consuming affairs,' said Saleh. He was on the way to landing in his cups, but he knew what this meant. The three men clasped themselves each to the other. Others gathered around them, whooping and cheering and slapping their backs. Saleh felt himself flooded with warmth; he reached out to clasp hands with other men as they gathered around the little knot of three at the centre.

He'd wondered, as a clever young medic leaving Alexandria Æsculapion, where modern medicine was made, what the legions would make of him. Now he knew.

Linnaeus felt the drop as Ben David took the Dead Sea road and descended into the poorest part of the Jewish Quarter, picking his way through a maze of tiny back streets and cheek-by-jowl tenements. The city was truly mud brick here, a jumble of yellow and red dust mixed with khaki smoke from thousands of cooking fires. Looped electrical cable was strung down one side of the street; it had been attached to every block of flats on both sides with care and skill. Even when curiosity got the better of him and he opened his window, his senses were not overwhelmed with reek. Pilate could take credit for that. Nonetheless, he noted, in the few wider streets, most of the streetlamps were broken.

If you shit in your own nest, people, we can't help you.

And now I'm starting to sound like Pilate.

Animals—scrawny goats, for the most part, although one camel tried to stick its head in through Ben David's window—dodged in between donkeys hauling lumbering carts, the occasional rusty bicycle, crowds of pedestrians carrying sheep trussed up on poles and street stalls selling everything from trinkets to hot food to spare parts. He was sure he spotted at least one table—tucked discreetly into a shaded alcove—covered with pistols and ammunition, gathered innocuously around an engine block with its polished steel finish. Ben David leant on the horn to get the animals and pedestrians out of his way. Linnaeus smiled when he saw groups of teenage Jewish boys liming on street corners next to battery-powered radios, listening to Roman music. He wound up the window and relaxed back into his seat, observing from the quiet of the vehicle's interior.

'They shouldn't be playing that music, should they, *Domine* Linnaeus?'

'I hope their parents don't understand the lyrics, David.'

Women dressed in black gowns eyed the large black cab with suspicion, but when they saw the sidelocked driver they turned away, satisfied he meant no ill will. Sometimes, however, they lingered long enough to see his passenger and note the short hair, clean-shaven features, gold headband and pierced ear. When this happened, children made signs to ward off the Evil Eye and men spat on the ground.

Some of them were collecting pats of dried camel dung and putting it into cloth sacks.

'What are they doing that for?'

'Fuel, *Domine* Linnaeus. It's much cheaper than wood, and you don't have to walk as far.'

Linnaeus lost his sense of direction as the streets became

narrower and darker. The day was still bright: sometimes sunlight shot down between the tenements and almost blinded him. For the most part, however, the houses were so crowded together the sun could get little purchase.

Ben David pulled up beside one of the narrowest and darkest buildings.

'This is the house of the Bar Yonah family.'

Linnaeus stepped out onto the cobbles, taking care where he put his feet. There was goat shit, horseshit and camel shit everywhere. He collected his briefcase and stood back to allow Ben David to lock the vehicle.

'If you want to stay and guard your taxi, David, I won't object.'

'They may be poor, *Domine* Linnaeus, but that does not make them dishonest.'

Linnaeus made his way up the hewn steps, his fingers collecting fine, pale dust each time he reached out to steady his grip. After the first storey, the stairs became metal; his feet clattered on them despite his best efforts. The crooked towers bore down, dry and leaning, their flat roofs blinding in the sunlight. He reached a landing so high it soared above the tenement immediately across the street, which meant that the washing strung between the two hung lopsided. He looked at the slip of paper in his hand, checking and rechecking the address. The door in front of him had once been painted, he thought. A few green flakes still clung to it.

Painted at some point during the war against Hannibal.

Linnaeus knocked.

Petros Bar Yonah answered with a gorgon in his arms. Its outsized head rested on Petros's shoulder, while its twisted body seemed to curl around his, clinging as much as carried. There was a fleshy, russet lump at the base of its skull, making the head swollen and the ears lopsided. Its eyes were too far apart: they were shut at the present moment. As Petros turned to hook his door back and admit both of them, its body turned, revealing a livid scar that ran for about a third of the length of its spine. There was some sort of medical equipment hitched to its ear and neck; the tubes dived away into a place tucked within Petros's grey robes that Linnaeus could not see. And did not want to see.

Linnaeus flinched and stepped backwards. In so doing he stood on Ben David's foot and made him yelp. He turned and apologised, straightening up as a woman in black holding the hands of two small children appeared behind Petros. He said something to her in Aramaic. She faded into the background, where Linnaeus could see other figures—two or perhaps three men, shrouded for the most part in darkness.

There was a tidal wave of movement as the woman retreated; a young man sprinted past Linnaeus and Ben David, rattling down the metal stairs. Petros shook his head and called out to him in Aramaic. Linnaeus could understand the gist of his words: *Simon! He's not Fretensis! He's Arimathea's man!* The Simon figure turned as he ran, his beard streaked through with sweat, and shouted *Romoi, Romoi* in Greek. Another man joined Petros at the top of the stairs. He was young, clean-shaven and physically beautiful. His black hair—parted down the middle, something Linnaeus had long found attractive in men—fell in soft waves to just below his ears. He spoke in Greek, in a voice so melodious that Linnaeus was almost able to ignore the hideous monstrosity in front of him.

Simon the runner turned slowly and made his way back along the street and up the stairs. He glared at Linnaeus, spitting at his feet as he passed him and went back inside. Linnaeus recognised him from the CCTV footage as one of the more enthusiastic rioters; he'd clipped his beard since the riot, seemingly unable to go all the way and change his appearance by shaving himself clean. He retreated into the darkness.

'It is close to Passover, Roman, and I do not want you long in this house,' said Petros Bar Yonah, in broken Greek.

His hair was long and flecked with grey; his head—like Ben David's—was sidelocked, but Ben David kept his locks neat and distinct, curling them in front of his ears and at the sides of his beard. Petros's were a tangled mess, caught up with the thing he was holding and with the rest of his own hair and beard and clothing.

They all smelt of fish and sweat, save the pretty young man. He smelt of one of the inexpensive unguents one could buy at the public baths in the Roman Quarter. Linnaeus wrinkled his nose. He tried not to—he knew how it looked—but the impulse was instinctual. Petros smiled crookedly.

'You think I am filthy, and I think you are unclean, so we are even, Roman.'

Linnaeus extended his hand, stating his name. Only the young man took it—'I am Ioanne,' he said—although a man standing behind Petros, a neater, younger version of him, smiled when he heard Linnaeus speak.

'I am also Andreas,' he said. 'We have this name, too.'

'It's rare among Romans,' said Linnaeus, smiling and engaging his gaze directly. 'My mother is Sardi, and it's a common name among her people.'

At that moment, the thing on Petros's hip opened its eyes and began to wail. Linnaeus edged around it as Andreas invited him in. He tried to avoid both staring and showing his shock, realising that he was reacting in much the same way as Ben David had reacted to the young celebrants of the Rite just a few days ago. He saw Andreas and Ioanne shake hands with

Ben David, although he noticed Petros declined to shake the hand of even a fellow Jew. Simon hovered in the background, still staring at Linnaeus, his eyes on fire with hate.

No one offered Linnaeus a seat and he did not attempt to take one. He wasn't sure he wanted to sit down anyway. The hovel—for that's what it was—consisted of a single large room, a smaller room (hidden from view) and a kitchen. What looked like bedding was scattered all over the place; he suspected that all or most of the people in the room were currently sleeping on a patch of its floor. There was more drying washing hanging over the hob. The woman he'd seen earlier had hitched her two children to a rotating pin set in the middle of the kitchen with a type of harness. They could move around in circles, but could not come within range of anything hot. She fed wood into the front of the stove and perched a big silver kettle on the hob. The hovel began to heat rapidly. None of the men moved to help her.

No one spoke for a few minutes, and Linnaeus—he was unable to stop himself—went back to staring at the gorgon in Petros's arms. He noticed that his namesake stroked the monstrosity's head as he walked past, then paused again to stroke the two small children in harness in similar fashion.

Gods alive, it's a child.

Petros disappeared into the hidden room for a moment and returned with medical equipment sealed in sterile packaging. He set the gorgon down on a tatty couch on the other side of the big room and fiddled with what looked like a catheter. His movements were gentle and solicitous. Linnaeus worked at keeping his face neutral.

Petros finished what he was doing and cradled the gorgon in his arms again. He walked towards Linnaeus, rather pointedly holding the creature front and centre. Everyone in the room—even Ben David—watched the tableau.

'This is Shmu'el, or Sam to you, Roman. He's my oldest son.'

Linnaeus felt his gorge rising, and flapped his hands.

'It shocks you, doesn't it?'

Transfixed, Linnaeus nodded. The child's eyes were rolling in two different directions now. They were a startling hazel, flecked with green. On a sudden, it looked straight at him and cooed softly. The sound was sweet. Linnaeus felt himself taking a step backwards.

'You love only beautiful things, Roman. Beautiful places, you hope one day to conquer. Beautiful people, you hope one day to fuck.'

Linnaeus grimaced bitterly at this; Ben David could see his crow eyes close and darken without the movement of a single muscle.

'Your law not only lets people rip children from the womb, but crippled infants do not have the right to life until a month after birth. In that time, the parents are expected to kill them.'

Linnaeus spoke, soft and clear, holding Petros's gaze.

'This has been the Roman way—since the days of the Twelve Tables and the *patria potestas*—for some seven hundred years,' he said. 'It would never be possible to convince judges in Roman courts that parents who kill such an infant are criminally culpable.'

'It is easy to love beauty, Roman. It is harder to love ugliness, but God is love.'

The woman beside the stove spoke in Aramaic, looking at Linnaeus. He shook his head at her, indicating incomprehension. Ben David translated.

'She says the young Roman *medica* in the Æsculapion in Sepphoris tried to take Samuel away from them.'

Petros nodded. 'Rebekah went for her checks at your shiny new Æsculapion, and after the test with the needle...'

'Amniocentesis,' said Linnaeus.

'The Roman *medica* got the results and told us Sam had spina bifida.'

'The split spine, yes; now I understand.'

'She said to us, "you won't be wanting that". She had already contacted the baby butchers in another part of the building.'

Petros shifted Sam's weight in his arms and continued. Everyone in the room stared at Linnaeus.

'She gave us an appointment card for an abortion.'

Rebekah said something else in Aramaic; she went on for a long time. This time Petros translated.

'After Sam was born, the *medica* said, "you have a month, the state will not prosecute you". We said, we want him to live; we have heard there is surgery to close up the back so that he can live. The *medica* did not want to give it. She called two other *medicae*, ones above her, women from Alexandria and Rome. The Alexandrine convinced the two Roman *medicae*, and Sam lived, but the Romans complained about the cost.'

The woman filled a metal bowl with water and walked to each man in the room in turn, offering it to them, ending yet another awkward conversation. Linnaeus was grateful.

He watched as each man dipped his hands in it and then flicked his fingers out straight in front of him. She approached him as well and he copied the movement, although he suspected that the process had actually made his hands dirtier. She poured the water down the sink and then handed each of them a bowl. Petros walked over to the stove, Sam on his hip, the bowl in one hand. The others followed him. Linnaeus looked at Ben David, one eyebrow raised. Ben David nodded.

'This is chicken soup, for Passover,' he said in his slow and careful Latin.

'What if it's got cooties in it? I don't want food poisoning.'

Ben David chuckled at him. He didn't know the slang term, but he could guess at its meaning.

'Drink it anyway. It has been boiled.'

She ladled the clear soup into his bowl and handed him a piece of round flat bread.

'Thank you, Ma'am,' he said, remembering his manners. He noticed that none of the men—save Ben David—had thanked her. She smiled at him; the expression touched the muscles around her eyes with its genuineness. He retreated to a point in the room furthest from the rest of the group, watching Ben David and taking his cues from him. He looked at the soup; he couldn't see anything obviously doing backstroke in there.

To his surprise, the soup and bread were very tasty, and he said so. The tone of his gratitude—and he would never quite know how this happened—punched through the hostility permeating the room. Petros looked at him from his spot on the couch beside Sam, his head on one side.

This is the best of Rome, Mary had said. *You do not pretend.*

'We make it with *shmurah* wheat, special wheat that has never fermented. No yeast, it has to be unleavened.'

Linnaeus always welcomed an opportunity to talk about good food.

'This bread looks homemade. Is it?'

Andreas spoke up. 'Yes, but not by Rebekah; you need a special kitchen.'

'An expensive kitchen,' said Simon.

Simon the runaway had not said anything until this point.

'Well, it's very good. I shall have to get the recipe for the soup at least.'

Simon looked at him, his expression quizzical. 'You cook? Like a woman?'

'I'm not a bad cook. I have servants, though, and they do

most of my cooking. New recipes always go down well.'

Simon nodded and went back to his spot against the wall. He looked at Linnaeus, at his lean frame and elegant fingers, his long, dark robe, heavy gold watch, diamond earring and polished, pointed boots—marked, now, with fine white dust—with a mixture of curiosity and contempt. Light caught the clockwork mechanism in the watch and spackled his face with luminescent dots.

Seizing his moment, Linnaeus began to outline his case and what was needed. He stepped through the CCTV footage, relying on frank fascination with his calculation engine—he set it down on the only table in the room—to hold their attention. Simon ran his finger around one of the lion's feet. Sam smiled and stared from Petros's arms. He passed around the evidence photographs and a set of model statements. Without revealing its contents, he held up Arimathea's, explaining his own role in framing and editing what went before the court. He was careful to leave the torture point for now.

He looked at Petros. 'Everything I've read so far indicates that you are chief among Ben Yusuf's followers. Mary Magdalena said as much to me this morning, and everything in the dossier'—he indicated his briefcase and the paperwork circulating around the room—'confirms it.'

Petros handed his bowl to Rebekah. Linnaeus followed him.

'I'm serious about that recipe,' he said to her in Greek, very slowly, his face a mask of urbanity. She nodded, indicating that she understood him.

'I will fetch it for you, Roman,' she said, smiling as she released her two smaller children from their harnesses.

Petros's face had become thoughtful.

'I'm surprised Mary spoke well of me.'

Linnaeus made brief eye contact with all four men in the room.

'She spoke well of all of you, to be fair, and also of some that I haven't met.'

'I can call us all together, if you like,' Petros said. 'Only Matthias will not come, as he is in fear of his former employer.'

Linnaeus raised an eyebrow.

'He used to work for *CreditGallia*, in their debt collection division.'

'A tax collector?'

'Yes. He quit to follow Yeshua and left them with a great deal of incomplete paperwork.'

Sam began to cry; Rebekah collected the remaining bowls and took them away.

'Excuse me a few minutes,' Petros said, 'I have to attend to Sam.'

He disappeared into the small room, Sam in his arms. Ioanne spoke up in his excellent Greek.

'*CreditGallia* are much better than the previous lot of *publicani*, but they're not above strong-arm tactics, and they were very angry with Matthias. He left two weeks before they were due to file. They sent two thugs around to beat Matthias up. Luckily, he wasn't there.'

Linnaeus had an unpleasant mental image of ex-gladiators with chains around their fists kicking in someone's door at the behest of the worst sort of bent provincial tax collector.

'I wish the Imperial Taxation Office would stop using debt collectors in the provinces.'

Simon's face registered surprise.

'So Romans object to them too?'

'Many do; every policy you see implemented in this province or any other has been debated among Roman citizens.'

Ioanne dragged the conversation back on point.

'You would like some of us to appear as witnesses, then?'

'And provide a statement, yes. The main thing I need is

evidence rebutting the State's contention that Ben Yusuf has a history of violence, because that's what they'll argue. All of you have known Ben Yusuf for many years. Those of you without any criminal history—Petros, or yourself—are most useful, as it is difficult for the State to impugn your testimony.'

'I was in the Temple that day, Roman,' said Petros as he re-emerged, closing the bedroom door behind him. 'They'll lock me up.' He paused, looking at Rebekah. 'I've put Sam down for an hour or two with some of the drops the *medica* gave us. He needs sleep.'

She looked up and nodded; one of her younger two was rubbing his eyes. She sat him on her lap, rocking him back and forth. The girl—she looked about two or three—was fast asleep on the couch, her thumb in her mouth. Ben David sat on the floor, offering to take the tetchy one from her. She accepted with gratitude.

'I know you were involved in the riot, and so does the State, but you haven't been convicted, so the State can't jail you. That requires a separate trial. The prosecutor can attack your credit, but that's all.'

Andreas shook his head in wonder. 'That is very fair.'

'I don't want to go to law in a *kufer* court, not just before Passover,' Petros said.

Linnaeus's expression became quizzical.

'Why? Some trouble has been gone to by the Procurator and the State—and by me—to ensure that this trial proceeds before Passover. Frankly, it would have been easier if the whole thing had been postponed.' He pursed his lips. 'I should be on holiday—this is *Megalesia*.'

Simon spat. 'Having the trial before Passover suits the High Priest, not Judaeans generally, or you Romans.'

Even Andreas was angry. 'I don't think you gentiles appreciate how Caiaphas makes people dance like a puppet on a string. He has your courts doing his bidding now.'

Simon butted in, his voice rising. 'He has even befriended Iscariot—'

'Iscariot is a most unpleasant human being.'

'Because he fought against Rome, and wanted your filth out of our country?'

Linnaeus flapped his hands.

'Please, I do not live in Judaea; I am here to act as defence counsel for a man many people seem to hold dear, including you. When the trial is over—whatever the outcome—I will go back to Rome and you need never see me again.'

'Would that all Romans did likewise.'

Linnaeus felt very tired. Even though he had not been invited to do so, he pulled out a chair on the opposite side of the rickety table where Petros and Simon were sitting.

'If you want to save Ben Yusuf, you're going to have to work with me here.' He paused, partly for effect and partly because he needed to gather his thoughts. 'The Procurator needs to hear from Ben Yusuf's ordinary Judaean followers and friends; he needs to see that the Temple riot was an aberration.'

He placed his palms on the table, speaking very deliberately.

'Mary Magdalena and Joseph Arimathea will both make excellent witnesses, but they can't do it on their own.'

'All you Romans will be dreaming of fucking Mary,' Petros said bitterly.

'That may be true; if you haven't done likewise, then you're a man of remarkable restraint.'

Petros looked hard at Linnaeus.

'If you haven't sinned, Petros, then you can judge this man.'

The voice was Ioanne's; he was gazing through the shutters and down into the street, his fine young head backlit.

Linnaeus continued; he ignored the byplay but formed the view that Ioanne would make an excellent witness.

'I will call Nic Varro to prove the extent of the corruption in your Temple—'

Simon spat again. 'Roman filth.'

Petros touched his arm. 'That's enough, Simon.'

Simon shrugged his shoulders, turned his back and stormed out of the building. His footsteps clattered on the stairs. The slamming door woke both Rebekah and her children, who'd fallen to dozing on the couch. The little girl began to cry; the boy crawled off Ben David's lap.

'I'm sorry about Simon,' said Andreas. 'He's angry.'

'I'm not sorry he's gone. We may actually accomplish something now.'

Andreas pulled the shutters to one side, tracking Simon's movements up the street.

'I think I'd better make an effort to get him back, Petros. He doesn't know Jerusalem. If he wanders around in a funk for too long, he's likely to get lost. Ioanne can help me once you've gone.'

Petros was grateful; Linnaeus could see the relief on his face.

'Simon is a Zealot,' Andreas said, by way of explanation, looking at Linnaeus. 'That's why he hates you.'

'This really doesn't look good,' said Linnaeus, an edge in his voice. 'First Iscariot, now this one. You tend to know people by the company they keep.'

'Ben Yusuf does not want to drive Rome from Judaea,' said Petros. 'Simon does, and Yehuda does, but not Ben Yusuf.'

'For what it's worth, Petros, I believe you. The point is I have to get Pilate to believe you as well. I've interviewed Ben Yusuf. Joseph Arimathea will visit him in Antonia. The contrast between his behaviour and Iscariot's couldn't be more marked; I've got a couple of little birds among his Roman guards. Some of them even like him.'

Petros's eyes grew wide.

'Romans? *Like* Ben Yusuf? He thinks your people are cesspits of depravity. He may not want to drive Rome from Judaea, but if you left voluntarily, he'd be a very happy man.'

'That may be so, but he's adroit enough not to show it around his Roman guards.'

Ioanne spoke from his place beside the window.

'I didn't know he could have visitors.'

'Of course he can; for pity's sake pay him a visit—tomorrow if you can—I'm sure he'll appreciate it.'

'I will. You should come too, Petros.'

'Go into a filthy Roman barracks? Where when they're not concocting more killing and conquest they're fucking whores from the Greek Quarter?'

'All leave is cancelled from midday tomorrow, Petros. Any unregistered women there—and that's a privilege only extended to officers, I might add—have to be out by then. Men who break that rule are liable to be flogged.'

'You will be clean in time for Passover, Petros.'

'There's another thing I need to tell you,' Linnaeus went on. 'And now that Simon has left, I can.'

Petros looked up.

'The State can put both Iscariot and Ben Yusuf to the torture; the water torture is favoured among Romans. It leaves no marks.'

Petros nodded. 'I knew that. Yeshua said if he fell into Roman hands, you would torture him.'

Linnaeus shook his head. 'It's unlikely he'll be tortured, to be fair. He's compliant. He's represented. He's been pleasant to his captors.'

'But Iscariot?'

'I'd say he's in a great deal of distress as we speak.'

Linnaeus scratched his bristly chin with one hand, trying

to be tactful. He looked searchingly at both Ioanne and Petros.

'If there is anything that Iscariot knows about Ben Yusuf or the rest of you that you do not want the men of X *Fretensis* to know, then they'll know it soon enough. If not today, then at some point in the near future, when the torturers do not have a trial in prospect.' He paused. 'Is there anything?'

'Apart from Simon's politics? No, I don't think so,' said Petros. 'The worst that could be said of any of us is already known among the garrison in Galilee. I presume the other lawyer—'

'Cornelius Getorex, the military prosecutor.'

'—Will talk to them and hear their complaints. Yeshua was very rude about some of them.'

'He once said they were machines built only for lust and conquest,' said Ioanne. 'Like you were making them in a special factory somewhere.'

'There's a percentage of Roman legionaries who'd take that as a compliment, I'm afraid,' said Linnaeus, grimacing. 'I know my own people.'

'He would also identify soldiers by name who engaged in *porneia*, wrong sex,' Ioanne continued. 'This did not make him popular.'

'Including Irie Andrus?'

'Sometimes, yes,' said Petros. 'Although there were things he liked about Irie Andrus, so perhaps he's a special case. When Andrus shot Iscariot and his brother over Sarah, Iscariot expected sympathy from Yeshua, but Yeshua said he had it coming, walking up to a Roman *castrum* like that and interfering with a Roman's woman.'

'This was in Nazareth?'

'Yes. The main garrison is in Sepphoris, but there are patrols all over the Galilee. There had been problems in Nazareth and the surrounding area, and Andrus came himself with around eighty men and stayed for about a month.'

'They don't normally stay?'

'Not for more than a few days at a time; one group arrives as the other leaves, and usually only about fifteen.'

'I see.'

'Andrus saw Sarah in the market when he first came and took her away with him to his quarters in the *castrum*.'

'She's his wife?'

'Yes, under your law she is, now,' said Ioanne. 'She's pregnant with his child, too. He told Ben Yusuf he took her because he wanted a wife and children, although he waited for a couple of years first.'

'That is the Roman way, especially where the marriage has been arranged.'

Petros paused, gathering his thoughts.

'Sarah was the most beautiful girl in Nazareth, and probably in Sepphoris as well. All the young men wanted her, but her parents knew they could get a good match for her. She was eighteen and still not married because they were always looking for a better one.'

'They'd finally arranged a marriage for her—a rich man in Tiberias—but she did not like what they had chosen,' said Petros. 'She said he was old and ugly.'

'When he first came to Nazareth, Andrus saw her taking a tray of dried figs into the market,' Ioanne continued. 'He was smitten—this I saw with my own eyes—and followed her with some of his subordinates in tow. He walked up to her at the family's stall, beckoning to her, and asked her in Greek if she could read and write. She said "yes", so he took something out of his pocket and got her to read it off. I think it was some ammunition specifications.'

'In Greek?'

'Yes. Her father sent her to school in Sepphoris to improve her marriage prospects. Then Andrus put his fingers in her mouth and forced it open, like he was buying a brood mare. Finally, he pulled her scarf off her head and ran his hands through her hair, nodding and smiling all the while.'

Ye gods, all the bits of Roman custom not for export.

'I think he knew she was his,' said Petros. 'Yeshua says our ways of thinking are wrong—and I agree with him now—but she had been touched all over her face and hair by a strange man in the middle of the market and did not move away. She even smiled at him. No man in Galilee would have her after that, she was dishonoured already.'

'Then he asked her if she wanted to be a Roman citizen,' said Ioanne, 'and she said "yes". Then he asked her, "with me?" And she said, "yes" again. So he picked her up, threw her over his shoulders and took her out into the street, to the Roman armoured vehicle. His subordinates clapped and cheered as he took her inside. We could see him kissing her through the windows.'

Well, we know his history lessons stopped with the Sabine women.

'This is marriage by capture,' Linnaeus said in wonderment. 'I've been a family lawyer for twenty-four years and this is the first time I've ever seen it. Extraordinary.'

'She does love him, I am not sure why or how,' said Ioanne.

'She did not want the marriage her father had arranged for her,' said Petros. 'We must accept that. I've always thought a girl who rejects her parents' love for her in the form of a well-chosen husband the worst sort of ingrate, but Yeshua made me see it from Sarah's point of view. A woman can burn for a handsome man just like we can burn for a beautiful girl. No matter how rich he is, a man who is old and ugly stays old and ugly.'

'And Andrus is a good-looking man?'

'Yes, he is handsome,' Ioanne puffed out his chest and

pulled his shoulders back. 'Very strong, with one green eye and one grey eye.'

'That means good luck in my country,' said Linnaeus. 'You're called a *merle*.'

'His eyes are frightening,' said Petros. 'There are some in Sepphoris who think he keeps order in Galilee just by staring at people.'

'Rest assured he had to work for her,' said Linnaeus. 'A man who captures a woman must convince her to stay with him, like we did with the Sabine women. Traditionally, this has meant civil and property rights, a careful and beautiful seduction, and a promise of children.'

'Yeshua said that what Sarah was doing was *porneia* and that she should go back to her family,' Ioanne said. 'He told Andrus this to his face the next morning. Andrus laid him out cold; I didn't think it was possible for one man to hit another man so hard.'

'If it's any consolation, both Getorex and I have called Andrus as a witness.'

Petros laughed bitterly.

'About a week later, Iscariot and Binyamin tried to kill both of them.'

'My understanding is that they were, ahem—'

'Fornicating outside, *under the arch* like it says in your language, yes. He took her to see one of your licentious mimes in Sepphoris and it gave her ideas. They both came back with a skinful and couldn't wait.'

Linnaeus laughed at this little detail.

'Yeshua was much angrier with Iscariot than he had been with Andrus and Sarah, though,' said Petros. 'This is when I came to understand his view of, what do you call it, honour killing. Before Yeshua, I thought this was just our law with respect to *porneia*; she was already betrothed to the man in

Tiberias, so it was like committing adultery with her. The punishment under our law for a man who has sex with a betrothed woman has always been death by stoning, for both of them.'

'Romans see that as honour killing as well.'

'Yeshua said that trying to kill them was a grave sin, because murder is worse than *porneia*. This was hard for the rest of us to bear, because she was dishonouring her family every night in the Roman's bed, and Binyamin was dead.'

'So he argued that Binyamin's death and Iscariot's wounds were self-inflicted, because they interfered?'

'Yes.'

'Do be aware that before Andrus took her to the mime, he would likely have only penetrated her once, probably on the previous night, as the capstone to his seduction.'

Linnaeus was careful to say nothing further, letting Petros continue.

'This is what Yeshua said, too. I wondered how he knew that. We saw them on the balcony outside his quarters after the shooting. She could not keep her hands off him. We knew then she wanted him, too. The next day, Andrus went to her parents' house and offered to pay bride price for her and blood money for Binyamin, but they would not accept it.'

I think I've just overdosed on primitive provinces of the Roman Empire. Really.

'After that, even Yeshua was surprised when Andrus helped him.'

'Helped him?'

'Yehuda's father and uncles were furious. They said that Yehuda was not a man, and that as he had a gun, he should use it to avenge his brother's honour. That way he could be a man again. Then they came for Yeshua, because Yeshua took the Roman's part.'

Something tells me this is going to end badly.

'Yeshua would sit in a little room off the market teaching. Nazareth doesn't have a proper synagogue, but we have more than enough at any one time for a *minyan*.'

'Minyan?'

'You would call it a *quorum* in your language,' said Ioanne. 'It means enough Jews in one place for prayer and worship.'

Petros continued.

'One morning they rushed him. Most of the town joined in.'

'Nazareth is just a scrap on the hillside,' said Ioanne. 'There can't be any more than nine hundred people there, absolute tops. There's no electricity, not even in the *castrum*. The Romans use gas for cooking and light and bring field radios with them so they can communicate with Sepphoris and Caesarea.'

'So nine hundred people tried to kill Ben Yusuf?'

'I think maybe half that number tried to drag Yeshua up the hill above the town with a view to throwing him off it.'

'Nic Varro told me a similar story,' said Linnaeus. 'I take it Andrus effected a rescue.'

'Yes,' said Petros. 'He and some other legionaries came on horseback—it's very steep there, you can't use vehicles—and drove the crowd back. At one point he fired his carbine into the air. One of Iscariot's Zealot friends had a pistol and shot at Andrus from within the crowd. We thought we were all going to die, that the Romans would just open fire—'

'Roman troops will not fire into a crowd of civilians,' said Linnaeus. 'They'd run you out of the legions on a rail if you did that.'

'So we learnt. Andrus and his soldiers formed themselves into a wedge with Andrus at the head of it and rode the man down. One of the soldiers was shot in the leg and another lost his horse, but no one died.'

'They beat the Zealot with their rifle butts, though,' said

Ioanne. 'His face swelled up like one of those poisonous fish.'

'Then the media people came,' said Petros. 'First JTN and later some people from Rome.'

'Vista?'

'Yes, that's who it was. They were making a programme about honour killings and blood feuds, and what the Empire was doing about it. This was after Andrus had taken Sarah back to Sepphoris with him. I don't know what happened with it.'

'I understand Yeshua has prevented quite a few of these honour killings.'

'Yes,' said Petros. 'He has. It was hard for us at first—his followers, I mean. Your soldiers are encouraged to take provincial women—'

'That's not strictly true. The policy is meant to make our soldiers a "good catch" for a provincial woman, and to encourage Roman men to settle in the province after discharge. That's why they must be unmarried when they enlist, so there's no woman binding them to their home province. They're meant to find a woman in the province where they're posted, and to make a citizen of her and their children. If their sons also join the army, that's a useful follow-on effect.'

'—But it dishonours our men. If we cannot protect our women, we are mocked all around the village.'

'I see.'

'You must also understand that Yeshua is critical of the soldiers, too, for *porneia*. Wherever your soldiers appear, there are whores *like that*.' He snapped his fingers.

'They are young men,' said Linnaeus, 'and if a young man cannot woo a woman in the normal way, he will use a sex worker. Your morality means there are more sex workers in Judaea per head of population than anywhere else in the Empire. It's a source of amusement in Rome every time the

Imperial Statistical Council releases the census data.'

Petros suspected Linnaeus was needling him. He chose to ignore it.

'Sometimes Ben Yusuf saved women from stoning and told them they must stop sinning, but they just went back to their soldier.'

'Well, they're hardly going to be welcome back around the family hearth, are they?'

'I suppose not.'

'You've witnessed Ben Yusuf doing this, this rescuing of women?'

Both men nodded.

'That's potent evidence in his favour, and will help to sway a Roman judge. Seriously.'

Ioanne turned to face him, 'I will come to court.'

Linnaeus handed him a sheaf of printed documents. 'That's very helpful, Ioanne. Thank you.'

Petros was still shaking his head. 'Not the day of preparation for Passover, Roman, I will be made unclean.'

Linnaeus rubbed his face with both hands. 'We need an older witness, Petros. If necessary I can have the court issue a summons ordering you to appear. I'm reluctant to do that, but if it becomes necessary, I'll do so. A fair trial for Ben Yusuf is more important than your religious sensibilities.'

Petros pursed his lips. 'I'd tell you to stick your summons up your arse if I didn't think you'd enjoy it.'

'Where did that come from?'

Petros pointed at Ioanne, 'I see the way you look at him.'

Ioanne stood up and faced both of them, 'I also see how he looks at me, Petros. If I were angry about it, I would tell him to stop.'

Linnaeus was unsure if that was an invitation or a reproach, and he smiled awkwardly. Ioanne shook his finger in front of

Linnaeus's face, a mocking glint in his eye.

'We do not partake in the Greek vice here, Roman. Nor should you.'

Linnaeus flapped his hands and shrugged his shoulders. *Don't know what you're missing out on.*

'You've got to understand how it looks if you don't front,' he said, returning to the matter at hand. 'Pilate has a dossier and is empowered to undertake his own researches. He will be aware of the esteem in which Ben Yusuf holds you. If you fail to appear it will look like a betrayal.'

Ioanne sat beside Petros and put his hand on the latter's shoulder.

'He said you would put yourself before him.'

Petros burst into tears. The suddenness of the outburst caught Linnaeus by surprise.

'Am I missing something here?'

'Some history,' said Ioanne. 'He will provide a statement, and he will appear.'

Petros nodded, tears pouring into his beard. His daughter had woken and skirted around her sleeping brother and mother—and a sleeping Ben David, too—and clambered into his lap. He enfolded her gently in his arms, rocking back and forth.

Linnaeus looked out into the street as Ben David began the climb out of the Lower City; he wasn't sure what had happened in the interval—apart from the fact that a couple of hours or so had passed—but the street was rapidly emptying of people. Two little girls seemed to run away from the cab as it approached, their colourful print dresses streaming out behind them, but when he craned his neck and looked up, he saw a woman yelling and beckoning to them from a top-floor window. Another woman in black robes marched into the middle of a group of boys and ordered them inside. When this had no effect, she picked up their radio, tucked it under her arm and proceeded to walk away with it. They followed her, fuming but compliant. Traders folded their stalls and stowed produce and wares. He saw one man loading melons into a bicycle basket. The man who'd been selling small arms from behind an engine block had similarly vanished, although his stall—complete with engine block—was still outside.

'They roll up the pavements early round here.'

Ben David shook his head, 'Normally this part of the Jewish Quarter will have traders out in force at midnight. This is the first day of the market week, too.'

Linnaeus struggled to catch a glimpse of the sky between the crumbling mud-brick towers, 'Weather?'

'No, it's clear. Passover usually falls on the cusp of the seasons, not too hot or cold. I did hear on the news some Zealots ran a flag up the pole in the Court of the Gentiles, though.'

'How serious is that?'

'I don't know. It was earlier today. Maybe they're expecting a security sweep.'

Linnaeus flipped the watch around his neck open and contemplated it.

'I really should talk to another witness. I wouldn't mind rounding up the young one, to be honest.'

'Ioanne?'

'He was making sense. I think he'd make a good witness, too. In some ways better than Petros.'

'Does he have any, what do you call it, of the previous convictions?'

'Yes, but very minor.' He rummaged through his briefcase. 'Hindering a tax official in the execution of his duty.'

'Which involved what?'

Linnaeus turned Ioanne's criminal history on its side so

that he could read the notation. 'Chaining him to a lamppost and dropping his trousers around his ankles on market day.'

Ben David chuckled at this. 'He'd have been conspicuous, then. I can take you back to Petros's if you like, so we can find Ioanne.'

Linnaeus looked at his watch again, thinking.

'No, take me back to the Empire, David. I've had my kosher quotient for the day. If I were I at home, I'd be on holiday. Instead, I'm working until ten at night for people who hate me. I'd like a little civilisation.'

Ben David looked at him; his crow eyes had narrowed to slits.

'A very early finish, then.'

Linnaeus shrugged, appreciating the taxi's unimpeded path and contemplating the prospect of an agreeable afternoon at the Empire.

Baths. Massage. Fotini. Yes. That will do nicely.

Ben David made his way out of the Jewish Quarter, pulling up outside a post office. He waited while Linnaeus went inside to place a call; he could see him standing up and gesticulating through the front window, smiling.

CRISPUS

'Ah, Lonuobo, you've seen fit to join us.'

Gaius Crispus was seated opposite a pair of well-dressed civilians Lonuobo did not recognise. One of them was wearing a *Parti Optimates* pin on his collar. Crispus had a bottle of *garum* in one hand and a large lump of bread in the other. The man with the pin was slicing cheese on a central platter and distributing it across three small plates; the other was pouring wine. Lonuobo read the label; Crispus's parents were footing the bill while their son drank fifteen-year-old Falernian.

A month's salary for a bottle of booze, there you go.

'Where is *Aquilifer* Getorex, sir?'

Crispus sniggered. 'At this very moment? On his back, exercising his cock, I'd say.'

'I need to talk to someone in authority, sir.'

'I'm in authority, *Centurio* Lonuobo. What is it?'

Lonuobo walked over to him, leaning across the two men and waiting for them to shift out of his way. He spread both the ciphertext and plaintext message out in front of Crispus.

'Three Zealots using a book in the Agrippa Memorial Library as a dead drop. They'd accidentally left this message in the wrong place. I've just spent the last hour decrypting it.'

Crispus leaned forward, his curiosity piqued.

'It means—I think—that when this "go signal" happens—raising a Zealot banner in the Court of the Gentiles—there will be a series of planned attacks on targets around Jerusalem.'

'You've got no date, Lonuobo. This could mean anything, and on any day.'

'It's today, sir. It's happening now. On my way back from the library, I saw two Zealots run a menorah symbol in their colours up the pole in the Court of the Gentiles. They'd removed Caesar's Eagle.'

Crispus dragged the two slips of paper towards him.

'And another thing—I'm reasonably sure this is number *three* in a series, to take place at fifteen fifteen hours. That means two others before it, and it's already fourteen hundred hours. I think—in less than an hour—there will be an attack on number one, whatever number one may be.'

Crispus' jaw appeared to have stopped working. He turned to his companions, both of whom looked suitably stunned. Crispus stood up.

'Gentlemen, you have obtained some excellent wine at my expense. Duty calls. When you're finished, one of the enlisted men will see you out.'

They both nodded.

'And the conversation you've just heard doesn't leave Antonia. Bad for the Empire.'

They nodded again, properly awed now.

Crispus fell into stride beside Lonuobo, collecting his jacket on the way out of the mess. His movements were sharp and struck Lonuobo as brusque. He buttoned his jacket as he walked, swearing at his fingers at one point. Word around the Legion was that Crispus planned to follow his father into politics. Lonuobo suspected the two well-dressed civilians were potential backers.

Crispus eventually made eye contact with him.

'I'd order a strike unit to deploy at the station, if it were me. Put a sniper at each end of the railway shed for a start. Discreetly, of course.'

'We have no idea what they're going to do, sir.'

'Some things would work rather better than others,

Lonuobo. The station is elevated; it's not as though you could drive a truck bomb in there.'

'We've got the two men who ran their banner up the Temple pole in custody, sir.'

'We also have Iscariot, Lonuobo, and he has form.'

'What do you suggest, sir?'

Crispus stroked his chin, looking at Lonuobo. The skin around his eyes crinkled with a faint smile.

'Do you think there's more where the thirty Tyrian shekels came from, Lonuobo?'

'*Aquilifer* Getorex wanted to wait until after trial before we exploited him fully, sir.'

'Don't be obtuse, Lonuobo.'

'*Aquilifer* Getorex will put me on a charge if I step over the line again.'

'I'm sure *he* would, Lonuobo.'

Crispus let the statement hang between them.

'The *Camera* CCTV is alarmed, sir. Any attempt to disable it...'

Crispus was beginning to look exasperated.

'What is it with this Brit and his hold over people?'

'I know how to disable the CCTV without setting off the alarm, sir.'

Crispus stood in the entrance to the Enlisted Men's mess and scanned the room. He soon found what he wanted. At the far end, Saleh, Vero and Eugenides were singing and extemporising. As far away as he was, he could see fine, red, blood-brotherhood cuts on the upper inside of Saleh's forearms, and when Rufus Vero gesticulated expansively his sleeve pulled up and a similar cut became visible. Various men stood around the three of them, backslapping and celebrating. Eugenides was showing something to Saleh, holding it out in his hand. Crispus squinted so he could make it out: with something of a shock he realised it was a small *tauroctony*, very finely made and painted. Eugenides turned it in his hand while Saleh admired it. Crispus caught himself making a face. Last year he'd sought membership in the Antonia Mithraeum, only to have someone drop a black cube in the ballot box. He was eligible to reapply, but had chosen not to. Cornelius Getorex was the Antonia Mithraeum's Pater; Crispus suspected that he was behind the blackballing.

He walked into the mess. He did not remove his officer's insignia.

'Saleh, Vero and Eugenides,' he called as he approached the group. Heads in the mess turned and men stood as he strode past. He waved them down. He made eye contact with Saleh, who handed the *tauroctony* to Eugenides. He had removed his officer's insignia.

'We need to do the work, gentlemen.'

Saleh stood, *kylix* in hand. Vero and Eugenides struggled upright after him.

'How much have you had to drink?'

'*Aquilifer* Getorex released us for the afternoon, sir,' said Rufus.

'That doesn't answer my question.'

Crispus craned his neck over the table and counted off the empty bottles. Saleh watched him do some mental arithmetic, his fingers pointed out in front of him.

'You'll do. Your presence is required in *Camera*.'

Saleh put the *kylix* down; Crispus could see the blood draining from his face.

Lonuobo fitted his goggles, lifting one eyepiece so he could see to find the wiring he needed. He clambered down into the bowels of the great engine that ran Antonia's security systems, making his way along an elevated stone platform and carrying a box of fine tools tucked under one arm. The place he wanted was beyond the main engine body with its rods and pins and gears arranged in serried ranks. He counted his steps along to the spot where he could see cables connecting CCTV units to recording boxes that in turn were attached to alarms. Some of these were designed to sound only in a confined space, or even in a single office. Others were meant to drown the entire barracks in a wall of sound. He was looking for one of those.

He had an engine blueprint, and even though he was trained as a tool and die maker—he'd often milled component parts for calculation engines—he found the blueprint faintly terrifying.

Don't fuck it up, Marcus.

Fortunately, someone—probably *Optio* Marius Macro, whose attention to detail bordered on the obsessive—had labelled the alarms for each CCTV unit. He isolated the relevant circuit. He could just sever the wires between the alarm and the recording box—that would be enough to kill the sound. However, that still left the CCTV recording until it was manually switched off from within the *Camera*. Whoever reached up towards it would have his face recorded. He flipped his goggle eyepiece down, pulled on a pair of latex gloves and pushed the manual slider on one side to increase magnification and illumination. He used a pair of narrow-nosed pliers—now enormously fat and rather shocking under magnification—to trace the wires backwards from the alarm to the correct recording box, cutting each one as he went, isolating the triggering contacts. He left the punch cartridges in their slots; there was nothing for them to record.

He flipped up one eyepiece again and admired his handiwork; he'd need to be back in here as soon as they'd finished their business to replace the wires and reclaim his scissor clamps. His chopping and cutting did not look like the work of a trained electrician.

Shortly after one of the guards had come to retrieve his empty metal lunch bowl, Ben Yusuf heard raised voices in the corridor. He was surprised at this; his cell was close to soundproof. The only noises he'd heard—and considerably muffled—were a Celtic war cry and some of the music one of the torturers had played at a prisoner he now knew to be Iscariot. Even when the soldier who'd brought him his latest reading material had stopped by, he'd shut the door behind him and killed any sound from outside.

Ben Yusuf stood up and went to his cell door, running his thumb along the seal joining the shelf where they left his food each day. The guard hadn't pushed the hatch all the way home; Ben Yusuf wriggled his fingers into the small space and levered it open another inch or so, trying not to reveal himself. Drunken singing floated down the corridor. Loud music started playing, infectious and happy. He hadn't grown up with music like that and now he could hear it at volume—especially after so much silence—he found it disorienting, even frightening.

He drew back with a start when he heard screaming coming from the same place as the music. As he watched, one eye at the slit in the metal, he saw five legionaries, some of them obviously tipsy, hauling Iscariot at speed along the polished stone floor. One of the drunkards was the medic who'd examined him when he first arrived. The medic was trotting backwards, trying to supervise the two men—one muscular and black, one white with a bald spot—holding Iscariot's wrists. The black man was sober; the white man was on his way into the bottle. From time to time the medic yelled something in Latin at the two draggers. It sounded like 'go easy' or 'not so much' but his words were unclear. Another drunkard—a blond man—brought up the rear, laughing uproariously from time to time, but otherwise not speaking.

A tall, fair officer he hadn't seen before directed the other four. This man was sober—aggressively so. Ben Yusuf watched him step ahead of the group and open a reinforced door diagonally opposite. He turned his head as far as he dared, trying to see what lay within. The fair man threw a switch and held the door open while his underlings dragged Iscariot inside. Ben Yusuf could see electrical cable running across the floor.

When Cornelius let himself into his quarters, Mirella was curled up on his bed, her chin tucked in and her knees drawn up into her chest. She was wearing one of his old shirts and—this surprised him—underwear. At first he thought she was asleep, but then he saw her eyes were open. He moved across the room and knelt beside the bed, reaching out to touch her cheek. He suspected she wasn't very well, but it was hard to tell.

When I get sick, I change colour.

She looked at him and smiled weakly.

'Are you all right?'

'My period came early, baby,' she said. 'You fucked it out of me, and now I'm sore and horny, both.'

He leaned towards her and kissed her forehead.

'I've got painkillers.'

'I couldn't find them,' she said. 'I searched and searched.'

He went into the bathroom and rummaged around for a minute or two, returning with a glass of water and a bottle of tablets. He looked sheepish.

'I left them on top of the medicine cabinet. You wouldn't have been able to see.'

She chuckled at this, sitting up and taking the water and

tablets from him.

'Not everyone is ten foot tall, Cornelius.'

He sat beside her on the bed, removing his boots and jacket and pulling off his shirt. She could see mottling across the top of his chest. He curled his arms around her, putting one hand on her belly. He began massaging her, taking his time.

'That's nice.'

'You know, sex is a good cure for period pain.'

'Cheeky, Cornelius.'

'I want a bath, first, though. Give those painkillers time to work.'

She followed him into the bathroom, watching him undress as the bath filled. He slid under the water and then began oiling his skin. She sat against the wall, drawing her knees into her chest again.

'I used your *strigil*. I hope you don't mind. I was careful to clean it up afterwards.'

He held the metal hook up in front of his face, grinning.

'Can't see a thing.'

After he'd dried himself, she watched as he threw his shirt and socks in the laundry and then retrieved a black towel from the cupboard. He pulled back the bedcovers and spread it over the sheets, tucking in the end. She smiled at his neat, controlled movements.

Think of everything, don't you, Cornelius the clever?

He took her hands and guided her first into his chest, and then into his bed. She shivered—her period sometimes did that to her—and he saw. He drew the covers up over both of them and then lay facing her, his hands tucked under and over her waist. She noticed he was erect.

'I'm not ready yet,' she said.

'Despite appearances, nor am I,' he said.

He slid his head towards hers and kissed her once. She

found herself responding, but he moved his head backwards after a little while.

'Truth or dare?' he asked.

She smiled.

'Truth.'

'If you were a man for a day, what would you look like and what would you do?'

'I'd look like you, Cornelius, and I'd ask me out.'

He chuckled at this.

'Your turn, Mirella.'

'Truth or dare?'

'Truth.'

'What's the longest you've ever gone without taking a bath?'

'This is fairly foul, but twenty-one days.'

'You can't be serious.'

'I am. On a joint exercise with *Legio III Gallica* in Syria. Mind you, we all stank by the end, so no one noticed. It was funny marching back into Damascus after it was finished. People on the footpath were disappearing into shops and doing everything they could to get out of our way. All our armoured vehicles reeked. I remember *Centurio* Calpurnius had to go to his quarters for some reason or other before going to the barracks baths. His kids ran away from him. His son hid in the hall cupboard and his daughter asked him why he'd painted himself black. His woman said that if he ever set foot in there smelling like that again, she was filing for divorce.'

She laughed and rested her hands on his chest.

'Truth or dare?' he asked.

'Truth.'

'What's the most recent thing you've done that you're ashamed of?'

She looked uncomfortable and bit her lip.

'I went through your big photo album. The one with the

map in the front. I'm sorry.'

This time she let him pull her to him and kiss her. She could feel his cock against her thigh.

'There's nothing in there I'm not proud of, Mirella.'

'Your daughter is gorgeous. And your concubine, with that ivory skin.'

'Under Celtic law, Bella was my wife, but any time a Roman lawyer sees a time-limited relationship contract, he calls it concubinage. Just as well, really, because at that stage I still couldn't marry. That's army rules, it's not allowed in your home province.'

'Didn't she want to stay married?'

'As long as I was in Britannia, yes. She loved me very much, which is why she chose to bear my child. Most short handfasts like that don't result in children. I knew I was going to be posted away, and didn't want to bind her to me.'

'Just like that,' she said.

'I also knew that Brennius liked her, and that she had eyes for him, too.'

'The man in the wedding photograph?'

'Yes. He's my blood brother. And he's from Germania Inferior, and will be in Britannia for the foreseeable.'

'Ciara wants to see you.'

'She's seen me twice this year already, which is good going. I've been able to wangle spots on Imperial Navy ground effect vehicle transports.'

'Truth or dare?' she asked.

'Truth.'

'What worries you right now?'

'Right now? *Advocatus* Gaius Crispus.'

'Another lawyer?'

'In this very legion, too.'

'Why?'

He pulled a face and pressed his lips together, struggling to find the right words.

'He cuts corners. He doesn't think the rules apply to him. He's dishonourable.'

'This is the first time I've ever heard you say anything bad about anyone, Cornelius.'

He pulled a face again. 'It's been playing on my mind. I do try to give everyone an even chance.'

'I know that, Cornelius.'

'Look, he did a really ordinary thing when he was in Rome. Half the legion knows about it so it won't hurt if you know as well. He had a concubine while he was at *Collegia Roma*, five-year contract I think. His old man's a senator, stuffy *paterfamilias* of the old school. Didn't like the concubine, although accepted it because she *was* a concubine...'

'What was wrong with her?'

'Playback singer.'

'I don't get it, Cornelius. What's wrong with a singer?'

'I don't fully understand either, but some old-fashioned Romans don't like actors and singers and whatnot. They're low occupations. Back in the day there used to be laws against marrying one if you were a senator or had a close family member who was a senator. Honoured almost entirely in the breach, of course. It's still considered a bit racy.'

'So he joined the army and voided the agreement?'

'Worse. He hopped on a troopship and refused to pay her out. It still had two years to run, too. The old man came good with the money for the two years, but only because she'd threatened to litigate. Pilate's firm handled it all—Pilate and Crispus senior are old political chums—kept it all hush-hush and out of the papers.'

'Men who do things like that should come with warnings attached.'

'Yeah, it's pretty poor.'

He kissed the tip of her nose and ran his fingers along the space between two of her cornrows.

'Truth or dare?'

'Truth,' she said.

'How long have we known each other?'

'Four years, Cornelius. And yes, I have been waiting.'

He cupped her face in his hands, moving his thumbs back and forth across her cheekbones. He did this for several minutes, blinking a great deal.

'It's time to apologise for using you as a festival fuck, Mirella. I'm sorry.'

She wriggled closer to him and stroked his face in her turn. His cheeks were wet.

'That's worship, Cornelius.'

'It doesn't feel like worship to me,' he said. 'I didn't grow up with it.'

She noticed he was having trouble looking at her. She lodged her fingers under his chin and turned his head so he faced her. He pulled the covers up over both their heads. A sliver of silver cut across his face where the material admitted a little light; it looked like someone had painted a stripe across his hair and one side of his head.

'When Marius first invited me and we all went to the notary's office in Caesarea to do our consents, I couldn't believe it. I thought all my Saturnalias had come at once,' he paused. 'Please don't take this the wrong way, I'm not being disrespectful...'

'I'm not cross with you, Cornelius. I am curious, though.'

'After the first time, and I'd had this huge thrill... the best time of my life, I think...'

'I like the Temple in Caesarea. They don't have to pretend to be something else.'

'Whenever he invited me, I'd always ask if you'd be there.'

'That's allowed, Cornelius. I'd always ask Camilla the same thing about you.'

'It's just that they can, I don't know... Romans are like taps, they can just turn it on, then turn it off.'

He mimed opening and closing a stopcock. The silver sliver danced on the back of his hand.

'We're Romans too, Cornelius.'

He laughed.

'You know what I mean, though.'

'Yes.'

'See, I wasn't going there for the Goddess. I was going for you. And I didn't know if that was, you know, mutual.'

'And you were afraid to ask?'

'Terrified. Used to wake up in cold sweats worrying that only the second woman I'd ever loved was going to tear my head off for impiety.'

'Oh Cornelius, you are so good, you *shine*.'

He began kissing her. She felt one hand slide up under his shirt; she let him pull it over her head and drop it on the floor. The other hand began working her pants off. She helped him, twisting her backside and lifting first one leg, then the other. He grabbed a handful of her rear.

'I really like this.'

'I hope that's a thick towel,' she said, expecting him to laugh or at least raise an eyebrow. Instead, he continued kissing her, moving his lips over her neck and breasts.

After a while, he stopped and stared at her, his face above her belly now.

'Truth or dare?' he asked.

'It's my turn.'

He smiled and repeated the question, ignoring her objection.

'Truth,' she said.

He seemed to be mastering himself for a moment. He reached for her breasts and began kneading them gently.

'Mirella Tanita, will you be my woman?'

Cornelius was a big man, but the intensity of her response came close to turfing him out of his own bed. She sat upright and wrapped her arms around his back, then pulled him towards her as she lay down. His face was directly above hers. He steadied himself with one hand. She hooked her legs around him.

'Fuck me. On my back. Do it now. I belong to you.'

I take it that's a yes, kiddo.

Ioanne looked out over Gehenna landfill from the lowest point of the Jewish Quarter, covering his mouth and nose as the wind changed, scanning the area for Simon. If he squinted, he could see figures scrabbling over mountains of rubbish looking for things they could sell or reuse. He wished that he'd brought his binoculars with him from Capernaum. He'd left them behind, locked up with his fishing gear.

Whole families lived on the tip; some of the tin huts they'd built for themselves had taken on a semipermanent appearance, with crisscrossing streets swept clean to reveal the ochre coloured earth. From time to time the Romans would chase them off, bulldozing the shanties. They were at it today. The legionaries had tied bandannas around their faces to keep out the flies and stench while they did it. The waste management company's employees stood off to one side, watching as the soldiers cleared the tip of its unwanted inhabitants. Occasionally the tip's residents would lob rubbish and rocks at the soldiers, but there didn't seem to be much of that going on today.

Ioanne had no particular desire to go scrabbling around Gehenna in his search for Simon, but it was a known Zealot stronghold. He also had to admit that the young hothead had defeated him. Ioanne now suspected he'd left Petros's place with a plan in mind, and knew Jerusalem rather better than Ioanne had given him credit for. With some irritation, Ioanne made his way out the city gate, through the swirling dust, down the slope towards the tip, hoping against hope that the Roman bulldozers would turn Simon up, or at least someone who knew where Simon could be found.

As he reached the outskirts of the tip, scaring scavenging birds out of his way as he went, he got close enough to see one of the legionaries crying into his bandanna as he flattened most of a 'street'. He watched as the soldier first used a loudhailer to chase the families out of their homes. The children came first, followed by their parents, followed—in some cases—by the elderly. Ioanne saw one old man being carried out on a door. They seemed to know the drill, standing mute and still to the side as the soldier did his work, their cotton print rags fluttering around them. Only one seemed to object; a woman with a toddler in her arms. She stood in front of the blade and remonstrated with the soldier in Aramaic. He rubbed the back of one hand under his eyes and gunned the dozer's motor, but she did not move out of his path.

Ioanne saw movement out of the corner of his eye; he turned to see a lean, brown man with Centurion's insignia striding towards the bulldozer and its young driver. The officer gesticulated, first at his subordinate and then at the woman defying him. The bulldozer inched forward, but the woman still refused to move. The Centurion strode towards her, pointing at the rest of her family. When she refused to move again, he raised his carbine above his head, aiming the butt at her. Ioanne suspected this was only for effect—Pilate didn't like his troops belting people with their rifle butts, that was a Gratus thing—but she wasn't to know that, and she scurried out of his way, swearing at him in Aramaic and shielding her child's head with one hand. He clambered up into the vehicle, sitting in the cab beside the crying enlisted man. Ioanne watched as he turned the young man's head to face him and backhanded it with some force. He bellowed something in his own tongue at him and then took over the dozer's controls. He flattened the street himself, at speed.

He's lucky he didn't make him drop and do fifty in the middle of the town tip.

I've seen them do that.

There was no sign of Simon. Ioanne decided that he'd done his bit and scrambled up the slope to the Jewish Quarter, not relishing the prospect of the long walk back to Petros's. He turned once, just in time to see the legionaries handing the bulldozers over to the waste management people. They formed into ranks and marched up the hill towards waiting armoured vehicles, singing. Just before they clambered inside, he saw an older ranker throw his arm around the crying legionary's shoulders. He was not crying now, although his eyes were very red.

'Hey,' the older man said. 'Get you to the baths and then find a nice girl in the Greek Quarter to suck your cock and you'll be good to go.'

The young man smiled.

As Ioanne watched, the tip people began sweeping the streets clear of debris while looking for straight sheets of tin.

He lay on his back, looking up at Fotini. She sat beside him, leaning on one arm, her legs tucked in. They'd planted themselves next to one of the fountains. Water cascaded musically down a series of clamshells, twisting and shimmering. Light from the *tepidarium* skylight backlit her, picking out flyaway hairs and making her look darker than she was. Although she was Greek, he suspected—with that elegant and rather retroussé snout, and her coffee-coloured skin—that there was an Ethiopian somewhere in her woodpile. They'd spent a leisurely hour or so washing, oiling and scraping each other, Linnaeus moaning all the while about Petros Bar Yonah, Petros Bar Yonah's ugly son, Simon the Zealot, trying to build a strong defence case for Yeshua Ben Yusuf, and dealing with Jews who hated him for what he was rather than for anything he did. She made sympathetic noises throughout, massaging him with her long, clever fingers and kissing him chastely on the cheek or forehead; part of the ritual of the baths involved public probity and delay of gratification. Suggestive mosaics and frescoes throughout the complex were there to provide inspiration for what came *afterwards*.

'I don't know how you Greeks put up with it, I really don't. It's a wonder you don't all up and leave.'

'A lot of Greeks make a very good living in Jerusalem because the locals refuse to, shall we say, come across.'

'Ah, yes. That's well known. It's just not being able to build your own temples, and being confined to your own quarter would grate, that's all.'

'Caesarea is close. We take cruises to the islands. We have summer houses on Cyprus.'

She ran her fingers around his gold headband; she could see his scalp when his fine straight hair was wet, and it fascinated her. Very few Romans had such straight hair; it was like it had been ironed.

'We learnt not to get in between a Jew and his religion the hard way,' she said. 'They threw Antiochus Epiphanes out on his ear. He tried to Hellenise the Jews in the same way as you're trying to Romanise them.'

'Surely there were some Jews who found Greek civilisation attractive?'

'Many. Jewish athletes competed at the Olympics and the Heraea. The Maccabees killed them. They went through the villages, destroying our temples and circumcising adult Jews who had become Hellenised.'

He winced at the thought. 'Why does that not surprise me?'

She smiled at him; her expression was somewhere in between wry and fey.

'It didn't help that Rome wanted the Seleucids to fall, so you could claim their territory for your own.'

'Yes, we'd have been busy coming up with gunpowder at about that point.'

'And selling arms to both sides.'

'That is the Roman way. *Divide et impera*.'

'Congratulations, Rome. You get the booby prize otherwise known as Judaea.'

He propped himself up on one elbow, laughing and then scanning the room.

'You know, I'm starting to wonder if I smell, or if I've grown an extra head that no one's seen fit to tell me about.'

'Why?'

'Look at this place. It's deserted. As a general rule I'm looking to leave around now because the baths are starting to get a bit popular.'

She stood up to look, her hands on her hips. 'You know, you're right. No idea what's going on.'

'As long as I haven't grown an extra head,' he said. 'That I can really do without.'

He stretched out on his back and curled a hand around one of her ankles, looking up at her.

'You know, that's a lovely, lovely view, Fotini.'

She knelt down beside him.

'I take it you'd like a closer one?'

'I would indeed.'

She took his hand and led him to the changing rooms. She'd retrieved a set of casual clothes from his room for him and she watched as he dropped a dark-blue tunic over his head and checked his watch, sliding the chain around his neck as he did so. She held out his boating shoes; he sat down to put them on, then rummaged in his locker for his wallet and the soft leather holdall he always took to the baths. She handed him her towel and clothes from earlier in the day; he stowed them neatly with his own. Finally, he brought out an amethyst amulet of Cybele he liked when he wore blue. In turn, he watched as she dressed in a diaphanous—and he thought very pretty—Greek gown, pinning her hair back with a comb. On a whim, he hung the amulet around her neck. The Goddess in profile with her crown of towers nestled between Fotini's breasts.

'It looks better on you,' he said. 'Keep it.'

She held it up in front of her eyes, turning it so that light bounced off the faceting. There was no one else in the change room, so he pulled her towards him. She put her arms around his neck.

'A fair day lies in prospect,' he said.

'There's a reason you finished so early,' she said.

'Oh yes,' he said, kissing her.

From behind his right ear, he felt something cold touch his ear. Fotini's eyes grew wide as he watched her face; both of them raised their hands without being told to do so.

'We got two more,' a voice said in bad Greek, loud enough to make Linnaeus start. The pistol pressed into the flesh behind his ear now.

'A Roman pig and his Greek whore,' the voice continued.

'Bring them out,' another voice answered from outside the baths. It sounded curiously familiar, although Linnaeus could not place it. The man stood behind them and walked them out of the Empire's baths. He took them through the palaestra, with its racked weights and rubber mats. There were free weights, bars and dumbbells scattered around the floor, and Linnaeus could see two pale feet sticking out from behind a marble pillar. The supervising trainer had been shot at his counter. Linnaeus noticed that he had his hand in a drawer on one side; its fingers were coiled around a pistol. His brains were distributed over a matte *Visit Judaea!* poster behind him. Linnaeus took Fotini's hand; the gunman made no attempt to stop him.

Standing next to the counter and its butchered occupant was Simon the Zealot. Linnaeus felt the blood drain out of his face. About the only consolation was that Simon's face had also gone pale. If anything, he looked even less happy to see Linnaeus.

'Fancy meeting you here, Simon,' he said.

Fotini stood on his toes and pinched his fingers, hard. He winced and shut up.

I've got the Midas touch in reverse. Everything I touch turns to shit.

Fotini looked at him, then at Simon, her face a mask of perplexity and horror.

'How do you know him?' she asked in Latin.

'He was at the witness interview I've just come from. The Simon I was talking about.'

Simon's mouth was working, but nothing came out.

'Take them up to the banqueting hall,' he said at length.

As they made their way through the ground floor bar area, Linnaeus started to count the bodies. He saw Armin, the concierge, collapsed next to his desk, his body riddled with bullets. He hadn't been killed cleanly and had left a wide blood slick where he'd crawled back to his desk to raise the alarm.

Linnaeus could see a red light flashing under the counter. *That'll go through to Antonia.* An elderly couple seated in plush chairs to one side of the bar had been executed where they sat. Fotini gasped again and he turned to look at what she was looking at. A young woman laid spread-eagled on the floor in an expanding pool of blood, her skirt hitched up above her waist. A Guild of Sex Workers card had been shoved into her mouth. The barman lay beside her; he'd been executed from behind. The front of his face was in tatters.

The Zealot prodded them into the lift.

The Empire Hotel's banqueting hall was on the top floor; it opened out onto a rooftop garden that could be customised for wedding receptions, coming-of-age celebrations and conference functions. The hall itself was expensively decorated with a mixture of religious and secular mosaics. In a central roundel, an ivory-crowned Bacchus danced with his maenads, while around the walls mythological scenes were interspersed with scenes of everyday life: fishing trawlers in the harbour at Caesarea; a Roman magistrate on a raised dais; a man and a woman shaking hands over legal documents spread across a table. On one side, floor-to-ceiling windows provided a panoramic view of the city and the Temple.

Linnaeus did not need to guess that today the gardens and hall would have been rigged up for a Roman boy's coming of age. The first thing he saw on emerging from the lift was a tall, slim teenager in a formal grey gown overlaid with the *toga virilis*. He had his arms around a beautiful woman some years older than him. He seemed to be consoling her; her head was on his chest and he was stroking her hair. His parents and relatives and various other guests were ranged behind them.

Fotini clung to Linnaeus; he noticed that the windows were all shut, and that the hall was getting stuffy. He looked past the family group and saw, then, the extent of the terror.

Upwards of two hundred people were crowded into the banqueting hall. There was a big group of dark foreigners—*Indoi, probably*—bunched together at the back, along with a large number of wealthy Jews from outside Judaea visiting the city for Passover. Several of the Jewish men were praying, rocking back and forth. Those not praying looked thunderous, with one man in particular glaring at each Zealot in turn. Two of the Jewish women had young children; both were screaming to beat the band. He scanned the room for bodies, expecting to find carnage similar to that in the lobby.

No one dead. Yet.

As he watched, a Zealot with a gun ordered the Roman family group to sit. The *paterfamilias* glared at him, rather pointedly sitting down last.

Gods alive, don't get yourself killed trying to prove a point, old man.

The Zealot kept his weapon trained on the man. He sat beside a stout, formally dressed woman—presumably his wife—his face defiant. He ran his fingers though his hair—it was auburn, flecked with grey—and grasped his son's shoulder. The boy still had his arms around the woman. Her face was still buried in his chest. Other Zealots—there seemed to be three or four of them—made everyone else in the room sit as well. Long lines snaked crookedly across the mosaic. Linnaeus felt the pistol in the small of his back; he and Fotini were shoved in between the family group and what he suspected were people affiliated to the hotel. He saw Cynara in the midst of the hotel's wait staff and several contract cleaners. He crawled towards her, hoping she'd notice him as he sat down beside her.

'What the fuck is going on?' he whispered.

He need not have whispered; the Zealots were making no

attempt to keep people quiet.

Cynara turned to face him. She had been crying: her mascara had run and her cheeks were streaked with iridescent blue kohl. Even though she'd turned towards him when he spoke to her, she stared through him, not recognising him.

'They shot up the lobby. They killed everyone. Half my people are dead. They gang raped a woman in the bar—'

'We saw, Cynara,' he said, reaching out to pat her cheek. Her pupils were almost completely dilated.

She responded to the sound of her name, focusing on him. Fotini wriggled over and sat on the other side of her, clasping her shoulders.

'Cynara,' said Linnaeus, leaning close to her, this time intuiting that whispering was necessary. 'Armin got back to his desk and raised the alarm. I saw the light flashing. They know in Antonia.'

Cynara nodded.

Simon was annoyed, because things had gone well to start with. Fewer Romans than he'd expected had been carrying weapons, and he'd only lost two of his fighters to people determined to choose death before dishonour. He'd acquired a decent arsenal of Roman machine pistols and ammunition in the sweep, which he distributed among his men. His problem now was the lack of coverage; he'd turned on the solitary functioning screen in the lobby to see whether their efforts had made the news as yet, but nothing doing. CR was reporting—in shocked and scandalised tones—that a member of the imperial household, one Gaius Caligula, had checked into rehab for the umpteenth time. JTN was replaying an old movie. The main Greek station had reverted to a test pattern with scrolling text wishing everyone an enjoyable *Megalesia*. For some reason he couldn't pick up the Alexandrine station—the screen was full of snow and distorted voices. This meant the boy he'd sent to the kitchens was either lost or wool-gathering.

Have to do it yourself, Simon.

Unwilling to trust the lifts, he made his way up the fire escape towards the main kitchens on the sixth floor.

He was also none too pleased at encountering Ben Yusuf's lawyer and his whore in the baths. He hadn't expected the lawyer to be staying at the Empire. He'd heard Romans say they didn't like spending time in Jerusalem on account of it being full of Jews, and he'd mentally labelled Andreius Linnaeus as that sort of Roman.

He found the Galilean teenager who was supposed to be lighting up the kitchens standing in front of a screen set flush into the marble outside the sixth floor restaurant. He was watching the CR story with a kind of awe.

'Started that fire yet, Yaakov?' Simon asked.

The boy spun around and looked at him.

'It's thirty inches across, that screen,' he said. 'I measured it.'

'You were supposed to start a fire, you fool.'

'It's beautiful here. Look.'

Simon followed the boy's finger towards the ceiling, which was indeed very beautiful—a fresco of young people dancing in a circle, alternating boy–girl, holding a coloured scarf in between each pair of clasped hands.

'You're not supposed to be admiring their filthy art, Yaakov.'

The boy dropped his eyes. Simon marched into the kitchen and began flicking gas burners on. He lit the end of a rolled-up newspaper on one of them and tried to light the curtains, but they were made of some sort of flame-retardant material and would not ignite. He swore and began looking in various cupboards for something flammable; he started breaking bottles of olive oil on the floor. He dumped the burning newspaper into the middle of the slippery mess and waited for it to take, then started to set paper towels on fire, dropping them into bins and leaving the lids up. The unmistakable smell of pork and fish assailed his nostrils. He walked around the stainless steel benchtops and saw several of the small fat rodents the Romans considered a delicacy cut open ready for seasoning. The cook who'd been working on them was now on the floor, a basting brush still clutched in one hand. He'd been shot in the temple.

Simon picked his way around the corpse and, judging the fire to be fierce enough, started to open windows. The oxygen intake was dramatic and effective, and both he and Yaakov hightailed it out of there, hearing bottles of gas and cooking oils explode as they went.

Simon went downstairs again; Yaakov followed him obediently.

Yaakov loved Simon, but wondered at him, too. He remembered telling Simon—when he was six or so—that he'd taken sweets from a Roman soldier. Simon had flogged him until he was unable to sit down. Yaakov also hadn't wanted to use the woman in the bar, but Simon had picked out three of them and told them, 'Fuck her, she's worthless.' He'd hung back while the other two went at her like madmen, holding their pricks out in front of them. Simon explained that she made her living fucking rich Romans who came to the hotel, a different one each night, unless he stayed longer than one night. Then he could buy her for the duration of his stay. Yaakov felt his cock get hard. He waited for one of the other men to finish and lay on top of her, pulling her dress down so he could touch her breasts; he'd never touched a woman's breasts before. She was crying, so he patted her head. 'Don't cry, pretty lady,' he'd said in Aramaic, but of course she couldn't understand him. He soon lost control of his hips, bucking as hard as the other two had. Simon shot her before he had the chance to pull his cock out.

Simon stood in front of the screen in the bar; he'd tuned it to JTN. As soon as they picked it up, he knew CR would follow. Yaakov watched as Simon unfolded the Zealot statement and sat it in the telegraph machine in the lobby. Simon took what Yaakov knew to be a JTN reporter's business card out of his pocket and dialled the telegraph number. The machine sucked in the paper and spat it out on the other side, a process Yaakov found intriguing. Soon enough, JTN cut into the thirty-year-old black-and-white movie they'd been showing with a breaking story and images of billowing smoke.

'Now it begins,' he said, and made for the fire escape. Yaakov followed him, struggling to keep up.

Linneaus began to reconnoitre the people around him. He encountered a nervy Ligurian businessman with the strongest Genuese accent he'd ever heard, a burly cook from the ground floor restaurant, a young woman who sold flowers and soft toys, a large number of people with connections to the arms trade and a tall Bactrian who now lived in Caesarea. The latter's name was Ashok, and he was ropeable.

'I was just about to close out a deal, and then this happens,' he said. 'I thought we had a mortgage on religious nutters at home.'

'In Caesarea?'

'Gods, no,' he said. 'In Alexandria of the Caucasus.'

Linnaeus now found himself a leader of sorts. When the infant children sequestered in the midst of the Jewish guests really began to scream, one of the Zealots mimed sticking his fingers in his ears. Another stood over one child and its mother and bellowed in Aramaic. The child's screams became louder. Linnaeus watched as other women pulled on the yelling Zealot's trousers, supplicating and pointing to the baby. The man rounded on her, lifting his weapon to his shoulder.

Linnaeus stood up. He was starting to develop a headache.

'The baby needs water,' he said in Greek.

His movement and voice cut through the hubbub; everyone in the room fell silent, apart from the wailing children. Two of the Zealots dodged around people crouched on the floor and trained their rifles on him. He made calm eye contact with both men.

'The children need water, that's why they're crying. If you want to stop them crying, you need to give them a drink.'

The Zealot closest to him cocked his head on one side and touched the barrel of his gun to Linnaeus's forehead. The Jewish mother spoke up again; she'd taken off her child's nappy; the stench permeated the room.

'And if you want that smell to go away, you'd better let her change the baby's nappy. Please.'

The Zealot lowered his gun slowly, cocking his head to the other side now. He pointed to the woman and her child, then pointed at the sign indicating the toilets, wrinkling his nose at the astrological symbols they used for 'male' and 'female'. The woman made eye contact with Linnaeus as she walked past; he could see her mouthing *gratia, gratia* as she went.

'The other child still needs water,' Linnaeus said softly.

The gun came up again, touching him between his eyebrows.

At that point, Simon the Zealot stalked into the room, followed by a younger acolyte. The man with his gun trained on Linnaeus turned away, losing interest. Linnaeus waited until he was most of the way across the room before sitting down.

Simon had a loudhailer in his hand. He raised it to his lips.

'Take out your identity cards and hold them up above your heads,' he said.

There was a ripple of movement as people dived into handbags and wallets and jackets and withdrew either a purple or yellow card.

Fotini looked at Cynara, her yellow card in front of her nose, the words 'Non-Citizen' stamped across the top.

'What are they doing?'

Cynara shook her head; her hands had started to tremble. She had difficulty withdrawing her own purple card.

'There's a story in Jewish folklore,' she said softly, 'that at the end of time God will judge the unbelievers, that he will divide the good from the evil as a shepherd separates the sheep from the goats.'

'What happens?'

'The sheep go to live with God,' she said. 'The goats go to the lake of fire.'

'The Underworld?'

'Worse. Much worse.'

'Do all Jews believe that?'

'No. It's a folk story, used to frighten little children who won't do what they're told.'

Cynara looked at her own card, turning it over in her hand and remembering how proud she'd been after the citizenship ceremony in Rome. No one in her family was a citizen; she'd been recommended by the Hotel School on the strength of her good results and 'contribution to the life of the school'. She remembered having to take a series of examinations in a fusty hall off the Forum. Because she had a sponsor, she didn't need to achieve 100 per cent on the exams, although as the woman administering them pointed out, 'It is customary to attain 100 per cent.' She'd had to brush up on Roman history and the final essay on 'the meaning of citizenship' had flummoxed her for a good while. The ceremony itself had required attendance in one of their temples—she'd temporarily baulked at this—but the grave seriousness of proceedings swept away any lingering doubts. Together with thirty or so others—all sponsored by various educational *collegia*—she'd raised her right hand and recited the Oath before a statue of the Divine Julius.

The *praetor* administering the Oath congratulated them, told them how they should say *civis Romanus sum* with pride, and encouraged them to be 'active citizens, to be leaders in their community'.

She held her card above her head.

The Zealots walked up and down the rows of people, looking at the distribution of yellow and purple cards, apparently confused about what to do. Simon had his hands on his hips and sucked his bottom lip. He brought the loudhailer to his lips again.

'Citizens, over by the windows; non-citizens, over by the mosaic.'

This time there was consternation in addition to a tidal wave of movement. Fotini looked at Linnaeus, curling her arms around his waist.

'I want to stay with you,' she said.

'I don't think that's wise,' he said. 'I can't imagine Zealot solicitude being directed at Roman citizens.'

'I want to stay with you,' she repeated. He nodded now, drawing her to him and then standing. He took her hand.

It also transpired that three of the Jewish guests were Roman citizens. This seemed to enrage the Zealots. In a sudden explosion of fury and speed, a sidelocked man was hauled into the widening gap between the two groups. Simon pushed him onto his knees and shot him in the back of the head. He pitched forward, his blood seeping into the interstices of the great Bacchanalian floor mosaic.

'They're killing their own people,' Fotini said. 'Like in the days of Antiochus.'

Simon pointed towards the two remaining citizen Jews—a man and a woman—splitting them from their non-citizen spouses and ordering them to join the Romans under the windows. The man folded the woman into his arms—she was gibbering—and guided her towards Linnaeus. They stood beside him.

Well done, Andreius. Make yourself conspicuous and everyone wants to be your friend.

Some of the Jews began to say Kaddish for the dead man. This incensed the Zealots even further. Two of the praying men were pistol-whipped into unconsciousness. Simon approached a third, but he did not stop praying, his voice somehow filling the room. Linnaeus could see admiring looks on various Roman faces, and not just because the prayer was beautiful. The man continued to pray. Simon let his pistol hang at his side. He spun on his heel and walked away, standing with his back to what Linnaeus suspected were kitchens and offices. It was at that point that Linnaeus noticed the Ligurian businessman had inserted himself among the non-citizens.

Simon raised the loudhailer to his lips once more.

'Cards above your heads again.'

The Zealots walked between the two groups, examining the cards and talking quietly among themselves. The young Zealot who had followed Simon in from the fire escape looked at Fotini's yellow card and pointed her to the other side of the room.

'She's mine,' Linnaeus said in Greek, but the boy shook his head, uncomprehending. He put his arms around her and pulled her close, doing his best to demonstrate sexual ownership in the way a Galilean peasant might understand. The boy turned her card over in his hand, trying to puzzle out the Greek letters. He was illiterate, or close to it. He handed it back to her.

There was a loud thump and a scream from the non-citizen side; Simon had turned up the Ligurian businessman and was holding his identity card up in the air like a trophy. Two more Zealots converged and dragged the man by the arms towards the dead man already in the middle of the floor.

So they'll execute him, too. Nice.

They stripped him to his underwear; the two men pinned him to his back and Simon knelt beside him. He was holding what looked like a shoemaker's awl in his hand. Another Zealot raced up the stairs leading to the rooftop garden and began winding the handle to open the roof; cool air flooded the hall as he did so. Linnaeus leant as far as he dared towards the windows, peering down into the streets below. Standing in front of the stolid classical edifice of the *CreditGallia* building opposite was an expanding crowd of onlookers and—this he particularly noted—three screen crews. *Colonia* police kept them back at some distance, although he knew that modern cameras had big telephoto lenses. If they wanted to show what was happening in close-up, they could.

Come on Fretensis, we need to get our arses out of here.

The man on the floor screamed as Simon cut something into his upper chest with the awl. Linnaeus squinted but couldn't see—but Fotini had young eyes and she could see. She tracked the movement of his hand.

'He just cut S.P.Q.R. into him,' she said.

Linnaeus turned; Ashok the Bactrian was dry retching over his Buddhist prayer beads, but nothing came out of his mouth. Cynara stooped and put her arms around him. He fed the beads forward through his fingers. Two Zealots dragged the Ligurian up the steps and onto the roof.

Saleh watches as Crispus draws deeply on his cigar, making the end glow, sometimes blowing smoke rings, sometimes not. He seems to be contemplating something esoteric, and hasn't spoken for several minutes. For his part, Saleh is saturated; Lonuobo has been vigorous with the watering-can and there's been too much overspill for the channel under the table. Water is pooling all over the floor. He's managed to keep it out of his medical equipment but at the cost of his own fatigues. It looks like he's pissed himself. Rufus Vero and Lonuobo are also wet, although Lonuobo is very wet. He has some sort of silver dye in his hair; it's mixed with the water and run in chalky rivulets down his face. Rufus holds his dripping towel by one end, letting it swing back and forth. Only Eugenides is dry, standing off to one side, in front of the painted S.P.Q.R., his hands in his pockets.

Crispus stands up, leaning over Iscariot. He jabs his cigar in the captive's direction. Iscariot's head is uncovered now.

'I do believe you've been using that clock to time your resistance.'

Saleh looks at Crispus, impressed despite himself with this bit of deduction.

'Eugenides, take the clock down. He's been able to hold us off because he knows when the first target is going to go up.'

Iscariot flinches as Aristotle removes the clock, pulling the wires out of the back of it far enough to allow him to turn it wrong way round.

'You know, I like this duty,' Crispus continues, his voice sibilant. 'Not because I'm a sick fuck, but because there's no smoke alarm in here.'

He blows a smoke ring, leans over the table and then stubs out his cigar in Iscariot's navel.

'Waste of a good cigar, that.'

Saleh still feels lightheaded from the afternoon's drinking, so when Iscariot screams—and that's what it is, a scream to wake the spirits—he bounces backwards, slamming into the wall and disturbing his medical monitor. He reaches out to catch it and then glares at his superior. He was willing to go along with Crispus once Lonuobo explained what was afoot, but the sharp tang of Iscariot's burning hair and flesh snaps him out of his compliance.

'That's forbidden under the Military Interrogation Code, sir,' he says.

Crispus looks at him.

'Quite the lawyer, aren't we, *Medicus* Saleh.'

Rufus belches while Eugenides and Lonuobo both titter.

'Maybe you'd better mind your own business, and leave the lawyering to me.'

Saleh bites his lip; the alcohol in his system seems to want to force its way out of his tear ducts and humiliate him.

Crispus rubs his hands together, making a raspy sound. His palms are still dry and warm.

'Lonuobo, would you be interesting in going electric?'

Lonuobo's head jerks up; he'd been standing, watering-can under his arm, waiting for another 'Put him down, thirty seconds' directive from Crispus. He smiles.

'I might be, sir,' he says.

Saleh stares at Eugenides, then at Rufus. Eugenides—for the first time—looks uncomfortable. Rufus strokes his hair back, making it stand up. His face is blank.

'Sir, this is the kind of thing that lands people in front of a Senate Select Committee.'

'Undoubtedly, Saleh, although I have taken certain precautions.'

He glances sidelong at the CCTV. It's at that moment Saleh

appreciates the reason for Crispus's failure to announce the interrogation earlier. The green light above the word 'Record' isn't glowing.

'And my father is Consul. Subject to the Veto and the Plebiscite, he runs the Empire.'

'And wouldn't he be proud of you now, sir.'

Lonuobo turns towards Saleh, the control box nestled in his hands.

'This is necessary, Saleh. People are going to die otherwise. You keep this one alive for now, and we'll save hundreds of others.'

Saleh has trouble arguing with this, in part because it comes from Lonuobo.

Lonuobo configures the control box while the rest of them wait, then gathers the two electrodes up in his hands. He rummages in a filing cabinet behind him for a roll of gaffer tape and tears off a length. Iscariot lifts his head, watching them.

Lonuobo grimaces, his eyes smouldering. He speaks in Aramaic.

'Continuing the Empire's modernisation policy, Iscariot, we're going to introduce you to the concept of electricity.'

Iscariot spits.

Lonuobo leans over Iscariot and speaks into his ear.

'You murdered my wife because she had to have an abortion. I'm going to make sure that's a situation your wife never has to face.'

Saleh's eyes widen as Lonuobo tapes the electrode to Iscariot's penis, his face focused and intent as he works. He picks up the control box, plonks it on the desk nearest Crispus and flicks the switch on at the outlet. He holds the remaining electrode out in front of him like a sword, grinning.

'Ready to go, sir,' he says.

'You've done this before, haven't you?'

'No, sir, but I have seen it done. In Syria.'

Saleh watches as Crispus leans over Iscariot, only stopping when his face is a couple of inches above his captive's. The whites of Iscariot's eyes are showing.

'Time to sing, little bird, because this stings like fuck.'

Saleh watches as they start with his lip, then move to his armpit, then finally to each nipple in turn. He's never heard a human being make noises like that, not even people he pulled from carriages after the Alexandria rail disaster. Crispus has Lonuobo apply the shocks in rapid succession, firing his questions like bullets: 'What's first?' 'What method?' 'What time?' The electric charge makes Iscariot writhe and contort, his fingers contracting and retracting with each application of the electrode. The water is making it worse; much of Iscariot's body is still very wet.

Saleh can see that even Rufus is having his doubts now: his hands are cupped around his nose and mouth. Perhaps unconsciously, Eugenides is shaking his head.

'Sir, I'm getting *Aquilifer* Getorex.'

Crispus rounds on him.

'You'll do no such thing, Saleh, and that's an order. This is my show, and I'm in charge.'

'The Empire,' Iscariot spits during this brief respite. 'The Empire Hotel. Top floor. Hostages. Through the front door. Now.'

'What's second? What method?'

Iscariot shakes his head.

'He said *now*, sir,' Eugenides yells. 'We've got to go upstairs with this shit.'

Crispus ignores the entreaty and twiddles the knob on the control box.

'Right armpit, Lonuobo.'

Saleh hears Iscariot's humerus fracture as he writhes on

the *parrilla*. It takes him a moment to realise that the bottom half of the bone has pierced the skin just above the elbow. He doesn't move fast enough to prevent blood spattering his face and the front of his uniform.

'Stop, stop, you fuckers, you've cut his brachial artery!'

'Fleet Fox, arson, the basement,' Iscariot sputters. 'At three.' Blood is seeping out of his mouth.

Saleh begins binding Iscariot's arm as best he can, his hands shaking, but not before blood sprays the ceiling and walls. The light is dappled, now, dark spots hovering like flies.

'Central Station, two shooters with auto Ravennas, three-fifteen.'

'We know that.'

'Jerusalem Academy, grenades in the watchtowers then shooters with Ravennas, I don't know how many. Three-thirty. No more. Please.'

Crispus is slapped diagonally across the head with a lash of blood from the jetting artery. He takes a silk handkerchief from his pocket, unfolds it and dabs at his face, then carefully refolds the handkerchief so the blood is on the inside. He puts it back in the same pocket.

'Very good, my friend. Lonuobo, bring that cipher. Now we go to Capito.'

The two officers leave the *Camera*, slamming the door behind them.

Saleh keeps working, staunching the flow of blood.

'For fuck's sake, Vero, don't just fucking stand there. Release him. He'll bleed to death if you don't.'

He sends Eugenides to the infirmary for medical equipment while Rufus unlocks the restraints around Iscariot's hands and feet. He rights the table at Saleh's command, gazing around the room for the first time as he turns the gears.

'It sure looks like a torture chamber now, sir.'

Saleh snorts, drawing up an antibiotic shot and injecting it into Iscariot's undamaged arm.

'Nice observation, Vero. Just lovely.'

Eugenides returns with a bottle of oxygen, a mask and a bag of clear, viscous fluid. Saleh sets to work, preparing what looks to Eugenides like a blood transfusion.

'Where's the blood?'

'He needs platelets, not blood. He's only lost about fifteen per cent.'

He succeeds in staunching the bleeding and uses his jacket to cushion Iscariot's head. He strokes his captive's hair back from his forehead, leaning over him. Iscariot's breath flows over his cheeks, warm and ragged.

'I'm sorry,' Saleh says in his accented Aramaic. 'This is... the state's idea. The state's idea.'

His work done for the moment, he slumps into his seat; his hands hang between his legs. He is covered in blood.

Capito is in the office adjacent to his quarters and standing next to a very red-faced Horace when the orderly opens his door. The office is austere carrara marble, white shot through with soft blue-grey. There is only one concession to ornament, one borne of necessity: a great mosaic map of the city on one wall, each major landmark picked out with an LED. Horace fidgets as both Crispus and Lonuobo stare at him, at the rills of sweat around his hairline and his flushed complexion. He looks at Capito, his eyes glistening with the flat sheen of hero worship.

Capito looks distinctly pissed off at the interruption, fastening the webbing around his waist as Crispus and Lonuobo present their findings. Lonuobo pushes the ciphertext and plaintext across his desk while Crispus outlines what Iscariot has revealed under torture.

Just as Capito stands up and looms over Horace, the light picking out the Empire Hotel begins flashing on the big city plan on the wall. He rubs his chin with one hand.

'You'd better get the Procurator, Horace,' he says. 'We have a problem.'

Horace straightens his robe and pats down his hair as he bolts out of the room.

Pilate is standing just outside Antonia's War Room, diagonally opposite his office. He's watching the Empire Hotel's emergency alarm light flash on a mosaic map identical to that in Capito's quarters. The emergency signal dragged him out of his office a few moments ago, and he strokes his chin as it flashes. Horace sees his back as he gets to the top of the stairs. Pilate listens to Horace outline things, his hands on his head. The attempt to radiate calm is a failure. When Lonuobo and Crispus arrive, the three men can see a vein in his temple pulsing and hear him grinding his teeth. For his part, Pilate can see lines of blood spatter across Crispus and Lonuobo's uniforms. He wants to ask questions, but the situation climbs on top of him.

'And it seems the Empire Hotel has just gone up, Procurator.'

'Capito, I grant leave to solve this as and how you see fit. You will need to notify Vitellius if you make use of the Air Force though.' He paused. 'Horace, get Vitellius up on the Eye.'

Horace faffs around for a bit; he starts going red in the face again. He's unfamiliar with the War Room. Only used in emergencies, it's dominated by the great city map, two vast engines and several large screens hung from brass clasps in the ceiling. A niche with a fine gold bust of Caesar overlooks the wall opposite the map. Surrounding the bust is a vivid fresco outlining *Legio* X *Fretensis*'s service history. Various bits of equipment are stored around the walls. The area is large enough for mass briefings; Capito is preparing for one now.

Pilate reads the service history for a while, but can feel himself getting edgy.

'Come on Horace, get your finger out.'

Capito moves to assist him.

Vitellius, it emerges, is visiting the East Empire Stock Exchange on official business and has to be dragged out of a meeting with the *praetor* in charge of developing exchange regulations. Pilate watches as Capito, Crispus and Lonuobo outline things for a third time, obtain Vitellius's consent to use Air Force resources and then field his blunt security questions.

'Any and all means necessary, gentlemen,' he says at last, looking pointedly at Pilate.

'They've overstepped their Form 23,' Pilate says, despite the fact that the three men are still in the room.

'That's your problem, not mine, Procurator. If you need more *striges*, let me know. I can scramble them quickly; their base is here.' He pauses; Pilate is sure he's noticed the state of the men's uniforms, especially Lonuobo's. His collar is drenched, dark brown against the tan and sand camouflage.

'Good to see you got that haircut, Procurator,' Vitellius adds.

The Eye winks off.

Capito dispatches two snipers to Central Station—as Crispus had suspected he would—then contacts the Station Master to warn him of their impending arrival.

'They'll be in plain clothes with disassembled equipment, and will arrive from a couple of different directions. You're to admit them, find them a discreet place to assemble their weapons and let them deploy as and where they see fit, including in the railway shed roof.'

'Yes, Officer.'

Lonuobo can hear him directing his men as to an acceptable ratio of civilian to military deaths.

'Ideally, one shot, one kill,' he says. 'These men are not going to be hiding. They're going in there expecting to die, and wanting to take as many of us with them as possible. Take them out quickly and this whole problem goes away.'

Lonuobo watches as the snipers start disassembling their weapons, strapping bits to various body parts and then dressing in loose fawn robes like the locals.

'Put something on your head, soldier,' Capito says to one of them. 'You won't fool anyone with that haircut.'

'Yes, sir.'

Another soldier is reminded to change his footwear.

'Those boots look like standard Roman military issue to me, and will to anyone else, too.'

Lonuobo smiles.

A bit more to disguise than you thought, eh?

Pilate sets about contacting the Fleet Fox. Capito looks up at him just in time to see him swear. He seems to have gone through a dozen *vocale* numbers.

'They're all busy or ringing out, Capito. I've even called the line in the *cella*, which has probably made me less than popular with the Goddess.'

Lonuobo sniggers at this.

'Contact the Academy while I break the call, Procurator,' says Capito. 'Probably in the middle of a whole Temple gabfest.'

'Or a whole Temple fuck,' says Crispus.

'That's enough,' says Pilate. 'Don't be impious.'

'We need someone who takes this seriously, Crispus,' says Capito. 'Go get Getorex. Wherever he is, whatever he's doing, he's needed here.'

Having arranged his face into a suitably neutral expression, Crispus stands with care.

Lonuobo is cycling through the Empire's networks on the War Room's screen, the sound muted. He turns to Pilate.

'Procurator, the Empire is on JTN.'

Billowing smoke pours from half-a-dozen windows about halfway up the building. The hostages are corralled on the top floor. A large number are standing at the windows. One or two even wave. JTN are reporting from in front of the *Credit-Gallia* building opposite; bank staff and sundry bystanders are on the footpath, watching and pointing.

'They've lit the fire *underneath* themselves,' Pilate says, staring. 'All the Gods and Goddesses.'

Capito stands beside him.

'We have to issue a general terror alert, Capito.'

'Procurator, the moment we issue a general alert, the terrorists know that we know and will change their plans accordingly. We'll thwart two out of four, maybe even three out of four of their attacks as things stand. That means we can contain the situation in the Empire.'

'That,' he points, 'is going to be on every network in the Empire in less than half-an-hour, Capito.'

Pilate rubs his face with both hands.

'There are some things lawyering doesn't prepare you for.'

'If it's any consolation, Procurator, there are some things soldiering doesn't prepare you for, either.'

Cornelius brought a platter of the simple but tasty fare that sustained him and sat opposite her on the bed. He set it down between them and they ate companionably, occasionally feeding something to the other, but for the most part chewing in silence. She noticed he was liberal with the *garum*.

'You know, that's one Roman thing I've never been able to like,' she said.

'I got addicted to it when I was studying. I like salty savoury things, and this stuff saw me through my finals. I shared a house overlooking the Tamesis with three other men. The army was paying for all of us. I would watch the river glide past my window and just eat bread dipped in it while I was trying to grasp the concept of quasi-contract, or whatever it was.'

'I think I just dropped breadcrumbs in your bed.'

He shrugged and grinned.

'I'll get used to it.'

She looked at him, perplexed.

'I presume you want to move in with me.'

'I didn't know I could, Cornelius.'

'Perk of the job,' he said, chucking her under the chin. 'I just have to register you with the CO. Takes about a fortnight for permission to come through, while they do security checks. When we want babies, though, you have to go to the *colonia* once the first one's born.'

She looked around his quarters, noting that they were generously appointed and likely designed with a married man in mind. They also screamed *boy*, right down to the hand-painted model trains on top of his bureau.

There was a knock at the door, loud and insistent. Before Cornelius had a chance to stand up, it was repeated.

'Coming, coming,' he yelled, dragging some trousers on and fumbling with the webbing at his waist.

She heard low and urgent consultations, followed by a burst of swearing from Cornelius and movement into the kitchen. There seemed to be two or three new voices; one of them had the same edge to it as the voices of women who've just realised they're in for a long and difficult labour. Mirella moved the platter onto his bedside table. The bedroom now smelt only of sex, overpowering even his aftershave. She luxuriated on her back, stretching and wriggling, retrieving his shirt and pulling it over her head. She looked at the ceiling, decorated in geometric red and black, and was shocked to realise that—tender as she was—she would gladly go round with him again if he asked.

Contrary to reports, it is possible to overdose on sex.

She collected the platter and took it into the kitchen, walking carefully as she went.

Three strangers—another officer and two enlisted men—were crowded around Cornelius's small kitchen. All three were covered in dark brown splotches.

'My woman, Mirella,' Cornelius announced, pointing at her. 'Saleh, Eugenides and Vero.'

The three men inclined their heads.

'If you'll just excuse me for a moment,' Cornelius said. She noticed his voice had the same throttled quality as when he'd called her on the ward. She heard a single loud expletive come from the loo.

The officer leaned forward and proffered his hand; she realised when she shook it that he was a medic.

'That doesn't look like the regulation camo pattern.'

'We had a bit of an accident,' he said, touching the caduceus on his collar with almost familial distress.

Cornelius reappeared, now wearing a shirt in addition to his trousers. Mirella noticed as he buttoned it that his upper chest was mottling the way it did when he wanted sex. This time, however, the mottle was close to purple. His jaw was set.

'*Medicus* Saleh wanted to get you, sir, but Crispus ordered him not to,' said Rufus, continuing the conversation that had started before her arrival.

'He went too far, sir,' said Eugenides. 'You should see it down there. It looks like a kosher butchery.'

'There's that thing about the ranking officer taking responsibility for interrogation deaths on his watch, too,' said Saleh. 'And I guarantee it won't be Crispus.'

Mirella watched Cornelius usher them out of his quarters and bid them farewell with exaggerated calm and restraint. His neck had begun to mottle purple as well. He closed the door behind them and turned to face her.

'We can add insubordination to corner cutting and general dishonourable conduct.'

'Crispus?'

'Yes.'

His voice was very quiet; his face was mottling now. In a single swift and graceful movement he spun around and punched the wall. She flinched.

'If I get him by himself, I'll strangle the little cunt!'

He examined his right hand with a degree of detachment; the knuckles were abraded.

'He's flouted Roman military law. He's pissed all over the chain of command. He's put three young men's careers at risk. He's a cunt.'

He was screaming now, and stomped around his quarters.

'If I had my way he'd be cleaning latrines with his tongue until he didn't know the difference between shit and bread.'

At no point did she feel in any danger, but there was something terrifying about such a big man displaying so much aggression. It made her realise that she'd never heard Cornelius swear save in a joyful, sexual context before, and that he wasn't even given to raising his voice.

She went to attract his attention and try to console him when there was another knock at the door. He spun on his heel and crossed the floor towards it in three long strides. He paused, struggling to master himself. Another blood-spattered officer—one with fair hair pushed back from his forehead—stood outside his quarters.

'Cornelius, you're wanted in the War—'

As she watched, he wound up and smashed the fair man in the face; the latter flew backwards and thumped into the wall opposite, sliding down it. Once he reached the floor, he lay there, only moving to form a tent over his nose with both hands. Cornelius slammed his door and turned to face her.

'That's Crispus,' he said.

'I guessed.'

She covered her mouth with her hands and shook her head. He reached out and drew her to him.

'I'm sorry. You've just seen the worst of me.' He clasped her hands in his. 'The terrorists have gone after four targets, starting with the Empire Hotel. They've got hundreds of hostages. Promise me you'll stay until we know it's safe.'

'Women aren't going to stop having babies, Cornelius.'

'On the way to the Jerusalem Æsculapion from here, you'll have to pass both the Empire Hotel and Jerusalem Academy—that's another target. You won't get through the roadblocks, apart from anything else. If you leave Antonia, it won't be to go to work. It will be to go into danger.'

The intensity of his desire to protect her was overwhelming.

'I'll stay, Cornelius.'

He went to move away and retrieve his uniform jacket, but she held him.

'When you come back, I want you to register me here.'

He rested his hands on her backside, the mottling on his face and neck fading now. He began to kiss her, gentle non-sexual kisses across her cheeks and forehead. She put her hands on his face to still his head.

When Crispus reported to Pilate and Capito that *Aquilifer* Getorex was on his way, his nose was rapidly colonising the rest of his face, the undersides of both eyes were going purple, tissue was shoved up his nostrils and fresh blood spackled his uniform. He requested permission to go to the infirmary for some painkillers, which Capito granted.

Pilate smiled grimly once he'd gone.

'I think *Aquilifer* Getorex takes Form 23s even more seriously than I do.'

'You always were a good poke, Cyler Lucullus,' she said, rolling off him. 'You should come to me more often.'

He'd first gone to her on a recommendation three years ago and she'd only become more alluring in the interval: heavy busted, long limbed and fair. He thought she was about forty, but he'd never asked and she'd never told. He also suspected the blonde came out of a bottle, but he was happy to be deceived on this point. She filled him with lust, which is what he cared about.

'I want a woman,' he said. 'I want children. Not right now, but once I'm *immunis*. That's why I haven't been.'

'So you've been looking?'

'Yes, but no luck so far. You can't meet women the normal way here. They don't let them out of their sight.'

She stroked his cheek.

'Poor Cyler. You want a provincial woman?'

'Yah, I do. I like it here, except for the shy women part. I can set up in Caesarea as a sole practitioner after discharge, or maybe in-house counsel somewhere. They're always short of military lawyers in the contractor firms.'

'So you like Caesarea?'

'There's nothing close for me in Italy except my sister and my parents and my brother. She's married well now. There are four of us. We can all care for our parents in their old age; we've all got jobs, except my little brother—he's still at school. And there are good perks for taking a provincial woman.'

'This is true.'

'And if you get a Jewish woman, she'll give you a big family. I want four.'

'You might get killed first.'

'I might. It's do or die.'

That always gave her a little shiver of mixed wonder and fear, the way they were trained to be indifferent to death.

'Will you still come to me?'

'Course I will. Can't expect a wife to do everything I like.'

He crawled towards her, reaching out and pulling her hips against his. 'I've still got one more in me, and I want to eat you out. Then we can do that other thing.'

She laughed, throwing her leg across him and leaning forward; he pulled her into his chest and began kissing her face. Their teeth clashed and he tasted blood—his own, probably—and slowed himself, letting her respond to him with kisses of her own. He used the power in his forearms and wrists to pull her onto him, hooking his fingers together across her lower back.

'Is this from firing a gun all the time, Waterboy, such strong arms?'

'Naughty naughty, Laia, those are different. In the legions, we have a call about the difference. Your rifle you kill with, your gun—he bucked his hips under her—you fuck with.'

She found this funny; she knew the call.

'Get them mixed up and you'll have lots of *shitty* duties.'

She seemed to have spent her life in Roman garrison towns listening to their bawdy and patriotic cadence calls. The Centurions had good voices; the calls and marching feet would carry through the still morning air and act as alarm for everyone for miles around. And she'd seen them run ragged, flogged, bawled out and then let loose after completing their basic training, strong and brown and fit and fierce.

The Romans like them fierce.

She had to admit she liked Cyler Lucullus, though, for all his Roman ferocity; she'd told her current apprentice that Cyler would 'make some woman an excellent wife one day'. He had something of a reputation among his fellow soldiers as 'the man who can', securing willing women or tax-free Persian hashish or duty-free German beer for them for a fee. They teased him by calling him Waterboy, but he didn't care, wearing the name earned for defending his sister with pride. He was also loyal and bold and shrewd. If he turned those talents to marriage and *paterfamilias*, she thought, he would be very good at both. There were three of her clients where she would—were her income not so high or the age gap not so great—gladly sign a contract of concubinage. Cyler was on that short list. Today, he'd amused her by negotiating for bareback sex by showing her his sexual health card, neatly filled in by one of the legionary medics.

'Using a condom is like washing your feet with your socks on.'

'You'll still have to pay a premium,' she said.

She gave herself up to him now, trusting him as he ate her and then turned her over, taking her from behind. He made her come with his usual skill, shouting with joy. He coiled his arms around her, burying his face in her blonde curls. She rubbed her cheek against his bristly scalp.

'Cyler, you are such a *fine* poke.'

'That was good, Laia. Only thing is, I haven't got another one in me, at least not for a long while.'

'Four is very impressive.'

'We can do that other thing now?'

'What do you say, Cyler? What's the correct form of words?'
He went down on his knees beside the bed, looking up at her. 'Please, *Domina*, I need discipline.'
'*Serve*, I will give it to you.'
'*Domina*, thank you.'

She disappeared, and he sat up on the end of the bed, enervated but elated. He pulled his knees into his chest and admired the room.

He liked the decoration in the House of the Spirits, so very similar to what he'd seen in fine country houses as a boy when he'd gone to wealthy folks offering to do odd jobs, this so he could buy his high school textbooks. The voucher covered the cost of education—for those who'd done well enough to stay at school until eighteen, and he had—but not books or stationery. He'd clipped and mowed and whitewashed to put himself through. In his final two years, he'd sliced meat in the market for a local butcher, followed by a stint in a blacking factory mixing vats of polish. He suspected the polish was destined for boots worn by members of the Praetorian Guard.

He'd taken a set of enlistment forms to his parents on the day school finished. His father signed in the blank space marked *paterfamilias* and they'd both wished him well. He'd marched under the arch in Reate's Forum to have his hair sheared off inside a week. He remembered citizens standing around watching—enlistment was a large and public ritual—their arms folded. They were clippered and screamed at and taken away to be made into men.

He stood up and went to the House's shrine, dipped his fingers in the perfumed water, flicked his hands over the *lares* and lit a stick of incense, touching the wet fingers of one hand to his forehead. He did not notice that Laia had re-emerged, wearing the traditional fine gown of a wealthy Roman woman in the days of slavery, modified to sluttish effect, exposing her breasts. She stood behind him, waiting for him to complete the ritual. She gently looped a metal slave collar around his neck and fastened it. She attached a long leash to it and drew him towards her, walking backwards across the corridor and into the House's dungeon. He followed obediently. She shackled his hands both together and to a hook in the wall above his head. She had a cane in one hand, and held his leash in the other. She put her lips to his ear, running her tongue around it before speaking.

'Count the blows, *serve*; nice and clear, or I'll make the next one count double.'

He'd counted up to twenty-three when he heard the unmistakable sound of a siren; he cocked his head back. She took this as encouragement, hitting him harder. Welts came up on his back. The siren sounded again, followed by an announcement in Capito's voice over the city-wide alert system.

'Battle stations, battle stations! All men report to Antonia for roll call. This is not a drill. Repeat: this is not a drill. Battle stations, battle stations. General terror alert, General terror alert!'

'Laia, stop, I've got to get back to base!'

Even though he'd not used his safe word, there was something in his tone that stalled her. She let the cane hang at her side, breathing heavily; sweat beaded her top lip.

'Listen,' he said, as the announcement repeated.

She shook her head, a mask of fear stealing across her face.

'Get me down now. This is serious, serious shit. I haven't heard that in all my time in the army.'

She unhooked his hands from the wall and brought him his fatigues, wallet and pistol. Both of them were so distracted he stood in the corridor and began dressing with his wrists still shackled. He dragged his trousers up and tied his bootlaces regardless.

'Keys, Laia,' he yelled. 'Shackles.'

She rummaged around in another room for what seemed like an inordinately long time.

'Don't tell me you can't find the fucking keys. I'll be needing a welder if you can't.'

At the same moment Laia returned with a circle of jingling silver—and dressed in a knee-length shift, he noted—a striking young woman, seventeen or eighteen, came in through the House's front door with a large cardboard box full of groceries in her hands. A taxidriver with two more boxes followed her. Both of them looked terrified.

'What's happening? A *strix* just left from Antonia.'

'Corinna, my apprentice,' Laia said, unlocking his shackles and unclipping the slave collar from around his neck.

Corinna noted Cyler's camouflage and looked at him. 'What's happening?'

'I don't fully know, except that it's serious. We don't put out calls to battle stations like that except in the most extreme circumstances.'

The siren sounded again. This time Capito's message was directed at civilians, advising them to stay indoors and await further instructions. He repeated it in Aramaic and Greek.

He pulled his shirt over his head and—as they watched—loaded ammunition into his machine pistol, hanging two more magazines to hand at his belt. The taxidriver put his boxes down inside the doorway.

'Do you have a screen?' he asked in Greek.

'Yes, in the Workers' Room upstairs.'

Cyler's brain started to work. He thumped up the stairs, Laia, Corinna, and the cabbie behind him.

'First door on the right, Cyler,' he heard Laia call. There was a large poster stuck to the door: *Guildworkers, Know Your*

Rights! it read, with two columns below, one marked *Acceptable* (with a circle), the other marked *Unacceptable* (with a line). Cyler pushed it open.

Every House employee and half-a-dozen clients were standing around the big wall screen in the middle of what was a converted banqueting room. Some of them turned to face the four who'd just barged in. Several people were crying. One woman let out a low whimper. Some looked reassured when they saw that one of the newcomers was an armed legionary. Cyler strode into the middle of the group, looking at the screen. It was tuned to *Communicatio Roma*. He watched as—in what seemed like slow motion—two masked terrorists propelled a man with considerable force off the rooftop garden of the Empire Hotel. The camera tracked his descent.

'That's twelve stories,' Laia said, her voice sounding far away.

He landed on his back. Blood spattered everywhere.

'They did it because he was a citizen,' the whimpering woman said. She had a strong Greek accent.

'The Zealots stuck his identity card in his mouth,' said a man with silver hair, who stood beside her. 'It was still there when the paramedics arrived.'

'They've got hostages.'

'They shot at the *vigiles* when they tried to put the fire out.'

Cyler picked up the remote control and cycled through the Empire's four main networks. All carried similar footage, following the same story. One focused on a billowing fire that seemed to be coming from windows above the main hotel kitchens. Sirens sounded both from the screen speakers and from outside. There was a couple of seconds time delay; Cyler felt like he was hallucinating.

Simon was sharing the wealth, and Yaakov knew that he

was next. He'd watched as Simon—at reasonably regular intervals—called out one of his underlings and then pointed to a particular hostage.

'Your turn,' he'd say. 'Shoot the pig.'

Early on, he got two of them to don masks and roll the bodies off the roof, but after the first couple he became concerned about snipers on the *CreditGallia* building picking them off as they stood up, so he ordered that the bodies be stacked in a corner. There were six there now. Yaakov kept counting their feet.

Yaakov had avoided his turn at shooting first time around, this because Simon ordered him to take the members of the *Indoi* trade delegation out of the building. The *Indoi*—many of them from Taxila—had been forced to wave their travel documents above their heads in lieu of identity cards, and presented Simon with a problem.

'We'll have to get rid of them,' he said.

'We could just shoot them,' Eleazar—his most trusted confidant—suggested. 'The Kushans will blame Rome.'

'No,' said Simon. 'The Kushans will blame us. They're not so rich or so clever as the Romans, but they want to be. Like the Romans, they believe that progress means a long, lustful life without a thought for God.'

'They don't even believe in God,' Eleazar persisted. 'They have religion without God.'

Simon shrugged and directed Yaakov to lead the fifteen *Indoi* down the fire escape.

Yaakov was now regretting his decision to climb back up the stairs. The pile of bodies in the corner was getting bigger, there were pools of blood all over the floor and Simon was furious that the Romans had cut media broadcasts into the hotel. Every screen in the building now showed a test pattern.

Eleazar had thought to bring a wind-up radio—thinking it would avoid the general media blackout—but it seemed radio signals were being jammed as well. He was so angry he was getting hard to deal with.

There was also the problem that Romans from Italy proper would not kneel to be shot. They stood—men and women alike—confronting their would-be executioners and pointing at their throat or head.

'And look me in the eye while you do it,' was a common challenge.

Two of Simon's lieutenants had crumbled at this, turning their backs and telling Simon to get on with it himself. One Roman man—he had auburn hair and a strongly military bearing—rushed Eleazar, dropping him with a single, rapid jab before Eleazar had a chance to pull the trigger. Other Romans in the room cheered him on; they seemed to feed off the aggression. Simon intervened and shot the man, but not before the latter managed to stand and face him and yell 'Romans die on their feet!'

Yaakov took his chance to slip down the fire escape during the commotion, his shoes clattering on the stairs. He coughed and sputtered as he passed the sixth floor—black smoke was billowing across the street—but if nothing else it concealed his flight. He got to the bottom of the stairs and looked around. Apart from the growing knot of spectators across the road, the area seemed deserted. Pausing only to identify the spot where the smoke seemed thickest, he followed his nose. He knew the Romans were watching, even though he couldn't see them. He waited for the shot to come. It would not be fatal, he knew. They would cripple him and capture him and take him away for torture. When it didn't come, he simply wandered. He did not think, trying only to place one foot in front of the other. Sometimes he turned slowly on the spot, as though dancing, his eyes heavenwards.

JTN: The scene you can see unfolding behind me appears to be the first release of hostages from the Empire Hotel. We were aware from events earlier in the week that there was a Kushan trade delegation in Jerusalem this week and it seems that it's the *Indoi* who have been released. We're being held back for safety reasons but I'll see if we can get a comment.

[...]

JTN [Greek, Aramaic subtitles]: Can you tell us what's happening up there?

***Indoi* trade delegate**: They really, really hate you.

JTN: Who?

***Indoi* trade delegate**: Romans, you Romans. They hate you. Please can I get past?

[...]

JTN: In other news just to hand, the Zealot statement has now been translated into Aramaic; it appears it was written in Greek deliberately. It reads as follows:

'Enough of words. It is time to take action against the iniquitous and faithless force that has spread troops through the Holy Land. You are all forfeit, not just the soldiers who do your bidding, but the citizens who pay their wages as well. We consider you an enemy if you kill us or pay taxes to kill us. To kill the Romans and their allies—civilians and military—is an individual duty for every Jew who can do it in any country in which it is possible to do it, in order to liberate Jerusalem from

> their grip, and in order for their armies to move out of all our lands, defeated and unable to threaten us.'
>
> **JTN**: It is unclear if this means the Zealots wish to broaden the conflict to other provinces with significant Jewish populations, such as Cyprus, Egypt and Cyrenaica [...]

The street he'd chosen was narrow but straight with shops and offices and small workshops on the ground floor and apartments above. Everything was shuttered. If there were people watching above, he could not see them for the smoke. He thought he saw a child's face through a door opened just a crack, but he blinked and it was gone, the door shut tight. He slung his Ravenna over his back, the strap across his chest, leaving his hands free. Ammunition rattled in his pockets. The smoke was clearing now, and he realised that he was climbing steadily. He looked up, seeing a vast and ornate residence on the top of the hill. That, he knew, was Herod's palace. The Procurator lived there, but only for a month each year. A purple *vexillum*—unadorned out of respect for local sensibilities—fluttered from a horizontal crossbar in front of the palace. That meant the Procurator was present. As he climbed, he noticed the houses he passed were further apart, with spacious frontages and extensive gardens. These, too, were shuttered.

He reached an intersection and, knowing nothing of Jerusalem's Roman Quarter, he turned left. He felt himself descending now. This street was wider; its streetlights—the elegant gas variety—were each decorated with two baskets of flowering plants hanging from a metal crosspiece below the lamp. He had no idea what the flowers were, but he thought they were beautiful. He walked towards one and looked up.

He flinched as the woman in the lobby appeared before him. 'We make beautiful things,' she said. That's what the soldier who gave him the sweets said, too.

I'm sorry, pretty lady.

Then, he'd been standing admiring Roman legionaries while they built a railway bridge, one of the metal ones.

'Shouldn't you be in school, little man?' the soldier asked. His Aramaic was careful but clear.

'I don't go to school,' he said.

'That's a shame,' said the man.

The soldier was looking through an instrument with a polished brass lens; it was set on a tripod and had a lever he used to move the lens both vertically and horizontally. There were complicated marks all over it. His fingers adjusted and measured and he bent down to look through the lens. He settled on what he wanted and spoke into something just below his collar.

'What's that machine called?'

'A *dioptra*,' he answered.

'What's it for?'

'It's so we can make sure the things we build are aligned.'

'What happens if they're not aligned?'

'They fall down.'

Yaakov smiled at that, and the soldier reached out to ruffle his hair. 'I like your bridge,' he said at length.

The soldier smiled now, turning away from his machine and sitting on a convenient boulder. He reached behind him and retrieved his pack, rummaging in it for something. He pulled out two small round bread cakes. He handed one to Yaakov.

'We make beautiful things,' he said.

'I want to learn how to use one of those,' Yaakov said with

his mouth full, pointing at the *dioptra*.

'School would be a good place to start,' said the legionary. 'Why aren't you in school?'

'I don't know. My papa doesn't want me to go.'

'If you go to school, when you turn sixteen you can join the *auxilia*; tell them you want to learn how to be a surveyor.'

'I'm not a citizen.'

'Not the legions, the *auxilia*; I don't know the Aramaic word. If you serve for twenty years, you get citizenship.'

Yaakov nodded. He knew the soldier was talking about what the Romans called 'allied troops'.

'That's a lot.'

'Well, a woman has to have three babies by a legionary before she gets citizenship. That's a lot, too.'

The little thing by the soldier's collar spoke to him; he turned it up in his fingers and responded. Yaakov finished the cake and dropped the waxy paper it came in on the ground. The soldier leaned forward and picked it up.

'Don't litter,' he said. He was smiling, but there was a hard edge to the smile. 'No wonder your cities get so filthy; people litter all the time. Do that in Rome and you'll get fined on the spot.'

Yaakov felt himself colouring. 'No one told me.'

'Well, now you know.'

The soldier ruffled his hair again, smiling.

He came to another intersection, a much bigger one. He turned left again, walking down the street parallel to the one where the Empire Hotel was located. He suspected he was looking down the *cardo*; it was wide, spacious and paved with blocks of white stone. The offices and apartments were beautiful, faced with coloured marbles and fronted by fluted columns. Several multi-storey, multi-use buildings dominated the street—there were a couple of banks, some law firms, JTN's offices, and a selection of restaurants and cafés. Residences with small balconies topped all of these, overlooking the street. This time he stopped before going very far, because there was something happening below him. He felt very tired now, and did not want the woman to come back. He sat down under an umbrella pine planted in the middle of the street, drawing his knees up to his chest, and watched.

He saw a dozen Zealots—skinny militiamen in loose shirts familiar to him from a childhood spent in the Galilee—sprint around from the rear of an ornate building on the right. They dodged over construction equipment and slabs of marble scattered about the building site next door. Steel reinforcing poked up out of several incomplete concrete pillars. He could not see what was pursuing them, although from time to time they turned to fire on their attackers. Two of the Zealots went down in the middle of the street, their blood staining the white stone. The others took cover in the buildings opposite and settled down to a war of attrition against the unseen shooters in the ornate building.

His curiosity piqued, he ran down towards the next umbrella pine, squinting up at its rounded crown. Part of him knew he should be helping the Zealot militiamen, but every time he reached for his Ravenna, he saw the woman's face. She would say *we make beautiful things* when he looked at the safety, reminding him that the thing he held in his hands was Roman, too. You could get copy Ravennas and copy Capuas from the Kushan Kingdom, but the Zealots had learned the hard way that they were shite. They jammed all the time and he'd even seen one explode in a fighter's hands. Roman weaponry was nigh on indestructible.

At some point—perhaps while the attackers were reloading—the Zealots shot out the glass in the front of the ornate building. Sparkling fragments whirled and spun upwards in a graceful parabola before tinkling to earth. Yaakov could see people peering out of shutters on the top floor, watching proceedings unfold below. The Zealots now seemed to be getting the better of their attackers, with two crossing the street and entering the shot-out frontage. It was then he saw a civilian move swiftly onto his balcony, lift a rifle with the longest barrel Yaakov had ever seen to his shoulder, and calmly shoot twice into the blown out building. Yaakov heard one militiaman screaming from within. The civilian did not pause to admire his handiwork, vanishing inside so quickly that the Zealots below could not identify where he'd come from. One militiaman began firing indiscriminately into top-floor apartments in response.

Yaakov trotted down the hill to the next umbrella pine.

Gunfire was now coming from several of the top-floor apartments, while three of the Zealots had made their way up a fire escape and onto the roofs opposite the ornate building. When the civilian with the long rifle emerged again, one of the rooftop Zealots shot him; he pitched forward and landed on the street below. Just as he did, a Roman MRAP—one of the big Jupiter-class vehicles—roared past. A legionary popped out of its turret and began bombarding the Zealots on the roof with what looked like a cannon. He took out two of them; Yaakov watched them fragment as the huge rounds hit them. The third dived for cover behind the wall surrounding the flat roof, but the legionary with the massive machine gun kept firing; the weapon rapidly chipped the wall away. One of the Zealots on the ground thought to turn his weapon on the man with the cannon, hitting him in the cheek. He collapsed backwards into the vehicle; Yaakov heard one of the others yell 'Someone get on that fifty,' before a dozen legionaries emerged from the vehicle and began sprinting down the street in an odd, zigzag pattern.

Another Jupiter-class MRAP followed the first just as more Zealot militiamen—he suspected they'd come up from the Jewish Quarter using the sewage system—took on the man with the roof-mounted machine gun. They appeared from the narrow street directly opposite the ornate building.

'The fucks! They're coming out of the fucking drains!'

'We *own* those drains, motherfuckers!'

He watched with mounting dread as a legionary called for cover and emerged from the second MRAP wearing a gas mask. He had something long and shiny in one hand and a crowbar slung over his shoulder. The militiamen opposite the ornate building tried desperately to take him out, but half-a-dozen legionaries mounting a solid wall of fire covered him. More militiamen emerged from the sewer, pouring out into the street opposite the ornate building. Yaakov knew it was stupidly dangerous but he scuttled down to the next pine tree.

The legionary in the gasmask approached a manhole about fifty feet from the ornate building and used his crowbar to lever it up. The legionaries from the first MRAP engaged the Zealots pinned down in the buildings opposite what Yaakov could now see was a modified Roman temple of some sort. Just as the legionary with the gasmask broke the shiny canister on the rim of the drain and yelled 'Eat that, sewer rats,' Yaakov heard someone in the first MRAP scream 'RPG!'—it sounded like the gunner—and throw himself out of the vehicle. The driver and navigator were less fortunate; Yaakov could see the rocket had gone through the front of the vehicle and exploded in the driver's chest. The MRAP's reinforced windows did not blow out, which surprised him. They went brilliant scarlet instead. The front of the vehicle caved in, but the hull was undamaged.

He saw the gunner crawl into the vehicle's rear and retrieve his predecessor; the latter touched his hand to his bleeding face and held it aloft to show he was fit. He had real trouble standing up, however, and Yaakov watched the second man half carry, half drag him behind the MRAP and yell 'medic!' A man from the second vehicle came to his aid.

Out of the corner of his eye, he saw another civilian—a woman, this time—emerge onto a top-floor balcony directly above the bulk of the Zealots. She had something large and white in her hands. He thought he saw a hand try to draw her back inside, but it missed, only catching the edge of her robe. A stereotypical Roman *matrona*, she was robust, large busted and shapely. Her steel-grey hair was swept up in combs and held together with fine silver bands, and she looked thunderous.

No wonder they conquered the world; you'd do whatever you could to get away from one of those.

She raised the large white thing above her head and then hurled it into the densest part of the militia. It was food of some sort, bright red and plentiful, enough to feed a dozen people or so. It landed square on one militiaman's head—the one with the RPG—and shattered, spraying its boiling contents across a dozen others. She then just stood there, looking down, hands on hips. Within seconds, Yaakov could smell the pork.

Pork mince. She's just coated them with pork mince. A *lot* of pork mince.

The man who'd been hit directly passed out in the street, but many of the others betrayed their positions by attempting to clean themselves of the Roman filth. The legionary with the gasmask and the gunner on the second MRAP had themselves a picnic now; the men from the first MRAP soon joined them. For the first time, Yaakov saw the three men who'd been defending the temple. They were legionaries, all right, but wearing black body armour and black trousers shot through with silver. Two of them had S.P.Q.R. tattooed across the bicep; the other had a wild boar pawing the ground. They joined their comrades, closing in. The Romans took a couple of casualties—Yaakov saw a man shot in the arm and another in the foot—but it was clear they knew they'd gained the ascendancy.

Yaakov watched as the second MRAP disgorged all its crew save the gunner and the wounded man. The gunner now leaned amiably over his weapon, grinning. They stretchered away their two wounded comrades. The Zealots refused to surrender, forcing the Romans to shoot them down one by one. Two more bursts of fire echoed along the street. Yaakov saw a militiaman he vaguely knew get his weapon shot out of his hands; his fingers landed on the footpath along with his carbine. He saw a couple of deliberate shots to the kneecap—*they want prisoners then*—and some rapid banter between the three men in the black body armour and their uniformed fellows.

'Handcuffs and shackles? Not a problem, sir. We cater to all tastes,' said one of the former. 'Be right with you.'

Moments later, he emerged from the temple basement, crunching over broken glass with a selection of restraints in his hands or draped over his arms. He handed them over.

The legionaries started to roar with laughter.

'Leopard skin? Seriously? I'm about to lock down a prisoner with a set of leopard-skin cuffs?'

'Look at this, sir,' said another man, holding what looked like a long metal pole with three holes in it up in front of his face. He loomed over one of their prisoners and snapped the larger hole around his neck, clipping his wrists in the smaller two on either side of his head. He prodded the man to stand.

'Now, ain't that a picture?'

Soon the Zealot captives were all restrained in various items of bondage equipment, some of it brightly coloured and decorated with feathers. Quite a few of the soldiers were laughing so hard they had difficulty standing up. Civilians emerged from the apartments and joined in the mockery. The Centurion spoke into the radio at his collar, calling for transport.

Yaakov saw movement behind the man who'd brought out the shackles and cuffs and realised that people were now coming from within the temple, picking their way over broken glass, fallen masonry and spent shell casings. One he recognised as a Roman priestess of Cybele in full regalia: he'd been to Caesarea once as a boy and seen a woman in a flowing gown wearing a crown of towers with trailing silk pinned to each turret. He'd asked and had it explained to him what she was. He remembered the word *whore* was added to the account as an epithet. Half-a-dozen younger women flanked her, but they lacked her odd headdress. He looked hard at one of the young women, realising at length that 'she' was a 'he'—of sorts: one of the *Galli*, men who emasculated themselves for the Goddess and whose identity cards bore the letter *I* for 'indeterminate' instead of *M* or *F*. He shuddered; the *gallus* was very beautiful. A larger group of about twenty young people followed the priestesses. Some of them were eating, others were drinking wine, looking cheery and flushed in the face.

The senior woman did not look whorish. She looked fearsome. Yaakov clung to the tree trunk. He really didn't want her to see him. She terrified him—at that moment—more than the legionaries did. All of them blinked in the bright afternoon light; the young people in particular looked up and down the *cardo*, stunned at the wreckage, the shot-out frontages and partly demolished MRAP. He noticed that they were less fazed by the corpses than by the property damage, picking their way around the former without concern.

The woman whose husband had been shot off his balcony emerged at last, pointing at one of the captives. She did not mock. Her face was white with rage.

'He killed my husband,' she said. 'I want his blood.'

'We're taking them all into custody, *Domina*,' said the Centurion.

'Charun claims his blood,' she said, not moving. 'My husband's blood is spilled on the ground, it must be repaid.'

Yaakov watched as two soldiers hauled the captive the woman indicated into the middle of the street, directly in front of the temple.

'She's invoked Charun, sir,' said one, looking at the Centurion. 'And we've got plenty of prisoners.'

Yaakov clung to the tree trunk and felt the blood drain away from his face, hands and feet. He watched as a legionary forced the man to his knees before the tower-crowned priestess and her temple.

They're going to make him worship their Goddess.

'Head up, sunshine, you want to see who rules you,' the soldier said, sneering.

They did not make the man worship, although the priestess and her acolytes and the young people watched what followed in grave stillness. Instead, the Centurion ordered his troops back and pointed at the large crowd of civilians—Yaakov noticed the woman who had dropped the pork mince among them—who'd gathered behind the mourning woman, clutching skillets and pans and garden tools in their hands. Someone passed her a mallet; she swung it smoothly around her shoulders and brought it down on the prisoner's head. The others soon joined her.

When two legionaries found what appeared to be a sleeping

boy underneath a nearby pine tree, they were half inclined to leave him be, but the weapon propped up against the trunk forestalled that. The two men called the Centurion, curious as to what to do with him. The officer turned the child's face up with his boot, expecting him to stir. The body was limp. The Centurion called the medic, who opened each eye in turn and shone a torch into them.

'Accommodation reflex present, but slow, sir,' the medic said. 'Looks like a true catatonic stupor.'

'Maybe a Zealot who lost heart for the fight,' said the Centurion. 'Better bring him in and see what we can do with him.'

'He's just a baby,' said another soldier. 'Barbarians, making their boys fight before they turn sixteen.'

The two legionaries slung the boy into the prisoner transport and piled into the front with their fellows. The Romans drove slowly in convoy towards Antonia, singing a lament for their fallen comrades. The gunner had a strong lead; he stood behind his weapon and filled his lungs; tears streamed down his face as he held the vehicle's amplifier to his lips. His fine voice soared over the sound of the engines. Roman civilians stood on balconies as they passed, joining the soldiers' voices coming from the street with their own.

Nic Varro had done some dangerous and stupid things in his time: none of them, however, involved having a rifle shoved in his face. He sat in JTN's Production Control Room and looked at the young legionary who was menacing him. The various fire-fights and running gun battles taking place throughout the city played on different monitors behind his head. His technical director and production manager were both being similarly menaced; both had their hands in the air. Nic gripped the armrests of his chair.

'I thought,' he said evenly, 'that this kind of crap had

stopped thanks to the Constitutional Settlement reached between Augustus and the Senate sixty years ago.'

Democracy with Roman Values, eh Augustus, just to keep us all in line.

The soldier looked towards the more senior of the three men—the one holding the technical director hostage. Nic could see he had *Optio* insignia.

'You need to shut down that live feed,' the officer said. 'You're giving them publicity.'

'In case you hadn't noticed, Officer, the Fleet Fox is four doors down from here. It's a trifle difficult to miss.'

'You're also compromising our operations.'

Nic heard two soldiers clatter onto JTN's roof and start remonstrating with the cameraman who'd ensconced himself up there to film events as they unfolded in the street below.

'Romans need to know that this is what some people think of them.'

'They're throwing citizens off the *fucking roof*, Varro. If you were there, they'd do it to you, too.'

'Spare us from the Roman military and the Roman government worrying about citizens' delicate sensibilities.'

'You've provided no fatality warnings, Varro.'

'This isn't the *ludi*, Officer. This is a major terrorist attack. These people hate us. The more I know about them, the happier I'll be.'

'If you don't stop broadcasting voluntarily, we'll be forced to jam you.'

'You do that, soldier. Feel the power.'

Cassius of the violet eyes lay stretched out on a wooden platform at the very top of the railway shed, his Capua 28-4 with the customised long barrel nestled into his shoulder. He'd been waiting for quite a while, now—long past the 'go' time Capito had given him for the attack on Central Station—and suspected the terrorists had been waylaid elsewhere.

He watched commuters milling around the station: Jews arriving from Caesarea, Romans leaving for Caesarea. Many of the former were in traditional garb, with long shawls and black leather straps wound around their arms and head; many of the latter carried elaborate feathered headdresses and multicoloured costumes ready for Caesarea's grand street parade in a week's time. He'd never had the chance to sit so high up in a railway shed before, and he watched the light as it danced across the glass and the wrought iron and polished stone. *You know that phrase, 'the play of light'? Well, the light does not 'play' up here. It's deadly fucking serious.* He saw two Romans turn up in their full parade costumes and begin to dance on the platform. Someone saw them and decided to play something appropriate over the loudspeaker.

Other Romans—costumed or not—joined the first two and soon there were twenty-odd people all dancing on the number two platform to Caesarea. Cassius tapped two fingers gently against the stock. He found himself wishing hard at that moment for a transfer to Caesarea or even the provincial frontier. He was sick of pretending to be something other than what he was, of frequenting the Greek Quarter for nights of furtive lust with a boy for whom he cared little and—in the long run—wanted less. There was a time when he'd thought of trying to find a lover outside Antonia or the Greek Quarter, but then there'd been that news story about what the Zealots would do to Jewish lads who'd gone Greek with Roman soldiers. They'd kidnap them and take them miles north, somewhere in the Galilee. Then they'd crucify them and leave the remains draped over a barbed-wire fence. Cassius hated the Galilee. He secretly hoped that its inhabitants would do something so egregious as to justify their wholesale extermination.

The world does not need people who believe shit like that.

He watched the man with the golden gown and the feathered headdress whirl his woman around and draw her into his chest. Cassius thought the man had a sweet body. He lifted his eyes slightly above his scope to get a better look.

At that moment, a man walked into the station and took it upon himself to fire his weapon into the air, blowing out a chunk of glass from the roof and causing people to scatter or throw themselves on the ground. Cassius trained his Capua on him—as did his opposite number at the other end of the shed—and pulled the trigger as the man squealed with delight and brought his weapon down to fire indiscriminately on commuters. Both Roman snipers must have struck at once, because the man's body, then his head exploded. Another Zealot followed the first into the station, but seeing his comrade felled unmanned him, and he put his weapon down at his feet, raising his hands above his head. Cassius curled his lip, chambered another round and fired.

Suck on that, Galilee, he thought, *suck on that.*

At first, Linnaeus had thought rescue would come when the Romans used three *striges* to cover the *vigiles* while they put the fire out. He'd watched through the windows as the great winged machines sailed over the roof, drawing Zealot fire while the building released its pall of black smoke. At one point a *strix*—one of the smaller, nimbler ones—came so close to the window he could see the whites of its aviatrix's eyes and her elaborate biomechanical helmet through the insect-like canopy. He watched her flick something fleshy down in front of one eye; her *perplexae* glowed silver in the gathering dark.

'They're scary,' said Fotini. 'Well, they scare me.'

'I think that's the idea,' said Linnaeus, watching the Zealots in the room crouch down in fear as the wings beat twice, lifting the *strix* over the roof. 'There's no other reason to make them look like bats or falcons. Well, I don't know of one.'

As he spoke, the lights in the banqueting hall winked out, and it occurred to him that *Fretensis* and the supporting aviatrices were waiting for dark; none of the Zealots, so far as he could see, had night-vision goggles. Sunset scythed across the city, glowing orange and gold as it flowed through the windows and picked out those parts of the mosaic floor not smeared with blood. He took the sudden darkness as an opportunity to grab both Cynara and Fotini by the hand and move them towards the complex of offices and kitchens at one end of the hall.

'What are you doing?' Cynara asked.

'When they come, I'd like to be less exposed.'

'The internal walls in here won't withstand an armour-piercing round, Andreius. It'll go straight through the wall, us, and the opposite wall as well.'

'They'll use hollow points, Cynara; we're inside. If we get in there and get down, we may live.'

Fotini watched the two Romans casually discuss their military options with a degree of awe.

'How do you two know all this stuff?'

'It's called a Roman education,' said Cynara. 'It's something they care about.'

Linnaeus sat down, dragging the two women along with him.

'The Guild office is just there,' said Fotini.

Linnaeus waited until his eyes adjusted to the deepening dusk. The office door was ajar. In front of it was a tall semicircular desk—something like the concierge's desk in the lobby—where interested parties could make bookings or assignations. He poked his head around the side and looked around its internal shelving. He could vaguely see piles of paperwork, a stapler, a box of rubber bands, paper towels and assorted stationery—even a block of yellow legal pad. He smiled at this and began scrabbling around with one hand. He looked at Fotini.

'Nothing so useful as a pistol in here, by any chance?'

She shook her head. 'In the office, yes, but not here.'

His fingers butted up against something cold and metallic, and he drew it towards him, feeling for a seal or something to indicate what it was. It gave off a chunky rattle as he moved it.

'That's the petty cash tin,' said Fotini. 'Some people still like to pay in cash, rather than adding us to their hotel bill.'

He nodded, making sure—for reasons he found obscure—that the tin was within easy reach.

Cynara, meanwhile, was peering into the office.

'I think someone's dead in there,' she said at last. 'I can smell powder burn.'

She went to stand up and look inside, but Linnaeus dragged her back.

'Don't you dare,' he spat, with more force than she expected from him. 'Draw attention to yourself in there and they'll treat you like the woman downstairs.'

The last splinters of orange light faded into the clouds; the Credit Gallia building opposite was swathed in darkness, and none of the streetlights had come on. Linnaeus could hear Simon cursing in his own tongue; Eleazar seemed to be much the calmer of the two, remonstrating with his superior.

Linnaeus touched Cynara's shoulder.

'What are they angry about?'

'Only two torches,' she said, 'and there must be five or six of them.'

Beams of torchlight flickered and swept over the hostages; many were sleeping. The room reeked of piss—they'd stopped letting people go to the toilet nearly an hour ago—and Linnaeus had a dreadful feeling about the smallest of the infant children. He hadn't heard it cry for the best part of two hours. He heard Eleazar's voice again, from the far side of the room. It was low, almost conspiratorial. He heard a woman's voice in response, angry at first and then frightened. A few moments passed, and she began to scream.

Lovely. They're having themselves a field brothel.

Torchlight settled on Fotini's face; Linnaeus and Cynara both felt themselves squinting, even though it wasn't directed at them. Fotini shielded her eyes with one hand. Simon's figure swirled up out of the darkness and crouched down beside her. He put his pistol under her chin.

'Show me your identity card,' he said.

She rummaged in her clothes and handed it to him. He shone his torch on it, turning it over.

'So useless Yaakov was right,' Simon said. 'You're just a whore. You don't belong to this man at all.' He jerked his head at Linnaeus and dropped the card on the floor. Cynara picked it up.

'Leave her alone,' said Linnaeus, at a loss as to what else to say. 'She's done nothing to you.'

Cynara said something in Aramaic. Simon's head jerked up; he stared at her.

'You're all whores, anyway. Look at you. You're as bad as them. Look at that gown, I can see the shape of your tits.'

Cynara repeated whatever it was she'd said previously, her eyes huge and terrified but her voice even. Linnaeus thought he heard the Greek word *porneia* in there somewhere, but he wasn't certain. Simon dragged Fotini upright and slammed her into the Guild office wall. He began grinding his hips against her as he took her by the wrists, pinning her arms above her head. He still had his pistol clutched in his right hand and was forced to hold one of her hands down with his wrist. He tried to kiss her, but she turned her face away from him.

'Come on, you do a different man every night. What's one more?'

Linnaeus could see Cynara building up to say something and he held up his hand to quiet her. *Do something*, she mouthed at him. *For God's sake, do something.*

Linnaeus did not consider himself a man of courage. He looked down. Simon's torch was on the ground, illuminating the base of the wall and throwing just enough light to show Simon sticking his tongue in Fotini's ear. He thought of using the torch as a weapon, but suspected that moving it would alert Simon, even in his distracted state. *Do something*, Cynara mouthed again.

'Now, I'm going to let your left hand go,' Simon said. 'And I want you to drop my trousers and lift your skirt so I can get a nice fuck in.'

Linnaeus watched as—with glacial slowness—Fotini unbuttoned Simon's fly. He used his pistol hand to pin her shoulder to the wall. She began dragging her skirts up as he started to kiss her again. She looked at Linnaeus sidelong. Where it came from he never knew, but in one swift movement he stepped back, bent down behind the counter and retrieved the petty cash tin. He balanced it across both hands for a second or two.

Well, if I have to go, I'm going to go out swinging, friends and neighbours.

Just as Simon touched his penis against Fotini's vulva, Linnaeus brought the petty cash tin—corner first, and with all the force he could muster—down on his head.

Several things happened at once. Simon collapsed forward in front of the desk, screaming and clutching the back of his head. Gunshots began to echo around the hall. Linnaeus hugged Fotini to his chest as his feet went from under him; they fell behind Simon. He heard the unmistakable sound of a *strix* close-range missile shatter the windows on one side of the building. Cynara kicked Simon's pistol a good thirty feet along the office wall where it was picked up by an enormous legionary wearing night-vision goggles.

'Thanks, lady,' he said, running past, 'but we've got plenty.'

Cynara bent down and crawled into the Guild office, crouching under a desk and clasping her hands around the back of her head. *Amazing how school comes back like that.* She realised she was sharing the underside with a pair of bare feet. She pushed them away; a male body rolled off the chair and onto the floor; a foul stench reached her nostrils. She closed her eyes.

Linnaeus could feel Fotini clinging to him. He rubbed her back and stroked her hair and made soothing noises, but she seemed to be doing her best to crawl into him. She was stronger than her slight frame would indicate, and at one point he found himself having to unpeel her fingers from around his back.

'Fotini, I can't breathe.'

Her grip loosened, but only a little.

Gunfire in the banqueting hall intensified. Linnaeus heard the whine of one of the fat-bellied pushprops—designed to transport troops—through the shattered glass. The thump of legionary boots sounded on the roof as men fast roped down from it. A fire had started among the wooden religious props stored at the other end of the banqueting hall. It was enough to backlight a Zealot standing with an RPG balanced on his shoulder. He was about to fire when a legionary shot him in the calf and planted a foot in his back, sending him out the window. People yelled at each other, trying to find family members and friends in the dark. He heard Eleazar scream and a legionary swear in Latin.

A Zealot had succeeded in climbing into the roof cavity and onto one of the chandeliers. He blasted away from up there while other Zealots covered him. Linnaeus suspected the Romans were hiding around the corner across from the toilets and taking pot shots at him and his confreres.

'I can't get a clear shot at the fucker,' one of the enlisted men was yelling.

There was more shooting and swearing, and then maniacal laughter. Linnaeus did not know from whom.

'Oh, sod this.'

The very tall legionary who'd claimed Simon's pistol earlier aimed his carbine at the mounting rather than the Zealot and blew the chandelier out of the ceiling. It cannoned into the floor, shredding its occupant in the process. An expanding circle of glass shards skittered across the mosaic. Linnaeus waited, expecting more gunfire. None came. He felt Fotini's hand snake around the back of his neck, pulling his face close to hers. He could hear dripping.

'Is it finished?'

'I think so.'

'I hadn't thought of that, sir,' the enlisted man said, his voice tinged with awe.

'That's why they pay me the small sesterces, Lucullus.'

Linnaeus sat up slowly; she twisted in his lap, turning to face him and twining her arms and legs around him. The position was only tangentially sexual: she was trying to stay as close to him as possible. She rested her head on his shoulder and he stroked her hair.

The legionaries rigged up a synthetic fuel generator; he heard the motor cough into life and watched it bathe the hall with light. More boots thumped on the roof, followed by the whining rotary engine and heavy *clunk* of a Sagittarius-class transport aircraft. Medical teams began to come down the stairs, stretchers in hand.

'Fuck me sideways,' he heard one of the medics say as he saw the shattered chandelier. 'What'd you do to this one? Mince him?'

Linnaeus turned his head just in time to see Simon push himself onto his knees and grab at something concealed in his sock. The tall legionary noticed the movement, whirled around, levelled his weapon and fired. Linnaeus closed his eyes; Fotini whimpered.

I hope that's a hollow-point round.

I hope he's a good shot.

When he opened his eyes, most of Simon's head and throat now covered the two of them. Fotini began to scream. He joined her. He could feel bits of something or other slide down his face. Fotini began shaking her hands beside her ears. Blood and muck and—he was sure of this—most of an eyeball spattered the wall behind them.

'Are you all right there?' he heard the tall legionary shout. The soldier ran over and crouched down to look at them, taking off his helmet and night-vision goggles.

'They're all right,' Linnaeus heard Marius Macro say from the other side of the room. 'No one who makes that much noise is gonna die any time soon.'

Linnaeus wiped blood out of his eyes. As he did so, he saw the tall legionary's brilliant ginger hair, silvery on the tips thanks to the harsh light.

'I'm sorry we couldn't meet under better circumstances,' said Cornelius. Linnaeus resisted the urge to laugh maniacally. The *Aquilifer* fished in his pocket and handed Fotini a spotless white handkerchief. She blotted her face with it. Linnaeus wiped the worst of the blood and mush off his face with one hand.

'Cornelius Getorex, my opposite number; Fotini Kallenike, my concubine.'

She raised her fingers and gave the ginger soldier a little wave.

'I think I've ruined this,' she said, holding up the handkerchief. He took it from her, his face unperturbed.

'I'll get you two cleaned up just as soon as we get the emergencies sorted out,' he said, standing up, turning and walking into what now looked like a field Æsculapion.

Linnaeus reached into the desk and laid his hands on the paper towels; he tore open the brown paper wrapper with his teeth and began to clean first her face, then his own.

'Not the softest things in the world, I'm sorry.'

'Did you mean that? About taking me as your concubine?'

He began to blot her hair.

'Only if you want it, of course.'

'I do want it,' she said.

Cynara emerged from the Guild office, picked her way through the glass and identified herself to the two officers, watching as the legionary medics treated the wounded. She noticed that most of them were soldiers. She did see one woman who'd been hit in the back by a ricochet, and another man who—although otherwise unharmed—was staring off into space and dribbling. One soldier, a young man with a premature bald spot, died while she stood there, clutching Marius's hand and making an oral will, as legionaries were allowed to do. She noticed then that Marius had a wound across his cheek; a flap of skin hung down over one side of his face. From time to time he folded it back up, but it fell down again. Blood streaked his neck and uniform.

Linnaeus and Fotini—looking like a pair of bleeding

statues—approached her and asked to go to his rooms.

'You'll need to use the fire escape, I'm afraid. The lifts are out.'

'I'm also going to have to check out, Cynara. I need power to run my portable calculation engine and right now I want to get as far away from this building as possible.'

'I don't blame you,' she said. 'I think we're about to close for remodelling.'

'I'm also going to relieve you of one of your *hetaerae*.'

She raised her eyebrows, looking from one to the other. Fotini was grinning through the coat of gore.

'She's coming back to Rome with me as my concubine,' he said, pulling her close.

Cynara smiled awkwardly. She never knew quite what to say in these circumstances, although she'd seen it often enough, now.

Linnaeus washed and oiled both his and Fotini's hands with devoted attention. He then began using a torch to help with packing things in his trunk. He'd tried running the bath, but there wasn't enough water pressure for any more than an inch or so. He took her property from her and packed it in with his own.

'A lot of my things are still in the Guild office upstairs.'

'We can go back—'

'No,' she said. 'Not just now; not after today.'

He sat down on the end of the bed and hung his head between his knees. She noticed that the blood had caked dry on his short fine hair, making it stand on end and gluing his gold headband to his forehead. She touched her own curls; they were near solid as well. She sat next to him and he curled an arm around her shoulders. Both of them began to cry. They cried together for twenty minutes or so, tears streaking their messy faces and leaving pools of bloody damp on already ruined clothing. He flopped backwards in the dark and she lay across him; it was the first time in his life he could remember being this close to a beautiful woman without wanting to fuck her. She went to grasp his penis—instinctual, this—but he shook his head and held up one hand.

'Not just now; not here; not after today.'

She nodded and rested her head on his belly; he laid one hand across her cheek.

Later, he took her hand and led her down the fire escape, somehow managing to haul his trunk in the other. She looked out over the city, noticing the column of black smoke rising into the air from two streets away.

'They tried to destroy the Goddess's Temple,' she said.

'Looks like it,' Linnaeus said. 'They like destroying things.'

Linnaeus was about to detonate: on top of everything else, now Ben David was being difficult. He stood outside the driver's side window, remonstrating with Ben David with one hand and holding Fotini close to him with the other. His trunk was propped up on one end in the space marked *valet*.

'What is it with you people and sex? You all need *help*, you really do.'

'I won't have her in my cab,' Ben David said. 'She's a whore.'

Linnaeus felt himself getting snaky, now.

'You take soldiers from Antonia to the Houses. You told me so yourself. How is that different?'

Ben David flinched at this. He kept forgetting that Linnaeus was a paid professional arguer.

'It just is, *Domine* Linnaeus.'

Ben David could see Linnaeus's crow eyes narrow and harden; he looked at the two of them, marvelling at how

Linnaeus retained his air of superiority—even command—despite his encrusted state. The woman nestled protectively under his arm.

'How so?' Linnaeus asked. 'How is it different?'

Ben David bit his lip.

'You said a Zealot tried to rape her. You can't rape a woman like that. She has sex all the time, with a different man every night. She wouldn't know the difference.'

This time Linnaeus did detonate. With surprising speed, his long-fingered hand darted through the window and wrapped itself around Ben David's face. The latter's eyes widened with shock; he didn't think Linnaeus had that in him.

'David, listen to me. Listen carefully, because I'm only going to say this once.'

He tapped his right index finger against the car door, emphasising his points as he spoke.

'Women have sex for all sorts of reasons, including—sometimes—for money. The point is, they choose to give it away. If a man steals it from them—well, it's rape. And he has no self control.'

Ben David looked from Linnaeus to the woman and back again. She eyeballed him, defiant.

'And another thing,' Linnaeus added, his dark skin reddening. 'I contracted for this cab for the rest of the week. If push comes to shove, I'll leave you here and we'll drive it to the Procurator's residence in the Upper City ourselves.'

'She's a whore,' Ben David repeated stubbornly, although his voice lacked conviction. Linnaeus had a point about the contract, and if Romans had a god they really did get on their knees before, it was the law of contract. The woman leaned into his window now, her hair stiff with blood.

'*Kyrios*,' she said softly; his head wrenched up at the respectful form of address. 'This is how I choose to make my living. No one else chose for me. I had no scholarship at the *collegium* in Alexandria. I did this to pay my fees. I liked it. And people—mainly men, but some women, too—like an educated and skilful companion.'

Ben David felt himself reddening almost as much as Linnaeus. He looked down.

'Now I am with this man,' she went on, 'and yes, he does give me pleasure.'

Ben David flicked the release on the dash; the rear doors unlocked.

Even Nero did not know what to make of them, circling both slowly, his tail hanging down straight. Fotini held her hand out, palm up, inviting the dog to sniff it. He approached her cautiously and licked it once, sitting down and whimpering. His tail thumped the floor, just the once.

'I don't dare ask how you came to look like that,' Claudia said.

'I assure you that none of it's ours,' said Linnaeus.

Camilla stood off to one side, looking on with fascinated horror. She'd wanted to ask after Marius, but there was something terrifying about the blackened vision the two of them presented, their faces pale and moonlike in the midst of caked-on filth. She bit her lip. Antony stood beside his sister. According to his father he was supposed to know the man with the gold headband, but he couldn't recognise him—at least not while he looked like *that*. He went downstairs to play with his racer and wait for supper. He was already hungry, and hoped it wasn't too far away.

'Dana! Zoë!' Pilate called. 'Take Fotini to the palace baths and help her clean up.'

'I'll come too,' said Claudia. 'You'll have to have a backwards bath, I'm afraid,' she said, looking at Fotini. 'You'll need cold water to get the blood out of your hair.'

Claudia arrived in the *frigidarium* with a wooden box of combs and hair oils; she set it down on the side and slid into the water beside Fotini. The latter shivered as Zoë and Dana tried to clean the dried blood out of her long dark ringlets.

'If you have to cut it off, *Kyria*...' she looked at Claudia, 'then cut it off.'

Claudia shook her head vehemently.

'No, we are not cutting it off. You have beautiful hair, and as far as I'm concerned, you're keeping it.'

Fotini smiled. She liked Claudia already. Claudia listened to her with infinite patience as she blurted out what had happened at the hotel.

'He saved me, *Kyria*, then took me as his concubine.'

'Not something he would do lightly, either. I've known Linnaeus for a long time, and he's never been one to do anything in haste.'

Fotini smiled at the thought.

'And do stop calling me *kyria*. You're not a servant.'

Claudia poured something mildly astringent into the palm of one hand, running her fingers through Fotini's hair. She passed Dana and Zoë a wide-toothed comb each.

'We'll divide it into three and clean it from the bottom up, girls.'

Fotini bobbed gently in the water as the three women worked on her hair and chatted amiably.

'I watched what was happening on screen until they shut it off,' said Claudia. 'I must admit I thought our soldiers gave a very good account of themselves outside the Fleet Fox.'

'I'm glad they stopped the shooting in Central Station,' said Dana. 'That would have been terrible, otherwise.'

'You wonder what they want to achieve,' said Zoë.

'I think that's very clear,' said Claudia. 'They want us out of Judaea, and were it not so strategically useful—what with all the current problems in Persia—I'd want out of Judaea, too.'

Fotini saw movement at the other end of the *frigidarium*; Linnaeus was clean and spruce already. He walked towards the women, Nero at his heels and wagging his tail.

'He's remembered who I am.'

He stopped beside Fotini and her three companions and knelt down at the water's edge, leaning out over the surface to kiss her forehead. Wordlessly, he stood and walked into the hot room. Claudia watched Fotini's gaze follow his back.

'You love him, don't you?'

'I think so, Claudia, although it's a bit soon to say. I do like him a lot, I know that.'

'He's a very easy man to love.'

'He likes what I like,' she said.

'Yes,' said Claudia. 'That explains many things.'

Dana and Zoë looked at each other, knowingly. Nero settled next to the bath, his nose on his paws.

Pilate passed Linnaeus the water pipe and exhaled. He stood and poured wine for both of them; Aristocles and Milos clattered and tinkered in the kitchen. Rich food smells mixed with the smell of cannabis. Pilate had watched how—with unusual devotion to detail—both Linnaeus and Fotini had lit incense before the residence's cut-glass portrait of the Emperor and Pilate's fine bronze of the matronly woman who embodied the city of Rome.

Pilate sat down heavily, the bottle clutched in both hands.

'I shouldn't complain after what you've just been through, but I'm *this* close to telling them where they can stick their job.'

'This isn't to do with the Ben Yusuf matter?'

'That's part of the mix, but only a small part.'

'Perhaps I'm not the person to talk to about this...'

Pilate ignored the lawyerly caution.

'There's a reason we rolled up the Zealots so efficiently today. It might not have seemed terribly efficient from the Empire Hotel, but we nearly had something that big across four different targets, including Jerusalem Academy. The press are writing it up as a great intelligence coup and singing the praises of our brave boys in *Legio* X *Fretensis*, and on one level, that's true. It's only a matter of time before the rest of it gets out.'

Linnaeus finished his wine and held his glass up for a refill.

'Torture?'

Pilate filled his glass.

'Yes, and then some; one of my officers redecorated the Antonia *Camera* with Iscariot's innards.'

'Not Cornelius Getorex, surely?'

'No, not Getorex, Andreius; he's the best officer in the legion, and I say that knowing that my daughter *isn't* promised to him.'

'One of Getorex's juniors?'

'Yes. Gaius Crispus.'

'Any relation to...?'

'His son.'

'Jove on a pony.'

'Don't worry, Getorex dug up enough nasty to last a good while just with the water torture, and there was some very good sleuthing by one of the counter-terrorism people. Crispus put two and four together and took it upon himself to go a few steps further, blowing the lid off what happened this afternoon.'

'That's why you had snipers in Central Station.'

'Yes, and why the Temple was prepared in advance for a firebombing that would have baked everyone inside like pizza. Not to mention the school.'

'Antony and Camilla.'

'Yes.'

Linnaeus rubbed his face with both hands. He felt very tired, and he wanted Fotini badly.

Where is she?

'Pontius, you need to stop talking about this to me. Much of it will be ventilated at trial.'

Pilate ignored his caution once more. 'I've also been bloody railroaded, and I made a decision today that I just know is going to stick around until the day I die.'

Linnaeus raised his eyebrows.

'I shut down the JTN broadcast. I did it on advice, but the decision was mine.'

'What about *CR*?'

'Vitellius. I don't have enough authority to roll them up. Nic Varro—I used to know him well in Rome, when he did the *CR* market wrap-up—is now my sworn enemy.'

'Varro's a witness in the Ben Yusuf matter, Procurator. I think we'd better save the rest of this conversation until after the trial.'

Pilate startled at the use of his formal, legal title.

'I'm sorry, Andreius. I shouldn't have... it's unprofessional, with you being counsel.'

'No more, Pontius.' He paused, speaking very softly. 'Sometimes I don't want to know what the Imperial Roman Army is doing in my name.'

Both men turned and stood, glasses in hand, as the women made their entrance. Zoë—with her background in dance and theatre—had made up both Claudia and Fotini's faces, while Dana had oiled their skin—arms, back, neck—so they both shone. Fotini seemed to have a peacock feather around each eye; fine silver lines as brilliant as her hair decorated Claudia's eyelids and temples. Zoë and Dana stood to one side, smiling hugely at the drama their ministrations had created.

Pilate could see that Fotini was wearing one of Claudia's cast-offs, but that meant little. Claudia had impeccable taste in clothes. Linnaeus noticed the severe cut of the blue silk, and that she was faintly uncomfortable with it; her fingers clutched the amethyst amulet he'd given her. She'd always favoured loose and diaphanous Greek dresses at the hotel, never anything so close fitting and unforgiving. Her hair—every bit of it saved from calamity—hung down over her shoulders in shiny ringlets coiled to the circumference of a man's little finger. Claudia—as she often did—wore a long black robe threaded with silver. She never changed her glossy silver mane, and it curved sweetly under her chin.

'Someone's been having a good time in here,' she said. 'I can smell it.'

Pilate remembered his manners and poured wine for both of them. Aristocles rang his little bell, summoning Antony and Camilla to the table for supper. They also gaped. In an unguarded moment, Camilla touched Fotini's bare shoulder and said, simply, 'You look gorgeous.' Antony—only a month away from turning thirteen—had the dizzying sensation of responding to a woman as a woman for the first time in his life at the same time as being aware that he was doing so. Camilla reached out and closed his mouth as the grinning soldier on the residence's front door opened it to admit Marius. He was still in his uniform, dusty and streaked with blood, although his hands and face were clean and his cheek had been stitched. Camilla flew to him, Nero behind her. He wrapped his arms around her and lifted her off the ground. She kissed him gently and raised her fingers towards his cheek.

'That's, what is it, a lot of stitches.'

'They have to make them small on your face.'

'Did you get shot?'

'No. This is from flying glass.'

'We're about to eat,' she said.

'I'm tired and hungry from battle,' he said. 'Food is good.'

Of all creatures, the dog has made man's joys his own, and Nero now danced around the table and the women and Marius, his tail high, barking. Pilate did not try to quiet him. Dana and Milos began serving up food, dodging the animal while they dished out hearty ragù with beans and bread. Pilate palmed Nero a piece of cheese, confining the dog to his side of the table. Linnaeus stepped around Pilate and put his glass down. He took Fotini's hands in his own and guided her to the seat beside him.

'You are beautiful and good,' he said.

'I don't feel very good,' she said, 'not just yet.'

He leaned his face close to hers. Their foreheads touched.

'I think you're good.'

Pilate poured wine and gave his position at the head of the table to Marius. The latter hesitated at first but Pilate insisted. Linnaeus backed him.

'Two of us would be dead were it not for you and your men.'

Claudia stood and proposed a toast.

'To the men of the Tenth,' the rest repeated, standing and raising their glasses.

The four servants stood to one side, watching as the members of *chez Pilate* and their friends unwound and indulged. Someone poured Antony a glass. His first encounter with wine made him pull a face, although he queued up for a second glass when it was offered to him.

'He's thirteen in a month,' Pilate said. 'And he got chased out of school today.'

It fell to Marius to report on what had gone before in the day.

'That's why I'm so late, and so unwashed,' he was saying. 'I had to go to the *vicus* and tell two women that their men were dead. One has a new baby.'

'At least she'll be a citizen now. And the child, too,' said Claudia.

'Yes, *Donna*. More often than not another man will take a provincial woman in those circumstances. Normally we'd put her picture up in the enlisted men's mess, but she's very pretty; one of our officers has taken her and her baby.'

'I didn't have you pegged as a matchmaker, Marius,' Linnaeus said.

'The army looks after its own,' he said. 'I take that seriously.'

'Where are we with casualties?' Pilate asked.

'It could be a great deal worse, Procurator. We lost one civilian at the Fleet Fox and fifty-one at the Empire.'

Pilate winced.

'And military personnel?'

'Two at the Fleet Fox, five at the Empire. There's a lot of glass wounds and abrasions. One man will have to be invalided out; he's lost most of his foot.'

'Shit,' Pilate said softly.

'*Aquilifer* Getorex thinks we were looking at upwards of three hundred civilian deaths had there not been, ah, intelligence.'

'Yes, I know.'

'About the only consolation is that there are relatively few injuries. People either lived or died; military personnel are being treated in Antonia. I had terrible visions of a blood transfusion cock-up at first.'

'How did you get such good intel?' Fotini asked, her peacock eyes focused on Marius.

'That's classified, I'm afraid.'

And just as well, thought Pilate.

When they'd eaten and drunk and smoked once more—and some time after Camilla had taken Marius by the hand and led him away to the baths—Claudia took Linnaeus and Fotini to one of Herod's suites. They walked for a long time, following a complicated and confusing path through vaulted passageways. At length they went down a flight of stone stairs, the way lit with gas lamps pinned to the walls.

'We didn't know this was here,' she said. 'Not until Camilla went exploring last year, trying to work out just how Herod built this place. Somehow, she got hold of a set of plans in Caesarea. It was impressive, how she went about it.'

'This is an internal maze?'

'Yes. There's an identical one on the opposite side of the structure, but at the other end. Each has a similar suite of rooms.'

'I've heard he was paranoid.'

'Herod? Went right off his rocker by the end; although he'd have wanted to be paranoid about this, to be fair.'

'Was it something he had to hide from the religious authorities in Jerusalem?'

'I think so,' she answered, unhooking an ornate metal object from a heavy brass ring at her waist. 'It's not on the security system.' She held up the key. 'Look at this thing. It makes me feel like a jailer.'

She buried it in the oaken door, turning it and pushing the door open.

Linnaeus took Fotini's hand and led her inside.

It was a recreational dungeon, magnificently appointed and decorated. There were spanking benches and crosses and a wall with whips and chains. Padded leather restraints hung from the ceiling. There was a cage set into one wall and shackles trailing across the floor. The walls—decorated with frescoes depicting some sort of religious rite intermingled with exuberant scenes of sex and bondage—leapt out at them. A woman flogged another woman with a cane. A woman fellated a man while he spanked her; another man took her from behind, whip in hand. Red and purple dominated; people whirled and spun in the brightly coloured, heavy robes fashionable fifty years previously.

Linnaeus goggled, turning slowly on the spot.

'What did Pilate say?'

'He doesn't know what you like,' Claudia said, 'I've never told him; but he's not a fool. He's probably guessed at some things. We use Herod's official suite—the one Gratus got to with marquetry that wouldn't be out of place in a brothel—but we've always known there were at least a dozen others, appointed to taste. It just took us a while to find them all.'

'It's quite a find, Claudia.'

'If you don't want it, I'll put you elsewhere, but I knew you'd never take a woman unless she liked what you like.'

Fotini nodded.

'That's right,' she said. 'Not everyone's as squeamish as you.'

Claudia pursed her lips.

'After what happened today, I wonder at how you can do this.'

'With my man,' she said, '*I* choose to.'

Linnaeus smiled, licking his lips and dragging the back of his hand across his mouth. He pushed the canopy surrounding the bed to one side.

That's a very big bed, friends and neighbours. It'll spread her legs nicely.

'Look at this,' he said to Fotini. She poked her head around the material.

'My opinion of Herod just went up about a hundred points,' he said.

'The servants have been sworn to secrecy, of course.'

Claudia added.

Linnaeus pulled a face.

'No one in Rome will care.'

'Yes, but people in Judaea might, and at least some legal matters in this province are lucrative.'

She watched as the two of them began exploring the contents of various cupboards, noting where their property had been stored. Linnaeus took a set of shackles from one drawer, holding them loosely in one hand. She saw Fotini take the stopper out of a jar of perfumed oil and hold it to her nose, then to his.

'Myrrh,' she said, 'in a carrier oil. It's lovely.'

He smiled.

'You've just given me an idea,' he said.

Claudia handed Linnaeus the key.

'Breakfast is at seven,' she said. 'If you get lost, the left hand on the wall trick works; it'll take you to the baths.'

They watched her leave, waiting for several minutes. Fotini began to giggle. He stood behind her, kissing the top of her head and resting his hands on her hips.

'You look so beautiful I don't want to undress you,' he said. 'I don't want to smudge that lovely make-up.'

'But I want you to undress me,' she said.

'So we want a service top tonight, do we?'

'We do, very much.'

She felt his fingers undoing the buttons down her back; the silk dropped to the floor around her feet. She kicked off her shoes and turned to face him; he started to suck on an earlobe.

'I want you to chain me to that bed and have your way with me,' she said.

He led her under the canopy and shackled her hands and feet to the four corner posts of the bed; he could see her watching herself in the mirror above.

And, yes, that's a well spread pair of legs.

He poured a quantity of the myrrh into one hand and rubbed his palms together, kneeling between her legs. He leaned over her and, starting with her breasts and belly, began to massage the oil into her body.

'This is good,' he said. 'This is very good.'

'We lived,' she said. 'We're not dead yet.'

Walking past Camilla's bedroom and what had become a noisy, lusty celebration of Marius the warrior had put Pilate in mind of something similarly enjoyable with his wife, and he'd gone to look for her. Not to mention that Claudia looked fabulous in that silver make-up. Nero's claws ticked along the tiles beside him. Pilate looked at the dog; he could still hear the hero's return being played out on the other side of Camilla's door. Nero sat down outside it.

'Looks like you and I are the only two spare pricks in the house.'

Nero settled down again, sighing, his head on his paws.

'You'll be waiting there for a while, dog.'

Nero's tail thumped the floor. Pilate went in search of his wife.

He watched Claudia as she appeared at the top of the stairs, heavy keys looped around one wrist. He'd only realised where she'd gone when he'd seen some fine silver dust outside the entrance to the maze. He'd touched his fingers to the floor and brought them up to his face.

'Why did you put him in the maze?'

Claudia startled when she saw her husband; she hadn't expected to see him there.

'Did you follow me?'

He reached out for her; she realised what he wanted and coiled her hands behind his head and stroked his hair. He began to kiss her with real feeling.

'Let's go to our rooms and Gratus and all his mad marquetry,' she said.

He laughed, cupping one of her breasts.

'Why did you put Andreius in the maze?'

'I thought he'd like it.'

This wasn't the ideal answer, because it meant Pilate broke away from her for a moment or two, working out exactly where he was in the maze. A dawning realisation about his closest friend's tastes and proclivities commingled with a strong desire to bed his wife. Her right hand slid up under his tunic and for a moment there he really did think the back of his head was going to blow off with lust.

'That's the kinky suite,' he said at length, through clouds of pink mist.

'Yes,' she said. 'They're both kinky.'

'I didn't know that.'

'Andreius is very discreet about it.'

He leaned back, looking at her. Her hand cupped his balls and he found himself playing with her breasts.

'That means you're a bit kinky, Claudia my love.'

'No. That was always the problem. I'm not.'

'Hence the flying crockery incidents. I heard about those, you know. It got around. I was warned about them when we announced our engagement.'

'Yes.'

'I suppose I'm bland by comparison.'

She shook her head with real insistence.

'No, never; you are the best of our people, what any Roman woman would want in a husband.'

He'd lifted her gown above her waist now; he pulled her hips into his at this suggestion.

'Why didn't you tell me?'

'You never asked.'

This did make him laugh, because it was true.

'And I wouldn't have wanted to know, either.'

'No, you wouldn't.'

He wrapped his arms around her, gazing up at the curved ceiling and its intricate pressed metal. The gaslight picked out the pattern in blazing white, consigning everything else to deepest shadow.

'I didn't take this job to learn about myself.'

She cocked her head on one side at this, sucking on her bottom lip. She was hoping his introspection would wind up soon; it was a decent walk back through the palace maze to their rooms and she wanted him badly.

'Or to learn private shit about my closest friend.'

She saw that he was smiling; she kissed his neck, drawing some of his flesh up in between her teeth.

'I've been avoiding learning about myself all my life. Long may that process continue.'

The gaslight in the maze backlit his head, making his eyes and skin seem to smoulder. She felt his fingers between her legs.

'I'm too old to fuck on a tiled floor,' she said. 'It's hard on the knees. Let's go to our rooms.'

'Yes,' he said, 'let's.'

When Rufus Vero was killed by a combination of flying glass and a Zealot bullet at the Empire Hotel, *Optio* Marius Macro sought Saleh out.

Saleh was busily extracting a bullet from a woman's back.

'Be with you in a minute, sir. We can't move her until I've shifted this and I'd rather not send her back to Corinth a paraplegic.'

Macro waited until Saleh held the projectile up in front of

his face in a pair of tweezers, grinning triumphantly.

'Thank the Goddess that was only a .22,' Saleh said.

'She'll be able to walk?'

'She will; as long as she doesn't sit with her back in a draft too often, she won't even know she once had a sizable lump of lead in there.'

He dropped it onto a surgical tray.

Macro took his elbow and led him away from the other medics and nurses. He pointed at a body bag off to one side. Saleh saw a familiar face distorted by a bullet in the eye.

'As of now, Rufus Vero's left everything to a Rachel in the *vicus*,' Macro said. 'He also nominated you as his son's guardian, subject to Rachel's wishes.'

Saleh felt like he'd been punched in the guts. He knelt down beside Rufus's body; the bullet had mashed the night-vision goggles into his face. Saleh removed the metal and glass instrument with long, steady fingers. He put it to one side and closed Rufus's one undamaged eye. He fished in the webbing at his waist for a coin, holding it to his chest and then putting it in Rufus's mouth. He felt Marius's hand on his neck.

'I'm sorry. He died with great courage. He'll be remembered well in our stories.'

'He's now my blood brother, sir.'

'I know that. It's my job to tell Rachel she's lost her man, though, which I'll do immediately.'

'Yes, sir. Rather you than me, sir.'

Marius smiled his twisted smile at this.

One thing I won't miss when I finish up with Capito's job.

'I want you to hop in that pushprop back to Antonia with the men from the First Cohort and wash up for her. We'll meet at twenty thirty hours in the Officers' Mess and I'll tell you what else to do.'

Saleh took extra care in the baths. He'd already dropped his bloody fatigues into a bucket of cold water and soap. After he'd finished scraping himself clean and dunking himself in the *frigidarium*, he headed back to his quarters. Once there, he shaved his face and clipped his sideburns. This was in addition to a particular effort to smell nice. He donned his dress uniform and slicked his curly hair flat with pomade. He admired himself in the mirror; the effect was good. He hoped Rachel would appreciate it.

He waited for Macro at the bar, drinking wine to give him a little confidence. He'd tried this once before, but the woman in the *vicus* had chosen an *architectus* in the Galilee. Saleh hadn't begrudged the 4th cohort man a woman; she'd clearly been impressed at the thought of officer's quarters in lovely Sepphoris, and he'd clearly been waiting for a long time. The Galilee messed with men's minds.

Macro—still bloodied and dusty—joined him and ordered a double nip of brandy.

'She's distraught,' he said. 'A wreck. In one of those peculiar quirks that can only happen in Judaea, she's actually from the Galilee.'

'Where, sir?'

'North Galilee. Yes, you heard right. Vero rescued her from a burning building and because a Roman had touched her arse she was pretty much forfeit.'

'Gods alive.'

'He brought her back to Jerusalem and made her his woman. She's had a lot of Latin classes and seems to be quite fluent, but there's no Greek in there to speak of, at least not spoken Greek. She's a citizen now and will inherit his pension, but she's still terrified that she'll be out on the streets with her baby.'

Saleh could feel tears prickling his eyelids.

'I'll look after her, sir.'

'Well, you better. I've told her how we do things, that I'll put her picture up in the mess, and that she has a month to mourn before she takes anyone.'

Marius put Rachel's photograph on the bar, nudging it towards Saleh with his fingers.

'That's a good-looking woman,' said the barman.

Saleh looked down, self-conscious.

'Can she, ah, you know...'

'Please a man in bed and keep the keys? Of course she can. Rufus taught her the first himself and sent her on a course for the second. She'll budget all right, and entertain you, too.'

He sniggered at his mirthless wit, while Saleh fidgeted. Saleh had only been concerned about Rachel's ability to keep the household in the black; her sexual talents were not, he thought, something about which Marius should speculate.

'She's also desperate for a mercy fuck—she threw herself at me—but if you do that, then you have to take her.'

'Yes, sir.'

'If you do take her, let me know tomorrow and one of my headaches will go away.'

'Yes, sir. I'll do that.' He paused. 'Do you think she'll be happy with me, sir? It's just... I'd like a woman.'

Marius laughed at this; the mess was nearly empty—everyone was out fighting terrorists or patrolling the city—and his voice echoed around the marble and granite. He took a small notepad from his pocket and tore out a page, writing something on it. He folded the paper and handed it to Saleh. Saleh unfolded the paper.

LAW OF ONE PRICE was written on it in Marius's neat, sloping hand. Underneath was the sentence: *In an efficient market all identical goods have only one price.*

'I don't understand, sir.'

'What would you rather be, cohabiting or single?'

'Cohabiting, sir.'

'What about most of the men in Antonia? In Judaea?'

'I'd say cohabiting, sir. Playing up in the Greek Quarter starts to pall after a while. We want children.'

Saleh could see Marius smiling his twisted smile. Sometimes that smile frightened him: it seemed to smoulder slightly, to give off a faint whiff of brimstone.

'What about the women of Judaea? Do they want to cohabit?'

'Not with us, sir, not in any great numbers.'

'So the ones that do want us have scarcity power, yes?'

'We compete for them, yes. I've seen that a lot. There's some nasty stuff gone on, especially in the Galilee.' He paused. 'Maybe she won't be happy with me.'

Marius wagged his finger in front of Saleh's face. He was grinning now.

'When the women have scarcity power, what's a rational response on the part of those men competing for their affections?'

Saleh had had conversations like this at Alexandria Academy back in the day. They, too, gave off a faint whiff of brimstone.

'To make themselves more attractive in some way.'

Marius reached out and flicked the caduceus on Saleh's collar.

'Yes, Saleh, to ensure they're not identical goods.'

Saleh understood, now, what Marius was driving at. He had the unpleasant sensation that he'd just been upended and had someone go through the contents of his pockets.

'I'm an officer and a medic, sir.'

'Exactly.'

Saleh rolled onto his back, turning his head so he could watch Rachel feed Rufus's baby. He wanted her, but she needed to stop for little Marcus's midnight feed. He waited patiently, watching her guide her other nipple into the infant's mouth.

'Greedy,' she said. 'Just like your father.'

He chuckled at this; she heard him do so and gave her breast a swift pump; milk squirted over his lips and chin. He licked it away.

'That tastes good,' he said. 'Like coconut.'

'You're greedy too,' she said.

He liked the *vicus*, the way its tall, haphazardly arranged flats tiered awkwardly down the slope behind Antonia. It looked like it should be poor and dirty—probably because it was built of breezeblock and rebar—but the enlisted men who kept women in it were tradesmen who knew how to maintain a settlement. The apartments were small, but they were all plumbed and drained. It was often possible to see rebar poking out of the wall and a couple of legionaries building an apartment around it, levels and hammers and trowels in hand. Sometimes the woman in question would stand to one side, all her worldly possessions in her hands as her man and his comrades built her somewhere to live. There was even a baths complex at its very heart, concealed from the public and available only to the women who lived there. To walk into it was to walk into an elaborate but scrupulously clean labyrinth and thereafter—unless you knew where you going—to lose your way in a matter of minutes. Saleh had a good head for directions, however, and he'd found the right place after only a couple of trips up dead ends or the wrong flight of stairs.

Rufus—or one of his tradie friends—had stuccoed the breezeblock and built solid timber furniture for his woman and baby. The stucco was attractive, topped and tailed with red and black with ochre in between. Saleh reached across her and her nursing infant and ran his fingers around the top of the bedside table.

Whoever built that can work with wood.

The Antonia *vicus* was smaller than others elsewhere in the Empire. Finding a willing woman in Jerusalem was no little thing. This fact accounted not only for the booming trade in the Greek Quarter but also for intense competition among the men for local women who were willing to take up with them. There was a high turnover, of course. As plots of land with purpose-built houses became available at the *colonia*, women would leave to have their places taken by other women who had paired off with Roman soldiers. Sometimes, too, women stayed because they only wanted one or two children and a small apartment was enough. This latter group accepted that the prize of citizenship would be conferred only on their children, not on them.

'He's a sleepy boy, now,' she said, rubbing the baby's back and listening to him belch contentedly.

'Sleep, baby,' she said, as she laid him in his cot beside the bed and swaddled him.

'He'll sleep just like that?'

'Yes. He's very good. I don't need a clock, I have Marcus.'

'I like that noise he's making.'

She smiled.

'Rufus called it yarkling. He'd say, the baby's yarkling Rachie, better get him something to eat.'

'You can hear it, you know, "yarkleyarkleyarkle".'

She dragged herself over to him on her elbows and rested her head on his chest. He folded his arms around her, rubbing her back.

She'd answered the door with the baby on her hip, her eyes

red-rimmed and raw. He'd brought her a cameo that had once been his mother's and a bottle of good red from the mess.

'You are Saleh?' she'd asked, her Latin clear but accented.

'I am,' he answered. 'Vero sent me to be Marcus's guardian, and to be your man, if you'll have me.'

She'd appraised him, looking at him and her baby in turns and wiping away tears with the back of one hand. He watched her gaze pause at the caduceus on his collar.

'He looks like a good daddy, yes?' she said to the child in Aramaic, not realising that Saleh—with his Nabataean dialect, the language of Petra—could understand her. She'd cried and gibbered then, desperate to ensure that he intended to stay with her. He'd reassured her over and over again that he would, that he would not shirk his duty, that his mother had raised him not to wish his life circumstances away. She'd offered herself to him then. He'd hesitated at first, despite her loveliness; her distress at his wavering and his own desire for a woman and family overwhelmed his resistance.

He traced her thick, dark eyebrows with his fingers and admired her alabaster skin, pale against his own brown body. He was aware that the two of them fitted the Roman ideal of beauty, lying there together: the fair woman and the dark man. He'd seen that in any number of their artworks, in photographic exhibits, even in the people cast to take leading roles in theatre and cinema.

'Help me make another one,' she said, one hand straying to his cock.

'Not just yet,' he said, showing her the inside of his left forearm. She saw the trident-shaped contraceptive implant a lot of Roman men used.

'It's still got two years to run, and anyway you need a bigger gap between children.'

'Trust Rufus to find me a nice responsible medic.'

He smiled and kissed her, wriggling so she could stretch out along his body.

'We can still do the fun part.'

She touched the implant with her forefinger, then moved above it to the fine blood-brotherhood cut.

'It's actually pretty in a way.'

'It's good I can use it. Some men can't.'

'Why?'

He giggled. 'It makes the whites of their eyes go pink, like a bunny rabbit or after a big night on the skunk. A few it makes sick as well.'

She found this especially funny for some reason and began to laugh. He realised then that her laughter sounded like the baby's yarkle, and that perhaps the yarkle was a type of laughter, too.

Fotini needed to put her left hand on the wall and take the scenic route to the baths. The first time she tried to find her way out of Herod's maze, she'd become hopelessly lost and it was all she could do to find her way back to their room. Linnaeus was awake by this stage; she went over and kissed him.

'I want a bath,' she said. 'I'm all smudgy.'

'So am I,' he said, 'but I think a little more sleep is the first order of business. What is it...' he leaned around the canopy and flicked his watch open. 'It's only five in the morning.'

'I got lost just now. I'm going to try to find my way out again.'

'You do that. I'll see you at breakfast.'

She was alone in the baths and took her time. The kohl that Zoë had used on her face had some sort of fixative in it and it took her a long time to get it off. Her eyelids and cheeks glowed pink afterwards. She did loiter in the *tepidarium* for a while, oiling her skin and replaying the night's amusements.

I have been fucked silly.

She dressed in her own clothes this time, one of the loose-fitting gowns from the hotel. She really was going to have to go back there at some point and reclaim the rest of her things. Cynara still had her identity card, while her pension plan and health insurance paperwork were in a drawer in the Guild office. *With the dead body.*

Pilate and Claudia were already at breakfast when she finished in the baths. Pilate had a pencil tucked behind his ear and was reading the newspaper; Claudia was drinking espresso and gazing out over the city as the sun came up. They were both immaculate: Pilate in his formal work robes, Claudia in a long, conservative gown.

'I thought breakfast wasn't until seven,' she said.

'We like to start early,' Claudia said. 'Force of habit.'

'Morning, Fotini,' Pilate said. He did not look up from the newspaper. She saw him take the pencil from behind his ear and write something on it, pushing his coffee to one side.

She sat down; Zoë spread a napkin across her lap and brought her coffee and a roll.

Fotini noticed that Pilate had a pile of papers at his elbow. She could see 'CONTRACT OF CONCUBINAGE' written across the top of the first one, with 'WARNING: Do NOT sign the attached contract without reading and signing this warning. Do NOT sign if you feel pressured. You should obtain INDEPENDENT LEGAL ADVICE.' There was more writing underneath, most of it obscured by Pilate's sleeve. She could see *before signing or during the five-day cooling-off period* but not the rest of the sentence.

Pilate pointed at the front of the contract.

'As you can see, you're supposed to get legal advice. Not everyone does, of course, but Andreius is a skilled and clever family lawyer and you're going to need all the help you can get; there's nothing like a little equality of arms. He can advise himself.'

'But you're Andreius's best friend; he told me. Can you be independent? I can go to the Guild notary in Caesarea if need be.'

Claudia looked at Fotini, her eyebrows raised. She was a picture of sweetness and innocence, this little Greekling, but she was also sharp and self-aware.

'That's a good and fair point; if I were you I'd listen to me *and* go to the Guild notary in Caesarea.'

'I'll do that, Procurator.'

'Please, my name is Pontius. You are my best friend's chosen woman.'

'Sorry, Pontius.'

Pilate spread his paperwork out across the table as Zoë and Milos cleared away some of the plates, bringing Fotini some melon and more coffee.

'The essence of Roman concubinage is threefold: it allows a man to take a wife if he wants to; it protects his estate in the event of breakdown and it allows you both to time limit the relationship if you so wish.'

'Andreius wants five years with an option to renew.'

'Yes, he told me. As is becoming the modern trend, he is uninterested in maintaining a wife at the same time as a concubine. He wants you in much the same way as a wife.'

She nodded.

'However, he wants to preserve his estate. I think Andreius has political ambitions—'

'He does,' said Claudia.

'—And like many lawyers, he is blessed—or perhaps cursed—with an overabundance of caution, and he wishes to ensure that he maintains his property qualification for the

Senate.'

'Yes, he told me that last night.'

Pilate had a sudden and rather vivid vision of legal horse-trading going on during the breaks between enthusiastic and kinky sexual romps. He shook his head to chase the images out of his mind's eye.

'The essence of this contract, then, will be a promise from him to acknowledge and support any children born under the agreement, and to keep you in the manner to which you have become accustomed for the next five years.'

She giggled.

'This means working out what you expect in the way of support for your children. I will then draft the terms and run them by Andreius. Remember, too, that he is entitled to ask for a paternity test.'

'Yes, although I don't intend to have children.'

'Doesn't matter; the law of contract is a type of insurance. You draft for contingencies so that they don't leap up and bite you later on.'

'I'd forgotten how good you were at this, Pontius,' said Claudia.

Pilate raised his eyebrows.

'You also have to value your time. If he breaks off the arrangement before the time is up, he pays you out for the remainder, adjusted for inflation.'

'Yes.'

'If, however, you break off the arrangement, the default rule is that he only pays you fifty per cent of the agreed sum for the remainder. You can contract around this, but most people don't bother.'

'Why is that?'

'In most cases, people are more realistic in their approach to a contract of concubinage than they are to *sine manu*, Roman marriage. I remember when I was in practice that the Imperial Statistical Council published a major study showing that people who are about to marry have an accurate sense of the likelihood that *other* people will get divorced—about twenty per cent over time—but simultaneously believe that they are certain or almost certain not to get divorced themselves. It's completely unrealistic.'

'I didn't know that,' said Claudia. 'That's very impressive.'

'By contrast—when it comes to concubinage—parties do not have unrealistic expectations of either permanence or fidelity. They tend to last for their allotted span with all the other arrangements intact. The main difference is that concubinage produces fewer children, which is why the tax system favours marriage.'

'How?'

'With a married couple with any children under six, the father's income is split into two and treated as two lower incomes, rather than one higher one, allowing the woman to stay at home and care for her family. This means that couples where there are children with a single income around average male weekly earnings or lower pay no income tax; it's a powerful incentive to marry, have children and stay together. It is the principle reason our divorce rates are not higher. Augustus introduced it in the days when our divorce rates *were* in the stratosphere, and it's been very successful.'

He opened the contract and began to fill in the blanks using the pencil behind his ear.

'So your Guild lawyer can change anything she's unhappy about,' he said.

'What about my pension plan?'

'That's part of valuing your time. I've always advised concubines to ensure that their pension contributions are maintained at the same or even a higher level for the duration of the agreement. Which fund are you with?'

'It's the one through the hotel.'

'And fully portable?'

'Yes.'

'Good.'

He turned the document towards her.

'I always advise clients—both in concubinage and marriage situations—that the default terms are well drafted. People who care about good public policy and well-designed incentives wrote them, and only after extensive empirical study. Varying the defaults is fine—and many people do so—but don't vary for the sake of variation. Good defaults matter.'

'That's code for go away and read them, isn't it?'

She ate in silence, reading through the document.

Linnaeus emerged from the baths—in a plain grey tunic while towelling his hair dry—on the stroke of seven. Pilate was standing, preparing to leave for Antonia while Claudia had retrieved a manuscript covered in fine blue pencil edits. There was no sign of Antony, Camilla or Marius.

Aristocles rang his little bell. Antony emerged almost immediately, his hair also wet from the baths. He went to the shrine, lit a stick of incense, touched wet fingers to his forehead and then sat at the table, immediately beginning to eat. Dana brought him coffee, which he sniffed at but did not drink.

'You're nearly thirteen,' Pilate said. 'Drink up.'

Antony nodded and took a sip. He still felt itchy and weird after last night, even though he'd washed himself with surpassing thoroughness when he awoke, stripped the sheets off his bed and thrown them in the laundry before Milos could do it for him. He avoided looking at Fotini, whose head his sleeping mind had stuck on sundry frescoed images in the

Caesarea residence.

If I have to put up with this until I'm sixteen, I'm going to explode.

Please Venus, get your hand off it.

Saul watches the Empire Hotel burn on a giant screen in Jericho's Market Square. Upwards of a thousand people are gathered around him; it is easy to be anonymous. He watches as the Indoi trade delegates gather outside telling Romans how much they are hated, sees a man pushed from the roof and then explode on the footpath, the falcon-like Roman fighting machines making short work of any Zealots trying to flee. The CR cameras linger lovingly over this, and at one point the footage comes from a camera mounted on a strix; blood drops spatter the lens.

Not privy to the full details, it is nonetheless clear to him that at least some of the attacks have been stymied thanks to Roman intelligence. It's hard to maintain contact with people at the best of times, but the suddenness with which Yehuda has vanished from Zealot networks gnaws at him. He has a vivid vision of Yehuda stretched out on a sloping table in Antonia's bowels, spotlit by pale-green light. A generic bristle-headed Roman interrogator leans over him, speaking softly, whispering that the drowning feeling will stop soon, oh yes it will, all one has to do is tell, tell, tell.

Saul knows that the cells under Antonia are painted green, because a soldier told him once. Saul was in Konstantinos's dark and grimy bar in the Greek Quarter. The soldier had been in his cups thanks to too much Caledonian firewater, and alternated unpredictably between wild laughter and maudlin sobbing. Saul did not speak Latin with an identifiable Aramaic accent, and used this fact to pump the man for information.

'You know, sometimes they talk shit just to make us stop,' the soldier went on, 'and we go up the country on wild goose chases, but so often, they try to be heroic, try to say nothing. When those ones

break, they tell us everything, and not just about this or that bomb plot... but about how they cheated in their high school alchemy exam or fucked their brother's wife. It's hilarious and sad.'

Saul asked the soldier if he liked the torture in the pale-green cells under Antonia, and the man shook his head, saying he always had to throw up afterwards. 'Some like it, though,' he added. 'They like it so much they can't get enough of it, and even volunteer. They take pictures and show their concubines.'

Saul closes his eyes, pushing his memory of the soldier's gormless, dribbling expression to one side. He hopes Yehuda has not encountered Antonia's torturing photographers.

The sun is in his eyes, now, and he turns away from the big screen, excusing himself as he passes through the growing crowd in the square. He crosses the street in front of the newly constructed Roman Ministry of Health (Jericho) building, its frontage decorated with geometric patterns and a sunburst motif over the main entrance. Around the foyer are stylised murals of doctors and nurses vaccinating children, their gestures grand and sweeping. Bas-reliefs above and below the painted murals read, 'Eradicate Polio!' 'Eradicate Smallpox!' 'Eradicate Diptheria!' Saul knows that in all three cases, the eradication in Gaul and Italy has succeeded, and that rapid progress is being made in Judaea and Syria.

He fishes in his pocket and takes out his identity card, the purple background glittering in Jericho's hard light. His card is a new one, and in addition to the S.P.Q.R. is watermarked with the same sunburst pattern as the Ministry of Health building. For the first time, he notices that there are words, repeated over and over, behind the sunburst image.

'Eradicate Ignorance!' 'Eradicate Ignorance!' 'Eradicate Ignorance!'

He turns his back on the Ministry of Health and walks down a shadowed side street.

GLOSSARY

Ab urbe condita: from the founding of the city (of Rome), traditionally dated to 753 BC, which is thus a.u.c. I. As in our system, there is no 'year zero'.

Advocatus/a: lawyer, advisor.

Aquilifer: standard-bearer, a position of considerable honour.

Andronites: men's quarters in a traditional Athenian household.

Architectus: military engineer (either sapper or civil).

Basiliké Stoà: town hall.

Brituncculus: An unpleasant diminutive for a person from Britain.

Caldarium: the 'hot room' in a Roman baths complex.

Chametz (Hebrew): leavened bread, forbidden in a Jewish household during Passover; a Jewish baker is obliged to 'sell' his bakery before Passover and then 'repurchase' it afterwards.

Cardo: main street *or* high street.

Cinaedus: rent boy.

Coleones: balls (slang).

Collegium (sing.): the Roman law version of a limited liability corporation with a separate legal personality.

Contubernium: squad or section in the Roman army; comprised of eight men.

Corona: the Roman Victoria Cross or Congressional Medal of Honour.

Culpa: guilt, blame

Curo! Terra minae: 'Caution: Land Mines!'

Decumanus: secondary main street; always intersects with the *cardo*.

De gustibus non est disputandum: 'There's no accounting for taste'

Delict: the Roman law of tort (civil wrongs).

De sua pecunia fecit: 'Built with his/her own money.'

Divi Filius: son of a god.

Divide et impera: 'divide and rule.'

Dolus directus: murder with intent.

Dolus indirectus: murder without intent, but where death is seen as inevitable.

Dolus eventualis: murder without intent, but where death is seen as probable.

Dominus/a: Master/Mistress; *Domine* is the masculine vocative form (the 'calling' case).

Duumvir: mayor, always elected as one of a pair by a system of census suffrage.

Erastes/Eromenos: 'official' names for the older man/younger man in a Greek homosexual relationship.

Feria: Festival, usually somewhat bloody.

Fideicommissa: the Roman law equivalent of a trust.

Fretensis: 'Of the Straights'; indicates originally formed as marines.

Frigidarium: the cold bath in a set of Roman baths; often large, even swimming pool sized.

Gallus: ladyboy. The plural is *galli*.

Gveret (Hebrew): Madam.

Haruspex: An individual who practices divination based on the dissection of livers.

Hetaera (Greek): a highly educated courtesan.

Immunis: a soldier with a skill; if a professional (lawyer, medic), something akin to a staff officer, but among subordinate ranks corresponds roughly with 'specialist.'

Instrumentum vocale: 'The tool that speaks.'

Ita, recte: yes, indeed.

Kohanim (Hebrew): priests at the Jerusalem Temple, tasked with management and organising animal sacrifices; always descendents of Aaron.

Kohen Gadol (Hebrew): High Priest.

Kyrios/Kyria (Greek): Sir, Madam.

Lanista: a trainer or manager of gladiators and cage fighters; considered a low-status occupation, although many of them are very rich.

Lararia: god-shelf, family shrine; similar to Japanese *kamidana*.

Lares: household gods, gods of place; similar to Japanese ***kami.***

Laudatio: Eulogy.

Legatus: General.

Leno/a: pimp/madam

Libellus conventionis: indictment.

Licentia: trade or professional qualification.

Limes: Border.

Ludi: games, entertainment (plural).

Magister/Magistra: teacher, used as a title, much like 'Sensei' in Japanese.

Magna Mater: the Great Mother, mother of the gods (*mater deum*); used of Cybele.

Manes: the ancestral spirits.

Materfamilias: mother of the household, but only ever used of a woman who has, in fact, borne children.

Medicus: doctor, usually in the military.

Megalesia: The Roman Festival of the *Magna Mater* (the Great Mother, Cybele).

Mezzadri: sharecroppers.

Mitzvah (Hebrew): blessing.

Mos maiorum: 'way of the ancestors'; the plural is *mores*.

MRAP: Mine Resistant Ambush Protected armoured vehicle; has a distinctive v-shaped hull, making it difficult to destroy with IEDs.

Niddah (Hebrew): period during and following menstruation when a woman is ritually unclean.

Novus actus interveniens: 'New intervening event'; break in the chain of causation.

Optio: the second in command of a legionary century, although Marius, as *Optio* of the first century, first cohort is a senior officer.

Optimates: Tories.

Pais, padika (Greek): 'boy lover.'

Parrilla: 'barbecue.'

Paterfamilias: father of the household. His duties extend beyond those in the nuclear family, taking in servants, colleagues of lower status, friends down on their luck and—occasionally—children-in-law. Considered honourable, something to aspire to; commands considerable moral authority.

Payot: Earlocks.

Perplexae: Complex, intricate, and beautiful pattern

Pietas: filial piety (in a sense similar to that in Confucianism).

Philotimia: private philanthropy for the good of the *civitas* or *polis*; it is always *for* something (education, entertainment, construction, commerce).

Populares: Whigs.

Potestas: power, especially derived from respect or rank, not violent display.

Praetorium: courtroom, especially in the provinces.

Primus Pilus: 'First File'; equivalent to a senior colonel.

Publicani: Private firms contracted to exercise the tax collecting power by the Roman state.

Scientia est potestas: 'Knowledge is Power.'

Senatus consultum de re publica defendenda: Emergency edict, 'state of emergency'.

Septuagint: A Greek translation of key Jewish scriptures.

Seriatim: one after the other.

Shabbat goy: A non-Jew who runs errands or completes tasks for a Jew on the Sabbath.

Shiva: Judaism's traditional period of mourning.

Sicarii: 'knife men', used of an extreme faction of the Zealots; they particularly target those they consider collaborators with the Roman occupation.

Simpliciter: without qualification or condition.

Sine manu: literally, 'without the hand'; form of Roman marriage where the husband and wife's property interests were kept separate. The most common form of marriage, it ensured a husband had no control over his wife's property, and that he could not interfere with her income or investments. It also forbade joint bank accounts and wives standing surety for their husbands in a real property transaction.

S.P.Q.R. (*Senatus Populusque Romanus*): The Senate and People of Rome.

Stuprum: General term for sexual immorality, often of a quite sensational sort.

Tabula recta: Alphabet tables, used in cryptography.

Tamesis: The Roman name for the River Thames

Tauroctony: Mithras slaying the bull; principle cult image of the Mithraic Mysteries.

Tekton: Carpenter or stonemason

Tepidarium: the 'warm' room in a Roman baths complex.

Tribus: Roman constituency; originally geographical, the system was diluted over time until characterised by rotten boroughs and disproportionate electorate sizes and populations.

Vasco: Basque.

Vexilla/um: Flag

Vigiles: fire brigade, and in some cities, the police as well.

Yeshivot: Rabbinical school

AUTHOR'S NOTE

Kingdom of the Wicked had a long gestation—some thirteen years.

Two years after *The Hand that Signed the Paper* was published, I began to research and write an historical novel set during the reign of Vespasian (AD 69–79). The idea was good and I had lots of research available. A local television station even flew me to Italy, allowing me the time and resources to do further research, in exchange for appearing on one of their programmes. There was one problem: the book I started to write (and by that stage, there were 40 000 words) was very bad. I persisted for a while, thinking I could draw on what I hoped was a developing literary skill to 'iron out' the wrinkles. Unfortunately, the manuscript turned out to be all wrinkles, so I abandoned it. The idea of some sort of Roman-era book never went away, however, and when *Kingdom of the Wicked* came to mind, demanding to be written, I knew the book I originally wanted to write was the wrong book. This, I hope, is the right one.

In between writing the two novels, I became a lawyer, and, consequently, *Kingdom of the Wicked* is a product of legal, rather than historical, theological, or scientific imagination. This isn't to say that history, theology, and science aren't important in the world I've written, but to highlight that the book began with law. Let me explain.

While I was in my second year at Oxford, a friend asked me if I'd seen Mel Gibson's *Passion of the Christ*. I had to admit I had not, and at his suggestion watched it. Leaving the immense controversy and success of Gibson's film to one side, at its conclusion I found myself thinking about the Gospel accounts of Jesus's trial and execution from a lawyer's perspective. I realised I hadn't read them for many years, and certainly not since qualifying in law. 'If I were counsel, how would I make a plea in mitigation...' is a favourite parlour game, although more commonly applied to errant footballers and wayward celebrities, not religious figures.

What struck me at once was the attack on the money-changers in the Jerusalem Temple. All four Gospels record it, and their combined accounts do not reflect well on the perpetrator's character.

Jesus went in armed (with a whip) and trashed the place, stampeding animals, destroying property and assaulting people. He also did it during or just before Passover, when the Temple precinct would have been packed to capacity with tourists, pilgrims, and religious officials. I live in Edinburgh, a city that has many large festivals—religious and secular. The thought of what would happen if someone behaved similarly in Princes Street during Hogmanay filled my mind's eye. This was not a small incident.

It seemed obvious to me that Jesus was executed because he started a riot. Everything else—the Messianic claims, giving Pilate attitude at trial, verbal jousting with Jewish religious leaders—was by the by. Our system would send someone down for a decent stretch if they did something similar; the Romans were not alone in developing concepts of 'breach of the peace', 'assault' or 'malicious mischief'. Those things exist at common law, too.

I shared this insight with my friend, and he suggested rather wryly that while Pilate was locking up the ringleader, perhaps the disciples were each subjected to an anti-social behaviour order (ASBO). I laughed, but I also started thinking.

How, I wondered, would we react to Jesus Christ if he turned up now?

My answer was not one I liked very much: I thought we'd mistake him for a terrorist. There was a period in the sixties and seventies when Jesus was conceived of as a bit of a hippy, certainly a pacifist. But the figure belabouring the ancient world's equivalent of bank tellers with a whip did not look like a pacifist to me. Then there was his politics: socially conservative (he railed against divorce), redistributive, even socialist (he railed against the rich), egalitarian (he railed against the treatment of the poor). He wasn't too impressed by the Great Satan of his day, the Roman Empire, either. His Judaean contemporaries referred to the Roman Empire as 'the kingdom of the wicked', whence the title of this book.

For a little while, I thought of transplanting Jesus to Britain or the US and watching the story unfold (and unravel) as I told it, but every single version that played out in my head turned into Waco or the People's Temple. Those stories are terrifying and confronting by turns—as well as fascinating—but they are not the stories I wanted to tell.

Finally, instead of bringing Jesus forward in time and placing him in modernity, I thought to leave him where he was and instead put modernity into the past. What, I wondered, would have happened had Jesus emerged in a Roman Empire that had gone through an industrial revolution? Other things being equal, what would modern science and technology do to a society with very different values from our own? Would they react with the same incomprehension that we do when confronted by religious terrorism? I did not know the answers, but I suspected that writing a book based around the idea of a Roman industrial revolution might help me develop *some* answers, if not *the* answers.

This meant I tried to conceive of a world where a society

unlike ours produces the 'progress and growth' template that all others then seek to follow. It is commonplace to point out that Roman civilisation was polytheistic and animist, while ours is monotheistic but leavened by the Enlightenment; that Roman society was very martial, while Christianity has gifted us a tradition of religious and political pacifism; that Roman society had different views of sexual morality, marriage, and family structure. In short, I had to imagine an industrial revolution without monotheism.

I could not stray too far from 'the West as we know it', however, for while we may have lost ancient Rome's ancestor worship, multiplicity of gods and goddesses, candy-coloured religious art (Roman statues and temples were brightly painted, as they are in Hinduism) and filial piety, Europe in particular has kept much of its law, and the great bulk of Roman law was conceived of and employed by polytheists. Sometimes this non-Christian heritage is obvious: the toleration of homosexuality, abortion and concubinage, easy divorce, the importance attached to appointing an heir whose job it is to undertake regular ritual appeasement of ancestral spirits.

Sometimes, however, Roman law is different from the English common law only in its details. It also provides an orderly way of resolving disputes over everything from who owes money to whom, to who sideswiped whom. Both systems (and, in the context of human history, neither Roman law nor common law have any serious rivals as legal systems) were clearly developed by peoples with a genius for intelligent legal organisation and the ability to change bad law and retain good law. Both systems show a sophisticated understanding of the gains to be made from trade and the embedded nature of private property.

How, then, to create this mixture of familiar and foreign?

The best speculative fiction persuades you that its

alternative world is real. It does this by constructing plausible points of departure from actual history, 'our timeline'. In *The Man in the High Castle*, Roosevelt is assassinated and replaced by a nonentity. In *SS-GB*, Operation Sea Lion is successful. In *Pavane*, Elizabeth I is assassinated and the English Reformation doesn't get off the ground. While I am more interested in working out the way people relate to each other and to society rather than in the intricacies of interlocking technical developments, I have been as careful as I'm able in constructing my points of departure.

My industrial revolution has its origins when Archimedes survives the Siege of Syracuse in 212 BC and is treated to a Roman version of 'Operation Paperclip' (the American retrieval of scientists from defeated Nazi Germany). As a consequence he (or his students) develop calculus and a variety of practical military technologies. In keeping with Roman militarism, the first place the new technologies manifest themselves is in warfare. They then propagate. We know that the Roman general Marcellus was furious when Archimedes was killed contrary to his specific orders, and also that Archimedes was close to developing calculus (with its immediate and obvious practical applications). There are lots of reasons why you'd want to graph a curve.

The rationale for pushing technological innovation of this type back to the Middle Republic—rather than having it occur later—is that industrialisation is predicated on using machines as labour-saving devices. While Roman-era scientists later developed designs for things like steam engines (Heron of Alexandria) and built fabulous mechanical instruments (the Antikythera machine), they did so in a society that had been flooded with vast numbers of slaves (the late Republic and early Principate), and large-scale chattel slavery and industrialisation are simply incompatible.

Chattel slavery undermines incentives to develop labour-saving devices because human labour power never loses its comparative advantage. People can just go out and buy another slave to do that labour-intensive job. Among other things, the industrial revolution in Britain depended on the presence (relative to other countries) of high wages, thus making the development of labour-saving devices worthwhile. The Antikythera mechanism is a thing of wonder, but it is also little more than a clockwork executive toy; no wonder the great lawyer Cicero had one. It's just the sort of thing I can imagine an eminent silk having on his desk in chambers.

Rather than science and technology being deployed to amuse and entertain, operating at most as an adjunct to labour power, I used Archimedes to give the Romans what a friend of mine calls a 'machine culture'. That is, machines become part of everyday life, and many individuals participate in the development of further innovations. This means that the abolition of slavery becomes a live issue.

Slavery—and its near relative, serfdom—have been pervasive in even sophisticated human societies, and campaigns for abolition few and far between. We forget that our view that slavery and slavers are obnoxious is of recent vintage. In days gone by, people who made fortunes in the slave trade were held in the highest esteem and sat on our great councils of state. This truism is reflected in history: *The Society for Effecting the Abolition of the Slave Trade* met for the first time in 1787. It had just twelve members—nine Quakers and three Anglicans. And yet, in 1807, Parliament passed *An Act for the Abolition of the Slave Trade*. The Quaker role in abolition was so vast it is difficult to overestimate. And in the context of both Christianity specifically and human religion more generally, the Religious Society of Friends is theologically distinct. Who in antiquity could perform the Quakers' role?

In the end, I lit upon the Stoics, and came to admire many aspects of their philosophy when researching *Kingdom of the Wicked*. Ancient Stoics shared many characteristics with Quakers, apart from a common dislike of slavery. They were thrifty and hard working. They thought that people should participate in public life and so improve it. They were successful in trade and commerce, elevating prudence to an art form. Their ideas influenced Adam Smith when he came to write *The Wealth of Nations*. Of course, there are important differences: Stoicism is intensely martial, and influential modern Stoics (Admiral James Stockdale comes to mind) are often in the military. Stoics did not accept the existence of an afterlife. They were pantheists who considered suicide in the face of suffering or oppression to be virtuous.

At the same time, we know that the Romans didn't think some people were 'naturally servile', which is at the heart of Aristotle's argument in favour of slavery. The Roman view (consistent with their militarism) was always 'you lost, we own you'. Roman law—even in its earliest form—always held that slavery was 'contrary to nature'. Human beings were naturally free; slavery was a legally mandated status, however cruelly imposed. It is also important to remember that ancient slavery was never race-based. No Roman argued that slaves were lesser forms of the human. Middle- and upper-class Roman children educated at home by slaves who were manifestly cleverer than them (not to mention mum and dad) knew this, intimately. These factors allowed me to yoke Stoicism to the sort of enlightened economic thinking that led to the repeal of the Corn Laws and the promotion of free trade in Britain. The Quakers and the Whig free traders were on the same side. Often they were the same people: David Ricardo, the theorist of comparative advantage, was a 'Quaker by convincement'. The prudent and thoughtful Stoics made useful

Quaker analogues.

Both before and after Quakers agitated for the abolition of slavery and free traders advocated the repeal of the Corn Laws, England and then Britain witnessed the long struggle between Crown, Courts and Parliament for supremacy. Parliament eventually won, but not without bitter conflict and much loss of life. There were periods when it could easily have gone another way. This is important to remember because in Roman history we know that a similar struggle did go the other way, and that their society became increasingly autocratic over time. Augustus gave himself powers roughly analogous to those of Charles II (although both rulers exercised authority judiciously). By the time of Diocletian, the emperor's powers were akin to those of Charles I. Further down the line, Constantine could reasonably be mistaken for Henry VIII (including the major religious transformation).

Because the Constitution of the Roman Republic—like Britain's Constitution—was unwritten and ordered according to constitutional conventions, I have always seen it as more Westminster than Washington, despite Washington's extensive borrowings from Rome (right down to the electoral college, for example). This means that when depicting constitutional change in response to social shifts and economic growth in *Kingdom of the Wicked*, I must admit to adapting a fair bit of British constitutional history (including elements from the Glorious Revolution of 1688 and later movements, such as Chartism).

The broad historical outline of the implosion of the Roman Republic remains (you cannot have that much power and wealth floating around without the lads wanting a piece of the action). However, the rough political distinctions of the late Republic (between *Populares* and *Optimates*) later harden into something approaching political parties, much as it took time for Britain's rough political alliances to coalesce into Whigs and Tories.

The system that emerges in my early Empire is less autocratic and more constitutional, with an Emperor executive combined with a representative (but not democratic) legislature, the Senate. The latter is elected by census citizen suffrage and retains its Republican property qualification for admission. I have also retained the Roman tendency to draw a sharp distinction between citizens and non-citizens when it comes to doling out rights. Westminster blurs legislative, executive and judicial functions in ways most Americans find discomforting; so did Rome, which is why I conceived of other senior Roman magistracies coming to form the cabinet, and the non-imperial consul taking a role akin to that of prime minister. The main difference between Westminster in its long evolution and my modified Roman system is my use of census suffrage. Census suffrage is the opposite of *equal suffrage*, meaning that the votes cast by those eligible to vote are not equal, but are weighted differently according to the person's rank in the census (for example, people with high income have more votes than those with a low income, or a shareholder with more shares in a company has more votes than someone with fewer shares). Suffrage may therefore be limited, usually to the propertied classes, but can still be *universal*, including, for instance, women or ethnic minorities, if they meet the census.

I did this for two reasons. First, the Romans themselves often made use of male census suffrage, as well as setting property qualifications on holders of high public offices. Second, the status of women in ancient Rome in the first century BC and the first century AD was higher than it was, say, in nineteenth century England. Both married and single women retained ownership and control over their property; married women could initiate divorce and retrieve their dowry (indeed, a divorced man had to repay his ex-wife's dowry before he paid any other creditors). There are records of Roman women in trade, commerce, law and scholarship. The Romans were also well aware of the 'no taxation without representation' principle. In 42 BC, the Second Triumvirate attempted to enact a law taxing Rome's wealthier matrons in order to help fund the Republic's many wars. Led by a prominent lawyer, Hortensia, Rome's women objected on the basis that until they were given seats in the Senate and a role in the affairs of state, they should not be taxed for poor decisions that other people had made without consulting them. The Triumvirs backed off, instead increasing the taxes levied on men.

To my mind, it would not take much technological and social change for an economically hard-pressed government to go the other way, enfranchising women in order to tax them. After all, governments are almost incurably addicted to revenue. The corollary, of course, is 'no representation without taxation', which is why I can imagine the Romans enfranchising propertied women before they enfranchised the poor—the opposite of what happened under the various Reform Bills, where women were last in line.

This quirk of gender attitudes (no one knows why Roman women had such high status; Roman society was thoroughly militaristic and male dominated in other respects) meant that two of the biggest battles fought by first- and second-wave feminism respectively (married women's property rights, then unilateral divorce) were already 'settled' matters. Add reliable contraception and industrialisation to a society like that and who knows what would have happened to the status of women.

In order to give some substance to Roman cultural difference—the status of women being one component thereof—I made use of Roman religion. Or, rather, Roman religions, as it emerged. They had hundreds to choose from. Those enumerated in *Kingdom of the Wicked* are but a tiny sample. Edward Gibbon's statement that the 'various modes of worship which prevailed in the Roman world were all considered by the people as equally true; by the philosopher as equally false; and by the magistrate as equally useful' is an accurate summary, although it ignores the fact that some Roman magistrates could be religious, too, just not in ways we would necessarily recognise.

Laid over the top of this plethora of religious practices was the Roman civil religion, which was ornate, public, characterised by elaborate parades, animal sacrifices and festivals, and, it would appear, similar to the system of State Shinto that prevailed in Japan before 1945. Like the Japanese, the Romans had a strong sense of filial piety, and even used similar images (a young man carrying an aged parent on his back) to express it. They worshipped before a god-shelf (in Latin, *lararia*; in Japanese, *kamidana*) with identical conceptions of the numinous gods and goddesses (gods of place, gods of the hearth, the ancestors, the Imperial Household). You didn't have to accept a shred of the civil religion as 'true', but you did have to do your 'bit'. It was about ritual, not content. Even out-and-out atheists did their 'bit'.

In order to depict a plausible modern paganism (one that doesn't resemble much of what passes for paganism now, which one classicist friend derides as 'fluffwicca'), I relied on some excellent classical scholarship. I read hundreds of articles, but two books that brought paganism alive for me—and also showed how different Christianity was, even when it pinched aspects of paganism, such as the cult of the saints and Mariolatry—were Robin Lane Fox's *Pagans and Christians* (1986) and Ramsay MacMullen's *Christianity and Paganism in the Fourth to Eighth Centuries* (1997). Both convey how paganism was alive and central to the way people lived their lives.

I've taken some guesses at religious culture, based in part on trying to conceptualise the sort of music that would accompany mass pagan ritual. Both MacMullen and Lane Fox emphasise the importance of music and dance to pagan tradition, and its heavy use of percussion (which the early Church Fathers hated with the same intensity as the Puritans hated the English theatres). Christianity has in large part exiled the joyous from its tradition. (This is possibly why evangelical Christianity does so well; it takes Larry Norman's question seriously. 'Why does the devil have all the good music?'). I did get the distinct impression that Christians turned up the treble, while pagans turned up the bass. When Camille Paglia describes rock music as 'pagan', I think she's right.

I've also had fun portraying a pagan society that is strongly pro-family. It's important to remember that once upon a time, polytheists and their filial piety, law and order, joyous rituals, and civic virtue were the conservatives. This meant taking parts of Augustus's actual pro-family legislation and tweaking it in ways in which I imagine he'd approve. Some bits, however—like the payments he made to parents of three children—I've hardly changed at all. I've added things like income splitting (which reinforces the sexual division of labour) and citizenship perks, because they're the kind of incentive-based policies that tend to work in light of modern economic research. I have also preserved the pagan sexual double standard. Technology may attenuate it, but some form of double standard (it manifests differently in different cultures) seems to be culturally universal.

Finally, there is the effect differing religious and cultural values have on technological progress. It is not an exaggeration to suggest that medicine and biology are the

Johnny-come-latelies of science. We knew a great deal about physics and chemistry, while we were astonishingly ignorant of biology, with the inevitable corollary: as our economies exploded in the eighteenth century our lives nonetheless remained, for the most part, nasty, brutish, and short. A disproportionate chunk of our scholarly endeavours were poured into communications. Women were still dying in childbirth in droves at the time Alexander Graham Bell was granted a patent for the telephone. In the society I have depicted, by contrast, the lack of a religious prohibition on medical and biological speculation (as well as the absence of a moral code that draws much of a distinction between humans and animals) means that my fictional Romans have directed their scientific and technical resources towards medicine and biology. They are brilliant doctors and geneticists but, as with Britain in the '60s, there are only three channels and all those sign off just after midnight. After playing the National Anthem, of course.

If religion is something that sets us apart from the Romans, then—as mentioned—law brings us closer together. At its heart, *Kingdom of the Wicked* concerns a trial, and workable trial procedure depends on the rule of law. In my experience, many writers concerned with alternative worlds do not build believable legal systems; it is always disturbing to see developed and sophisticated fictional societies resorting to trial by battle, or having no mechanism for the enforcement of contracts. Much as it may be painful to admit, law has a reasonable claim to being the second-oldest profession. People may indeed want to 'kill all the lawyers', but building civilisation without us is surprisingly difficult.

Because the Romans produced some of the world's greatest lawyers, and because we know a lot about their law (it forms the basis for every legal system in western Europe save

England's and Ireland's), I made a deliberate decision to depict a functioning legal system in *Kingdom of the Wicked*. I am qualified in both Scots and English law and have ransacked both systems for legal ideas, something for which I will no doubt have to apologise to professional colleagues on both sides of the border.

Procedurally, however, I have used the adversarial method characteristic of the common law, rather than the inquisitorial method now used on the Continent. This is for two reasons. First, my initial training and practice was in a common law jurisdiction. I have seen a lot of trials, and have an understanding of the cut and thrust of a common law trial. Second, the Romans themselves used a mostly adversarial procedure. I am convinced that, absent the introduction of inquisitorial methods via Canon law, a non-Christian, industrialised Rome would have retained its adversarial practices.

I have, however, gestured towards three characteristics of Roman law that set it apart from common law. First is the capacity of judges to investigate matters on their own motion. This explains why Pilate is able to source evidence independent of counsel, something considered most improper at common law. Next is the importance Cornelius attaches to obtaining a confession, and the lack of procedural safeguards for the accused. To a Roman lawyer, a confession is the 'Queen of Proofs', while his common-law counterpart always suspects that confessions come about thanks to the judicious application of lengths of rubber hose. Finally, there is the absence of a rule against hearsay, something that is peculiar to the common law.

Of course, in addition to being a fictional contrivance, the system depicted is far from perfect. There is no legal aid for non-citizens. The prosecution is not independent. It allows an application to court seeking a warrant for torture—a system devised by Augustus and criticised by the Roman jurist Ulpian—a regime reanimated in recent times in controversies around the use of torture as part of America's 'War on Terror'. I wanted to expose the bones of a society where the rule of law contends for mastery with the rule of men, with lawyers, soldiers, civil servants, and businesspeople constantly pulled in both directions.

In depicting an evolving system based on what I know of both common and civil law I have relied heavily on arguments first articulated by economist and legal scholar F.A. Hayek in volume one of his *Law, Legislation and Liberty* (1973), a short book called *Rules and Order*.

Hayek argues that law is constitutive of civilisation and arises originally by custom; legislators do not make it, although it can take on statutory characteristics over time. Those customs that enhance individual and community survivability prosper; others are allowed to fall into desuetude. Hayek calls this process 'spontaneous order', with a clear nod to biological evolution. Law, if it is to work, undergoes heritable change over generations in the same trial and error fashion. Things I have shown evolving over time—a Roman law version of the limited liability corporation, to take one example—are speculative, but it is informed speculation. Industrialisation requires the ability to spread risk, and some of these risk-spreading mechanisms were already present in Roman law. Cato the Elder, for example, underwrote shipping contracts with 49 other investors. Roman partnerships (as they do in Scots law) already had separate legal personality. Limited liability, I am sure, would have soon followed.

My comments have strayed a long way from the story of Jesus and the moneychangers in Jerusalem's Temple, but context is useful, if only to illustrate some of the things that interested me when I started writing. I am wary of attempts to distil books into a single theme, but if there is one thing that exercised my mind while writing *Kingdom of the Wicked*, it is the relationship of the two missionary monotheisms, Islam and Christianity, to science, technology and the western use of a form of religious tolerance that a pagan Roman would recognise but for a long time was in abeyance, in both the West and elsewhere. Rather than attempt to say how that relationship should work in so many words, I used fiction to explore my own confusions, doubts and concerns.

ACKNOWLEDGEMENTS

No book this large and complex gets written without a great deal of help. The following institutions and people made *Kingdom of the Wicked* possible: the Institute for Humane Studies, whose three fellowships allowed me not only to pursue studies at the Universities of Oxford and Edinburgh but also bought me time to write; the law faculties at both Oxford and Edinburgh, which supported my studies and allowed me to engage in careful deliberation in the areas of jurisprudence and comparative law; Mel Richards, who taught me about the Religious Society of Friends and made me think about the relationship between religion and modernity; James Worthern, who introduced me to a wealth of classical sources, many of them obscure, all of them fascinating, and then helped with translation; Katy Barnett, who was a brilliant and attentive first reader; Sinclair Davidson, who clarified many obscurities in economic theory and provided one of the best lines of dialogue in the book; Paul du Plessis, my Roman law tutor at Edinburgh, Lorenzo Warby, who discussed the intersection of slavery and technological progress with me; Carlo Kopp, who brought his knowledge of military culture and technology to bear on many points in the story; Dave Bath, who introduced me to ancient medical literature and helped me understand how a different medical tradition might develop; Susan Prior, who was an astonishingly sharp-eyed editor, and Justice Peter Dutney, who was an extraordinary and insightful pupil-master.

Any errors, infelicities, and disagreements are my responsibility.

Oxford, Edinburgh, Sydney, London

BOOK TWO

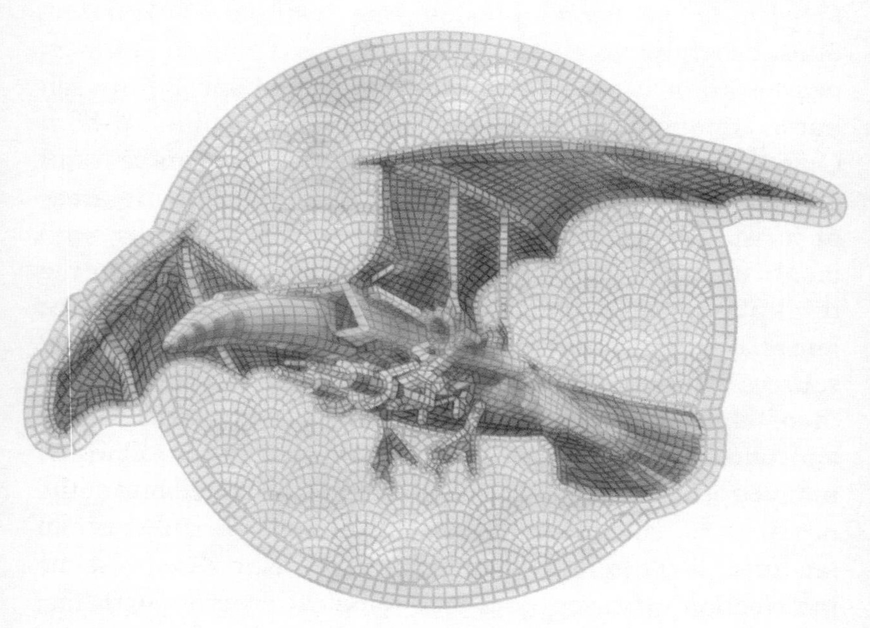

ORDER

COMING EARLY 2018

PANTERA'S STORY

'After I finished my basic, the Empire sent me to the Galilee, a part of Judaea province. It is beautiful but very poor. I don't know how far you've travelled outside Germania Superior but you need to imagine clear light and blue skies and dry ground the colour of old bones. The people who live there are resentful of Rome taking their liberty from them, more resentful even than you Germans. Originally there were no cities and everyone lived in villages, or on small farms, or fished in the lakes and rivers, growing just enough to live on—salad vegetables, some olives, apples and grapes—Jews and Samaritans side by side. As you know Romans do not suffer a place to be without proper cities, so we built them. One city was Sepphoris, the Jewel of the Galilee, the bird on the hill. Many of the city's pieces had to be sent by rail and over the sea from Rome. The one I remember is the Temple of Roma, which came unassembled and had to be put together by local craftsmen. It had Ionic columns that they hadn't seen before. All of these were installed upside down, with the scrolled bit at the bottom. This was very funny when the *municipium* inaugurated it.

'Judaea is not a safe province, so even though there was this new fine city, it still needed to be garrisoned. We soldiers built a permanent *castrum*, and very good it was, too. Each day detachments would go forth to watch over the people of the Galilee in case they were revolting. They revolted a lot. Once they tried to revolt in Sepphoris itself, but that was before my time. Afterwards the revolting went north, into the wild hill country. At first the Galilean revolters were mistrustful of Sepphoris and it was mainly Greeks who moved in beside us Romans in our *castrum*. In time they became less wary and soon there was a lively trade going on in the forum. At first the customers were the men who built the city, but soon people came from outlying villages to buy and to sell. One day a man stood up in the forum and said that buying and selling in the marketplace like this was immoral, because the sellers looked only to their own concerns, not those of the people who bought from them. Maybe he had been cheated in commerce, because he was very bitter. One of the shopkeepers came out of his store and said that this was well and good for the man standing and speaking in the forum, because friends supported him. That is, they paid for him to catch the train between towns and harangue people about their immorality, while the immoral people made a living the best way they knew how and so made life better for everyone.

'The Galilee is full of signs and wonders, even I have seen some. In one village there was a woman four hundred years old who could tell the future. In another there was a man who could conjure something out of nothing, like the Egyptian priests in days gone by, and which we do not see so often in our time. Once I went to the old woman to have her cast me a horoscope and she forecast that I would not recognise my first-born son. She was frightened by this prediction and so was I, although I put it down to having Sagittarius who fires his arrows one way and runs the other as my rising sign. Soon after this our Cohort fought in a battle on the border and I captured a dozen Persian mercenaries with my own hands, for which I was awarded Roman citizenship. When I marched them back to the prison camp one of them looked at me and took an eye out of his face. He held it up above his head and used it to see much further than a normal man. Once he'd seen where I was taking him and his comrades he put the eye back in his head.

'I wanted to know where I might get an eye like that but he said they only existed in Persia, that we Romans made many good things but not magical things. Once we were in the *castrum* I determined to show that he was wrong and went to the Cohort's leading *architectus* and asked him to show the Persian in the cells our most powerful magic. He laughed at me and said there was no such thing anymore, that Lucretius was right and that everything could be explained by means of reason. I asked the *architectus* how the Persian could still see with his eye out of his head, to which the *architectus* replied, "Are you sure he can see?" I had to admit I was not sure.

'Not long after the battle on the border I saw a beautiful young woman selling clothes in the forum in Sepphoris. She was too poor to rent a shop so she just had a table in the place set aside for street stalls. As soon as I saw her I wanted to fuck her. She had glossy black hair that she styled up with fine silver bands. She'd decorated these with what looks like silver coins except that the discs were too small and too fine to be coins. Some of these hung over her forehead. Then there was her skin, as fair as you Germans but without the high colour of the north. At that moment a breeze swirled up and showed me her sweet shape as it coiled her clothing around her. In my mind's eye her naked body was already in my arms and I was kissing her breasts.

'So that I could find out her name and stand closer to her I bought one of her shirts. It had long sleeves with a button and was embroidered around the neck. Her name was Miriam and she did the embroidery herself, as well as making the shirts. When I was on leave I wore it and everyone complimented me on it, so I bought two more from her. I began to think how I might convince her to have sex with me. I thought

I had a good chance at her, mainly because she did not have male relatives around her all the time. Normally in the Galilee a woman does not leave the house without a man. Among them a woman who does go out alone is often called a harlot, even when she is no such thing. In Miriam's case her parents were both dead. She told me that her family had once been well off, her father trading in the fine things that his wife and daughters made. He had no sons, she told me, so he put his womenfolk to work.

'One year they caught the ferry to Cyprus for a holiday in the Roman manner: the man, the wife and the daughters. You may remember it, when the Master slept and forgot to close the bow doors and the ferry capsized in little more than a minute. Miriam and her oldest sister lived—the Imperial Navy fished them up out of the sea—but the rest of the family drowned. After she told me that I felt sorrow as well as lust for her, so I told how my people were all seafarers and fishermen until a Roman senator built a pulp and paper mill by the waterway that ran through our town. The mill leaked dye into the river and the sea, and the fish swam away from us. Even the seabirds went from our skies; no more did we wake to their screeching cries as they followed the catch into the bay. My father sold his boats; he didn't have the money for the great trawlers that go out beyond the Pillars of Hercules into the Atlantic seeking whales as well as fish. My brother and I joined the *auxilia*, while my sister took an apprenticeship as *hetaera* in Antioch. She got to visit our father more than we did. She said he steered his trawler in his sleep.

'Miriam and I were two people who sorrowed for each other. I'd been a soldier for, what is it, four years at most. Miriam had been alone in the world for something similar. On the day in question her sister was there with her behind the table in the forum; the sister was doing the selling while Miriam had eyes only for me. The two women had rented a small room off the forum to store bolts of cloth and reels of thread and buttons and decorations of divers sorts, not to mention the machines Miriam needed to make the things she did. I realised they were living there, cooking on a little gas stove in the corner, going to the public baths to keep clean and washing their dishes in the tiny sink. She took me into this room and we lay on her mattress on the floor in the middle of the beautiful things she had made to sell. She trembled as I undressed her, so shy like all the women of her people and yet ardent, too, as I stirred her up. She knew not how to be clever in the Roman way so I taught her over many more visits how to please a man and how to please herself.

'I was twenty-two and didn't want woman or child, and told her so. I wanted sex, and to find it willingly—given up without recourse to *hetaera* or other women who pleasure men—was a great delight. Miriam seemed to think something similar, because we kept going back to the well and drinking from the same cup together. At first she insisted that we go to the little room off the forum only when her older sister was not there, but Elishiba was not deceived and at the end of one market day she walked in on us. I remember it was winter and cold—as cold as it gets in Judaea, at any rate—and Miriam was humiliated. She leaned forward and clung to me and I threw my army-issue coat over her. This covered her completely and allowed me to stroke her hair and back and soothe her. She said, "She's fourteen, Pantera."

'I said, "She likes it well enough".

'"So do you," she replied.

'A few months after this incident Miriam told me she was pregnant, and as I was her only man and I took her virginity I must be the father. At that stage the Æsculapion in Sepphoris was only half built so I offered to take her to Caesarea.'

'What for?' asked Gunda, her head resting on my chest.

'For an abortion. I told her that the Æsculapion there was finished and that we could stay on for a few days if she liked. Caesarea's nice. But she told me that she didn't want an abortion. So I told her that I didn't want a baby. Then she pushed her hands against my chest and swore at me. I said to her "I didn't want a woman or baby, Miriam. You've enjoyed this arrangement as much as me."

'"So you won't help me with it?" she asked. I told her that no, I wouldn't. Under our law, if a single man states clearly and explicitly beforehand that he does not want a child, the woman has no claim on him if she has one.

'Miriam then said, "And I suppose being Roman, you'll have that in writing." Which, of course, I did, with the legionary *Advocatus*. Miriam said that we truly were the wicked kingdom, we Romans. I offered again to take her to Caesarea. It's easy enough to get rid of it. Better to have an abortion, then she wouldn't be "shopsoiled". But Miriam didn't want an abortion; she said it was wrong.

'I shrugged my shoulders at this and told her to have it her way, then. I was sorry to lose her in those circumstances, but at least a line was drawn. Soon afterwards I was posted to Jerusalem, and I told her that I did not expect to see her again.

'Jerusalem was a city calculated to drain the hot blood from any healthy young man; the local women would not come across under any circumstances. At one point I hadn't had sex for six months and I began to regret leaving Miriam. I spent a lot of time standing in the sun on Temple perimeter duty or skulking around patrolling the countryside thereabouts, contemplating contacting her again and asking if she would have me back. This was presuming, of course, I could sit comfortably for long enough to get to Sepphoris on the train.

'My sister had moved to Alexandria after our father

died—still sailing in his sleep, she said, the housekeeper found him on the floor with an old tiller in his hands—so I made plans to visit her when I had some leave. Just before I left I had cause to think of Miriam again. There were honour killings in the villages outside Jerusalem, and one particularly terrible incident where a girl had talked to a Roman soldier who'd innocently asked her for directions. Her family did not consider her dishonoured but the village elders did, and she was murdered on the way back from the well. Her parents were willing to give evidence, but no one else would and they started to get threatening letters shoved under their door. I led a detachment that helped them move into the city for their safety. While I was there helping them pack their belongings, I saw a photograph of the dead girl; she was Miriam's double. I wondered if Sepphoris had any village elders like that. Yes, it was beautiful and civilised, but it was also in the Galilee.

'I spent much of the train journey feeling shame about what I had done to Miriam and longing for her, such that when I arrived in Alexandria and saw my sister on the platform the first thing I told her after we exchanged greetings was what had happened in Sepphoris. She insisted I incubate in the Temple of Isis so that I might learn what I ought to do. After spending that night in the arms of one of my sister's close friends from the same House I resolved to attend to matters of the spirit.

'If there is magic still in our Empire of steam and speed it is in Egypt, and so on my sister's recommendation I presented myself to a priestess skilled in the interpretation of dreams. I cleansed myself according to her instructions and took heed of her words when I arrived at the Temple. She held a tonic to my lips and bade me drink. Once the tonic began to take effect, she led me by the hand to the place at the Goddess's feet where I would sleep that night. She touched my head, noting how soldiers have little hair to stroke away from the forehead in the traditional way.

'A falling dream came to me, picked out in great detail thanks to the drink she had prepared. I stood on the highest point of the Pharos, its great rotating ray of light cutting across me at regular intervals. I could see ships of all shapes and sizes scattered out across the water: ironclads and fishing trawlers and ships taking cargoes to Terra Nova and other far flung places. I knew I must step off from my place of safety and did so. I fell alongside the wall, arms outstretched, then fell through the lighthouse's concrete foundations and then the sea and the seabed. I was not afraid that I would hit the ground and die, although I became afraid when I passed through solid objects like a spirit. I saw a green sea serpent eating its own tail and heard it speak to me but not what it said. At length I crawled up out of the sea and out of my dream and told the priestess what I had seen. She warned me most solemnly that I must not go back to Miriam and told me that everything was already fixed. She also stressed to me that Isis looks out for the weak people and that I must never again take advantage of weakness like that. The priestesses of Isis are not given to hysterical warnings and so when I saw her worried face from my place beside the statue I knew she was concerned for me. I promised I would abide by her instructions.

'I kept my promise for nearly nine years, requesting frontier duty and avoiding Sepphoris. I saw much action as a result and rose through the ranks, becoming Cohort Commander shortly before being posted here. It was when I heard about the terrible defeat in the *Wald* and then learned of my Cohort's imminent transfer to the *limes* that I broke my promise to the priestess. I remember the announcement over the radio in Antonia and how everyone stood to attention out of respect for our honoured dead. I wondered what had become of Miriam and her child and thought that it was safe to look in on her in the forum in Sepphoris.

'I made arrangements to meet Victor, a comrade of mine in the Sepphoris *castrum* and caught the train from Jerusalem. Victor took me into the forum and I was pleased to see that Miriam was doing well. She now had a nice shop of her own and lived in an apartment above it. Victor told me an older tradesman, Joseph from Nazareth, did not mind that she was shopsoiled and took her in marriage; I saw two of his children by her standing near the entrance to the shop. Victor pointed out my son to me when my son stepped outside to join the other two, although his dark colouring and height made it clear he had different paternity from them. I walked towards him but did not have the courage to cross the street and approach him directly. I just loitered there in front of the theatre opposite Miriam's store and hoped he would notice me. He was a good-looking little boy with my hair and his mother's fine features. He was wearing a brightly coloured kippah and great tufts of curly hair protruded from under it. He started to play a game of tag with the other two children and finished up beside me, in part because he had to keep stopping and holding onto his hat. I spoke to him and to my surprise he replied.

'"I am Yeshua," he said. "I'm going to be a carpenter when I grow up."

'I asked him "Do you go to school?" He told me that he did. "Here in Sepphoris, I can speak Greek. My father is *tekton*."

'I tried to detain him longer by making more small talk, but I've never been good at small talk and in time I could see he was becoming bored with me. He then asked if he could look at my beret, which I was pleased to show him as it was new and had my Cohort Commander's insignia on it. I handed it to him; he gazed at me. "You're my father, aren't you?"

'I did not know what Miriam had told him and so stood rooted to the spot. "Yes, Yeshua, I'm your father," I said.

'He went on, "Your name is Pantera," looking closely at my shoulder flashes. "And you've been promoted."

'He handed me my beret, staring at me. He had enormous dark eyes and at that moment I could not turn away from him. Then, solemly he said, "You did the wrong thing."

'By then Victor had joined me in front of the theatre. He was eating an ice cream and handed one to me. He said, "I got you *chocolatl*, so you owe me because it's twice the price of the others." The boy heard and asked for an ice cream.

'Here was my chance to redeem myself in a small way; I led Yeshua to the gelateria and let him choose two flavours, whatever he wanted. He ordered strawberry and chocolatl. His two siblings, I noticed, had retreated to the other side of the street and were heading into their mother's shop.

'Yeshua tucked into his ice cream. "This is nice," he said.

'Then a voice behind me said, "You haven't changed, have you?" It was Miriam, standing behind me with her hands on her hips. She was round and fat with a baby but still very beautiful. "Bribery will get you everywhere."

'I told her that he had asked for an ice cream, so I bought him one. At that point Victor wriggled his eyebrows at me and stepped backwards, smiling. He spoke in Latin, "This is getting into awkward territory so I'll just go feed the ducks in the park next to the baths."

'With Victor gone I asked her if she wanted an ice cream too. The three of us stood on the footpath in the sunshine eating our ice creams, not speaking, watching the customers go in and out of Miriam's shop to be served by her sister and two other women. When I'd finished eating, I held out my hand to her to shake, but instead she called me a prize shit. Her tone was amused, not hostile. She took Yeshua's hand and walked him across the street to her shop.

'She didn't look back at me.'

Helen Dale is a Queenslander by birth and a Londoner by choice. She read law at Oxford (where she was at Brasenose) and has previously worked as a lawyer, political staffer, and advertising copywriter (among other things). She became the youngest winner of Australia's Miles Franklin Award with her first novel, *The Hand that Signed the Paper*, leaving the country shortly after it caused a storm of controversy. Her second novel, *Kingdom of the Wicked*, is published in two volumes by Ligature.

Terry Rodgers is a Scottish graphic artist and photographer who has spent many years designing material for the Fringe, especially Skeptics on the Fringe. He lives in Edinburgh.

COPYRIGHT

First published in 2017

by Ligature Pty Limited
34 Campbell St · Balmain NSW 2041
www.ligatu.re · mail@ligatu.re

and Wilkinson Publishing Pty Limited
Alcaston House · 2 Collins Street · Melbourne Vic 3000
wilkinsonpublishing.com.au

National Library of Australia Cataloguing-in-Publication entry
Creator · Dale, Helen, author.
Title · Kingdom of the wicked / Helen Dale
ISBN · 9781925642247 (paperback)
Series · Dale, Helen. Rule; bk. 1
Subjects · Romans–Fiction · Rome–History–Fiction.

ligaturefirst